THE TELLING

THE TELLING

ALEXANDRA SIROWY

SIMON & SCHUSTER BFYR

NEW YORK   LONDON   TORONTO   SYDNEY   NEW DELHI

SIMON & SCHUSTER BFYR

An imprint of Simon & Schuster Children's Publishing Division

1230 Avenue of the Americas, New York, New York 10020

SIMON & SCHUSTER BFYR is a trademark of Simon & Schuster, Inc.

For information about special discounts for bulk purchases, please contact
Simon & Schuster Special Sales at 1-866-506-1949 or business@simonandschuster.com.

The Simon & Schuster Speakers Bureau can bring authors to your live event.
For more information or to book an event, contact
the Simon & Schuster Speakers Bureau at 1-866-248-3049 or visit our website at
www.simonspeakers.com.

Jacket design by Lizzy Bromley

Interior design by Hilary Zaryky

The text for this book was set in Adobe Jenson Pro.

Manufactured in the United States of America

First Edition

2 4 6 8 10 9 7 5 3 1

Library of Congress Cataloging-in-Publication Data

Names: Sirowy, Alexandra, author.

Title: The Telling / Alexandra Sirowy.

Description: First edition. | New York : Simon & Schuster Books for Young Readers, [2016] | Summary: A series of murders that are eerily similar to the dark stories Lana's deceased brother used to tell start happening in her home town, threatening her newfound popularity.

Identifiers: LCCN 2015023147| ISBN 9781481418898 (hardback) | ISBN 9781481418911 (eBook)

Subjects: | CYAC: Brothers and sisters—Fiction. | Murder—Fiction. | Grief—Fiction. | Self-Actualization (Psychology)—Fiction. | BISAC: JUVENILE FICTION / Social Issues / Death & Dying. | JUVENILE FICTION / Social Issues / Friendship.

Classification: LCC PZ7.1.S57 Te 2016 | DDC [Fic]—dc23

LC record available at http://lccn.loc.gov/2015023147

For the girls who are sharks,
and those who are kittens,
and those who are heroes,
and those who are villains.

THE TELLING

— 1 —

This is what *after* looks like: me picking my way up the ridge in my swimsuit; the swollen water of Swisher Spring at the end of summer; girls baking under an orange sun on the boulders; boys cheering for me to jump, even though they've been vying for bragging rights all day. *Boys.* Yeah, there are those in *after*—one in particular.

Right on cue, Josh winks up at me from where he treads water with the others. That one thing—a silly gesture he probably passes out like smiles—has been twelve years in coming for me, because I've liked Josh Parker since he wore red corduroy pants the first day of preschool. And up until a month ago, I'd never heard him say my name.

After doesn't feel as good as it looks.

I'm buzzed off one beer, breathless on the rocky ledge that might as well be a stage twenty feet above the others, with a hundred acres of wilderness preserve at my back, and fighting the urge to wrap my arms around my midsection because even after a month, I'm still not comfortable in this teeny-tiny bikini in front of the kids my classmates have called "the core" since the sixth grade. Definitely not with Carolynn Winters sunning herself below, keeping one bright fish eye on me. She's dazzling, confident, the kind of girl who never asks twice.

Everything is the wrong color and too bright and out of proportion.

There's space between what you see and what I feel. In my experience there's usually a line that separates what people choose to show the world and what they keep hidden.

My small life of *before* was like that too. I was the quiet girl, good in the way adults want teenagers to be: raising her hand for extra credit; more worried about what people were thinking than what I thought. Nights were early; days spent studying. There were millions of flash cards and the eight-semester plan.

I was an earthworm dreaming of being a python.

The wind whips my hair, and I tighten my halter tie. In the water I was knocked around by the boys' maelstrom. No matter how old boys get, they think it's freaking adorable to splash you in the face. And no matter how old girls get, we're always at the mercy of boys and their splashing.

If I said that out loud, Willa would add: *and their war.* She's on the shore, likely rolling her eyes behind her aviators and hoping that I'll jump fast so we can leave and she can watch whatever's been recorded from the History channel. She's already been patient with me *all day* (more like every day for two months) and she's sick of doing things she despises and hanging out with people she likes even less for yours truly. I flush guilty.

"Jump! Jump! Jump!" the boys howl, pumping their fists as the water slaps their chests. Rusty, Duncan, and Josh have been inseparable since preschool. Rumors always circulate about the three of them and one of their testosterone-fueled misadventures.

"Jump where it's deepest!" Rusty shouts, his indomitably curly, strawberry-blond hair wet and flattened to his scalp. I can see the hint of a waxy bald spot on the top of his head. A reminder that the best-case scenario is getting old and dying—not that I'm obsessed with death or anything. The opposite. My stepbrother Ben's voice is in my head. *Don't wait until you're dead, Lan. Exercise your nerve and mischief.* I'm obsessed with living.

"Don't land on the rocks," Rusty shouts again. He's a natural cheerleader, having played team sports since he could walk. I give him a thumbs-up. We've been at the spring for hours, lounging until the sun and booze induced comas, our skin sending up steam as we rolled into the water. No one's made their way up the rocky face of the cliff littered with NO CLIMBING signs to make the jump before this.

Four years ago, Terrance Finnsberg, a senior at Gant High, leaped from this peninsula and snapped his spine on a rock in the water below. Died instantly. I heard he was high when it happened, told his friends he could fly. In response, Gant Island passed a town ordinance that made jumping illegal. It didn't do a lot of good, since it's only one of those punishable-by-community-service crimes, and everyone needs community service for college applications. Moreover, *this is Gant*. A fog of boredom hangs over the island during summer months as tourists descend on us and Seattleites ferry over, crowding beaches. Kids around here are used to being entertained. Dangle something in front of their faces and tell them they can't have it, they'll stomp until you give it to them—or just up and take it.

Ever since jumping became taboo, it's everyone's go-to stunt. It makes or breaks reputations. What the core doesn't know is that Ben took me here way before this was Gant's preferred dare. When I was eleven, I could find my way to the top of this precipice in the dark and cannonball into the water between the rocks poking up like knuckles.

"Rusty's next," Duncan calls.

"Bro"—Rusty wags his middle finger at Duncan—"I told you I can't hurt my shoulder before season. The team would have my balls if I couldn't start. *You* go next."

Duncan tips his skipper hat and gives what he thinks is an irresistible smile. "I can't risk screwing up this perfect face. I'm taking Bethany J. out tonight." He says her name like it's an exotic delicacy he can't wait to gobble up. Bethany J. is a petite cheerleader with D cups. Bethany G. is a stocky flutist in the school band. To Duncan— and the majority of Gant High's male population—it's an important distinction.

Duncan shouts up to me, "This one time, Kara Moren jumped with her beer and gave herself a black eye."

"You could put your beer down to jump," Willa deadpans. No doubt she's glaring at his white skipper hat. "It's like he thinks he's the captain of the whole island," Willa groaned as we pulled up behind the others at the trailhead for the spring earlier today. "Promise you won't blame me if I knock it off his head; it'll be justifiable hat-homicide."

Duncan kicks up from the water, punching the sky with his free hand. "You can take my freedom but never my beer!" He's the only one staying afloat without relinquishing his bottle. With his drink, metallic-framed sunglasses, aforementioned cap, fitted swim trunks he brought back from Crete, and gold chain around his neck, he looks like he's starring in a music video and the others are his entourage. Knowing Duncan, this is by design.

"No one's jumping. *She's* going to freak," Carolynn gloats, not even deigning to say my name. She smirks only at her bestie, Becca, who's sitting cross-legged beside Carolynn on the rocks that rim the spring.

"It's okay, Lan," Becca calls. "I wouldn't even jump to save Duncan's life."

"Hey," Duncan shouts, lifting his chest from the water to see her. "What did I do to you?"

Becca props her huge-framed glasses on top of her head and gives him an innocent look. "I'm over Bethany J. is all. Bethany J. is blacklisted. She's all you talk about this summer." Her lips pout and she gives a little huff in place.

"Not true."

"Kinda, man," Josh says, laughing. Rusty grunts in agreement.

Duncan slaps the water, feigning anger. "Guys, she's *Bethany J.*" A pause, and he grins. "BJ?"

Becca claps her palms over her ears dramatically. "Stop traumatizing me," she moans. Duncan blows her a kiss. She mimes plucking it from the air and then slumps to the side in Carolynn's lap, giggling. "Why can't we all just marry each other?" Becca asks wistfully. "Then there'd never be reason to talk to anyone but *us*, and I'd never have to go on another date where the boy wants to go halvsies." Carolynn absentmindedly rearranges the bracelets stacked on Becca's wrist.

Despite being best friends with Carolynn Winters, Becca Atherton is not soulless. Becca pats my empty towel. "C'mon down, Lan, and we can predict hookups and couples for senior year." She says this as though it's the most alluring carrot she can dangle in front of me, a famished bunny rabbit. *Before* I would have whispered to Willa that *news flash*: All girls are not boy and gossip crazed. All girls are not kittens or bunny rabbits. Some are sharks. This is ironic, since although my former self would have acknowledged this, she never would have had the guts to act on her sharkish impulses.

After Lana grins at Becca and shouts, "Lemme jump and then I have a few predictions."

The sun refracts off the diamond stud in Carolynn's pinched nose as she tips her face up to the cerulean sky. "I've seen loads of guys jump," she says. "Girls aren't meant for stunts like that." She drops her chin and winks at Becca. "Pussies are pussy."

Willa sits bolt upright. She's the only one of us not in a swimsuit, since she doesn't swim and isn't the tanning type. The stripe of white sunblock down the bridge of her nose has the look of a landing strip. "There's a lot of disagreement about where that word came from. Pussy is actually a diminutive of *pusillanimous*, meaning cowardly. Although maybe the origin doesn't matter, since everyone equates it with the female anatomy anyway?"

Becca rocks back, barely able to say through her giggles, "Puss-a-what-a-lis? Are you speaking Snuffleupagus?"

Willa gives a perplexed shake of her head before continuing, "And why wouldn't girls be able to do everything guys can?" I know she's forcing herself not to make a fist at Carolynn—she considers Becca too easy a mark.

Carolynn groans and rolls her head until she's looking at Willa. "They're different. I like mani-pedis, and Rusty"—she points a pink nail at him—"likes jerking off." Willa snorts. The boys whoop. I don't know how it started, but the core is always joking about how much Rusty Harper *loves* himself. What would have made other guys outcasts made Rusty a comic hero. He plays right along. He even had RUSTY PIPE printed on his baseball uniform.

The core's like that. They defy gravity.

Carolynn eyes Willa like she's a bumbling foreigner clueless about basic customs. "I repeat: boys and girls are different," she states slowly, matter-of-factly. *In this country we drive on the right side of the road.*

Cue a din of pervy comments from the boys as Willa pops up on her knees, hands on her hips, her tone full of bravado. "What do you want to bet that not only will Lana jump, she'll dive?"

Like it's been choreographed, everyone's faces snap in my direction. They don't have a clue about the times I came here as a kid because *before*, Willa and I didn't lunch in the same solar system as these kids, let alone spend half the summer setting off fireworks at Shell Shores with the radioactive core of Gant High. Why radioactive? Because these six hold the power to make others treat you as the deformed victim of nuclear fallout or a superhuman with clear skin and flawless hair.

Willa and I were sipping iced mochas at Marmalade's Café a month ago when Josh invited us to play pool. Josh was all tumbling laughter and easy smiles, and after weeks of not being able to catch my breath, I could breathe near him. Before the first eight ball was sunk, Carolynn had called me *Lena* twice and shrugged once, purring, "Same difference," when I corrected her—which was a lot nicer than when she emptied a flask on my dress at freshman homecoming. She was trying to scare me off; she didn't bank on me sticking around for two more games or Josh driving me home afterward. I know Ben was the only reason Josh noticed us initially. Losing Ben cast a shine on me that I didn't have as the weird little sister of "a popular."

The corner of Carolynn's mouth quirks up and she pets her poufy bun's imaginary stray hairs, her gold and white bangles tinkling. She turns to Becca and says, "If *she* wants to jump, it'll be *her* funeral." Carolynn's the only one of the five who likes to remind Willa and me that we're not part of their *us*. We're add-ons. As temporary as the season itself. Maybe the sun will keep shining through the autumn, or maybe Willa and I will be iced out when classes start.

Here's a secret, though. Who cares? I never thought summers were boring before, and it's only this year, the first without Ben, that I need a distraction. I *need* the core.

Becca's green eyes turn up to me. "You sure it's a good idea, Lan?" She points in the direction she thinks the sun is setting—south. "Can you even see to dive?"

"I can. No worries," I call. I don't agree with Willa when she says that Becca would miss sarcasm if it were an asteroid soaring straight at her. Becca just wants to think the best of her friends and refuses to see their scratchy edges. She lives down the street from me, and as a kid she'd come over to play while her parents fought. They were divorced by sixth grade and she stopped coming after. That's when I learned that girls weren't all automatically friends based on their shared girlness. Becca's picked up with me like there's no obvious gap in our friendship. Willa doesn't understand how I'm not bitter over Becca ditching me back then. If Ben were here, he wouldn't get it either. It probably should bother me, except Becca has this way of tugging you in close and delivering a compliment on your eyebrows or the freckle above your top lip that makes you feel as pretty as you *know* she is.

I crave the giddiness that turns my knees, elbows, and knuckles to liquid around the core. I even feel weightless at the perceived peril of this stunt.

"Dive. Dive. Dive," the boys chant, except it sounds more like, "Die. Die. Die," by the time I tune back in.

Willa looks down her ski-slope nose at Carolynn, her chin jutting out with the result of a finger pointing. "If Lana jumps, you have to admit that girls can do everything guys can."

Carolynn's hands move to tame fly-aways. "No, I'll admit that *Lana* can do anything a boy can." She grins at her cleverness and adds, "Maybe she even jerks off like one?"

Rusty whoops like a monkey and Duncan erupts in a fit of giggles, cracking, "Lana's got lady-balls."

Josh whips an arm across the surface, splashing Duncan. "Bro, shut the eff up."

Duncan shields his face with the beer bottle, paddling away from Josh with the other arm. "C'mon. I'm kidding."

Rusty shouts, "Dude, she's gonna do it. She's *Ben's* sister." The way he says *Ben*, slightly awed, isn't new.

Duncan snorts. "Lana and Ben weren't blood related." The past tense burns.

Josh's limbs churn like eggbeaters as he faces me and shouts, "Don't listen to him. You can do it. Right in between the rocks." His torso and head bob up and down, buoyant on the surface. The three of them have the look of those moles in the carnival game where you rush to whack their heads. There's warmth radiating from my rib cage that you can probably see glowing through my skin, like I swallowed a bajillion glowworms. Josh Parker stuck up for *me*.

I step forward until my toes curl over the edge. It's the middle of August, but the spring is deep, fed by an underground stream Ben and I spent summers searching for. The shadowy forms of three boulders run like columns from inches below the surface to the spring bed; other than them, it's a clear twenty feet until you hit the bottom.

"On the count of three," Rusty demands. "One!"

I let myself picture the way Ben looked jumping the last time we came: freckled broad back peeling from a sunburn; blond hair drenched brown; a tattoo on his shoulder already fading because it was cheap and done when I was fourteen and he was sixteen by a guy who operated in the back of a Chinese restaurant and didn't check IDs. Even when it got really bloody, Ben didn't wince. He just kept saying, "Shhh, it's okay," to me, like I was the one in pain. I sniffled the whole time.

"Two!" Rusty and Duncan shout in unison.

That was *before*. I wouldn't cry now.

"Three," they howl.

I spring forward. Two seconds plummeting to the looking-glass surface, my reflection a bird diving from the sky, falling like it's not afraid of gravity, of what will come after it hits the ground. I slice into the water like a knife. A world of blue-gray envelops me as I shoot to the bottom. The water is lonely. The snakes that nest in the pockmarked walls aren't eeling through the shallows. Ben is not on the surface with a mouthful of water ready to spray in my face.

My toes glide along the fuzzy, algae-covered rocks. I beat my arms. I exhale, sending bubbles to the strobe-light surface. There's the outline of legs kicking, swirling bits of plant and dirt with the look of space matter in those posters of the cosmos. A featureless head bobs under the surface; whoever it is can't see me. I hope Carolynn is so worried I've drowned that she's peeing herself. It wouldn't be her fault; I would've jumped if I were alone; if it were snowing; if it were the middle of the night. Jumping is what Ben and I did here. It was my only nerve and mischief.

The veins on my neck swell. I need air. I resist for ten seconds. My mouth opens to gulp . . . can't help it . . . don't want to surface . . . don't want to admit that he's not even *here*. I exhale. My chest flattens.

I am stone. Unfeeling. Indestructible. I can take it.

I shoot from the bottom, break surface, scrunch my eyes closed, and show the whole world my teeth. *Grin, grin, grin until you feel the smile taking root in your belly,* my mother used to say. *Perception is nine-tenths of everything.* Mom said that too.

Everyone talks in rapid fire. "That's messed up," one of the guys shouts.

"Such an attention whore," Carolynn groans.

Becca chants my name in cheer.

"I knew she was fine. She's Ben's sister," Rusty says.

"Screw you," Duncan shouts, "You were pissing all over yourself."

"Told you," Willa gloats.

Warm hands slip over my shoulders. Josh dunks me for a split second as he tries to turn me to face him. "Sorry . . . sorry." He's coughing up water with the words. I laugh—can't tell if I feel it taking hold as I drag the hair from my face.

Josh grins, white teeth pearly and straight, water dribbling from the corners of his wide mouth. He yells over his shoulder, "She totally schooled you with that dive, Car."

"Bet I can stay under longer than you, bro," Duncan challenges.

Rusty accepts and they start dunking under, their gasps and splashes background static. Josh's dark-blue eyes stay on me. His hair is caramelized wet. His hands on my waist tow me to his chest. His touch is as warm as his tan skin looks. He feels like ginger tea tastes.

"What about you?" I ask. "You want to go under with me?" I can't believe the flirty girl's voice is mine. I feel my mouth making Mom's coy smile.

Josh blushes. "Yeah, what'll we do down there?" He says it like he isn't the kind of boy who expects stuff or throws away winks. *I hope.* I would have kissed Josh the first night he drove me home from Marmalade's. Becca says he's too decent to make a move while I'm sad. Willa says a girl shouldn't wait for a boy to ask her out.

My smile sends waves into my chest, and I do feel it taking root. Mom was right. Maybe Willa, too. The nervy words are citrus bright waiting on my tongue. I will ask him out.

Duncan explodes on the surface, sending spray into the air. The water runs from his plastered-down hair to his face and neck. Thin ribbons of blood connect his nostrils to his upper lip. His head bobs in a frenzy, eyes darting below. I look too. The water's darkening along with the rose-and-blue tie-dyed sky.

"Dude, what happened to your face?" Josh calls to him.

"Rusty's going nuts down there." He thumbs one nostril, then the other, and tries to snort up the blood. "He kicked my face." Josh releases me. I shiver as the water rises and falls, blackening with each crest as the sun sinks behind the shaggy wall of trees. I scissor-kick faster to lift up. Willa's on her knees, really paying attention to the boys for the first time all day—maybe all summer. She senses the shift in the air.

"You're getting blood in the water," Carolynn whines, flicking a hand at the discord.

Becca crawls toward the edge for a better look. She snatches up Duncan's skipper hat from where he tossed it and places it on her head. "Blood is soooo gross," she complains.

Duncan has ahold of his nose and is egg beating in a furious circle. "I think there might be someone else down there," he says.

My arms slash through the water as I whirl around trying to see under. Josh is asking what the eff over and over. Willa's soprano tells me to get out of the water, "this second." Carolynn's shouting for Duncan and Josh to go down after Rusty.

Rusty hits the surface hacking up a lung, arms flailing, palms slapping hard to the rope ladder hanging from the rocky lip of the spring. The chorus is drowned out by his huffing, "There's a girl. . . . She's . . . at the bottom."

— 2 —

What comes next happens fast. It's getting dark and everyone is out of breath, their panting magnified in my ears. Becca's whimpers are desperate and grinding, bouncing off the trees. I want to tell her to shut up already, I need to concentrate. Josh leaves the surface, and there's only black lapping water where he was.

Duncan makes it to the shore and his voice booms, "Carolynn, call 9-1-1."

And she says, "My effing cell is in the car."

Willa shouts, "Run for it."

And then they stop making noise—except for Becca, who's still wailing—so I assume Carolynn runs for her phone. I get caught up in the enormous unlikelihood of seven of us and not one cell, and then I want to smack my forehead because there's no service at the spring.

Rusty vanishes too. He and Josh are diving for the girl. And I think, *What is she doing down there?* A split second later, I dive also.

I swim blind, the surface gone too dim to illuminate below. I wriggle through the black, my chest squeezing with the increased pressure. My hands jab the bottom. It's soundless as death, and I wonder if Ben can hear anything where he is. Stupid to believe he could be anywhere, dead is dead. And I'm not dead, even if sometimes I wonder if we'd be together if I were. That's a nightmare thought, the kind that filled the first month after we buried Ben's empty coffin.

There's a ripple in the water to my right—Josh or Rusty scouring the spring for the girl. *The girl.* I was below a minute ago and there was no one except loneliness and memories of Ben—but aren't those two actually the same? My arms sweep back and forth, legs propelling me forward. Pressure behind my eyeballs. Too long since the surface. And that *must* be the case, because I have the inkling that I'm an astronaut in space and I'm only dreaming that I'm in water.

My arms close around something—no, *someone*—waxy and firm. I take hold and yank and yank, ripping the form free from an invisible grip. She's slender in my arms, all sharp angles and poking bones. I wonder if she's a kid as we surface, and I gasp so hard it's a punch in the lungs.

"Help," I sputter. Everything is silver edged. Rusty's arms windmill toward me. His hands skate over mine to get a grip on the girl, which is good because she's slipping, her breasts smushed against my arms as I try to keep hold. *Breasts,* so she's not a kid. Rusty floats her on her back, and with an arm hooked under hers, he cuts through the water.

"Over here, man," Duncan calls, crouched on the shore, blood smeared across his face. Josh jerks his head to the ladder, and we swim for it. Rusty must have reached the shore, because Duncan adds, "Lift her. Yeah, yeah, yeah, a bit higher."

My arms go shaky and dumb as I climb from one rung to the next. I'm at the top, swinging a leg over a boulder, when Duncan shouts, "Holy shit, I know her." Becca cries out from where she's curled on her towel, the skipper hat and her face ducking intermittently behind her knees. "It's Maggie Lewis," Duncan says.

I scramble for a handhold on the slick rock, anything to sink my nails into before I fall. Maggie. *Maggie Lewis.* The name is a fist around my heart, giving it an extra pump. Like a gossamer screen overlaying the here and now, I see Maggie in the halls at school, the hearts and quotes she doodled in Sharpie standing out against the washed-out denim of her jeans. I see Maggie on the field through the rear library windows. She's sitting cross-legged with the hippie-wanna-be, hemp-wearing, political kids, and she's tossing chunks of her sandwich to a scraggly seagull. It was the nicest thing I'd ever seen her do.

I walk haltingly toward the huddle. I want to collapse. Becca's already on the ground, arms latching her knees as she rocks, her wavy hair a mane she's retreating into. I decide I don't like the way completely-freaking-out looks, so I stay standing.

"Is she breathing? Is she?" Becca asks.

Josh kneels next to Maggie. He throws her pale arms to the sides and places the heels of his hands, one on top of the other, at her sternum, over her transparent white shirt. Her body jolts as he pumps. Josh's mom is a firefighter; he knows what to do. He'll save Maggie. Except that doesn't ease the fist's grip on my heart. It wouldn't. I hate Maggie Lewis. Maggie is the reason Ben was driving the night he died. He was taking her home.

Willa's arms go around my shoulders, and I angle against her like a kickstand.

Carolynn trips from the shadows between the trees and braces her hands on her knees. "I . . . called . . . for help," she wheezes. A cell falls to the towel at her feet. The flashlight app's white glow washes us colorless as snow. The chill of the fast approaching night pinpricks me everywhere, filling me with every bit of cold in the whole state of Washington. I blink hard when I see water crystallize in Maggie's hair. This isn't happening.

Carolynn looks to the familiar figure on the ground. "Shit, it's *her*."

"Why isn't the CPR working?" Becca cries. She's up on her knees now, swaying and wringing her hands.

Rusty paces, yanking on clumps of his hair. "Josh, why are you stopping?"

Josh is straightened up after suctioning his mouth to Maggie's a fourth time. He keeps his purposeful stare on her. "Because it's not bringing her back."

Rusty squints at the neon digital face of his wristwatch. "You don't know that," he says. "It's only been a few minutes."

"Spaz, we've been here the whole day. She's been under for hours." Duncan throws a sopping-wet towel at Rusty.

"But you can't just give up on someone." Rusty stoops over Maggie, gets right in Josh's face, and starts shaking him by the shoulders. "*Do something.*" Rusty's voice goes uneven. His seams are ripping.

"Get out of his face." Duncan steps forward and shoves him. Rusty trips back, catches himself with a wide, wobbly stride, and then a second later, pivots to throw his weight into a punch. Rusty's fist connects with Duncan's square jaw. Duncan absorbs it, groans, shrugs off the pain, and tackles Rusty. The exchange takes only five seconds, as the rest of us are frozen.

Rusty isn't as broad and muscular as Duncan, who spends mornings lifting weights. Rusty is corded and flexible, built for stealing bases, and he crashes to the rocks, landing with Duncan on top of him. Rusty's head snaps back and collides with the rough surface. Duncan's instantly off him. "Bro, bro," he cries, "are you okay, man?"

Carolynn rushes forward. Becca starts crying, "Oh fuck, oh fuck."

Rusty rolls onto his side. His eyes are squinched shut as he coughs big, whooping barks. I almost cry out in relief. Carolynn kneels at his chest. She looks to Duncan coldly. "Were you trying to give him a concussion?"

"He punched me first," Duncan says lamely.

"You pushed him first," Carolynn snaps.

"Car," Rusty wheezes. "*I'm okay.*"

Josh remains crouched at obviously dead Maggie's sternum. Carolynn keeps laying into Duncan. "Why do you have to act like such an animal? Why does everything come down to you trying to prove you've got more testosterone than everyone else?"

"Josh?" Becca whispers. "Can a hospital help her?"

"No, B," Josh says, scrubbing one hand over his weary eyes. "She's dead."

Maggie's dark hair is a curtain over her face; only a sharp nose peeks through as a white little iceberg. Her pale form stands out against the night. She has the look of a character from one of Ben's stories. My throat tightens. She reminds me of the lily-pad maiden who was strangled by a mad king and left in a watery grave. I never thought Maggie was pretty and now there's a celestial quality to her, like we fished her from the liquid moon of an outlying planet. I spent

THE TELLING · 19

years trying to figure out what Ben saw in Maggie. And now she's dead.

I thought I'd never see Maggie again after she went missing seven weeks ago. I was glad—*relieved*. It hurt to look at her off-center ponytail of brownish-red, henna-tinted hair, her coal-lined eyes glaring, her clomping, steel-toed boots missing their laces and pulled over fishnets, and her bony, long fingers always two seconds away from flipping me off. What right did she have to be alive, and as pissed-off and disaffected as she wanted to be, when it was because of her that Ben was dead?

As much as I didn't want to, I also *needed* to see her, needed to corner her and make her tell me why and how. And now, with water bloating her lungs, it's too late.

Her lines blur and bleed into the night, as if she's a wet ink blot spreading on paper. As if night has unhinged its jaw and is swallowing her whole, making her disappear like it did Ben. There's static in my ears. A wormhole opens up in time, and I can see clear through its passageway to a night two months ago.

The night everything that mattered changed.

— 3 —

It was June 8, half past eleven. Ben's and my movie night had been interrupted. We'd eaten lobster tacos and I drank two beers, which was two more beers than I'd ever had before. Then a pissy Maggie arrived.

She and Ben started fighting—a blustery, name-calling argument. He'd broken up with her five days earlier. She wasn't supposed to show up at our house anymore. She had to accept they were over. For good. Although I didn't pick up on it as it played out, it was suspicious that she had a friend drop her off, only to demand a ride home. *No*, she wouldn't let Ben call her a car when he offered. *No*, she wouldn't sleep off her buzz in the downstairs guest room.

I'd given Ben a sleepy and inebriated frown as we stood in the hallway while she used the bathroom. "Please." He bent nearer, the light in his eyes diminishing until his forehead touched mine. He was all I could see. "I don't want to be alone with her. Come. Save me."

The three of us braced ourselves against the early summer breeze as we filed along the path to where Ben's SUV waited in our driveway. I was pouting, letting my flip-flops spray pebbles at Maggie's heels.

She scowled at me before she climbed into the front passenger seat—without even bothering to call shotgun. I sat in the back, pulled my knees to my chest, leaned against the window. "Turn the heater on," I whined. I stuck my earbuds in and was listening to the kind of angry, screeching punk I don't even like just to tune her voice out. And here's the second worst thing I've ever done.

I fell asleep, and I couldn't tell the police what happened next.

Two hours later my ears buzzed with the sharp, stuttered *ding* of car doors left ajar as the police tried to make sense of the blood splatter in the interior. The engine had been left running. My earbuds dangled out of the rear door, where I'd thrown them after yanking my cell free to dial 911. Each time the breeze picked up they swung, grating against the road. I'd never use them again.

The wind hissed through the pines behind Maggie and me. The police had set up perimeter lights; they stretched our shadows and threw them back at sharp angles. Mine was trying to detach from my feet; it wanted to run and hide. A police officer, his finger on the trigger of a camera, blinded me in intervals. The light flashed in my peripheral vision as a second officer captured the splatter on Maggie's face, arms, and torso. Ben's blood had gotten in my mouth; it was all I could taste as we waited for the detective Gant PD had called in from Seattle to direct the investigation.

Detective Sweeny started a mile down the highway, with another group of officers examining the crime scene where Maggie and I had left Ben to his attacker. Sweeny was small and wiry, cutting through the blockish male cops in uniform. She sized us up with close-set eyes as she approached. Unlike every other officer, her gaze stayed steady, ticking over the details of us like Willa absorbing a study guide before an exam. Sweeny didn't flinch away from all that blood. *We'll be okay now,* I thought.

Sweeny introduced herself. She was a homicide detective. Then she held up her hand when my expression went runny and frantic and added, "Let's not get ahead of ourselves. The *detective* part is why I'm here." She asked me if I'd been able to reach my parents. They were in Seattle overnight and their phones were off, and she measured her words even more carefully when I told her there was no one else to call. Ben hadn't been found; the police were searching; the coast guard had been mobilized.

I wanted to help them look. Sweeny put her firm grip on my shoulder. "The best way for you to help is to tell me exactly what transpired. Leave nothing out."

Only Maggie knew the first half. She could lie and I wouldn't be able to contradict her. We were a couple of miles before the narrow bridge that connects Gant Island with the Olympic Peninsula. It was the only route to take Maggie to where she lived, off the island. Maggie told the police that Ben and she were arguing. The car slowed. Maggie looked up to see why. To the right there were rocky bluffs that plunged to the island's heaving waters. To the left there was a dark, meadowy slope that ran until a distant wall of pines.

"A man appeared in the middle of the highway," Maggie whispered.

"Where did he appear from?" Sweeny asked. "The trees aren't close to the road. Was he hiding behind something?"

"No. He wasn't there and then he was. *He appeared,*" Maggie insisted, her voice rising. "Ben stopped the car. Rolled down the window and asked if the man needed help. Um, I think he offered his cell or asked if the guy's car had broken down."

"Did you see another vehicle?" Sweeny asked.

"Don't think so."

"Then why would Ben ask about car trouble?"

Maggie shrugged.

"He stopped the car, rolled down his window, and offered help. Seems strange that Ben would have been so friendly if the man just 'appeared,'" Sweeny pressed.

Maggie said, "Ben is charitable and shit. How do I know what he was thinking? He is always *helping.*" She rolled her eyes. "But the guy was in front of the car one second and the next he was right at Ben. And I started screaming."

Sweeny's eyebrows shot up. "Did he have a weapon?"

"I didn't see it."

"Why were you screaming, then?" Sweeny said like she'd caught Maggie in a lie.

"Because his face was red. Painted," Maggie said. The clouds were disintegrating in the sky as she spoke, and the stars that were revealed began orbiting us. I had to work to keep my feet stationary on the road, which started buckling under me like the black, netted skin of a trampoline.

"What kind of paint?"

"How would I know?" Maggie snapped.

Maggie said that she hadn't recognized the man on the road.

"Is it possible you knew him and you just didn't recognize him because of the paint obscuring his features?" Sweeny asked her that night—and probably every time she questioned Maggie over the course of the week after.

"No, I saw him clearly," Maggie insisted. "He was a stranger. The paint was frightening, but I'm positive I don't know him."

Maggie was asked how the attack started. She was vague and confused—traumatized, I thought initially. "He reached through the window for Ben. To get to him, to stab, I mean. Blood squirted on my face and Ben was shouting. Then the door was open and Ben was out of the car and dragged across the road. The stranger's hand kept coming up and down, stabbing Ben."

"What was he stabbing him with? A knife?" Sweeny asked.

I lurched around and vomited onto the gravelly shoulder as Maggie answered, "I couldn't make the object out. . . . It was sharp." She added hoarsely, "I heard it cutting skin." I thought we were both in shock. I didn't notice the oddness of her story until I was out of the fog of that night.

Sweeny asked us both what happened next. I couldn't say why I woke up when I did. I'd been pouting, and then I was lulled to sleep for the first few miles. I wasn't dreaming exactly as much as thinking nonsense things dreamily. Somehow between watching the Cheshire smile of a tiger I'd seen on TV earlier drift through my head and sensing that I was in our dinghy on the harbor, I was struck with the conviction that something bad was happening. My eyes snapped open. I tugged the earbuds from my ears before I was fully alert. Maggie was screaming. *Shrieking.* The car wasn't moving. We were on the highway. The driver's-side door was open.

"Where's Ben?" I asked.

Maggie screamed more shrilly.

I jolted awake completely. Everything rushed in at once. The windows were tinted and it was night and there wasn't a moon. Unexceptional. This is Washington. Clouds always fill the sky. The car interior light was on and moths were fluttering inside the cab. I saw past the yellow papery wings to a figure. A shadow man, I told the police. He was lumbering, or limping, or dragging a clubbed foot. He passed through the SUV's high beams. He was dragging some living thing. He was immense, a part of the dark, darkness personified. He moved across the highway toward the rocky bluff that swung out above the tide pools.

It was the strangest thing. Surreal as flipping through TV channels and landing on a horror movie. You haven't been watching. Your pulse isn't racing. The gruesome scene is almost lost on you. But then I heard a broken grunt, and I put it together. The shadow man had Ben.

My hands shook. They were slick and slipped from the rear passenger-side door lever. When I finally got a grip, I yanked and nothing happened. The child lock was on—although I only realized this in hindsight. I was shouting at Maggie to go after them. To get out of the fucking car and to help Ben. She scrambled over the emergency brake to the driver's seat, and I thought, *Maybe her door isn't working either?* She had stopped screaming.

She pulled the driver's door closed. It didn't latch all the way, and the interior glow of the car stayed on. There was blood everywhere. Red graffiti sprayed across the black roof and smattering the leather seats. I looked to my hands and saw that it wasn't sweat but blood making my fingers slippery. Maggie hit the accelerator, the car swerving before righting itself on the road. I was sitting sideways, pushing against the door, and with the force, I shot back, my temple crunched against the window. My ears rang. Maggie wasn't rescuing Ben. She was leaving him. *We were leaving him.* I pressed my face to the window, trying to see. My eyes weren't working. Everything was fuzzy. The phantom man was stooped over Ben. Ben was a heap at his feet on the bluff above the sound. Neither of them were more than shadowy outlines.

The good and bad are indistinguishable in the dark.

I was in shock. There was a drumbeat in my head. I clawed at the window, leaving bloody finger streaks on the glass. I don't think I spoke, or else I never stopped. Finally the car parked. It was only a mile away, but it felt as if we'd been traveling for an hour. I jammed the window button and led with my head. I hit the pavement, scraped my shoulder, popped up, and started sprinting in the direction we'd come from.

I lost a flip-flop after a yard. I was dizzy and staggering. Maggie caught me easily, yelling, "Call the police. Call the cops." I tried to throw her off. She was stronger than me, her wiry fingers locking around my arms. She shouted right in my ear, "You can only help him by staying here and calling the cops." And that's the worst thing I've ever done. I didn't tell Maggie that she should call the cops. I didn't run for Ben. I trusted her. I called the police like I would have to report a dog in a car with the windows up on a hot day.

Gant's police force arrived. They searched for Ben and his attacker. They took pictures of the evidence. The investigation was hopeful initially. This was Gant. The police would do their jobs; they'd find the person who stopped our car; Ben survived the attack and the authorities would find him. I'm not sure if Sweeny doubted Maggie immediately. But the police told Dad that they were suspicious of Maggie's account the following day.

The first red flag was the improbability of Maggie's version. How did a man with a painted face just appear on the highway? Why would Ben have stopped the car for a man like that? There were flares of alarm as Maggie worked with a sketch artist the morning after the attack. Each time she described him, other than the paint, his features varied. Her descriptions produced twelve sketches of twelve very different-looking men. The police grew impatient.

Unfortunately, I couldn't help. I'd gone to sleep and woken up to a world more dangerous. One where I didn't know the rules, or else there were none. A shadow man, I told the police. No features. No identifiable details. A variation of darkness in the night that I'd opened my eyes to, watched steal Ben away, and then lost. Gradually, in the days after, the hopeful talk about finding Ben alive, or at all, tapered off, until on the third afternoon I visited the police station with my dad and the officers, and Sweeny began using that pitiless word, *murder*.

I got the impression that they'd been using it for a while, quietly, hesitantly trying it out. The experts said that Ben had been stabbed at least twenty times, and the first few and bloodiest wounds were inflicted in the driver's seat. The spatter in the car, on the highway, and on the rocks told the story. Ben had lost more than half his blood. It was a near impossibility that he could have lived, even had he not been thrown thirty feet.

They couldn't find Ben's body. He was gone by the time the police followed the trail of blood across the road, trickling over the bluff, and to the tide pools below. That didn't surprise anyone. Tides converge a few hundred yards offshore, and the sound is deeper and rougher on that side of the island. The shadow man tossed Ben over, his bones broke on the rocks, and the tide swept him away. The coast guard searched, the chance he'd never be found increasing with each passing hour. There are schools of fish that nibble at dead flesh, and sharks as big as cars, and inlets for a body to drift into. The waters are carved up, with shipping lanes full of tankers and ferries with blades that could chop up remains. Three years ago a boat sank off a neighboring island, and two of the passengers still haven't been recovered.

On the fourth day, there hadn't been so much as one false tip or sighting of a stranger in Gant. The police began to discuss alternative explanations, including Maggie not being as innocent as she claimed. On the seventh day, Maggie Lewis left her family's trailer—a neighbor reported seeing her load a suitcase into her trunk—and drove away.

The details of Ben's death were all over Gant, and everyone accepted the only reasonable explanation. Like everything in Gant, Ben's murder came down to money. We had it and Maggie didn't, so she was a liar. It was a carjacking gone wrong. Maggie either recognized the man responsible or else she was working with him. Maggie hadn't even belonged in Gant; she only came to school here from off the island because her rightful high school was overcrowded. Maggie was scorned and Ben was leaving her. The SUV was pricey and a gift from our parents. Ben had cash in his wallet. The man stood in the road or else he waved the car down. Who knows, maybe Maggie convinced Ben the stranger was harmless? *Pull over*, she urged. Ben didn't give the car up easily. *He wouldn't have*, people said, nodding at his bravery, *not with his little stepsister asleep inside*. Ben was tall, broad, and strong, and people figured he'd fought back. Yes, a carjacking turned brutal murder.

The police assumed that the crime went so badly that Maggie

made up an absurd tale about a man with a painted face who appeared on the road to confuse the authorities and escape suspicion. All the bizarre details were her embellishments to make the crime seem like so much more than what it had been. She kept his identity a secret, even as the police threatened to charge her as an accomplice without his name. Then, before the police could prove that Maggie was at fault, she ran.

By that time, other than to attend the funeral, I wasn't leaving the house. School was out for the summer—not that I would have gone to classes anyway. I remained curled into a ball when Willa sat at the foot of my bed. I refused to speak when Dad brought grief counselors; I didn't move when Dad sobbed and begged me to come downstairs, to eat something, to let him open the curtains for a little sun. I collapsed into myself—my knees to my chest, my heels to the backs of my thighs, my head tucked under my arms. The only way I could stand the pain was to be as small as possible. It was simple. If there was less of me, there was less to ache.

The whistle of the espresso machine traveled upstairs; the putter of the mail truck reached me as it crept by in the afternoon; the front door shook the house as Dad went for appointments; the bird cry of his phone woke me when he worked from his study. It was a fever dream of the ordinary. How was life going on as it had before? I wouldn't—couldn't—do it. Not with Ben gone.

So instead, for twenty-eight days, I relived our shared childhood. No. Lived is wrong. *Lived* means too much and *imagined* means too little. I wasn't a kid talking to her invisible friend or playing with a plastic castle. But I also wasn't a girl gone mental, gabbing on with the ghost in the corner.

I would stay in bed and watch our adventures as the curtain of my eyelids dropped. It was like watching the play of my life. As kids Ben and I were drunk off make-believe. At the spring we were natives taming the wild. In the dinghy on the harbor we were lost at sea, the pretend so real it would take a gallon of water for me to stop being thirsty. In the dining room we built elaborate and colorful blanket forts—*cathedrals*, really. We'd stay inside their walls for hours as Ben told stories of cannibal pirates, mad kings, pitchfork-wielding scarecrows, and bloodthirsty lunatics.

There were hundreds, all the sort of dark, twisted fairy tales you find in dusty, yellowed books. Except these weren't from books—they were out of Ben's head. *They were ours.* And no matter the faraway land or the plot or the crimes of the villains, Ben always made the two of us the heroes. We were better and braver versions of Ben and Lana McBrook. Ben's fictive self defeated beasts. Mine was the warrior, bloody-knuckled after every fight. It was good against evil, and we always won.

I was ten, eleven, and twelve when Ben told them. They'd dazzled me like thundering fireworks lighting up the sky or a traveling acrobatic circus. I was tipsy and amazed, and like all things magical, it was impossible to recall how they'd worked. Their acts became disjointed. The details were weathered by time. I hadn't bothered to memorize them just like I've never memorized my favorite books. They were mixed in with all the other random stuff of life: the birthday cake preferences of my family members; the whickering echoes of laughter as we roamed the canals in Venice on my thirteenth birthday; fireside ghost tales told during fifth-grade camp. I set about piecing our stories together, using the fragments floating in my head.

It was better than getting out of bed and leaving my lightless room. I didn't want to see that Gant had returned to its version of normal—the nowhere place everyone pretended was the center of the universe, population every single person worth a damn.

Ben was gone. Maggie had gotten away with her part in it. And I never thought I'd see her again, until she showed up dead, *here*, at the bottom of our spring.

— 4 —

The police bring flashlights; their beams make slices in the dark, cuts that heal as soon as they're opened. Voices intensify as they spot Maggie's body. Josh explains how we found her, what we were doing before, and how he tried to revive her. He pilots us forward. I wonder at the calm making him stand straight over the dead girl. Each sentence is delivered levelly. When questioned we give mostly identical answers, our words spiraling around us. I get lost on a tangent, yammering to an officer about coming here since I was little, learning to dive with Ben.

Soon we're herded away from the spring; told we'll need to come into the police station and wait for the detective who'll head the investigation before we're sent home.

I wonder if it will be Detective Sweeny arriving from Seattle. Before Ben, Gant never needed a homicide detective. It used to be the kind of idyllic place that sells postcards and waterfront homes to dot-com millionaires. I haven't seen Sweeny since the last time she visited our house, the day Maggie disappeared. Sweeny headed back to Seattle, I assume. No one could question Maggie if she was

MIA, and they hadn't had enough evidence to arrest her anyway. She vanished, and with her went everything she knew about Ben's killer.

This is why a shot of awful glee cuts through me as I glance at Maggie's body for the last time. It doesn't last. I want Maggie to look defeated. Instead the ground fades from under her and she's floating, luminous and otherworldly. She looks powerful and wicked, a sleeping, supernatural creature straight from my childhood. I swing my arms against my sides, trying to scrape off the sensation of Maggie, rubbery and goose-pimpled as raw chicken skin.

I'm guided into a police cruiser. I realize the others have been filtered in different directions. Someone's drawn a fist with a middle finger up on the outside of the cruiser's windshield. The defogger kicks in as we accelerate on the two-lane highway. I watch the picture disappear. Ben and I used to leave doodles in the steam on windows. More like Ben drew and I doodled. Ben loved to reinvent the ordinary. Using pencils and his sketchbook, he reimagined a potholed parking lot as a veiny metropolis for a civilization of insects. He'd draw sailboats in the steam on the kitchen windows that faced the harbor, giving the illusion that they were on water. Once, I went down to breakfast to find a whole fleet of them.

I rejoin the others as we're led through the back door of the police station and to the waiting room, its framed flat-screen TV on mute, showing a Mariners game. I sink into a leather chair next to Carolynn. Opposite a reception counter, there's a bank of desks, uniforms crowded between them, heads bent, little more than susurrant voices reaching us. I pull my knees into my chest to make myself small.

Willa is across from me, staring blankly at the tops of her shoes.

Willa is usually like the heroines of the mysteries she watches on PBS. Steady gaze, cool calculating mind two steps ahead, a snappy comeback that strikes the antagonist between the eyes ten minutes after she leaves the room and they belatedly grasp her true meaning. I've never seen Willa go catatonic.

Becca's feline eyes are shifty and concerned. "When can we go home?" she calls to the officers amid the desks. No response. She whispers under her breath, words coming fast, "If they tell my mom we were drinking out there, I'll get sent to live with my dad. Mom is just looking for an excuse. And my stepmom hates me. She doesn't wear makeup and never cuts her hair and doesn't believe in soy milk and they don't even have a Starbucks nearby."

"This is bullshit. They're treating us like we aren't islanders," Duncan complains. I cringe. The way some kids, even some adults, refer to themselves as *islanders* in Gant drives me crazy. All that *us* versus *them* stuff does. I didn't used to notice it. But then I got to see Gant through Ben's eyes, an outsider's, once he got older and started forming opinions. After that it was impossible to go back and act like Gant is normal. Willa moved here when she was nine and she's said similar things about Gant, albeit not as loudly. Most places don't have so many fro-yo and cold-pressed juice shops, and kids aren't given sparkly new luxury cars, and parents aren't usually new-moneyed, working in tech, or island families whose ancestors built Gant.

Carolynn twirls her finger in the air with the look of someone impossible to horrify. "We found a body—Maggie's. There were beer bottles everywhere, and we weren't supposed to be out there past dusk. It looks shady. They weren't going to give us gold stars and say, 'Drink on,'" she says.

Josh holds his head in his hands. His dry hair is the color of honey; wayward and fluffy. I don't want to think that he's sad about someone like Maggie, but then I think how I probably wouldn't like him if he were the kind of boy who wasn't sad about a dead girl.

Even though the fruitless investigation, the hunt for the man on the highway, and the search for Maggie had died down by the time I started hanging out with the core, they still know all about it. They went to school with Ben and Maggie just like I did. Ben ate lunch in the quad with the core and the populars. They belonged to the same little community at school; they went to the same parties; they played the same drinking games. And even though Maggie wasn't one herself, they put up with her for Ben. While it's true that Gant's the kind of place where grown-ups smile tightly over a subject as messy as Maggie Lewis, and they're apt to remind the speaker that Maggie wasn't from Gant, my peers don't have as much restraint.

Carolynn pats at her still-perfect bun. If it wasn't for the slight tremor in her hands, she'd look like she spends all her Saturday nights at the police station. Carolynn's mom and mine grew up on the point, south of the lighthouse; our families are two of the old logging ones who have been here for generations. A photo shows Carolynn and me as plump babies, dressed in white eyelet jumpers, our moms in cashmere cardigans and our fathers in chinos on my parents' sailboat, named after my mother, Mira. Our mothers shared the same honey-blond hair that fell in effortless curls, sapphire-blue eyes, coy smile, and clipped laugh. They were the kind of friends who were closer than blood, an early version of the core. Those pictures are the only evidence that I didn't dream those years. Carolynn pretended I didn't exist until middle school. By seventh grade she had every girl calling me Uni-Boob. To my chagrin, she even went out with Josh in the ninth grade.

Despite this tumultuous history, the other members of the core welcomed me into their fold. Before I got out of Josh's car as he dropped me off after Marmalade's that first night, he said they were bonfiring at Shell Shores the next afternoon. He didn't even ask if I wanted to meet them, just assumed I'd be there. Who wouldn't? Willa and I arrived and we sat in the car for ten minutes. "You can't crawl back into bed and sleep away the rest of your life," Willa said. This was back when Willa was just relieved to have me upright. "This moping is beneath you." She meant to be supportive, but all those comments about moping made me want to hide how sad I was. I forgot all this once Josh spotted us walking over the dunes toward their golden bonfire licking the white sky of late afternoon. He waved and jogged to meet us.

Then Becca showed up at my door two mornings later. "You have got to save me from myself," she pled. "I cannot be trusted around strappy sandals." We took the ferry to Seattle and didn't get back until almost nine at night. It was like being with Becca when we were ten on the swings. We giggled and she asked about how I felt about Ben and said all the right sympathetic things and none of the "move on" stuff others did. She was less judgmental than Willa when I said I still hurt. Becca grew dewy-eyed and told me, "I think people can die from broken hearts." Becca got it.

With everyone but Becca, I struggled with what to talk about until a few days in, when we were at Shell Shores again and Becca was wearing a bikini she kept calling *banger*. *Banger* is a term that Rusty and Duncan used for any girl they wanted to *bang*. Becca thinks *banger* is infinitely charming. And once the boys saw that the term wasn't scandalizing the girls, they lost interest.

We were all smushed together on a blanket. Becca had a pack of sparklers and was lighting one after another and sticking them in the sand in a giant heart shape around the throw. She made us pose for pictures. Then she mixed beer with lemonade and spoke in a bad British accent as she informed us that this was called a *shandy*. Becca had met a foreign exchange student from London in Seattle the previous weekend and considered herself very worldly for making out—*snogging*—with him.

We toasted the queen, and Becca proclaimed her a banger. Carolynn and Willa rolled their eyes, the boys cheered, and I tried remembering what the queen looked like until I fished out the image of my grandma. It was a good afternoon, the kind that makes you bright and weightless. With the core there are a lot of those, and they make it irresistible to forget all the years they ignored me. They provide the ideal distraction from missing Ben.

Becca develops hiccups at some point, and they punctuate the passing seconds like a stumbling cousin to the loud ticking of the clock. In this harsh light I see Duncan's upper lip is stained from his bloody nose, and there's a bruise setting in on his chin where Rusty hit him. Rusty has dried blood on his ear. Josh told the police about their scuffle, but still, the evidence of violence makes me uneasy.

I bury my face in my hands. Maggie shoves me back, closer to Ben. The adventures of this last month—setting the rental kayaks free at Shell Shores, getting fake IDs in Seattle, and tucking bottles of pinot noir into our bags at Island Spirits without paying—matter less. Those escapades were all about the thrill. They were adventures that made my hands too weak to form fists, and I forced myself through them because I'm done letting adventures pass me by. All the nerve and mischief I had put between me and the loss are disappearing. The earth's revolutions reverse and accelerate; every passing minute hurls me a day back in time.

A detective in a pinstripe suit and shiny black wingtips ambles in front of us. His jacket's boxy in the shoulders and short in the arms—working class, Dad would note as though it were a bad thing. His hair is slicked back with the look of Dracula in those old-timey movies. He's clean shaven, his skin pitted with acne scars.

"First off, kids, my apologies for making you wait. I'm Detective Ward from Seattle PD." He blinks at us, near-black irises giving him a wide-awake look. "Second off, I know you've been through hell tonight." His pink lips grimace. "Here's the good news. I've been able to deduce a lot from the scene at Swisher Spring." He claps his hands once, and I start a little in my chair. "You've recounted events for my colleagues. How about we send you home and if I have additional questions, I contact you tomorrow?"

I'm on my feet, shuffling after the group for the front exit, when Detective Ward calls out, "Ms. McBrook?" I take two more strides before Willa swivels. She furrows her eyebrows at me as if to say, *That's you.* I turn slowly. "Do you mind hanging back for a minute?" Ward asks when he's sure he has my attention.

He doesn't wait to see me shake my head; he makes a beeline for the huddle of uniforms. Willa places her hands on my shoulders. Her bottom lip is indented from where she's been chewing its dry skin. The others siphon through the front door without sparing me a glance. Not even Josh or Becca seem to care that I'm not with them. "He's going to ask you about how you knew Maggie," Willa tells me softly.

"He'll already know," I say. "We gave our names and they know Maggie."

Willa brings her face closer. "No, Lana. Listen. You don't need to tell him what you thought of her." Her brows go up meaningfully. "You don't need to be honest." This last sentence she mouths. I understand. Willa doesn't lie. For her to tell me I should, it's important. I'm going to talk to the detective about a girl who's dead. It wouldn't be smart to express that I despised her. This is okay. I am a sometimes liar. Always have been. I get it from my mother.

Willa leaves, and I unravel a loose thread on my distressed jean shorts, working the small tear that's supposed to be there into a gaping wound as I wait for Ward to return. While I do, I remind myself of this, my most important childhood lesson.

I was four years old, feather boa draped on my shoulders, Mom's lipstick smeared in a clown's smile on my face. It was the week before she died. I know because she was lighting sparklers left over from the Fourth. I called them fireworks. Mom would be gone by mid-July.

I remember the bottle of wine overturned at her feet, her heels across the terrace, the way all her words were sighed, and her twinkling eyes. Dad used to say they were the exact color of the sea surrounding Sardinia, where they honeymooned. He wasn't home then to coax a wisp of a smile out of her. She was beautiful and crying.

"Mommy, are you happy?" I asked. I had this baby doll that whimpered when you pressed the plastic palm of one hand and cooed when you squeezed the other. Both recordings sounded like a deranged goat, but I'd had a lot of practice identifying sadness.

"Yes, baby. Perception is nine-tenths of everything. Even of the truth, Lana. Don't I look happy?" She smiled tightly, little creases radiating from the corners of her mouth. I nodded. But she didn't fool me.

I can replay this dialogue because my memory's been helped along. Mom left journals and pastel sheets of perfumed stationery with letterpress roses along the borders and all her little idioms written out in cursive in her hope chest. I pored over them when Ben found the chest's key in Daddy's desk for me.

Ward's smile warms to the degree of an elderly lady eager to serve you scratch lemonade when he returns to the waiting room. "Lana, may I call you Lana?" I nod. "Good. I appreciate you staying behind. The officers said you mentioned being pretty familiar with Swisher Spring. You kids said you didn't see anyone hanging around its vicinity today, but I wondered if you'd noticed any regulars around the preserve during any of your previous visits. Any hikers or strangers you've noticed more than once?" His tongue flicks to wet his lips; a reptilian tic.

"Tourists don't usually swim at the spring, since there's no sign at the trailhead and they don't know it's there. There are hikers, yeah, but I don't know if I've seen anyone more than once out there." My eyes stray in the direction that Willa and the others disappeared.

"What about locals? There's a homeless man who camps in the area, no?"

"Skitzy-Fitzy." I suck in my breath. "Sorry. Fitzgerald Moore." Kids call Gant's only homeless man Skitzy-Fitzy or "the troll," which is brainless, since trolls live under bridges and Fitzgerald camps on the embankment of Swisher Tunnel. Kids throw soda cans at him along the road with his rusted, ancient shopping cart. After an incident with two boys from the baseball team a couple of years ago, he ended up badly injured. At best people pretend not to see Fitzgerald. Ben's the only reason I know his real name. Ben said he was schizophrenic and had a long-dead uncle who had lived on the island.

"And?" Ward prompts.

"I've never seen him at Swisher Spring," I say. Does he suspect Skitzy-Fitzy of something? And if not, why ask?

"All of you knew the deceased?"

My stomach does a flip at how quickly we move from Skitzy-Fitzy to Maggie. "Yes," I say. "Maggie was two grades ahead of us. Our high school's small and everyone knows each other."

He points at me. "But that's not how *you* knew her."

I bite the inside of my cheek, looking from the finger to his eyes. This is what Willa was worried about. "That's how I first knew of Maggie. She went out with a lot of guys, and people always talked about that. I met her when she started dating my stepbrother right before their senior year. That was two years ago."

Ward tilts his head at a sympathetic angle. "Yes, I'm aware of your and Ms. Lewis's history." My forehead puckers. It means something that Ward knew about my connection to Maggie and questioned me about it anyway. Did he suspect what Willa knew, that I hate Maggie Lewis? And why would it matter? "One more question, please. If you had to guess, what do you think happened to Ms. Lewis that she ended up at the bottom of Swisher Spring?"

I think *karma* loud and clear and I'm almost certain Ward's pupils dilate like he hears. "I don't know," I tell him.

A long moment of silence, his alert eyes fixed on mine. I shift my weight from one foot to the other. "I see," he says finally. "Well, you keep thinking about it and be certain to let me know if anything plausible occurs to you." He turns to go and then adds, "Thank goodness the lot of you happened upon Ms. Lewis's body. I wonder how long she might have gone undiscovered. I'm sure the last thing you wanted was to lose another close to you." He watches my reaction. "So sorry for your loss, Lana. Oh, excuse me"—his palm to his chest—"*all* of your losses."

I walk rubber-kneed to the station's front door. The whole way I replay Ward's words—*all of your losses*—in my head.

There are more than he knows.

— 5 —

I am a story.

My *before* predates Ben's death and my *after* postdates it. I have a prologue that I guess could be defined broadly as the whole history of the universe and as narrowly as my mom and dad meeting, falling in love, marrying, and ending up with me. I don't know those parts all that well, so I won't tell them. I guess by the same logic I'll have an afterword, and it will go on once I'm dead and can't dream or think anymore. All that does is make me panicky as a caged animal.

The story I know well starts when Mira McBrook drank two bottles of Sancerre, swallowed three antidepressants, kicked off her black satin pumps, told her four-year-old daughter that she was tired of pretending, and jumped from the upper terrace to her death.

It was dusk and Daddy was on his way home. The french doors to the kitchen were open and he heard me screaming as he came into the house.

Dad and I did fine without Mom. We mourned appropriately, and when it was time to move on, we did. I was a lonely kid, but it had nothing to do with Dad not being there. He often was. And when he wasn't, a babysitter was there to entertain me or I was getting bossed around by Mariella, who cooks and cleans for us and has a talent for making her voice heard over the roar of the vacuum. Sure, I pine for some people's moms. All motherless girls do that.

Six years after Mira McBrook said good-bye in her strange way, Dad met Diane away on business. They dated mostly over the phone. Dad was lonely, romantic, and impulsive. He proposed. The day I met Ben was the day they arrived to move in. The wicked stepmothers and bullying brothers I'd seen on TV didn't exactly send me bouncing to greet them. Diane turned out to be a bird-boned brunette, younger-looking than the moms at school, with a sweet smile and a way of speaking that made me think of air escaping my bike tires. She brushed my braids from my shoulders, and I saw that she was missing the middle finger of her right hand. I liked her more for the mystery.

Ben slunk from their van gripping a cat carrier. He blinked at me with these giant eyes and a tear-streaked face. He was all uneven, his limbs too skinny for his big, round joints, and he trembled while angling the hissing tabby between us.

"Hello," he whispered, hardly louder than the cat. He was almost two years older yet a billion times more afraid. Instead of threatening him with the knitting needle I'd commandeered and was holding at my side as a sword, I took his hand and showed him to his room. I didn't want a brother before I met him, and then once I had, imagining life without him was like laughing with one lung rather than two.

Most siblings want to be different. They want to say this is me and that is you. But we were amateur brother and sister from the start. Both survivors of things we didn't want to talk about. Instead of crying over what we couldn't change, we reinvented ourselves as two kids who had, and only needed, each other.

We wanted secret messages spelled out on scraps of paper, hidden in places only the other would look. We wanted fireworks on the *Mira*; Decembers spent festooning her sails with sparkly lights; gingerbread house–decorating with Diane and Dad after they'd had too much eggnog to care about us pouring ourselves glasses; and weeknights when Ben and I ate dinner on the upper terrace, the Scrabble board between us, the sun fading to chalky rose behind the tree-logged hill.

We wanted traditions and inside jokes and family pictures and secrets. We wanted to belong to each other, and so we did. Do. Present tense intended.

If I am a story, then Ben is also. His prologue is a mystery to me. Did his mother fall in love and marry his father? Where was Ben born? I know pieces. One year he and Diane lived in a double-wide trailer with a car thief neighbor. The next they stayed in a mansion with an ancient plot of graves on the grounds and a giant bloodstain on the floor of the ballroom. Ben talked about nests of fiddler crabs in marshlands, fortune-telling bag ladies in Savannah, and men dressed up as women singing opera on the street corners at night.

But: Where did the inspiration for his stories come from? All those marauding villains with their insatiable appetites for screams and blood weren't born out of air. You had to be sneaky asking Ben about before Gant. I understood he didn't want to talk about it. I didn't want him to have to, just sometimes the curiosity got to me. Ben would laugh and say, "When we met, you were holding a knitting needle at your side like a sword. Trust me, the stories don't take *that* much imagination."

Ben had imagination for days.

Perhaps more than imagination, Ben could play the shadows. He knew what words to use to make you laugh; he knew ten more to make you scream.

Most kids would think we were freaks to be so wrapped up in gruesome make-believe. It would take hours of me lying in bed at night before the jitters would stop and I could fall asleep. They weren't for nothing, though. Our stories weren't senseless like the video games where you run around shooting people, stealing cars, and pistol-whipping prostitutes. Good beat evil. I, *a girl*, was the hero.

Ben stopped telling them eventually. That sort of make-believe dries up as you get older. Our games evolved. Ben was in awe of our island initially. He wanted to explore every windswept beach and trail. We spent summers searching for the source of Swisher Spring. We performed high dives between the rocks. When we were old enough, we sailed the *Mira* without Dad; parentless we sunbathed on her decks and waved and yelled as ferries blasted their horns in the distance. We sailed to uninhabited bits of land and foraged for berries and slept under the stars and got bitten lumpy by mosquitoes and roasted near a million marshmallows. We had adventures and swore on everything that mattered to us—on *summer*, our favorite time of year—that we'd never have as much fun with anyone else.

Ben got older, and the awkward boy who showed up with the tabby vanished. The kids at school stopped calling him praying mantis. He grew into his limbs. Ben became golden, popular, and opinionated.

He had better luck than me. Being a teenager isn't as hard for boys as it is girls.

For girls there starts to be all this static in middle school: who likes who; who hasn't had their period; who has boobs; who's stuffing their bra; who's going to second base; what is second base; who's a slut; who dresses like a slut; who's a prude; who dresses like a prude. It goes on and on. I slouched. I dressed to avoid attention. I kept my eyes and head down. I could jump, hoot, and snarl on the wild adventures with Ben, but as soon as I got to school, I made myself small and unnoticeable. I focused on what was ahead.

The girls in college wouldn't know that I was excluded from sleepovers because I wore a sports bra that gave me a uni-boob. The boys wouldn't know me as Ben's weirdo sister, or half cousin, or foreign exchange student—no one ever bothered to get the step-thing right.

Luckily, Willa wanted out of high school too. We spent the first semester of ninth grade on our plan. We consulted every college preparatory resource, researched college admission stats, pored over Gant High's course catalog, and plotted out the remaining semesters of high school to maximize our chances of getting into the colleges of our dreams. It was our foolproof map to escape. And then, in a blink of an eye, all that changed. It turned out that I was rushing to a place and time where Ben wasn't real.

There's nothing I can do to change it. You can't go back in time any more than you can regrow a lung once you've lost it. The only thing to do is learn to breathe with just one.

When I emerge outside, the core and Willa are against the lamp-lit brick facade of the police station in various positions. Some of their heels are kicked up on the wall, heads rested on crossed arms, and butts on the sidewalk. Josh is in a squat; he pops to his feet like a tightly loaded spring released. The rest of them follow.

"You guys waited," I say as an exclamation and question.

"We weren't going to leave you," Josh says.

"Why did he want to talk to you alone?" Duncan demands. He's a full head taller than the rest, hovering with the look of a gargoyle—a handsome one, if there's such a thing.

"He wanted to know if I've ever noticed anyone hanging out at the spring or hiking in the preserve, since I told the police that I'd been there a lot before. Ben and I used to go," I add, looking to the washed-out sidewalk, hoping that my voice isn't shaking. "He asked if Skitzy-Fitzy camps near the spring also."

"But why ask you *privately*?" Carolynn presses.

I shrug, eyes darting to Willa. I worry that the answer has nothing to do with me knowing the spring better than the others and everything to do with Ben's death and Maggie's part in it. "The detective also asked me what I think happened to Maggie."

"What did you say?" Josh asks.

"That I don't have a guess."

"Hold up," Duncan says, waving in an exaggerated way. "He asks you if you've ever seen Skitzy-Fitzy or anyone else hanging around the spring—the spring where Maggie showed up drowned. Then he's all, 'What do you think happened to the dead girl?' He thinks someone offed her," he exclaims, eyes bugging sadistically out of his head.

"Try not to sound so excited," Carolynn remarks, her heart-shaped face cringing in displeasure.

"But they can't think any of us had anything to do with Maggie-it-doesn't-matter-she's-on-the-rag-ie drowning or whoever might have." Becca sings the nasty nickname like a little kid jumping rope.

Willa turns with a shake of the head from Becca. "Maggie's death was mysterious, and none of us had an explanation for it. It stands to reason that they're at least contemplating murder."

There that pitiless word is again: *murder*. I never questioned who put Maggie at the bottom of the spring. It didn't really occur to me that someone must have. But of course someone did. Maggie was very hateable.

"The whole island knows she's responsible for Ben dying," Duncan says. "That's a whole island full of people who hated her guts."

"Maggie didn't off Ben alone. She had a carjacking buddy," Rusty says. "Maybe it's that she was mixed up with this psycho that got her killed? Maybe *he* killed her?"

I think about this. Whoever was on the highway that night is loose in the world. No one knows what he's done. I can't believe that he'd take the risk of coming back to Gant. I also don't believe that Maggie would have returned to Gant *willingly*, not after she fled the police, not after her staying gone was the only thing preventing the police from pursuing her as a suspect.

"We shouldn't have even tried to save her." Becca says this for me. "Maggie was beyond shady—totally evil." She beams at me. I should be grateful. I shouldn't wonder who killed Maggie, or whether her death has anything to do with Ben's. This shouldn't drag me in reverse to the time when I couldn't stop wondering who Maggie's accomplice was. Now I wonder who had more reason than me to want Maggie dead. Who knew where she ran off to? Who hunted her down and lured her back to Gant to drown her? Possibly, she wasn't even drowned but killed somewhere else and dumped into the spring.

I look up the sidewalk. It's on the late side of ten, lampposts glowing like orbiting moons, and there are adults wobbling inebriated from restaurants and stepping over flower beds. A few middle-school-aged boys balance on skateboards outside the ice creamery under the candy-cane-striped awning. Maggie's killer could be somewhere, not too far beyond them.

There's an eerie symmetry between Maggie's death and our stories. They always ended in the same way. The villains weren't carted off to prison; they lost their lives. Maggie set the events in motion that led to Ben's death and she turned up dead, possibly murdered. It makes me sick and happy at once. If Ben were here—Ben, whose heroes always killed their villains—he would call this justice.

Willa shifts forward confidentially and keeps her voice low. "Lana said Maggie was caught under the water. It's possible that the killer tried to prevent her body from being discovered. They didn't want her to be found, and *we* found her. What if we're in danger for it?"

Josh winds himself up and gives a nod he thinks will settle it all. "We're careful until we know anything for certain. Nothing we can do but wait and see." There's an optimistic swing to his words, and it sends comfort fanning out over the core, like a security blanket, easing their frowns and paving the way for Becca to remind the group that Josh's birthday is tomorrow and that she will *so not tolerate a canceled party*. Then there's a lot of agreeing to wait and see—and presumably to not commit the unthinkable act of canceling a party. The specifics of being careful or waiting and seeing—what we're going to do after we wait and see or what we're waiting for—aren't discussed.

It's difficult in Gant to believe you aren't safe. Hard to make the adjustment even after you've seen proof. Everyone but Willa, who stares at her shoelaces, seems convinced that all will work out, somehow.

Danger didn't used to be real on our island. You have parents and house alarms. You leave your bags on the beach during a swim and no one touches your cell. In the winter you leave your car running with the heat blasting to duck into Marmalade's for mochas, extra whipped cream, dark chocolate shavings on top. Gant is a state of mind as much as a place. I learned this summer that the idyllic island doesn't exist. Bad things usually happen when you least expect them, in places you believe you're safest.

We trade good-byes, and Willa and I separate from the core. I eye the dark gaps between buildings.

I know these lessons better than the others:

Life is biting into a cupcake and finding an eyeball at its center. Going to bed with the covers to your chin, all snuggly and dreamy, and waking up without your teeth.

— 6 —

There's the smell of bonfires, sweet charred marshmallows, and the singed edge of fireworks in the air as Willa and I walk to where the police parked her car. Gant Island is perfumed by its coastal celebrations all summer long. The breeze parts my hair like a finger brushing my neck. I shiver and smooth it to one side.

To my right there's a grassy slope leading to the pedestrian promenade that meanders along the water the length of downtown. We slip between two clots of tourists gathered at the front of a gallery with strummed guitar chords floating from its open door. I sidestep a woman in tall, spiky heels. I trip from the curb before I catch my balance. My head snaps up to avoid any cars. When I focus ahead, I see Ben, kicked back on an iron bench, one arm folded behind his head, long legs extended and crossed at the ankles just above his Vans.

A surprised cry from me and I run. He points toward the sky. There's a girl kneeling beside him, gazing dreamily up his arm, her black hair cascading over her shoulder. A flick of his fingers and he produces an origami star he holds up among the real constellations. I'd sit for hours studying in the kitchen, and when Ben had given up on distracting me with silly faces, he'd toss paper throwing stars into my hair. When my attention finally strayed from the books, he'd be smiling. "You have stars in your hair," he said once, gray irises almost silver. I wanted to say, *You have them in your eyes.*

This memory plays as a transparent screen over Ben and the girl on the bench. They both laugh as he lets the star drop into her lap—a *shooting star.* His laugh is warm and liquid like Ben's always is. Was. I stop a yard away. I squint. All at once the boy looks nothing like Ben. His hair is too dark, his nose too small, his jaw rounded rather than squared, his posture not nonchalant enough.

"Lana?" Willa calls. The boy and girl on the bench blink at me expectantly. The remains of a picnic are at their feet. A date in progress.

"Sorry," I mutter. I spin to retrace my steps. Willa's elbows are on the roof of her car; she frowns, watching me. "I thought I knew him," I say, with a casual toss of my hair. I open the Prius's passenger door. My arm shakes. I drop into the seat and try to appear neutral as she climbs behind the wheel.

This does not happen to me. I do not see Ben in crowds at the beach. I do not catch the tail end of his laugh in the movie theater. I do not glimpse his shadow slipping around corners. And it isn't for lack of trying. I look for him on the deck of passing sailboats and in the clouds threaded in the trees on the ridge opposite our house. I look for his name spelled out in the pebbles of our driveway. I look for his profile in the bark of trees. He's never there.

Willa accelerates past the couple on the bench. The boy has next to nothing in common with Ben. His features didn't blur to resemble Ben's. He didn't gesture in a Ben-ish way. He *was* Ben. This leaves me feeling unreliable. I crack the window and let the breeze dry out my eyeballs.

We pass the grassy square and the amphitheater where bands play on Sunday nights. Then the historic cinema that features foreign films. Kids at school mostly go there to make out and for this truffle-and-sea-salt popcorn that's practically world famous. I had my first-ever date there with our school's math decathlon team captain. Theo had shaggy blond hair and dopey, sweet eyes. We dated for three months during my freshman year. He ate lunch in the one hundred hall at school, which is just one removed from the quad and its populars. Willa and I ate in the library with a rotating population of study groups. Theo and I shared a handful of closed-mouth kisses, and I liked the way his bangs swooped over his forehead, almost in his crescent eyes. Then he opened his mouth during a kiss and I got a mouthful of burp-flavored saliva. I didn't like him enough for that. He wasn't who I wanted to be kissing anyway.

Although I am usually nauseated recalling Theo's slippery tongue, tonight it helps to think of ordinary things.

I look left in time to see a single teardrop slide down Willa's cheek. "Willa?" I strain against the seat belt to take in her whole face.

"Just don't, okay?" she says. "Wait to talk to me tomorrow."

"Are you okay?"

"Rosalind-effing-Franklin, Lana, just don't." She slaps the steering wheel. Her eyes flick to mine, and she must see my bewilderment because she adds softly, "Rosalind Franklin basically discovered what human DNA looks like. You should know that one."

A sheepish smile from me. Willa's always used her idols rather than curse words. As a kid, Willa would tell me, "I'll know I've made it when people start taking my name in vain."

"I'm just so tired and I don't want to say something I'll regret," she says. "I want to get home and talk to my mom about what happened tonight, before she hears it from someone else and I'm in thirty more kinds of trouble that I didn't call her and that I was with *those* kids." Willa's mother is our school's principal; Principal Owen is not so affectionately called Gant High's P.O., as in *parole officer*. Although I've convinced Willa to hang out with the core a bunch this summer, Willa is increasingly worried that her mom is going to realize just how much time she's spending with the kids P.O. refers to as "fast." It's probably only because we have so many years built up of never getting into trouble that Willa's been able to fly under the radar the last four weeks.

My wanting to go to parties and Willa's reluctance and sometimes refusal to go hasn't caused a rift between us, because although Willa and I have been bests since the sixth grade, we were never the kind of inseparable girls who did each other's pedicures and shared a sleeping bag. Plus, I had Ben.

When we were younger, Ben and I invited Willa on adventures. P.O. rarely let her come, because Dad and Diane weren't there to supervise. *Supervision* was always a big deal for Willa's mom and not a priority at the McBrook house.

"Willa—"

"Tomorrow." She gives me a grave sideways look as the Prius glides soundlessly up the driveway. I add wait-until-tomorrow to the wait-and-see of earlier. Their comfort and optimistic promise carry me into my house. Basel, Ben's tabby cat, meets me at the front door and runs figure eights around my ankles as I double- and then triple-check that I've set the house alarm.

Although she's the last person I want to think about as I get ready for bed, I can't stop seeing Maggie's glowing figure on the dark rocks of the spring. In death she looked like the powerful villain I knew she was.

During those twenty-eight days when I let sadness swallow me up, I also let guilt in. How hadn't I seen what Maggie was capable of? I'd thought she was ordinary, nothing more than an alternative girl who liked thinking she was original but was actually a cliché. She wore safety pins in her ears rather than earrings. She had mostly wannabe-hippie friends, and when she wasn't with Ben, she hung out with the kids who thought they were all political and enlightened because they wore hemp jewelry and ate pot brownies at reggae shows in the city. She scribbled all over her clothing in Wite-Out and Sharpie: M + B, or MAGGIE MCBROOK, or B+M 4EVER. She wasn't subtle.

Ben was the first boyfriend she kept longer than a few months. Before him she'd mostly dated older guys, the kind who hung out in their cars behind the school tennis courts, waiting to sell kids *substances* in paper bags. Maggie's exploits were the kind that pinched-nose cheerleaders thought were outrageous, even though they weren't different from what their football-playing boyfriends got up to.

Most of all, Maggie was jealous. If Maggie saw Ben talking to a girl in school, she'd rush up and chase the girl off and then get into a yelling match with Ben. If Maggie suspected Ben was getting texts or calls from girls, his phone would disappear. During their senior year Ben stopped going to parties with Maggie at all because they'd had so many blowups.

I don't get why Ben put up with it. He'd say, *She's passionate* or *I don't mind fighting* or *She hates Gant as much as I do.* That was it. They railed on Gant together. She had an outsider's perspective too. She could roll her eyes and go on about the beastly waterfront houses. The only difference was that Ben lived in one of them.

Ben and I would glide into the harbor after a day on the *Mira* and he'd shout, mock emphatically, "*Gant,* the idyllic island where the millionaires of Seattle flock with their 2.4 kids, labradoodles, and trophy wives. Gant, where shit doesn't stink and bullshit is recyclable, where everyone gets to be white, rich, and an asshole." It was theatrical and true.

Ben probably hated himself a little for it. There he was, on the deck of a *sailboat,* complaining to his cashmere-clad stepsister about the kids at school who only got jobs driving carts at the course because they were bored. We didn't have jobs, period. I heard Maggie call Ben a hypocrite a bunch of times.

If I hadn't been so busy being jealous in the way only a younger sibling can be, maybe I would have seen some indication of what Maggie was capable of. Tonight that guilt gnaws at my stomach. Ben and Maggie graduated one year and two months ago. I go over and over that time, trying to find the clues, the foreshadowing.

It isn't there, or I can't see it.

They graduated. Maggie got a job at an old people's home near her house. Ben took a gap year because he wasn't sure about college— where to go, what to study, or even if it was for him. When it came down to it, Ben was as desperate to escape as I was. Not just Gant, though. Ben wanted to escape the neatly laid road at his feet. College. Job. Someday a family and house in a place like Gant.

As a freshman he'd liked this perky blonde in the Amigos Club, and because of her, he'd gone with them on a trip to dig a well in

Guatemala. He departed home talking only about how hot she was. When he came back, it wasn't about her any longer. He saw Gant in a new harsh light. He went on two more trips like that during high school, and he wanted to return to Guatemala after graduation. He wanted to spend his whole gap year digging wells and volunteering on a village farm. He probably would have spent forever there if our parents had approved.

Diane went pale and left the room whenever Ben talked about traveling after graduation, so it fell to Dad to try and talk him out of it. "What's the matter with studying abroad at university?" Dad intoned. "I'll send you and Lana to Paris to visit the Louvre if you want another stamp in your passport. But Central America? To dig a hole and plant some beans?"

Dad and Diane wanted Ben to find himself at college, *like a normal kid*, on the campus of Dad's alma mater. But Ben was stubborn and wouldn't give up on the idea. The difference between where he'd been in Central America and where we lived was big. The comparison made us look like jerks with our flavored bottled water and designer wellies. I remember the day after he got home from that first trip, he stood stock-still in front of our open refrigerator. "There's brie in the cheese drawer," I said, watching his back, "baguettes in the pantry."

He turned at me abruptly; he looked angry. "It's hard to worry about landfills or where your trash ends up floating when you have a million flavors of bottled water to choose from." Up until then, Ben had been smitten with Gant. He saw only the forests, sound, hiking trails, and beaches. We had our adventures. Then: the freshman trip. The change in Ben was immediate. Gant's magic had been washed away.

So when Dad refused to pay for the time abroad after graduation, Ben valeted cars at the club and worked at the farmers' market, selling organic preserves for Swisher Farm. It took six months to earn enough to leave for three months. Ben and Maggie dated off and on for those months, and they were bad ones. There were loud public fights.

Maggie was furious that Ben didn't want her to come to Central America. They weren't speaking when I dropped Ben off at the airport on March 1. At some point between March 1 and June 3, when I picked Ben up, he'd decided to end it with her for good. He was through with Maggie. He'd rethought college and he was ready to do what Dad and Diane hoped he would. He drove over and broke it off with Maggie that very night, right before his welcome-home dinner.

It wasn't the first time. Depending on your source, Maggie and Ben had broken up twelve or fifteen times. But this time was different. It would stick. Ben hadn't spoken to her once in the three months he'd been gone. She must have known she was losing him. I heard the desperation and anger in her voice when she showed up the night Ben was murdered. See, unlike the police, I don't suspect Maggie of only arranging to have a friend ready to take Ben's wallet and car. I think she wanted to hurt him. Why else did she drive us away? Why didn't she leap from the car and stop it from going too far? If she knew the man, she could have saved Ben.

I may feel guilty that I didn't see Maggie coming, but for the first time since Ben, I don't feel as though he's completely lost. Before Ben died, our house always felt full. Days at home meant Ben and me on the window seat in my bedroom, taking turns reading aloud; scouring for summer provisions to stock the *Mira*'s aluminum chest; abreast on the couch in the media room, sharing the same perspective of the movie on the projection screen. Ben had a theory about that. He thought that most people see the world too differently to love each other, and that a lot of that difference is perspective. If we sat side by side, then we'd at least perceive things in the same way. It was literal and silly and maybe a little profound, too.

While Ben was in Guatemala the house was quiet, but not empty. Why would it have been? Ben was coming home. He wrote e-mails from his hostel's computer. Ben was out there, far away in a different country, making noise that I could pretend to hear.

Since Ben's death our house has been quiet *and* empty. Not tonight. I almost hear the grinding of the pipes from Ben showering in his bathroom. I feel the tremors from the bass of his speakers. It's easy to imagine Dad and Diane in the kitchen, sipping espresso and talking about their days. It's a wonderful and pathetic game of pretend. It leaves me warm and sick to my stomach.

Basel senses it too. He paces in the hallway, even after I'm in bed, duvet up to my chin. It's as if he thinks there's a chance that Ben is arriving home tonight and he's waiting like he hasn't in weeks.

— 7 —

People wear sadness like they wear hats." Dad's latte is steaming and he pushes a mug full of the white, frothy mountain of a cappuccino toward the chair next to him at the table after I say good morning. I sit and wrap my hands around the warm ceramic. "You slept late. How are you feeling?" He regards me over the rim of his mug as he takes a sip.

I stare at the soft peaks of the foam. "I've been better and worse."

Dad's eyes narrow as he takes me in, checking for parts more broken than I'm letting on. He eases his glasses off once he's satisfied that I'm okay. He doesn't have a clue what to look for. "I'm glad you called me when you got home last night, Bumblebee. And that you're letting me support you through this . . . strange turn of events." He briefly covers my wrist with his hand.

Everything Dad says is loaded. By making a general statement about sadness and hats, he's initiating a conversation about *my* sadness. By telling me he's happy that I'm letting him "support" me "through this", the subtext is that I refused to talk to him when we lost Ben. I was inconsolable. Why let Dad or anyone else waste their time trying to console me?

I smile, tight-lipped. "What about sadness and hats?" I ask.

Dad rests his ankle on his knee. He couldn't stand being out here on the terrace before Diane and Ben came to live with us. It never bothered me; Mom and I had good memories here too. "It's something I read after Ben," Dad says. "That one line stuck with me. The author went on with the metaphor, of course." He gestures with his hands. "Some wear their sorrow backward like a baseball cap, some wear it to the side, some pull the bill as low as possible to hide their faces from the world." A graying, bushy eyebrow is raised. "Do you understand?"

"Everyone copes with grief differently," I say automatically.

"That's right, Bumblebee." He pats my wrist.

"I'm not grieving for Maggie, Dad."

"No, not how you grieved for Ben, but you went through hell last night. You kids pulled that troubled girl from the water. You knew her. Ben cared for her. I wouldn't be surprised if you were uncertain what's normal to feel in an inconceivable situation like this." He shakes his head as he lifts the latte to his mouth and continues shaking after a sip.

I watch a low-flying bird and its shadow cut across the harbor. *Troubled* isn't the adjective that comes to my mind when describing Maggie. Even though Dad believed that she had a hand in planning the carjacking, he couldn't fathom that a teenage girl had anything to do with murder. Dad put the blame firmly on her accomplice. He seemed to believe Maggie had no way of knowing that things would turn violent.

I don't like adults much anymore. It took Ben's case for me to see it. Adults let you down. They say *I'll handle this* and then they bungle it all because they have lousy imaginations.

Adults are judgey and terrible and disappointing.

Dad lifts my chin until he's looking into my eyes. "Just promise me that you won't wear your sadness like a hat covering your face from the world. You aren't alone," he adds tenderly. "If bad memories are resurfacing for you, you can talk to me, *confide in me*, or you could call Mariella. She's a mother, you know."

Mariella only comes over a couple of times a week now, to stock the fridge with meals and tidy up our barely-lived-in house. Mariella doesn't live on our island and has three sons to worry about, and even if this was not the case, she was never interested in being motherly to me, which is great, since I was never interested in being daughterly to her. "I'm fine, Dad," I say. "Really."

Dad's eyes cut from the glittering harbor, and his forehead puckers. I look away from his concern. It's late morning and there are only the barest wisps of fog lingering. The reeds of the marshy banks of the north end hold the snaking tufts in place. I watch as a patch of fog seems to spiral on the shore. The wind blows. The fog begins to take the shape of a boy, about nineteen, hand raised to me, beckoning. I know he isn't real. My brain plays Ben's voice: "C'mon, McBrook. Let's have a summer day." Ben always wanted summer days.

It didn't need to be summer. It was just one of those things we said. Summer meant freedom from school; summer meant idle days of being rocked on the water. Summer was the highest compliment we had. *That's awfully* summer *of you*, I'd say if Ben brought candy from the movies. *You're always so* summer, he'd say if I saved him the last piece of key lime pie. When we wanted to make the most serious promises, we swore on summer. We loved the word. I wrote it on the inside of my notebooks and scribbled it on the soles of my TOMS. Once, I wrote it low on my hip bone where no one else would see and pretended that it was a tattoo. We called all our supplies for the adventures we went on *summer provisions*. Butterfly nets, peanut butter and marionberry sandwiches, and beach towels for the spring. Fishing rods, life jackets, and a tube of sunblock on the dinghy.

I raise my hand to wave back to the dissolving fog boy as Dad asks, "Would it help if you went to talk to someone?"

My hand ends up combing my blond hair into wings resting on my shoulders. I know what Dad is hinting at. If he only knew what I was thinking, *seeing*. "I'm talking to you now," I say, a hint of irritation in my tone. "I talk to Willa."

Dad passes a hand over his face. "I'm glad that you have Willa to support you, Bumblebee. I'm suggesting you speak with someone who's an expert in coping with loss. Perhaps one of the doctors helping Diane at Calm Coast?"

Dad used to call Diane every night at her emotional health retreat. For the last two weeks she's refused to come to the phone. The doctors say to give her time; she's suffered a loss. A century isn't going to make a difference. Yes, mothers are supposed to be the fiercest beasts in nature, but Diane was never a tigress guarding her cubs. She isn't out of her mind with grief. Diane is on vacation from reality.

Diane began mysteriously. Ben was more interesting than anyone I'd ever met, so surely Diane had secrets and a story herself.

I asked her what happened to her missing finger a few weeks

after they came to Gant. She was sitting right here at this table with Ben and me. She was eating a croissant, one flaky layer poised at her lips, when I asked. The burnt golden bit fell to the tabletop, and her head dipped strangely as she turned away. I looked quizzically to Ben when she retreated to the kitchen. "Do you know?"

Ben leaned in and whispered, "A monster took it." Then he flicked the fallen crumb of croissant to a speckled bird at his feet. I didn't move. He looked up, all sly-smiled. "I had you going," he said with a laugh. "She got frostbite during a snowball fight when she was a kid and lost it. Can we not talk about my mom?" I agreed. Who wanted to talk about moms anyway?

My point is this: Diane was always spacey and lost. A bit like a windup toy right before it dies. Everything happens slower, if at all. When I brought good grades to her, and Ben brought sketches, she'd murmur *how nice* and drift away. When Dad was at work, she'd disappear. I'm sure it wasn't as dramatic as that. She went places and had friends. We didn't mind. We had freedom. Dad brought us to school and we rode the bus home until Ben got his license. We ordered takeout or heated a dinner left for us in the fridge. Diane was always way more Dad's wife than my stepmother—even more than she was Ben's actual mom, which he didn't appear to mind.

"Really, Dad, I don't need to talk to anyone else. I'm never going to end up as a hermit in my room again. I'm not even going to stay home today."

"Oh? You'll need to be vigilant going out." Dad flips over the *Gant Island Times* on the table in front of him. The headline reads SUSPECT IN VIOLENT CARJACKING FOUND DEAD. A small, faded picture of Maggie is below.

"How is it already on the front page?" I ask. "It was barely twelve hours ago."

"I'd say an officer called the paper last night," Dad muses. "In Gant, it's big news. You recall the coverage of Ben." A long pause, possibly fueled by Dad remembering that I actually don't know about the news coverage because no one delivered the newspaper or turned on Channel 5 under the covers in my bedroom. I avoided it then and sure, I could use the Internet now, but what would be the point? I was there. "You kids weren't mentioned by name, although the piece does state that a person related to the victim of the attempted carjacking was among those who uncovered Maggie's body. It won't take long for everyone to deduce who they mean. I think you'll be safe as long as you stick to someone's house. Maybe invite Willa—or even Becca and her sort—over here?" Dad suggests.

I turn the cappuccino in a 360-degree revolution in its saucer. "It's Josh's birthday and he's throwing a party," I say, glancing up at Dad. "I don't have to go, though."

Dad shakes his head. "Don't miss it. New friends are important. I'm proud that you're making them."

I cringe inwardly at this reminder that even Dad was aware of my relative friendlessness before this summer. "I'm going to call Willa," I say, sliding my chair away from the table.

Dad's flipping through the paper before I make it into the kitchen.

I curl on the window seat in my bedroom with Basel. He purrs into my chest and his heat lulls me sleepy. I try Willa three times on her cell with no answer. I toss my phone and it lands on the carpet below. Once it's there, I know I should have used it to dial

Josh or Becca to confirm that his party is really still happening. Minutes roll on and I mean to reach for it and make those calls. But after hours of the same position, a pleasant numbness spreads. There's the faint tickle on my toes that rest on the window-seat cushion, and I imagine that spiders have mistaken me for furniture and are busy shrouding me in their webs. My sticky eyelids part in brief, fluttery intervals to catch Ben standing in my doorway, watching me. I'm losing my mind. It isn't unpleasant.

Becca calls eventually, a giddy and frantic lilt to her voice that doesn't fit the conversation. "I'm a celebrity today—I've gotten like a zillion texts about Maggie. Pick you up for Josh's bash at nine." I picture her clasping her hands at her chest, dancing from foot to foot in anticipation of an event worthy of a cute outfit.

"Okay," I say listlessly.

I read for the rest of the afternoon, until the words rearrange themselves on the page and I'm squinting to make them out at dusk. I pull myself up, turn on the shower in my bathroom, and return to the window seat, waiting for the warm water to kick in.

I must have drifted off to sleep, because I open my eyes to a dark, steamy window. I haven't been out of it for too long, since the gushing hot water continues to send fog wafting through the doorway. I prop myself up on my elbow. At chest height there's a little boat, triangle sail and mast, drawn into the steam on the glass.

I rub my fingers together; not wet. Was I dozing off, doodling absentmindedly? Thinking of Ben so I drew a sailboat like he used to? I stand and try to stretch myself alert. This sailboat might be a little drawing left for me by Ben just like the drawings on the kitchen windows. But how many times have I showered recently? I always leave the door between my bathroom and bedroom open, allowing steam to enter, making the windows sweat.

I haven't been perceptive lately. I put flip-flops on the wrong feet the other day; the granola in the fridge a week ago. I let the weird, sleepy state wash away in the shower.

While I blow-dry my hair, I decide on wearing a black dress that Becca and I found at a boutique in Seattle a couple of weeks ago. She said it made me look like a *banger*. If I'd been alone, I would have passed on the too-short dress. Becca—with her fingers crossed under her chin, her tousled chestnut hair smelling of saltwater spray, and her pink lips pursed in a heart while she waited for my verdict— was too hard to say no to. I pull on a black cardigan, almost as long as the dress, and slip on flat sandals even though Becca says no girl over fourteen should ever wear flats. Maybe she really believes this; maybe she only wears heels and ankle boots to hide that she's slightly pigeon-toed. She creates camouflage to cover up her insecurities.

Three blasts of a horn come from the driveway. Dad's on the porch when I get downstairs. Becca's in the passenger seat with the window rolled down. "I told Lana to phone if you two need a ride home," Dad calls to her, waving toward her house. I remember Dad asking me years ago, *Why aren't you buddies with Sophia Atherton's girl anymore? You kids are three houses away. Wouldn't that be fun and easy?*

Becca leans out the window and waves as if she's royalty riding in Gant's homecoming parade. "Thank you, Mr. M."

"She looks a little enthusiastic, recent events considered," Dad says from the corner of his mouth when I stop at his side.

Becca's grinning like a happy lunatic.

"If you want me to stay home, I will," I offer.

Dad nudges my side and smiles encouragingly. "You should go. It'll be good for you to get out. Worst thing you could do is sulk and think about the past."

The foamy-looking clover bordering the front porch sparkles in the beams of the headlights. Carolynn gives one last belligerent honk as my fingers close over the door handle.

I slide in as Becca whispers, "Play nice with the other kittens, pleeeease."

She could be talking to Carolynn or the twin toy schnauzers straining for freedom in her arms. Winkie's and Twinkie's lavender-painted nails clack against the center console as they try to claw their way to me. The car is full with the smells of mint, the flowery perfume Becca dabs in no less than ten places on her body, and the four drained iced coffees in the cup holders. Carolynn has a serious caffeine addiction and will only take her coffee and espresso over ice and sugared up with whipped cream, chocolate shavings, and caramel syrup.

"Hey"—Becca twists around to blow me a kiss—"you look freaking gorg."

"So do you," I say. "Hey, Carolynn."

"Hi," she answers curtly, without taking her eyes off her car's backup camera.

Becca sticks a pink flask in my face and sloshes the liquid. "Peppermint schnapps," she sings. "Yum-yum-yummy!"

"Thanks." The liquid is cool and syrupy on my lips. It leaves me thinking about winter and hot cocoa. I shiver even though the leather's heated under my butt. The windows are fuzzy with steam. I trace half of a boat's triangle sail before I stop.

Becca props herself up on her knees to face me, folds her arms on the headrest, and cups her chin. Her eyes are sleepy, dewy, and drunk. Her smile is lazy and warm. The dogs are set loose, and once they avoid getting tangled in the long gold necklaces she's wearing, they make desperate leaps to the backseat. Their little lavender nails paw at my hands as they whine shrilly to be petted. Becca sways gently with the car's momentum around a turn. "My babies love Josh. They had to come celebrate," she says. "He's the only guy who plays with them and never complains that I make them look faggy or if I paint their nails."

I go rigid at the ugly word.

"B, you can't say the F word, not even to repeat," Carolynn says.

I give in and scratch Twinkie's head. He wears a pink collar, and Winkie wears purple, both encrusted with crystals. "I know, I know"—Becca's hand flaps—"I call pass since most people never have to see a dead person, let alone find one who's been *murdered*." She pauses, angular brown eyebrows knitting until she gives a little nod. "I get passes all night." Her arm is outstretched and her hand opens and closes spasmodically until I put the flask into it. She tips it to her lips.

Her inebriated smile has returned as she offers the schnapps to Carolynn, who waves it away. "Carolynn has her serious face on tonight," Becca says in a pouty baby voice.

Carolynn doesn't respond.

"Willa didn't answer my calls," I say, unnerved. Carolynn and Becca are always in sync, finishing each other's sentences and laughing before the punch lines of jokes. This tension makes me feel more like a third wheel than their closeness does.

Becca yawns into her hand and goes for a fifth cup that's half-full with what was probably iced coffee earlier. "I need caffeine," she says. She slurps the liquid. "No worries 'bout Willa. I called to say the party's still on."

I lean forward, seat belt scraping along my neckline. "What did she say?"

"She was quiet *forever.*" Becca pauses to return the coffee cup to the holder. "Blah, coffee mouth," she groans aside, and goes for a sip from the flask. She hiccups, giggles, and wipes her mouth on her bronze, bare arm before continuing. "She said she'd try to convince her mom to let her come."

I don't say that I wonder if Willa was just aiming to hang up and knew she needed to appease Becca to do so. She hasn't come out at night with the core for a couple of weeks. "I tried calling her cell and she didn't answer," I say.

"I had to call the landline. Talked my way past P.O. Told her I needed a summer tutor and wanted to talk to Willa. I'm something else, huh?" Becca smiles triumphantly.

I bob my head in agreement. I stop. I am a traitor. I shouldn't be talking about Willa with anyone other than Willa. I should have had the guts to call the landline. I could have braved Principal Owen.

Carolynn cracks a window. "I'm getting contact drunk huffing all that schnapps, B," she complains.

Becca drops back on her butt with a flounce and faces forward like a naughty child who's been scolded. After not too long she fiddles with the stereo, hitting next on ten songs before she finds one she approves of. "This is my anthem," she shouts happily. Her window is rolled down and her arm hangs out. It flaps uncontrollably against the wind as we go. It reminds me of how Ben's limbs were buffeted against the asphalt of the road as he was dragged and stabbed. I look away.

Josh's house is halfway between mine and Swisher Spring. Up until a month ago I bet I was the only upperclassman who'd never been inside. Even Willa had gone when she was paired with Josh for an AP biology assignment in ninth grade.

Beginning sophomore year, Josh hosted parties when his moms went out of town. Josh and I had third-period chemistry together, and I'd hear people asking him what time to show up and if there'd be Jell-O shots or pizza. Once he invited Jamie Nanderbosh, who sat at the desk to my right. Maybe it was because Jamie and I talked a decent amount that I felt bold enough to stare as Josh invited him to a party. Josh saw me drop my eyes as he caught me listening and added, "You're invited Friday too." I bobbed my head, sensing his gaze on me. I stared at my class notes and hid my shaking hands in my sleeves until he ambled up two rows to his seat.

I reenacted the invite for Willa: in pajamas, standing at the foot of my bed, Willa humoring the performance; before the first warning bell rang, sitting in Willa's car, as she wolfed down a marionberry scone and I paused to take sips of kale smoothie. Privately, I imagined all the ways it could play out. In the rosier scenarios, Josh pulled me aside and told me how happy he was I came. Or I did something amazing, like talked the police out of breaking the party up. Then Josh would apologize to me for not recognizing how great I was before. It was pathetic. *I* was pathetic.

Friday night rolled around and after all that, I didn't go. I told Willa I'd be happier eating Rice Krispies Treats while finishing my English lit paper. The invite was a fluke. If Josh saw me there, he'd be polite. Carolynn would spill a beer on me, everyone would laugh. Or worse, Carolynn would spill the beer and Josh would tell me to leave. Or worst, Ben would be there to witness all of the above. Ben would observe just how unlike that ferocious little girl with the knitting needle I had become. See, Ben could have solved all my problems in school. He had that same radioactive effect that the core has. I only needed to repeat what those cruel girls had said and Ben would have stopped it. My problem: This would have meant admitting what I was. How unlike my braver, fictional self I'd grown to be. I couldn't bear Ben knowing. Instead I acted like I wanted to eat lunch in the library. I pretended that parties and dances didn't appeal to me and that I wasn't interested in making new friends. I lied.

Josh's street is lined with cars. His two-story house is putting out amber light from its floor-to-ceiling windows. Becca drums her palms on the dashboard. "Gah," she says as a happy gasp, "it looks like half the school is here." She flips the vanity mirror open. "I think my lips are too skank red and not enough vixen." She purses her lips to Carolynn. Carolynn grunts. Becca twists and blows me a kiss before returning to her reflection.

We park in the driveway behind Duncan's SUV. "C'mere, babies," Becca coos. "Your fans await." Twinkie and Winkie leap from the backseat, scramble over the center console, and land in a squirming heap on Becca's thighs. They scale the walls of Becca's oversize quilted leather tote and perch expertly inside, so their little front paws are hooked and their heads poke out. They've been to more of Josh's parties than I have.

Outside, the crisp air nips only at my nose, the schnapps spreading over me like a flannel blanket dulling the cold. Surrounding trees bow gently, their triangular tops bending with the look of flexi-straws in the wind. Becca's arm loops mine. "The schnapps is sneaky like that," she whispers. Her face is close, and she smells of candy canes and spiked coffee. I grin. She's as intoxicating as the schnapps.

"I didn't know there were going to be so many people," I say as we follow the semicircular driveway.

Becca's arm tightens around mine, the dogs and the purse bouncing at her back. "Tons of people aren't even home from vacation yet," she laments.

"I bet less than half who showed up actually know Josh," Carolynn says sourly.

I frown. "*Everyone* at school knows Josh Parker. Every single person." I sound too impressed.

She eyes me. "You mean knows *of* Josh and his parties, right? They don't know him. Not like me or even you do." There's a difference between what we choose to show people and who we are. I'm surprised that Carolynn knows about the line separating the two. "Schnapps me," she says.

We pause on the front lawn. The flask is passed; she drains it. Carolynn dabs her fingertips at the corners of her mouth and gives a decided nod like she's just resolved an internal argument.

"Grin, grin, grin until you feel it in your belly," she says, an ironic twist to her voice. She gives what I'm sure she thinks is a devil-may-care smile. Her eyes are too big. She uses a mantra that I hadn't realized was one of our mothers' shared idioms. There's an invisible thread tying Carolynn to me, and in a glimmer of moonlight, I see the proof of it. I have this shared history with her, and it means crap to Carolynn because she's only ever hurt me. It strikes me as insanely unfair that this awful, exquisite girl is my oldest acquaintance. I've spent most of four weeks trying to pretend she doesn't exist as I've gotten closer with her friends. Both these truths make me want to reach out and snap the thread right here.

But Becca and the schnapps are warming me, and I don't feel anything for Carolynn other than curiosity. I just let all the hurt go and leave it on that velvety green grass to sprout as weeds. "Perception is nine-tenths of everything, and you only need to appear okay for them to think you are," I say. Carolynn's stare darts to me, and I swear she actually smiles.

— 8 —

Josh's house is what a home should be. It's usually warm, smelling of fresh-baked chocolate chip cookies and brewed coffee, and decorated with vintage chessboards that make me wish I was good at playing and oil landscapes that remind me of my grandmother's study. The Parkers keep extra slippers in their entryway closet for guests to wear after they've shed their shoes. There's always a fire burning and a pie under the glass bell jar on the kitchen counter. It's a difficult place to leave.

Tonight Josh's house is as inviting as a fraternity during rush week—at least those I've seen in movies. A group of senior boys are posted outside, scowling up and down the street that disappears into the dark.

"Ladies," one boy calls from where he's perched on the railing. His heels drill the house's siding as he swings his legs.

Becca waves. "Hey, Rob. Is the party that weak?"

He pats a baseball bat slanted at his side, and I realize all the boys on the porch are Rusty's teammates. "Nah, we're just keeping a look-out. Rusty Pipe said Maggie was offed by somebody, and you know, we can't have druggie pervs from the city thinking they can pick us off. First Ben, now Maggie—even if she got what she deserved and wasn't an islander." The guys behind him bark in agreement.

"Oh my God, Maggie could have been living in one of those tents near Capitol Hill, where all the runaways and hookers are," Becca says.

"Nu-uh," Carolynn says offhandedly, her attention directed at the kids visible through the window. "Why would Maggie have ended up dead on our island and not there?"

"True. A city douche over the ferry wouldn't have known about Swisher," Rob says, flipping his cap backward and winking at Becca. "Catch up with you inside." His teammates lift their cups in salute.

My pulse is too loud in my ears as we file in through the front door. The baseball team is standing watch for a killer on the front porch. Gant's had two murders in as many months. With her hair like that and haunted blue eyes, Carolynn is a vision of my mother's ghost. She's giving me sideways looks like she can hear my thoughts. And I have the sense that I'm not all the way awake.

Inside, the amber sconces and the fireplace cast distorted shadows that twist and turn to have their look at us as we enter. They linger on us too long. The space is packed with partyers. Red plastic cups cascade down the staircase. A group plays beer pong in the dining room, celebrating with whoops and hollers. I get glimpses of the kitchen as the swinging door opens and closes. The mob of bodies pressed inside chants, "Chug! Chug! Chug!" Duncan stands at their center, the ringmaster of a circus in his skipper hat. A tight cluster of kids hang out an open dining room window, a cigarette traded between fingers.

A stilted melody, interrupted by a drilling rendition of "Chopsticks," comes from the grand piano in the adjacent family room. The piano's keys shriek in pain. A competing stereo plays the summer's hip-hop, what amounts to a bizarre soundtrack for the muted, overexposed-looking film on the flat screen above the fireplace. Josh's moms, Karen and Lily, put together the video montage for the party, and because Josh is the kind of boy who isn't embarrassed by his parents and defies gravity, it's playing and kids are crowded around, watching a clip featuring a cast of children wearing white bedsheets over their heads with eyeholes. One of the ghosts has scarlet corduroy pants peeking out from under the sheet. The next sequence shows our first-grade class singing "Happy Birthday" over cupcakes to Josh. The camera pans over the class.

"Look, there we are," Becca squeals, pointing. The camera glides over Becca and me, huddled and laughing over our frosting mustaches, before it moves on to other kids. I'd almost forgotten that we shared a desk. "We've been friends for ages," she says, half hugging me. I want to point out that we were friends back then, until the first day of middle school, when I asked her if Willa and I could eat with her at lunch. She stared at her new, grown-up heeled sandals and mumbled, "There isn't room. Sorry." There wasn't room at the twenty-foot-long cafeteria table she shared with ten other girls. It was a see-through lie.

Jamie Nanderbosh, with his T-shirt wrapped around his head like a pirate, whoops loudly and slides down the banister, kicking the red cups, sending them tumbling to the landing. Becca bounces forward with the dogs and purse swinging against her hip.

Kristie Riggio and Liddy Smyth, both cheerleaders, are standing with Rusty and Ford Holland. Kristie and Liddy are inexplicably wearing their cheer uniforms. They have glossy buttons pinned to their chests, showing a smiling Josh with the words BIRTHDAY BOY arced over. I spot a few more kids in the crowd with buttons secured to their jeans and collars.

After hugging Becca hello, Ford says, "Carolynn, looking tasty."

"Flirt with someone you have a shot with," she says bitingly as she cuts through the circle, gives Rusty a peck on the cheek, and makes a beeline for the kitchen. It's hard not to watch her fierce, dazzling figure go.

Ford laughs softly, bitterly. Ford is a sometimes companion of the core. We have a long, bad history. Before freshman year he was a boy who made snide remarks about anyone who spoke up in class. But once we got to Gant High, Ford singled me out. He sat behind me in freshman English and he'd knee me through the gap in my chair or slide forward in his seat and breathe heavy on my neck. We were in astronomy together sophomore year, but after a semester of his harassment, I moved to journalism. Since then, he's had plenty of opportunities to go out of his way to knock his shoulder against mine in the halls. We crossed paths earlier this summer at a cookout with the core. I overheard Ford asking Becca why I was there. Why was everyone *still* kissing Ben's ass?

Every time Ford looks at me, I can feel his thoughts ticking over all the nasty comments he wants to make and measuring their desired effectiveness. His eyes run from my reddening cheeks, to the dress tight on my chest, to my revealed thighs. I brace myself. This will be ugly; it'll remind me that he doesn't believe I belong here.

Instead he grins and says in a cloyingly sweet voice, "Hey, *sweetie*, looking hot." He throws an arm around my shoulders. Kristie and

Liddy glance at me, offering brief, identically fake smiles before turning back to Becca and her dogs. Ford's armpit is damp through my cardigan. He presses me close and keeps looking at me like the compliment should be the highlight of my year and should have the power to erase the time I read *Fugly Slut* on a wadded-up piece of paper he gave to me. I shrug him off and look to Rusty.

"Here," Rusty says, tossing me a button from his pocket. I catch it. Its glossy picture of Josh is different from the ones Kristie and Liddy are wearing. Josh has one arm slung over Duncan's shoulders and the other over Rusty's. "Remember that day?" Rusty asks.

"Yeah," I say. It was the queen-of-England-is-a-banger afternoon. The picture was taken at midday; the boys don't have shadows. They're grinning in that doggish way some boys smile when there are girls in bikinis. Carolynn, Willa, and I were standing behind Becca as she snapped the picture. Duncan grilled steaks like kabobs afterward on knotty sticks he foraged from the bordering woods. Becca threw a fit because the sticks looked like they could be poison oak. Duncan had to walk Josh to the tree he'd broken them off, so Josh could vouch that they were safe before she'd eat.

I smile at Rusty. "Where is the birthday boy?"

"Why? You have a birthday surprise for him?" Ford interrupts, cracking the knuckles on one hand, then the other.

Rusty says something about Josh pulling kids out of the upstairs rooms, but my cheeks are heating up again and I want to be anywhere but standing next to Ford. I'm almost relieved when Kristie and Liddy begin gushing about Maggie. It's all over town that the seven of us found her. Liddy asks Becca if Maggie was shot between the eyes and then dumped in the spring or *only* drowned.

"Like, were her eyeballs still in her head, or did they disintegrate?" Kristie asks. Her voice is high and grating. She's cradling Twinkie like he's an infant. The little dog squirms miserably.

Becca is sipping off Rusty's cup, and she sprays her mouthful across the circle as she laughs. "That would be too sick," she says.

"Of course her eyeballs were in her head," I say. "Maggie *drowned*."

"But were there worms coming out of her ears? Was she all bloated and fat?" Liddy asks Becca as if I hadn't spoken.

I shake my head. It's throbbing like my high ponytail is banded too tight. "It wasn't anything like that," I say. "Maggie looked . . . beautiful. It was awful."

"It would be my bliss to see Maggie's face all gigantic and about to pop like a zit. She was always bending down right in front of Tyler freshman year, and I swear his staring at her butt was why we broke up." Kristie tries to hold in an explosive laugh with her palm. "Oh my God. That doesn't make me a suspect, does it?"

Liddy covers her mouth in mock horror. "No way would you survive prison."

"Only if I was the bitch of some lesbo gangster hottie like in that show about girl-jail," Kristie says, eyes shining as Rusty chuckles. "Swear it wasn't me, though, so who?"

"The cops don't have any real suspects," Ford says, shifting forward. "That's what I heard my dad telling Duncan's earlier." Ford's dad is Gant's lawyer. "Gant PD is full of college dropouts used to giving parking tickets." Ford thumbs the tiny animal emblem on his designer shirt like he's reminding himself why he thinks he's better than the cops. "Even the detective they called in from Seattle is an incompetent halfwit."

"He was all over us at the police station," Rusty says. Liddy and

Kristie make sympathetic noises. I narrow my eyes at Rusty's lie and attempt at impressing them. "Yeah, I was like, no way did I kill a girl. I don't have a motive. I should have been like, maybe Ben McBrook's ghost did it, dude?" The others laugh at this.

My mouth goes dry. I miss what follows. I stare at Rusty, and eventually his eyes meet mine and he grimaces, equal parts uncomfortable and sheepish for mentioning Ben. It was a stupid thing to say. Brain-dead for a billion reasons, not the smallest being that ghosts, ghouls, specters, all the stuff of childhood make-believe, do not exist. And yet, I sneak a glance at the shape-shifting shadows cast on the walls.

"What did Ben ever see in Maggie anyway?" Becca asks.

Rusty snickers, his perma-sunburned face deepening a shade. "I know what he saw in her."

"I'm just wondering because there were so many hotter girls who wanted a piece of that," Becca explains. "*I* sort of wanted a piece of that, but he never looked at me, not even when I streaked at a Halloween kegger here and I ran right past Ben."

"That slut got what she deserved," Ford says. "For Ben," he adds, dull brown eyes waiting for my reaction. What does he expect, a swoon? I've thought the identical thing, minus the girl-shaming insult. The words are so much cruder and more violent coming from Ford, who's cracking his knuckles in another round and failing to swallow down a beer burp.

Liddy looks up from adjusting her cheer uniform and blurts, "You didn't even like Ben, Ford. He and your brother were feuding." She presses her lips flat and looks uneasily away.

Ford's smile hardens. He takes a sip of beer, the red cup's rim cutting off all except his glaring eyes. I know what he's thinking about.

Gant High has this tradition where they donate the profits from homecoming tickets each year to a charity of student gov's choice. His junior year, Ben proposed that our school use the money to help Fitzgerald. Ethan Holland, Ford's older brother, and Max Riley were at that same meeting, both trying to convince student gov to donate the money to their baseball team. They wanted to hire some trainer to come in and give them a swing lesson. Ben argued with Max and Ethan. The money was supposed to go to charity, not to help pay some ex–pro baseball player's fee, especially when the team could have just asked their parents to cough up the money. Right there in student gov, in front of almost thirty kids, three teachers, and Max's and Ethan's girlfriends, Ben told the two boys that if they needed lessons on using their *bats*, he'd help them out. It was stupid and beneath Ben. He'd just wanted to embarrass them.

Instead of taking out their humiliation on Ben, Ethan and Max drove to Skitzy-Fitzy's tent that night. Fitzgerald was found on the shoulder of the highway the following morning, one leg bent behind him, face pulpy and misshapen. Rather than arrest the boys, the police took Fitzgerald to a doctor off the island and told him not to return. He didn't come back for six months.

Becca gestures between us. "Okay, fangirls and fanboys, Lan and I need to find the guest of honor." Her hands thrust out and Liddy returns Twinkie. With both dogs as passengers, Becca's fingers lace through mine and she tugs me away as Liddy nibbles on Rusty's neck. I squeeze Becca's hand. We're escaping. I sense Ford's eyes stalking us. I want to duck into the crowd, lose him. There's something else, though, that's making me feel tracked, hunted through the room.

Maybe Ben McBrook's ghost did it.

Rusty's words are alive and crackling in my head, they're sprouting legs and scurrying after Becca and me, and I want to stop short, whirl around, and kick them away. But I don't. However impossible—however wrong, stupid, *classic Rusty Pipe*—his statement is, it brings Ben into the room. It gives him a little life and takes away a little death.

And I'd want Ben back even if it meant he were a monster, changed, diminished, someone—*some half-living thing*—he wasn't before.

— 9 —

Ford and all them are such hangers-on," Becca says over her shoulder, hardly out of their earshot. She narrows her smoky lined eyes in disapproval and laughs a little to herself. "Not that they should be shunned or blacklisted. Ford wants to *be* Rusty, and Liddy has wanted to hook up with Rusty since forever, and I can smell their desperation on Mars is all."

A tiny ping in my chest. I doubt that Liddy's wanted to hook up with Rusty as long as I've liked Josh. In a former summer might Becca have sniped about smelling my desperation from another planet?

"It's Ford I can't stand," I tell her.

Her glance is thoughtful. "Carolynn hates him too." She frowns. "Maybe I don't pay enough attention to see it?" Her grin returns. "Destination kitchen?" I nod. It's hard to stay worried about Ford or what Becca might have said in the past when she's tugging me along, girls who are buckets more popular than me eyeing our clasped hands with envy.

Belonging is its own kind of magic, and Becca is its grand sorceress.

Duncan is at the center of attention in the kitchen, a bottle of whiskey raised in a toast above his head. Josh watches, his expression a mixture of amusement and concern. It's hot and stuffy with thirty kids in a spellbound knot, their conversations paused. Duncan clears his throat, more as an intro than a request for attention he already commands.

"Here's to my oldest friend, Josh Parker"—he sweeps an arm to Josh—"who's never gamed up any girl I was into. Not even once," he booms. The crowd cheers. Duncan throws his head back, bottle to his lips, and drinks. Josh bows dramatically to the applause. His blue eyes land on us as he rises. He mouths an emphatic, "You're here."

Becca hooks her hair behind her ear, setting her gold earring swinging, and says, "Duncan's been hammered the whole day *and* with Bethany J." Her green eyes glitter and she bounces her exposed, freckled shoulders. "He gets a pass just like me too, though." She wags her finger. "Car does not think so."

I go to ask why Carolynn doesn't think Duncan should get a pass, but Becca tugs me along. Duncan finishes his chug to louder whooping. His hat falls and I watch Bethany J., adjusting her crop top as she swoops it from the floor and places it on her sleek black hair like she's crowning herself queen. Duncan doesn't seem to notice. He's unshaven, giving him an older, dangerous look. His feet are squared and he's swaying like someone winding himself up for a fight. Duncan with his hard and shiny exterior, a glittery Easter egg of a boy, doesn't seem like someone who cracks after seeing the body of a dead girl he knew only superficially.

Becca cups her hand around my ear. "Not everyone can deal," she whispers. "Seeing a corpse." With her face this close, she looks like she did when we were ten and she used to whisper secrets about her dad's affair and her parents' fighting.

Willa and Carolynn are at the breakfast nook, each facing away from the other. I throw my arms around Willa and even though she's not a hugger, she squeezes me back. "I called you three times," I tell her.

Her features look naked without glasses, and by the gentle squint of her eyes I know she isn't wearing contacts. "I saw. Sorry. I wanted to think through some stuff before we talked," she answers quietly. Tiny blue plastic barrettes I haven't seen in years pin her bangs. Willa's angry with me. Why else would she avoid my calls, need to think through what she wanted to say, and then show up for a face-to-face?

"Josh," Becca squeals brightly. He's all smiles, bobbing head and waving hand like he's a small-town mayor greeting voters. He dodges a group of soccer players calling him over for shots. He delivers hellos to us as the kitchen goes quiet.

Only Duncan's raised fist gripping the bottle is visible over the sea of heads. "Here's to my best buddy, Josh, who always has my back, even when it gets him a broken nose and a split lip 'cause I talked shit about some senior d-bags frosh year." Applause fills the kitchen.

A strange noise comes from Carolynn's throat, and then in a deep, flat pitch meant to imitate Duncan's, she says, "Here's to Josh, who throws house parties so I can drink my face off like some alcoholic Neanderthal." Josh reaches to take Carolynn's hand.

"Don't get your panties in a wad." She holds her hands up in a state of embarrassed agitation. "I'm just messing around, okay?" She hugs herself and cuts a straight line, the crowd parting for her.

I watch Josh as he watches Carolynn escape into the backyard. He isn't himself tonight either. His tan skin isn't as warmly hued. There are twin frown lines between his brows. And there's something less tangible that's off, like his usual aura of well-being is calibrated wrong. He meets my eyes. They are light blue like the shallows of the sea. Infinitely compassionate.

"She's freaked out from yesterday and it's just easy to take it out on Duncan," he explains.

"Everyone is so bumming me out," Becca says, giving a little stomp of her heel. She digs through her purse, unceremoniously pushing Winkie and Twinkie aside until she comes up with the flask of schnapps. She jiggles it, is reminded that it's empty, and without a word, veers toward a group of popular junior girls passing around a bottle. Within seconds she's surrounded, the girls enraptured by her guest appearance. Becca beams, motions to her shoes, and gestures as she recounts some exploit. Her fans laugh, delighted, each made to feel special with a brush of an arm or a compliment. Becca smiles blissfully when she's given a bag of miniature marshmallows and control of the bottle. The natives lay sacrifices at their priestess's feet.

Willa mutters that she needs to lie down. Josh produces a key from his jean pocket. "I lock my bedroom so I don't end up with random couples in there," he says in an apologetic way. "You can use it, though." Willa starts toward the rear staircase. I should follow. She's my best friend and she looks like she's going to be sick. She came to Josh's party to talk to me. But I haven't been alone with Josh for days and I want to stay standing near him, on his birthday.

"I'm glad you came," Josh says. He's moved closer.

I try for calm and casual. "Where are your moms?" I ask. Fail.

What kind of social outcast brings up parents at a kegger?

"They went out to dinner and a movie in Seattle." Josh frees a bottle of water from the pack at the center of the kitchen table and offers it to me. We settle against the oak table, facing the drama of the room. I twist the cap off and drink. He runs a hand down the back of his neck. "Am I the lamest eighteen-year-old ever that I hope my moms get home early so the party can end?"

Duncan's done toasting and our classmates have grown rowdier without his performance distracting them from their own drinking. The laughter is forced and bawdy; flashes fire as selfies and group shots are taken.

"I don't think so," I say. "Up until a month ago, I'd never really been to a party." Josh is being honest, I should too. "I was surprised that most people seem to be too worried about fitting in to have actual fun."

Josh frowns and looks around the room for a few seconds. His eyes cut back to mine, and they're surprised. "You're right. Everyone looks miserable." He laughs. "Like they have to be here and they know they should want to be, even though secretly they'd rather be home playing Assassin's Creed in sweats."

"Or reading a Brontë novel," I add.

"Or eating an extra-large pepperoni pizza, drinking a gallon of orange soda, and watching old-school *X-Files* episodes on Netflix." He grins and then feigns embarrassment. "Or is that just me?"

"Everyone secretly loves Mulder and Scully."

"This"—he waves his water bottle over the kitchen—"isn't what I wanted. Some of the others needed a party. It feels weird to celebrate after yesterday." He slides closer, and our thighs meet.

Warmth washes up from our points of contact. "Not that I'm sad for her." He reaches for my hand resting on my leg and hooks his pinkie with mine. It's an innocent little touch, the crook of my pinkie on the crook of his. My breath goes shallow, though. "I know she wasn't a good person. I bet finding her . . . being reminded . . . I don't know . . . makes you hurt worse for Ben."

"Yeah," I chance. I worry that I'll scare Josh by letting the grief spill into my voice. I try to keep it light with everyone except Becca and her policy of zero judgment. The core likes to reminisce about Ben the keg-stand champion or Ben the hothead who threw the first punch. Those are good. Those are safe, easy things to talk about.

"I know that the others can seem stuck in their own world," Josh continues. "Seeing Maggie, how gone she looked, has everyone messed up."

We watch as Becca tosses miniature marshmallows into Twinkie's snapping jaw. She tires of the trick and throws marshmallows to the junior girls so they take turns catching them in their mouths. Soon she's over that, and in a last-ditch effort to amuse herself, she targets a hapless girl standing in a nearby group. I recognize the girl as a reporter for our school's news blog. Becca does a little victory dance when her marshmallow nails the girl between the eyes. The victim tries to laugh it off as everyone around her snickers.

I almost gag at the wave of shame rising in me. I'm reminded that belonging feels so good because not everyone does. Becca's as much the sorceress of exclusion as belonging.

"It doesn't look like Becca is upset, but she called Car at three a.m. last night. She kept having nightmares," Josh says. His pinkie tightens around mine. I look away from Becca. This is all I want to feel, our pinkies, hooked and pressing. "Then I got to thinking that what all of us are feeling is like a millionth of a percent of what you've been feeling for months. If B's having nightmares over a girl she didn't like . . . I thought about what you're going through."

I drop my eyes to our joined fingers. "You've made it easier. It helps to do the kind of things Ben used to do. He liked bonfires at Shell Shores, and he loved breaking rules."

"And spitting in authority's face." The corner of his mouth tucks up in a devious way that's exotic and charged on Josh. "Ben was always trying to turn parties into rallies for something, like protesting the school store because they got our mascot hoodies from sweatshops."

I laugh. "I hadn't heard that one."

"Yeah, but he'd be shouting about kid labor one second and then he'd be out-chugging every guy on the beer bong. That's why people loved Ben. He was so . . . *different,*" Josh says.

I smile without feeling it.

Josh chews the inside of his cheek and then continues staring at my shoes. "Is it weird that we were sort of friends with him, partying together and hanging out at school with the same people, but not you, and now he's gone and we're friends?" He meets my eyes.

"A lot's changed since Ben died," I say, my voice shaking. I take a deep breath. "I don't care about being *weird,* as long as I'm moving forward, away from sad."

Josh's side rocks into mine softly. "My grandpa died three years ago. My mom doesn't have other family, and she was really broken up about her dad. She stayed in bed for weeks. And my other mom still had to go to work, and when she wasn't, she was trying to be there for Mom. It was a rough time. I didn't know how to make toast or

wash laundry before that. You're going to think I was such a lazy shit."
He smiles guiltily. "I didn't know how to start the dishwasher, like, I
couldn't have identified where the buttons were for a million dollars.
I learned so that I could help out. I should have known how sad you
were . . . are."

We just sit there, the length of his side pressed to the length of
mine, and he doesn't seem afraid of me and the sadness I'm hiding;
nor is he telling me I need to stop grieving.

"Can I ask you a question?" he says. There are flecks of green like
sea glass in his blue eyes. I nod. "It's okay if you don't want to answer.
How did you get over it? Becca told me you said you stayed in bed for
weeks after. Then all of a sudden you got up and made yourself better." Phantom arms squeeze my chest. Becca spilled what I confided
in her to Josh. He squints like he's attempting to read the answer on
my face. "How did you do it?"

The air in the room is forced out by the size of Josh's question. Without knowing it, Josh is asking what started *after*. Ben's
death ended *before*. I couldn't have been the same after he died if I'd
wanted to be. Josh is asking what got me out of bed a month later.
It was the truth inside an origami crane pressed between the secret
pages of my journal.

Josh deserves the truth. But the words are giant and heavy, and
they'd flop uncontainably to the floor, smashing this happy, ordinary
house to bits. How do words have power like that? How can they
open and drain you of all the I-hope-I-get-an-A, I-have-to-make-
my-birthday-wish-list-for-Dad, and I-wonder-if-I-should-become-
a-vegan thoughts that I was used to?

How did they fill me with questions I've never entertained

before, bizarre ones, like what will happen if I let that spider crawl over my hand rather than smack it dead on the wall? Or if the boys can jump from Duncan's roof into the pool, why can't I? Or maybe I was never as odd or alone as I thought for feeling what I did. Those words made me new with nerve and mischief until I wasn't myself anymore. I can't explain this to Josh without sharing the secret in the paper crane.

Duncan appears beside us. The skipper hat is slanted on his head, covering most of one eye. "Here's to Josh, the only guy in the room who isn't wasted," he slurs.

Josh claps him on his back, an easy smile pulled onto his face. "Hey bro, you really had them going." Duncan plants his feet, swaying counterclockwise, eyes unfocused and expression mean. He's a second away from saying something snide and stupid. "You hungry?" Josh keeps his tone light, sensing what I do. "I have that lobster mac-and-cheese you go ape for." He mouths, "Sorry" to me over his shoulder and leads drunken Duncan away.

Becca's still surrounded by junior girls, and she's rearranging the friendship bracelets stacked on her wrist and—I guess—sharing the origins of each because she reaches the tangerine and gold and points to me, grinning. I brush its mate around my wrist. She bought them at a boutique that first morning she took me shopping. It was surreal, after all those years zipping by without so much as a text, having Becca confide her deepest, darkest secrets to me over lunch. She acted like we'd been separated by continents, cell-phone-less—*no one's fault we stopped talking*—rather than three houses away, an invisible wall that she put up between us. Becca sees me looking and waves me over to join them, the juniors looking over expectantly, studying me as they would an exotic species of monkey introduced into the indigenous fauna.

I make for the staircase. Willa is here, and if there's anywhere I belong, it's with her. *Before, after,* whenever. I reach the third step and meet her at the fourth. She's sitting in the dim corridor, just beyond the sight line of the kitchen. Her temple rests against the wall and her eyes are closed. "Are you sleeping?" I ask.

Her lids open. "There was a couple sucking face against Josh's door. I didn't want to interrupt them," she inflects, annoyed. "Actually"—she taps her cell—"Mom would only let me come if she dropped me off and picked me up. I called her for a ride."

"Already?"

A long pause. "You're kidding, right?"

I can't decipher her expression in the dimness. "About what?"

"Trust me"—she rubs at her eyes—"you won't notice that I'm gone. You came with Becca and Carolynn. You want to flirt with the birthday boy. You won't miss *me*."

I drop down a step to bring our heads level. "I do miss you. I tried calling you earlier. You were upset last night and you said we'd talk about it today."

"I'm still upset, and I didn't want to have the conversation over the phone." Her voice has a crackly, choked quality. "But I don't want my mom to come to the door and see that there's alcohol here."

"I'll wait with you out front, then," I offer.

My fuzzy schnapps blanket has thinned and the cool, fresh outside brightens my senses. The white liquid moon gives everything a silver skin. The porch is empty, other than a couple in the corner making out; the baseball team gave up their post.

Willa's arms are folded rigidly against her chest, and her hair lashes her cheeks as she shakes her head. She stifles a strange sob that comes from nowhere. "I get that you're sad." She holds a hand out, blocking me from approaching. "I don't understand how sad because I don't have a brother or sister." I turn away. Willa's always said we were sisters. "I know that loss changes people. And that's okay." Her tone softens. Her hand tucks in mine and she squeezes. "Lana." Now she sounds just like her mother with steel running through her voice. "I shouldn't have even been at Swisher Spring yesterday. We were lucky that the police didn't charge you guys for underage drinking. There were beer bottles everywhere. We dragged up Maggie Lewis's body. *We were brought to the police station.*"

I take my hand from hers and place it in the folds of my dress. "Ben died in June. Dead. I watched it happen." She flinches. "So what that the police brought us to the station? So what that *oh my God,* there was drinking going on around you? Someone is dead."

Her eyes, round and hurt, flick to me and then to the road. "*Two* people are dead." It smacks of accusation. "I came tonight to tell you that I can't be around *this* anymore. We weren't supposed to waste our final summer before graduation. What happened to finishing our early admission applications? We were going to edit our personal essays. The eight-semester plan is leaving Gant. I thought you wanted that. And it isn't just what's stopped mattering to you; it's what's *started* mattering to you. You used to be counting down the seconds until you could escape all this *islander* crap. The core is their own little island in a sea of regulars. The core is Gant."

"I've always liked Josh; I used to be friends with Becca." I'm aware these aren't my strongest arguments.

She gives me an inscrutable look. "You're kidding. You can't think crushing on Josh and doing the monkey bars with Becca when you were ten is the same as hanging out—*every day*—with Carolynn Winters and Duncan Alvarez. Tell me you see the difference. Tell me that you see what a hypocrite you are, complaining about how exclusionary the core is and how nasty all the populars are, and then you sell out and spend the whole summer with them the moment they'll have you."

I hold my stomach. There's pain there. "I don't just want to study and plan," I say. "We've been in high school for *three years* and what have we done? I don't want to go to college a virgin who's never been hungover, or gone to a football game, or piled into a limo with friends for winter ball, or even had more than *one* friend."

Her chin juts out and she gives me this sidelong look.

"None of it is real, Willa. Chem lab and honor society and Latin—my God, Willa, *Latin* is a dead language." I duck between her and the road she's so intent on. "I wasted three years on all that stuff."

Willa's expression, her arms at her sides, her bearing, all of her hardens until I don't recognize her. "I'm sorry that I've been such a waste of your time." There's a bitter lilt in her voice. "Now is when I need to concentrate on what matters to me. If I don't matter to you, I don't see how we can continue being friends." She pushes past me. I make to go after her, but P.O.'s station wagon has just pulled up and the passenger window is being lowered. I spin and retreat around the side of the house.

Tears build. The blood hammers in my forehead. Wait until tomorrow. Tomorrow, with brown sugar on her oatmeal, Willa will be thinking clearly. She'll see that it isn't about the core being popular. She'll remember how stuck I was in sadness.

Being around the core is like twisting an orange peel under your nose, its spray making you wince and sneeze and laugh all at once. Intense. Refreshing. Stinging. A relief. Willa will understand why I can't be stuck in my small life; why I'd rather *feel* chemistry than study it.

I unlatch the gate to the rear yard. I can't stomach cutting through the crush of bodies inside. I pass under a trellis with tiny buds dangling like a doll's upside-down teacups. I toddle from stone to stone until I make it to the expanse of lawn that ends at the woods. I stop short. A figure faces the tree line. The wind slips through the yard, and Carolynn's white dress lifts and dances before she flattens it against her thighs with her hands. She's ghostly. I cross to where she stands barefoot. It says volumes that between Carolynn and the party, I choose her.

Her gaze is focused on the dark spaces between the pine trunks. "You shouldn't be out here alone," I say. "It isn't safe."

She sniffs. "It's nicer out here than inside."

"Even with killers on the loose?"

Her head tilts my way; she's smiling like you would when humoring a child. "Yeah. It would be a fair fight, at least. Out here I don't have to watch Bethany J. fall all over Duncan or Duncan put on his usual 'I'm the king of the party' routine." She glances down at her hands. They're shaking.

I wipe the runny mascara from under my eyes.

"You shouldn't be crying."

"I'm not crying over Maggie," I say quickly.

She tips her head back and laughs, a ragged, belligerent edge to it. "I know that. You shouldn't let them"—she jerks her head at the house—"see you cry. Ever. They're worse than anything that could be out here." My classmates have superpowers for making one another feel small. It surprises me that Carolynn, the most popular girl in our class, arguably the entire school, knows this.

The grass is wet with mist, and the cold fringe tickles the sides of my feet. I bend to undo my sandals. My soles crunch the individual blades; a hundred tiny pleasant pinpricks make me shiver.

"There used to be a swing set right here," Carolynn says, toeing the grassy spot. She gathers up her hair and begins twisting it into a bun. "The boys used to push us off the swings. It was a game—knock the girls on their butts. Not Duncan. If he came up behind you, it was to push you higher. He wanted you to fly."

Abruptly, she tugs her hair loose from the bun. "He was so sweet right up until middle school, and then it's like he forgot how. It's his dad. He's just one of those guys. All that master-of-the-universe garbage. *Don't cry. Be a man.* He just unloads on Duncan, like it's so easy to retire at thirty. As if that's *normal*. And if you aren't on your way to coming up with some billion-dollar app, you're a waste of space." Her gaze meets mine. "I thought since you're more objective, since you're more distant, you might see Duncan better. Do you think he'd still push us higher or knock us off those swings?" She winds and unwinds her finger in the platinum chain of her necklace, waiting.

"Is he wearing the skipper hat in this scenario?" I ask, half to make her laugh and half because I think it would make a difference. She huffs softly. I consider Duncan. *Before* or *after*, he's never said anything mean to me. "I think that any boy who takes his little brothers bike riding every Sunday morning would probably try to push you higher."

I hear her sigh. Her head bows, shaking. "Jesus. Why are you such a sappy freak?" It isn't clear if she's insulting herself or me. Without a word she slips her heels on and walks toward Josh's deck. Blades of grass stick to her calves like dark slots in her skin. I stay at the edge of the trees. Their branches shiver in the night wind. I don't budge at the snapping of twigs behind the darkness. In this moment, I'd rather face what's outside the house than what's within, like Carolynn. I choose one point in the shadows and I stare it down. That hungry, daring voice in my head, the one with all the questions, urges me to walk into the trees.

For the last month I've given in to that voice, mostly. I'm not crazy. The voice is mine. It was with me the day I left my bed for the first time in four weeks to stagger to the lower terrace, where Ben and I used to hang out. I watched the flames in the fire pit after lighting the wood, and I thought, *I've always wanted to leap the blaze.* I wondered if I could do it, so I did. It singed my socks—pink cashmere ones that Dad and Diane gave me for Valentine's Day. It was thrilling. I was alive. That was the first thing I did in *after.* My inaugural act as a new girl.

At present that voice quietly urges me forward:

Come prove that you're as brave as the girl in the stories.

Prove that you still exist.

It begins to sound less like me and more like Ben's alto. What if all this time, it *was* him? My toes clench in the grass. I wish I could reach inside my brain and pinch the thought as you would the lit wick of a candle. Snuff it out. When you love someone, love them in your bones and know them until the backs of their hands are as familiar as yours, can they ever be gone? Is Ben all the way gone?

I take a step for the trees. Maggie's killer is on the loose and maybe he's concealed by the shadows, staring me down, inviting me forward. *Who* would I find if I looked?

"Ben?" His name slips out, an arrow aimed at the dark.

There's laughter from behind me, not from the trees I'm focused on.

"Are you talking to your dead stepbrother?" Ford asks between snide chuckles.

My cheeks burn hot and I've scooped up my shoes and am halfway across the lawn by the time I can bear looking up at Ford. He's a few stairs above the grass on the redwood deck, sneering like I'm a bug under his boat shoe he's about to squish. "Liddy and Kristie were all, 'I bet they only let Lana hang with them because they feel sorry for her.'" He makes his voice higher than either girl's is. "And I told them no way Carolynn Winters"—her name's said with contempt—"let some desperate wannabe join her crew, even for the summer, because that girl doesn't have a heart."

I stop short. This is not *before*. I am not Lana trying to listen to Mrs. Edgemont's Mary Shelley lecture and refusing to let on that I feel Ford's breath on my neck. This is not Mr. Gupta's astronomy; I have more options than transferring out, or pretending I don't hear Ford's sniggers each time I speak, or risking making the bullying even worse if I tell Mr. Gupta on him. All those little jabs took divots out of me. They reduced me to easy and frequently picked-on prey. But tonight, I am not afraid of fighting back or making it worse.

I smirk at him like he's told a joke. "You're calling *me* a desperate wannabe? Do you hear yourself, Ford?"

He clears his throat, surprised. "All I'm at is that I was wrong. Pity it is: they must know you're a desperate bitch who talks to herself when no one's around. You were just mid-séance."

I reach the bottom step and am about to jog up them and disappear into the house. It feels like retreating from this spiteful boy. With the woods at my back, the pressure of the breeze in my hair, and whatever presence I sensed in the trees still near, I refuse to.

I place my hands on my hips, channel Carolynn's glacial stare, and say, "If it had anything to do with pity, it would be *you* they included. I wouldn't normally say this, but you're not a nice person." I shift forward confidentially and enunciate each word. "They think you're a hanger-on. But not me. I know the truth, Ford. You're worse than that. Your brother was a sadistic asshole. But you are a zombie, completely unoriginal, feeding off his popularity and nastiness, hoping that no one will see how pathetic and *mind-suckingly boring* you are."

He takes a step back and spits, "Screw you, bitch."

I give a laugh. "Way to prove me wrong." I jog up the stairs, hands shaking and blood singing between my ears as I half turn to look down at him. "Guess what, Ford? *I see.*"

Three light-headed strides later, I'm in the kitchen, dialing Dad to pick me up.

— 10 —

I sit on the long, pale-yellow couch in the living room and cuddle Basel. Dad left for Portland before I came downstairs. I've been watching the harbor's water go from black to gray, replaying the exchange with Ford last night. Telling him off was as exhilarating as diving from the ridge into the spring. It was the feeling I used to get as a kid rolling down a grassy slope, building speed, world spinning, a giddy tremor in my chest.

The doorbell chimes and Basel wriggles away. He lets one angry meow rip. I fling the front door open, wishing for it to be Willa. Two uniformed officers stand on the porch. They stare at the welcome mat. There's a dead bird in the center of its monogrammed *M*. I inhale sharply. The bird is brown with a dusting of white feathers on his plump breast, one wing fanned and crimped.

The shorter officer glances up. "Lana McBrook?" he asks, revealing teeth that are crooked and crowded. He drops his chin to his chest. "You have a bird-catching cat?" The taller officer toes the bird with his boot.

"We have an indoor cat," I say, pointing at Basel twitching his tail beside me.

"Neighbor's cat, then," the shorter replies. The taller sweeps the bird to the side of the porch with the inner sole of his shoe. "Your parents home?"

I shrink back. Police asking for the adults of the house can really only mean dire things. As if reading my mind, the taller officer places his boot on the threshold, preventing me from slamming the door. I shake my head. He slides his jaw back and forth, thinking. "Can you call them at work?"

My hands make tight fists and I force a smile. *Grin until you feel it.* "My stepmom's on vacation and Dad is working a couple of hours away," I answer. *Vacationing* is what Dad and I say Diane is doing. From the way people smile sympathetically, everyone knows better.

The taller officer gives a decided nod and says gruffly, "You'll call them on the way to the station. You're needed to answer additional questions about the events at Swisher Spring, two nights ago."

I swallow. When I needed to answer questions about the night Ben died, they called Dad on the phone, requested we come in at our convenience. The police showing up to escort me doesn't seem like a good development. The shorter one's staring from my naked feet to my pj shorts with cartoon ponies on them. I know I look younger than seventeen. He tilts his head in a friendly manner and says, "If you promise to be quick, we'll let you change into something more appropriate."

Raindrops pitter-patter on the roof as I wriggle my pants on upstairs. This close to autumn, the rain comes out of nowhere. It's usually sprinkling on the first day of school, and that's just a week away. I find my pink wellies in the mudroom and squeak to the door. Basel is a sentinel on a console table, and he's swiping his tail back and forth and sinking into a crouch while eyeing the officers.

I scratch his head. "Bye, toots," I murmur. The cops start away, and I follow once I've locked the door. The bird rests against a big stone planter, its broken wing pinned up like it's waving to me. Our neighbors don't keep outdoor cats. Twinkie and Winkie get loose from Becca's yard and they go after anything fuzzy and smaller than they are. "I watched a bird fly into my bedroom window and fall to the terrace a few years ago," I say. The tall officer grunts as he holds the rear door of the cruiser for me. Seated, I dial Dad.

He answers after the first ring. "There you are, Bumblebee. You sleep in?" His voice is warm, light as it used to be.

I cradle the phone between my shoulder and ear and rest my head against the window. "Not really. Dad?"

"What is it?" His voice is instantly alarmed. I imagine him knocking over the latte on the table in front of him, the brown liquid bleeding into his shirt cuff without him noticing. "How are you feeling? Are you still in bed?"

"Dad, I—"

A sharp intake of breath. "Are you hurt? Is it Diane?"

I stare out the window at the tunnel of fog we're in the thick of. "They're bringing me to the police station to answer questions."

Dad wonders why the police would escort me down rather than extend the courtesy of a call, since I was the one who discovered Maggie. He proclaims me a hero. A hot flare of nausea spreads from my stomach. I don't want to be Maggie's hero. I'd rather be Ben's. I'd rather be the reason Maggie was sent to the bottom of the spring than the force that dragged her up. Neither of us understands why the police would want to speak with me. I don't know how or why she ended up where she did. I try to stop thinking about it before I consider what Rusty said last night. Ben is gone. *Dead.* There's no trace of him left. Nothing remains of the dead. Rusty was joking. Still, I feel paranoid, as though I know more than I've admitted, as though I'm hiding the truth. The officer driving watches me in the rearview mirror like he senses it too. My heart begins to thump louder.

"Don't say anything until I'm there, Lana. Thirty minutes, max. I'm already on my way home. And don't worry, I'm going to take care of this and you and I are going to watch a movie tonight, your choice, no comedies, I promise, and we'll order in from that new Italian spot. You tell Willa the same thing. She's invited if you like."

"Okay, Dad. Thank you," I whisper.

Willa. Did the police show up for her this morning? Are all seven of us being hauled in, or is it only me? I text Willa swiftly.

The police are bringing me to the station.

I wait for a response. What could the police want to ask me that they didn't the other night? We told them the truth, and in what universe isn't that enough? I smile bitterly at my hands. The truth usually falls short—or else it is entirely too much. The truth hurts you if you tell it and kicks you if you don't. I've wondered if losing Ben was my punishment for lying. If I'd been honest and brave and said, *Screw this small life, it isn't enough,* would Ben be here?

The shorter cop in the passenger seat half turns and slips a tissue through the divider that separates us. I wipe my running nose. "Your dad's coming?" he asks, concerned. I bob my head and try to look less guilty than I feel. "There you go. I'm sure he'll straighten this out."

The tall cop gives a warning glare, and the short one turns abruptly to the windshield.

We follow Harborview Drive as it winds in the direction of downtown. Before the city streets, the car reaches a fork in the road. To the left is Swisher Tunnel, a short pass-through under the ridge with railroad tracks on top. The tracks used to carry minerals that were mined from the island and trees that were logged to the commercial loading dock and warehouses on the far side of downtown. The tracks are abandoned, crisscrossing the undeveloped segments of the island. If we followed the road through the tunnel, we'd reach Swisher Spring. We go to the right, but for the split second the car passes the mouth of the tunnel I squint up the embankment for the lumpy outline of Skitzy-Fitzy's tent. It isn't there, and the only reason my thoughts travel in his direction is because Ward asked if I've ever seen Fitzgerald at the spring.

I don't suspect the guy with his threadbare parka and soiled cargo pants of killing Maggie, any more than I suspected him of hurting Ben. When the police were investigating Ben's murder, they asked about him, obviously. But Maggie knew Skitzy-Fitzy from around town and was certain it wasn't him on the highway. And even if I didn't believe Maggie, Ben would be the last person Fitzgerald would hurt.

Ben became aware of Fitzgerald, in more than just the passing way everyone knew of Skitzy-Fitzy, a few weeks after that first trip to Guatemala, freshman year. Ben hated that in the middle of all this *privilege*—he liked that word most for Gant—there was a homeless man living in a tent. Ben was always buying him deli sandwiches or ducking into the bakery to order a box of croissants for him. Fitzgerald was polite and at the worst, skittish, easily startled. On the occasion I was with Ben, he accepted the food with a brisk, "Thanks."

Ben wanted to believe he could make a difference—and not just with Fitzgerald. He started taking the ferry to volunteer in a homeless shelter in Seattle. I went with him up until Dad found out and said he didn't want us exposed to *those people*. Ben kept going in secret. This is why I wasn't surprised that he wanted to spend months digging in another country so strangers had clean water to drink. That was Ben.

Ben didn't like that Gant was removed from the world most people lived in. Gant was the picturesque, plastic island at the heart of a snow globe. As he got older, he started noticing the glass walls. He started feeling trapped inside them. Dad said once that Ben had twice the share of opinions of most and four times as many about Gant. Diane's usually mild expression became the saddest face I'd ever seen as she said, "Sometimes it's safer not to care so much." Ben pushed away from the dinner table and replied, "Most people can't switch their feelings off like you can." Diane's features went neutral, her wineglass traveled to her lips, two fingers tugged at the blush petal of a rose in the bouquet Dad had given her, and she steered us off the subject with a feathery sigh about the perfume of flowers.

At the police station I'm ushered through the rear door. All seven of us are here, and everyone, other than me, has at least one parent with them. Willa's mother's heels are clacking like a hammer on nail heads as she paces figure eights. Willa's eyes are cast on the yellow linoleum as I'm led into a corridor where folding chairs have been lined up. I'm told to sit between Josh's mom Karen and an empty chair, presumably for my parent.

I drop down as Willa's mother takes one, two, three strides, the *click-clack* of her shoes driving into my skull. Principal Owen, a witchy version of her daughter, stops over me, leading with a pointed finger and a scowl.

"You look me in the eye," P.O. demands. I do. Her usual stern calm cracks. Thick clumps of bangs stick out from her bun. She has gray hair rather than highlights. "I know that you're the reason Willa is here." She jabs a finger, and I shrink to avoid its nail. I meet Willa's puffy eyes beyond her mother's frame.

This is my fault. Willa didn't want to be at Swisher Spring; she wanted to watch the History channel. She's hung out with the core for me. *Only for me.* I'm the reason she was there to find Maggie, and I'm the reason she's been brought in by the police.

P.O. snaps for my lost attention. "There are consequences for loose morals, Lana."

"Mom," Willa calls.

"The parties and the boys and the broken commitments," P.O. hisses, a vein poking up through the tissuey skin of her forehead. "You've been spiraling and now you're dragging my girl down. Ever since that stepbrother of yours died—"

Karen hops from her chair and closes her hand around Principal Owen's finger. "Rhonda," she warns. But it's too late. She's right. Not about Ben but everything else, yes. I dragged Willa along on my misadventures. I made Willa compromise everything she loved and worked tirelessly for.

Karen continues in her friendly but authoritative way, "I think you should sit down. If you have something more to say, Lana's father should be here." It's as if Willa's mom only just realized we're in the company of the parents of her students, their individual conversations gone quiet. Principal Owen smooths her unwrinkled pencil skirt and nods once before returning to Willa, who is doubled over, her forehead on her knees.

Karen claps her hand over mine as she sits. Her skin is warm and calloused, and it cuts right through me to where I hide the longing for my mother.

Josh leans forward and smiles in a hopeful way. "It'll be okay, Lana." Lily, on his other side, inclines her head, her eyes creasing as she watches him. It's instantly obvious why it's easy for Josh to believe that everything will work out. Has there ever been anything in his life that hasn't? Has he ever been sweaty and puking with regret? Has he ever been so consumed by a secret that continuing to exist—to breathe and blink and sleep—becomes a lie?

I understand that it wasn't only the red corduroys that made me smitten with Josh way back when. I was a motherless four-year-old girl on her first day of preschool when I spotted two women flanking Josh. He had *two* moms. Josh has an extra portion of what I have none of.

"How long do *these people* think they can keep *us* waiting?" Carolynn's mother asks. Her vowels are liquid and her consonants candied. She subscribes to the wisdom that you can say anything as long as you remind others that you and yours are exceptional. My mother used to be one of those lunching, committee-sitting, tennis-playing women. She was always in the getting-ready or cleaning-up stages of going out.

Rusty's father, City Councilman Harper, is in a suit tailored like a second skin. He drills his heel impatiently. His hand never strays from cuffing Rusty's neck. He leans forward and, red-faced, bellows,

"Officers, are you aware that I'm your city councilman?" He throws the title out as a dart, anticipating that it will hit its mark. It usually does. Gant cares about titles. "We're tired of humoring you and will be leaving soon."

Detective Ward passes through a doorway into the hall. His voice and expression are carefully neutral. "If you wouldn't mind humoring the police a bit more, we need your children's help in understanding the circumstances of a young woman's death." Councilman Harper's face reddens up to his receding hairline. Dad sidesteps Ward and slides into the chair next to me. The anger is dimpling the corners of his mouth, and he looks like he's been biting into a lemon wedge.

Still, he manages a comforting, "It's going to be fine, Bumblebee. You don't have anything to hide." There are whispered deliberations among the rest of the parents.

As they die down, Ward continues, "I assume that all present are aware of Thursday's events at Swisher Spring. After forensic analysis of the body, I'm afraid additional questioning is necessary." Ward explains that there is one caveat to us being treated as cooperating witnesses. We must speak with the detectives alone. More loudly voiced protests, shaking fists and heads, folding chairs shrieking against linoleum as a few parents stand, threatening to walk out. After a brief standoff, the adults yield one by one. Ward's chest swells as though gathering strength from each parent giving permission.

"Ms. McBrook, care to go first?" Ward asks. I start in my chair and look to Dad.

He nods encouragingly and says, "Remember that you can get up and leave at any time."

It strikes me that I'm less afraid and feel less alone than I did when being questioned by Ward before. I am braver. I stand and march into a claustrophobic interrogation room. There's an additional set of lungs recycling the air inside.

"This is my partner, Detective Sweeny of Seattle PD. *Homicide*," Ward tells me.

Sweeny half stands. "We've already met. Good morning, Lana. How have you been?"

I lower myself into the lone metal chair placed across the table from the detectives. The single lightbulb overhead buzzes and flickers. Homicide. Sweeny. I work to keep the memories of June from creeping up, from bottlenecking in my throat. Fragments of that night flash: the clouds that disintegrated as they were blown across the sky while Maggie and I waited for the police; the blood drying on my hands; the yellow moth that landed in the splatter on the dashboard and was stuck there, wings beating in vain, stringy brown legs trapped as the blood clotted. I wonder how long it took that moth to die.

I am June. I am a hand shaking so badly it drops the phone twice before I can get out one sentence after my father finally turns his phone on. *Daddy, Ben has been attacked.*

Sweeny waits patiently for my response. Maybe she can see I'm not here, not really. My mouth is dry. "I was doing better," I say. "What about you?"

"Busy," she says, thin lines spreading from the corners of her downturned mouth. Intelligent brown eyes study me. "How are your father and stepmother?"

My shoulders rise and fall. "Dad started working again. He's in the hall. Diane needed some time away."

"I hope it does her well," she says. Ward's head is cocked as he listens. Sweeny doesn't explain our history to him; I assume he must already know, since they're partners. I can't remember Sweeny ever mentioning having one or that another detective was working on Ben's case. Ward could have been behind the scenes, back in Seattle. It makes sense that once Maggie was found dead, Seattle PD would send someone familiar with her and Gant. I pull my shoulders back and stare unblinking at him.

He clears his throat. "We've officially declared Maggie Lewis's death a homicide," he says, and waits. He waits for shock to register in my expression, or waterworks, or a silly wail—who knows. I don't give him anything, because *big freaking surprise*. We suspected Maggie's death was murder two days ago. Maggie the murderer was murdered. Maggie's killer did what I couldn't.

"You don't seem surprised, Lana," Sweeny says, her tone inviting me to explain.

I shake my head. "We figured it might not be an accident."

Ward leans forward, nostrils flaring like he's trying to scent the truth. "Why is that, Ms. McBrook?"

I hesitate over how abrupt his tone is. Sweeny bows her head, urging me on. "Lots of reasons," I say. "Maggie was attached to something at the bottom, weighted down. She supposedly left town once you—the police—suspected her of being involved in Ben's death. She wouldn't have been casually swimming at Swisher Spring or in Gant at all, like no big deal. She wasn't even in a swimsuit or her underwear. She had one shoe on."

What I really want to say is this: How couldn't it have been murder? Maggie was hateable, a cruel, vengeful girl. She was a villain.

Ward smirks. "Are you sure there isn't another reason you know it wasn't an accident?"

He says it in a you're-an-idiot-if-you-think-I'm-an-idiot way. I must be missing something. "Yes, I'm sure."

"Ms. McBrook," he says in a furious and tight voice, "if you refuse to cooperate, we'll have to treat you hostilely and move forward with booking."

I cross my arms at my chest. "I'm answering your questions." Sweeny's and Ward's expressions are only similar in that neither reveals a thing.

"When was the last time you saw Maggie Lewis before you *claim* to have pulled her out of the spring?" Ward asks.

June is there in the room with us, crooking her finger, urging me back. "Almost eight weeks ago, while the police were investigating Maggie," I say. I wait for Sweeny's corroboration. She stays as unmoving as her starched blue blouse. Ward's big pink lips spread into a smug smile, as if I've confessed to murdering Maggie myself. I get dizzy thinking it. "Why?" I ask.

"Wouldn't you wonder if you were me?" His brows quirk up and they stick there, making a home high on his forehead. "Think how this looks. Maggie was questioned regarding your brother's death. Not two months later you're in the very spot she's murdered with a group of your friends, and you just happen to be the one who surfaces with her body?"

"Ben was not my brother," I say moodily, half to be difficult and half because that's who Ben is—*was*. "His mom married my dad, making him my stepbrother." I finish less hotly than I started.

In a strained voice, Ward says, "I know what a step-sibling is. Answer the question."

I whip my ponytail back and forth. "And it wasn't that Maggie was *just questioned*. She was suspected of planning the carjacking. She knew who Ben's attacker was." I pause, searching his face for a muscle twitch or clue. "I—I don't understand what you're asking." My fingers press at my temples.

He takes his time, reclines in his seat, rubs the knuckles of one hand before switching to the other. "Would you be suspicious if you were me?" he asks slowly.

"Of what?" I cry. My heart is knocking against my rib cage like an unfamiliar and insistent fist on a door. At present Sweeny is squinting at me under the lone lightbulb, just as she was in the glare of the flashlight as she took Maggie's and my statements that awful night.

"There's one problem with the little tale you and your bosom buddies have woven," Ward says. "The coroner's report for Ms. Lewis came back this morning. Really, kids as smart as you lot should have foreseen the complication. You might have gotten away with it. You waited two months. You recruited six witnesses to lie for you. How long were you and your friends at Swisher Spring yesterday? Approximately?" He jabs his finger viciously.

"Seven hours," I say.

"And did you ever leave the spring as a group?" Both his elbows are on the table as he strains forward.

"No, we were there from two to after nine, when the police arrived."

"At what time did you find Ms. Lewis?"

"Um, it was almost dark. After eight, I guess."

"Is the spring large? Are there any sides obstructed from view or shielded by trees?" His chest presses against the table.

"No, it's not big. We were on the rocks." He saw the spring for himself. "We could see the whole thing, the whole day."

Both his palms strike the table. I jump. He raises one finger in the air between us. "Ms. McBrook, Maggie had been dead for one hour before you pulled her from the water."

I am sinking. Ward and I are on a seesaw, and I'm slowly weighing my side lower as I lift his. His ravenous scowl is bearing down on me.

"One hour," he repeats emphatically. "Placing her murder at Swisher Spring at roughly seven in the evening, when you and your friends swear that you were the only people in sight. And what's more, the deceased was fed a poisonous substance only hours before death. A poison that immobilized Maggie and prevented her from fighting as you held her under the water and waited for her to stop struggling."

— 11 —

I shouldn't stay in the room with the detectives, who are determined to drag me backward. June is wafting through the air duct in the ceiling as neon, toxic fog. It brings the snowflake petals on marionberry bushes into sharper focus than the ceiling tiles and the periwinkle of Sweeny's blouse. It hurts to think of firework stands at every turnout in the highway, the end-of-the-year assembly, the drive to the airport, and the promise of Ben home and then in college.

Sweeny leans forward, electrified. "Lana, was there someone else at the spring?" Her nail taps the table for my attention. I wince at the gentle click like I did at Ward's pounding. "The vagrant schizophrenic man who camps at Swisher Tunnel, did you kids see him? Did Maggie arrive with your group? The two boys, Mr. Harper and Mr. Alvarez, who were injured in a scuffle at the spring, did one of them hurt Maggie?" Her eyes beg me to open up like she's some after-school special. "You kids think you're doing everyone a favor by lying? You can tell me if there's someone you're protecting." She keeps at it with her gentle prodding, and Ward bursts in with intervals of shouting, not even coy about accusing me of orchestrating Maggie's murder.

Sweeny tries to lessen Ward's verbal blows by offering alternative explanations that all boil down to me lying because I'm protecting someone. One of my friends. Skitzy-Fitzy. A passing acquaintance. I watch the ceiling sag. A hundred yellowed squares stretch at the seams. Their corners break free and curl like the worn stickers on the inside of my school locker. Ribbons of tile peel slowly until they're shed as dead skin, falling to Ward's boxy shoulders like snow or dandruff. I rub my eyes. We didn't lie about Maggie. I didn't see her underwater when I leaped from the ridge. Maggie appeared as a fourth atom with the hydrogen and oxygen of the water.

There's a twinge between my brows as I ask Sweeny, "You're sure that Maggie was dead for one hour? They're able to tell even if the body's in water?"

Sweeny's head bows in confirmation. "The medical examiner is certain."

"Poison," I whisper.

"The autopsy confirmed that she ingested *Abrus precatorius*, a deadly neurotoxin, five to six hours before she drowned," Sweeny says. "It affected her nervous system after several hours. She would have been unsteady on her feet and afflicted by slurred speech."

"Abra-what?"

"Rosary peas," Ward cuts in. "But you knew that, Lana. The red berries that used to be threaded along with a cross to make a rosary. Clever of you to know that the berries and their seeds have paralytic properties when ingested. Did you conceal them in Maggie's lunch? Did the rest of you eat as you waited to incapacitate her for your attack? Did you drown her as a last resort once you saw the dose you'd given her didn't prove fatal?"

Rosary: a trinket held close by old ladies and priests in foreign films. Creased and papery fingers worrying over red berries as they mumble prayers like spells. There's a familiar quality to this scene, like a recollection you have in the morning and assume it's the flash of the previous night's dream because the details are vague and disjointed.

"Rosary peas aren't indigenous to this region, Lana," Sweeny says.

"We have officers contacting every hothouse in a day's drive to see if they grow the plant. This isn't something your parents are going to be able to save you kids from—it won't matter who they are. We'll get warrants. We'll find the proof we need. Soon. If you tell the truth now, save us all the trouble, we'll be able to say you're cooperating," Ward whispers like he's telling me a secret. "Lana, I'm told you're bright. One of your friends is going to come clean. It's just a matter of when. Don't you want it to be you? Is that where you got the poison? A hothouse? Or did one of you kids have an antique rosary? You have a flair for the dramatic?" He's hoping one of us will confess, thinking that the consequences might be lighter for whoever spills.

"Maggie wasn't with us," I say. It's the truth. "I haven't seen her for eight weeks." That's true too.

When the police told us there was likely nothing recognizable of Ben left to find, I wished it had been Maggie to die. Not only in the trading places scenario of Maggie dead meaning Ben alive. I wanted Maggie to die regardless—*in addition*. My mouth salivated for revenge. I even imagined taking it myself. Whether the police found her responsible or not, whether Dad believes that she meant to hurt Ben or not, there was something off about that night. It felt sinister. In my head, that night seems less like an ending and more like the beginning to one of Ben's stories.

Wishing someone dead is different from killing them. I know this, but as Ward stares me down, accusation written all over his face, I think, *Did I do it? Did I want it badly enough?* My thoughts land on Rusty joking that it was Ben's ghost. The chair screeches as I slide away from the idea. Sweeny's calm exterior falters; the muscle under her right eye twitches as she looks from me to Ward.

"I think Lana's been through enough today," she says coolly, calmly, but her gaze goes from me to the door. Is she telling me to leave? Should I run? Ward presses a firm hand to my shoulder as I stand.

"Detective," Sweeny says sternly, "Lana's given us her witness account, and she's clearly upset and has nothing more to offer at this time. To press the issue would be presumptuous without comparing all witness statements."

Ward's face goes purple. I don't wait for them to have it out. I mutter good-bye. As I pass over the threshold, Ward calls, "This isn't over, Ms. McBrook. You're looking far from innocent."

I don't doubt that he's right.

Each heartbeat bleeds into the next until there's a sustained, battering pressure in my chest. It carries me forward to vomit, or gasp, or scream. The faces in the hall are too similar to tell apart. My boots squeak as I dodge through the human obstacles. I angle outside.

My forearms hit the back door and I jog down the cement stairs to the parking lot, dark from the night's rain. The smells of wet asphalt and the brine of the neighboring oyster shack are a noxious blend. I lurch between two police cruisers, brace myself on my knees, and breathe deeply. Black spots wriggle like spiders on my field of vision.

A palm rests on my lower back, and I whirl around with a yelp. Josh has one hand in the air. "It's just me," he says. He smiles nervously, a bit out of breath. "You looked bad coming out of the interview." He scratches his head. "Not *bad*. You look like you." He says *you* as if it's synonymous with pretty. "Upset is what I mean." He shifts his weight, hesitates for a moment, and puts his arms around me.

My eyes scrunch shut against his shoulder. "This can't be happening. . . . I didn't survive this summer to—to go to jail."

His arms slacken and we're toe to toe, looking at each other. "No one's going to jail." A corner of his mouth picks up. "Well, maybe I'm going to jail since I'm eighteen, but you're going to juvie. Too soon for jokes, huh?" His blue eyes are apologetic.

I get a whiff of Josh's freshly laundered shirt. Josh is the kind of boy who eats kale salad at dinner with his moms and has a clean room and laundry folded in his dresser drawers and doesn't know what it's like to get picked last. What happens to boys like Josh in jail? "They said Maggie was dead for one hour," I whisper. "She was poisoned."

Josh is frowning. "I know. I was interviewed while you were, although mine lasted only half as long."

The tissue between my ribs constricts, knitting the bones tighter. "What did you tell them?"

"Nothing." Josh eyes the exterior of the building. "There's nothing to say. We didn't do what they're accusing us of. Duncan went in after me, and Ward called Carolynn in once you were done. Becca, Willa, and Rusty are still waiting for their turns."

"I should talk to my dad," I say.

"He's out front with my moms, conference calling a lawyer," he explains. He pauses, expression turning uncertain. "Look, I know we haven't really talked about what you saw happen that night and that Maggie was the reason you guys were in the car, and she planned the whole thing. I guess that goes without saying, since everyone in Gant knows. I mean that I get that you probably felt like killing her and you didn't even hurt her." His eyes grow big and sweet. "You're too good for that. And it's really unfair that we're—that *you're*—suspected anyway." His soft hands rub up and down my arms. "It sucks."

My smile is feeble. The other boys give Ben credit each time I do something that impresses them. When I jumped from Duncan's roof into the pool with the boys, Rusty whooped that Ben taught his little sis to be a badass. When I lit three Roman candles and sent them careening into the sky, the boys applauded and Duncan asked if I was sure I wasn't blood related to Ben. Ben. Ben. *Ben*. Never me.

Not Josh. He gives me credit. "Thanks," I say. I appreciate it even if deep down I know that I am not good or forgiving or honest.

We glance to where our chests are together. I step away, my cheeks warm. Josh shakes his hands out at his sides. Nothing's *actually* changed since two days ago. The police believe we're responsible for Maggie's death because the coroner's report is wrong. The mistake will be revealed. We either killed her or we didn't—and we didn't, no matter how much I may have wished for it.

"An officer my mom is buddies with took her aside and said they're hoping that if they scare us, one of us will spill." Josh flicks his honey hair from his forehead.

"We told them everything we know."

He hooks his thumbs in his front jean pockets. "They were suspicious of Rusty's and Duncan's injuries from the start. They let it go.

Boys get after each other all the time. Then they did the exam, and the results say we aren't being truthful with them. There's your connection with Maggie. There's Rusty and Duncan's blowup. We look suspicious." He exhales slowly; his shoulders shrink with the lost air and he never quite inflates again.

Perception is nine-tenths of everything, and if we look like liars and murderers, that's what the police will assume we are.

Carolynn and Duncan file out the back door of the station, spot us among the cars, and come toward us. Duncan's left his skipper hat at home, and he's stiff and uncomfortable-looking, closing his eyes in intervals. Beads of sweat cling to his greenish face. Hungover.

Carolynn avoids looking my way. Duncan glares at the station over his shoulder before speaking louder than necessary. "The jack-off who questioned me said that he'd find fingerprint bruises on Maggie from whoever held her under. I told him good." He thumps his chest and looks greener for it. "I didn't kill a girl."

Carolynn waves dismissively. "The c-u-next-Tuesday who questioned me with Ward said that they could tell by the food in Maggie's stomach that *I* fed her poison. As if I'd buy that there were fingerprints on digested muck in guts."

"What did you tell her?" Josh asks.

Carolynn coils the end of her fishtail braid around her finger and rolls her eyes. She's much more herself than she was last night. "That I have nothing to do with the vomit in anyone's stomach." She lifts her chin at me. "What about you, weak link?"

"Don't start." Josh rubs at the worry lines creasing his forehead. I don't remember the marks on his face before yesterday.

"What?" Carolynn shrugs a thin shoulder. "She is the weak link.

Good little Lana McBrook only comes out to play after she has a grief-fueled revelation that she's wasted her life sucking up to teachers." I squirm. Carolynn's reduced me to one sentence, and it isn't entirely off base. Her fingers brush Josh's hand, and she runs her other hand along Duncan's arm, staking claim to them both, naming me the outsider—as if I'd forgotten. "Lana and her wonder-scout BFF could tell the police it was the five of us just to protect their perfect attendance trophies."

I bite the inside of my cheek. Swearing on my vintage copy of *A Wrinkle in Time* isn't going to work with Carolynn like it does with Willa. I need to respond. Duncan's eyeing me like I'm a cobra that might strike at any moment and he's contemplating beheading me preemptively.

"Why would I lie to the police, when there are more of you who could accuse me in return? I'm the only one with reason to despise Maggie," I say.

Her nostrils flare delicately, and her diamond stud twinkles. Josh claps a hand on both our shoulders. Carolynn reluctantly breaks eye contact with me. "No one's throwing anyone under the bus," Josh says. "We told the truth. It'll be enough. We need to stick together until then."

Carolynn pops a hip. "That's just it, Josh." She sighs at being surrounded by idiots. "We weren't supposed to be out at the spring past dusk. We were drinking; there were beer bottles everywhere. Rusty and Duncan were all scraped up from a fight. We pulled Maggie Lewis from the water, and they can prove that she died while we were there. They're sure we're lying. Do you get how shady this looks? And for kicks and giggles, let's say I buy that Lana 2.0 has my back. No way does Willa.

Not if it comes down to her or us. Will they believe her? Maybe not, but it definitely won't help exonerate us if she points the finger."

I look from Josh to Duncan. Doubt is splashed all over their faces. "I promise you that Willa would never tell the police something that wasn't true." Willa said she couldn't be friends with me, sure. I don't believe that she would lie to escape suspicion herself. "Sticking together may not be enough," I state. "What's to stop them from arresting everyone? If no one lies and points fingers, won't they assume it's a conspiracy to commit murder?"

Duncan snorts. "She's effing right. They'll blame us all. Maybe . . . maybe we say it was Skitzy-Fitzy?" He bobs his head enthusiastically like it's a genius idea. "I mean, they're practically leading us in his direction."

Josh's eyes narrow. "What are you talking about?"

"They kept asking if I saw anyone else at the spring and if I think that bum could be involved. What if we tell them it was Skitzy-Fitzy who killed Maggie? We saw him do it and were afraid he was going to go all medieval on us if we told. Maybe we just tell them what they want to hear?"

Carolynn steps back as if she's been pushed. Josh rushes forward. He's red, grabbing for Duncan. "Are you joking, man? Do you hear yourself?" Josh is a couple of inches shorter than Duncan, but he winds his hands in the fabric of Duncan's shirt collar and yanks him to eye level. "You want to blame an innocent guy?"

"Bro, it was a suggestion." Duncan works to loosen Josh's grip. "And we don't know that he's innocent. We didn't see who hurt Maggie."

"You're a coward, a fucking dickless coward," Josh shouts. He tightens his grip and a button from Duncan's collar pops off and ricochets on the asphalt.

Duncan pushes forward, his skin turning violet with the insult. "Say that again. You try saying that again."

"You're a dickless coward," Josh shouts louder.

Carolynn thrusts her elbows into the boys' sides as she squeezes between their torsos. "Someone's going to hear you," she whispers urgently. "Please let him go, Josh."

"I should go in there right now, man. I should tell them it was you," Josh growls. He's shaking with anger.

"Duncan, tell him you weren't serious," Carolynn says, her expression fixed and furious. "Tell us *both* that you would never do that."

"I wouldn't do it," Duncan says between his teeth, looking only at Carolynn, and then to Josh. "Dude, let go." Duncan rears back. Josh keeps hold as he's jerked forward. Carolynn is sandwiched in the middle. Another button breaks off, pinging against a police car. Windows made of privacy glass cover the face of the building, which cops—*which Detective Ward*—could be watching us from.

"We go to the spring," I blurt. "We search for . . . for something to support our story."

"Evidence?" Carolynn asks, squirming out from the boys. The waist of her jumper is twisted and one of its straps is off her tan shoulder. "Aren't the, oh I don't know, *cops* supposed to have that covered?"

Josh's arms fall away from clutching Duncan.

"Not necessarily," I say. Josh is breathing hard, eyeing Duncan, who's rubbing his neck where his collar chafed the skin. "Think about it. They're focused on the seven of us as suspects and using the body and timeline to prove our guilt. They're probably not collecting more evidence at the crime scene. They're trying to track down where we got the poison."

"Lemme get this straight," Carolynn says, righting her jumper and glaring at a smudge on the suede of her right sandal. "*You* want *us* to hike back to the spring, where a girl was murdered, to look for evidence of who did it? And what if we find it? What if we figure out the identity of who offed Maggie? What if it is Skitzy-Fitzy and he's looking for his next victim?"

"I'll take a run-in with some prick who drowns girls before I take prison," Duncan says. Josh grinds his teeth at his voice.

My hands hook at the back of my neck and I give a helpless shrug. "We don't have a choice. If we wait to do something and they come to arrest us, we won't have a shot. We told the truth about Maggie, and maybe it's going to be enough—*maybe*—but we do this *just in case*." Just in case.

— 12 —

We agree to meet at Josh's house at six tomorrow morning, putting us at the spring before anyone else will likely be there. It falls to me to handle Willa. To recruit her for the mission. To make certain that she isn't contemplating throwing more suspicion in our direction to escape it herself.

I'm in Dad's car and he's taking me home. He huffs into the rush of wind from his wide-open window. He's indignant. He can't grasp how anyone with half a brain would dare to suggest that his precious, bright, well-behaved daughter had anything to do with such a sordid business as Maggie Lewis, dead or alive.

"To think," Dad says, "I heard what people said about that girl, and I know most of that gossip was small-town-mindedness, because she was a girl who apparently enjoyed dating a lot of boys before Ben, and remember, I let her date my stepson and welcomed her into our home, but for God's sake, you are my sweet little Bumblebee and that girl took your big brother from you, and you *still* tried to save her life."

Blood-warm shame washes over me. Indignation too that Dad says *Bumblebee* like I'm a doll he's kept in her box, all neat and innocent. I think that, silent and clear, and I hear Ben's laugh in response. It comes from behind me. I eye the rear seat. Why do I anticipate Ben's silhouette cocked against the window, his freckled knuckles obstinately rapping the glass?

Ben hated the way Dad called me Bumblebee. Before Ben and Diane came to live with us, it was just me and Dad. I spent the most time with a circulating cast of foreign nannies and teenage baby-sitters, who were mostly good at playing DVDs and ordering takeout and who didn't bother with pet names. But there were a couple of afternoons a week with the slightly more attentive and way bossier Mariella. She was fond of telling me that I should act like a lady, which as far as I could tell meant playing inside and washing my hands a lot. Dad didn't mind if she brought her sons over when she worked, so she did whenever they weren't in school. They played on the terrace and the dock in *my* dinghy. Mariella set me to work cutting the crusts from sandwiches and sent me for the boys when it was time for lunch.

Then Ben came along, and he thought the situation was weird and insisted I play outside with the boys. Ben wasn't afraid to get into it with Mariella; he wasn't intimidated by the way she'd strike the wooden spoon she cooked with on the counter in anger. She'd throw up her hands and give Ben whatever he asked for, because there was no winning with him once he wanted something.

We were on the dock near the dinghy one of those afternoons, soon after Ben and Diane moved in, and Mariella's oldest son—a pushy boy who was constantly sticking his tongue out at me—told me that I was just a stupid girl who should be playing with dolls inside.

Lightning fast, Ben shoved him into the water. I guess Ben figured that wasn't punishment enough, since he dunked the boy's head under as he tried to bob up. The boy howled and made a big deal. Mariella was furious. Dad was angry until Ben explained, and then Dad told Mariella that her boys weren't welcome anymore. Dad said to Ben, "We can't always talk with our fists, but good for you. You took care of our girl, *our little Bumblebee*." Ben frowned. Dad had missed the point.

Even though Ben had "taken care" of me, he didn't do it because I needed him to. He didn't do it because I was a girl and he was a boy. And he knew that Dad calling me *our girl* wasn't that far off from Mariella's kid calling me a *stupid girl*.

"Bumblebees buzz and make sickeningly sweet honey," Ben said after the incident, when we were the two of us. "You swat them away from your sandwiches on picnics. You aren't a bumblebee."

"I'm a shark," I said. He grinned. "And you're an alligator," I added, gnashing my teeth as a snapping beast. When I thought about it later, what he said made sense. Not just sense, it expressed what I had been thinking but was too young to know how to explain. I didn't want to be a bumblebee, or a kitten, or a sweetheart, or the million other babyish, trifling, fuzzy-animal names people call girls. I wanted to be Lana, brave and of consequence.

I watch the harbor flash between tree trunks. Its blues diminish and then richen. Memories like these aren't enough. I want my brain to draw Ben everywhere. In addition to feeling that a part of Ben is left, I want to see proof of it.

The dead bird is gone, dragged away by whatever killed it, probably. The big house manages to feel claustrophobic. Dad's filling it up with anxiety as he paces the kitchen. His cell chirps as I'm sitting at the island and Dad's at the sink, staring out of the bay window with an intensity that I'm surprised doesn't burn the fog away. I rest my head on the marble as Dad circles, drilling the lawyer. "Of course there were minor discrepancies in their accounts, they're children. . . . Adults give differing witness accounts. . . . What the hell is Willa Owen's mother telling the police? . . . Yes, I think it's possible that she'd pressure her daughter to lie if it meant clearing Willa's name. Would it be enough? If the six others stick to their story?"

I bite my tongue to keep from whining that it isn't a *story*. It's the truth and that should mean something, but all of a sudden the truth as a concept seems wispy. In my head the truth blows away as Dad pounds a fist on the island's marble. That's the way the truth is, you know.

The truth is a vindictive fuck.

"How can they be considering arresting all of them? Lana's answered their questions, and we're done speaking with them voluntarily. If they want to show up with an arrest warrant, that's what they'll need to do." Dad lowers his voice as he retreats, rounding hall corners. A few more seconds and the door to his office closes, ending what I can hear of his conversation.

I head down the stairs that run from our upper terrace to the waterfront one hundred feet below. On the dock I draw our wooden dinghy in from where it floats, climb aboard, and push off. I drift until there's a gentle tug as the rope tethering the boat to the dock goes taut. A blanket of fog fuzzes the borders of the harbor, giving it the look of a bathtub overflowing with steam. I recline on my back, my spine taking the shape of the bowed wooden floor. It's solid under me, slightly wet with rain from the previous night.

The water slaps the siding lazily. There's only blue sky, and rather than bearing down on me, the color is distant and faint. A pinprick of blue diffused in a vat of white icing. A thin strip of green-and-black mountains peek at me as the boat dips at the bottom of each crest. I can vaguely hear the rustling of papers, the clink of Dad's cup on its saucer, the periodic hiss of the espresso maker as he froths milk, and the click of his laptop keys on the upper terrace.

I let the sounds of land fade and pretend that I'm lost at sea. I am adrift in the Pacific, aimlessly sailing. Or not aimlessly. The current is washing me to where Ben waits on a golden beach, and we'll scavenge for driftwood and build a bonfire and toast marshmallows like we used to. I allow the make-believe to go on and on. It lulls me into a kind of spellbound state where I trace the halo shape of clouds.

A trio of pelicans flies at a slant overhead, and I pop up on an elbow to watch them. I love birds; always have. They can fly away; escape. My eyelids are heavy. Dusk is coming fast. The automatic dock lanterns buzz and flick on. Flying insects surge toward their burnt gold, all determined to capture the glow.

Dad calls down to me. "I'm headed in. Better come up." His words echo along the shoreline. Hand passes over hand as I reel myself to the dock. The water is black and opaque, and I tense as I lunge over the gap between the dinghy and dock.

I make it a third of the way up the stairs, to the landing that juts out from the hillside, our fire pit at its center. A far-off laugh skips across the water like a stone. It's from a man or boy. Familiar. It brings on the sense I had last night that Ben isn't all the way gone. If I turned around, would he be there? I shake my head. *Stop.* Ben is dead. His killer is on the loose along with Maggie's, and I shouldn't be down here alone. I can't help what I do next, though. The dusk is shimmery, full of magic. And I want to pretend a bit longer.

I close my eyes and picture the flicker of flames on Ben's face and the glow of a sky full of stars turning him silver. He loved to sit around the fire pit in the middle of the night.

A soft tap at my door and he'd open it a crack. "Are you awake?" he'd whisper, or, "Get dressed." He'd lead me down the stairs, my hands on his shoulders because I was half-asleep. I lived for those nights. Sitting until the sun broke over the horizon, Ben's voice syrupy in my ears, spilling over my shoulders, dripping from my fingertips, puddling wonder beneath me. I wanted to drown in it. It reminded me of the old days in our blanket forts. The whole world, the looming sky and the serpentine inlets of the sound and the far reaches of Central America, had become Ben's blanket fort.

Last December we were leaning dangerously close to the spitting fire to keep warm. I jabbered on about my plans to apply for college in the fall, and Ben talked about traveling the spring away. "What do you think you'll find in college, Lana?" His voice was hungry, ravenous. It scared me sometimes, having to defend my small life when I wasn't exactly thrilled with its size. When we argued, it felt like scraping my knees along the sidewalk. I worried about what might be revealed by the scraped-away skin.

"Everything," I said. "History and anthro and archaeology and poli sci and astronomy."

"That's why you're studying your ass off in high school? You want to land yourself in college and study your ass off again? You don't think you can learn more from going, seeing, *doing*?" He gave me an incredulous look.

"Sure, but in college I'll be studying so that I can go to law or business school."

He stood fast, came around the fire pit, and hit his knees at my feet. The flats of his hands covered the tops of mine. They were hot in my lap. "That's what you want? You want to bust your ass in school for more school, all so you can defend a criminal or oversee a corporate merger?"

The water stopped slapping the rocks below us, and a hush fell over the world.

It was ripe for a confession.

Actually, Ben, I only pretend to be the studious, well-behaved daughter of Cal McBrook, because I'm not brave enough for the alternative. I'm not brave enough to wear black fishnets, or flip off Carolynn Winters and those girls, or tell Ford Holland exactly what I think of him, or ask Josh Parker out, or take the chances I really want to, the chance I'm aching to.

I resolved to tell Ben all this after high school, when things were different. I'd come home the first Thanksgiving of college and I'd be myself: unafraid, bold, devil-may-care. I'd be Lana with a knitting-needle sword at her side. Even in my wildest dreams, I didn't blow off college, I went and made Dad and Diane proud. That's who I grew into being. I was wild and daring as a kid, uncontainable, then time passed and it rubbed off and other traits stuck. I became more of an earthworm than a python. Until I was jolted awake. Jolted brave again by losing Ben.

Ben was waiting for an answer, and my hands were sweating under his. I said pleadingly, "Come to college with me. We can apply to the same schools and because of your gap year, you'll only be one year ahead."

He pulled away abruptly. "I'm tired," was all he said. He jogged up the stairs, leaving me and the firelit night. Ben talked about escape more than I did. We both chafed at living in Gant. The island wore me smooth as a little stone on a riverbed. Ben grew more opinionated and blustery. He wanted to hitchhike through Canada, sail to the South Pacific on the *Mira*, trek through Borneo, and teach kids in a Brazilian *favela*. Everything was for after, after, after we got out of Gant. He wanted me to say, *Screw college. Let's go on an adventure.*

I open my eyes. Playing memories offers temporary relief. But I am emptier for it. I circle around the fire pit and go for our secret place. It's a nook concealed by boulders that fit like jigsaw pieces on the hillside. There's a crevice below the rock shaped like a three-quarters moon. If you glide your hand in, you reach the hollow spot behind the rocks' facades.

Ben and I used to hide what we didn't want to be found there. Mostly, I stored my contraband candy stash in a jar. As a teenager Ben used it for booze and cigarettes. We'd be at the market, or the movies, or Marmalade's, and Ben would turn dollar bills, or receipts, or gum wrappers into cranes while we waited. A few times Ben left these origami animals with notes scribbled in his messy, slanting handwriting in our hiding spot for me. I haven't checked inside the hollow since Ben's been gone. Holding anything that he hid away—even soggy cigarettes I don't intend to smoke—would be better than only remembering.

My fingertips run along the cold stone interior walls and close around an object. I pull it out. There's a bracelet in my palm. Its leather cord is worn soft and its beads are smooth and round.

Familiar. My fingers roll them side to side.

It's a rosary, threaded with *rosary peas*, like those that someone might have forced into Maggie's mouth as she struggled. I hear the choking gurgle she might have made as she was gagging on them. I see them swinging from this thin strip of leather, held by her killer. I am startled by an explosion of memory. A bulky, toothless monk runs his fingers like frantic spiders over a rosary. He's the villain from one of our stories, but the details of the plot aren't more than smudges of pencil that survived an eraser in my head. The monk was crazy, escaped from somewhere, roaming the countryside killing women by forcing them to swallow rosary peas. My heroic likeness hunted him down, killed him in the same way he took victims. Although I don't recall this specific ending, this is how the stories always ended: good trumped evil.

Ben never let the villain win.

I squeeze the rosary in my hand. It's real. It's here. And I've seen its mother-of-pearl crucifix before, outside my imagination, in the jumble of pretty tokens at the bottom of my mother's hope chest.

— 13 —

Ben and I huddled above my mother's hope chest on a stormy afternoon. It was a few months after he and Diane moved in, and we'd been trading secrets when I confided in him my desire to see the chest's locked-away contents. This was one of my most closely guarded secrets, since I'd taken to pretending I had no interest in learning more about my mom. I had never told my father that I was curious about what was inside her chest, which lived at the foot of his bed. I could have asked, but Ben setting out for the key was more fun.

He found it on the third day of his effort, at the bottom of a folder filed away in my dad's desk under the letter *M*. I remember the way Ben's fingers lingered over a similar file in the *W*s. Wright: Diane and Ben's last name before they took McBrook. He bypassed it and we moved on with the key to the trunk.

The journals inside were how I discovered all my mother's sayings. I scanned their entries and read tidbits out loud to Ben; I'd later study their pages. He leafed through the photo albums. He only had one from before he came to live with us and never let me look inside. I think he didn't want me to see how poor he and Diane had been—as if I would have cared. The rosary was at the bottom of the chest, a token from my mother's very Irish Catholic great-grandmother, who'd married a missionary and had lived in India before they'd immigrated and found Gant. Before Mom's death, the rosary, her only keepsake from her great-grandmother, dangled from her vanity. It was handmade and strung with rosary peas grown in India.

We replaced the chest's contents, all but the journals. So how did my great-great-grandmother's rosary end up in my secret hiding place? Did I grab it along with the journals and dump the rosary in one of my cluttered jewelry boxes? Did Ben hang on to it because he thought I'd want to keep it close? But then how did it make that final leap from our house to the hiding spot? Had Ben told me the story about the monk before we rooted through the chest? Yes—I think. I remember the rosy cast of light on Ben's face as he held the rosary up and said with a devilish wink that was too grown-up for his face, *Just like the monk's*, I think.

I see the strange link between Ben's story, this rosary, and Maggie's poisoning. But I'm the only person Ben told stories to, and however he knew rosary peas were poisonous—a comic, or a TV show, or a movie, or a book, or Wikipedia—there are probably a hundred other ways Maggie's killer could have known. It's a fluke. I could pick up the newspaper and find threads of Ben's narratives in half the articles covering knife fights, kidnappings, animal attacks, and murders.

More mysterious is how this rosary came to be in our secret place. There's no evidence that this is the rosary used to poison Maggie. There's no evidence that the rosary peas that poisoned her even came from an antique rosary instead of directly from the plant. And our hiding spot was a secret. I am the only living person who knows about it. Ben knew and he might have placed this here before his death, but I can't see why. If he didn't, someone else must have, and I am wrong thinking that I'm the only living person who is aware of our hiding spot. The rosary didn't just appear here. Living hands hid it. Unless . . . I fling the rosary back into the hollow. This is insane. I am Lana McBrook. I have a 4.20 GPA and took anatomy last year in school, and I know that when the human body dies, there's no speck of consciousness left. There definitely isn't a murderous force. I don't believe that death has an *after*. I am sad and losing my mind, and if I didn't think I'd end up with Diane at Calm Coast, I might tell my dad that I need professional help.

I pound up the stairs, every few steps glancing over my shoulder. The sense that I'm being watched from the outcropping of rocks or the vines separating our property from the neighbor's is as maddening as the itch of a mosquito bite. Last night I wanted to stare the shadows down; today I want to run from them. Either I'm crazy and put my great-great-grandmother's rosary in the hidey-spot ages ago and forgot about it or Ben did for some inexplicable reason before he died. In both those scenarios, my rosary isn't the murder weapon.

I'm jumpy at the wind rattling against the kitchen doors as Dad and I eat dinner. My fork clatters against the plate as I drop it for the fifth time. Dad goes to his study once we finish. Upstairs I contemplate toeing Ben's door open, slipping in, running my fingers over the things he loved, and drinking up the comfort.

Not until I saw Josh's room, his walls covered in football heroes, photos of family and friends, and the blue-and-gray zigzag wallpaper did I realize how most teenage boys decorate their rooms.

Not Ben. His is full of trinkets: charcoals and sketch pads; a foot-tall wooden drawing mannequin; a bookshelf sagging with falling-apart, age-darkened books; intricately carved wooden boxes in a range of sizes from our family trip to Prague; a three-foot-long ostrich feather; a replica of a reindeer skull he ordered from Mongolia on the Internet; and a varnished bedside lamp with Sanskrit characters etched into the base.

The walls are speckled with the abandoned corners of posters. Each tear of glossy paper and masking tape is evidence of Ben changing his mind. First Che Guevara went up, followed by Karl Marx, then two German philosophers whose names I mix up. Ben liked the idea of standing for ideas. He wanted to emulate the thinkers of times when the stakes were higher. Ultimately, he was bound to find some tidbit he didn't like about them. Then down went the poster and up went someone new.

If not for these paper triangles on the wall, the room could belong to an antique dealer who drove his rickety car along the Silk Road. I spent hours sizing up Ben's new additions, a tiny framed Turkish coin or a book where the font was too faded to read, trying to decipher what Ben loved about the item. I only understood the posters. The rest remain mysteries, and this is why I haven't gone into his room since he died. Yes, I look for him everywhere. And there he would be: Ben, a version I don't understand. At times I think we were so close that there were things we couldn't see about the other. The alternative—that we weren't close enough—stings too much.

I lie on my bed and dial Willa's number. Voice mail clicks on immediately.

"It's me," I say. "I'm going to get us out of this. I know you wouldn't have been at the spring if I hadn't made you come. *I know.* I should have said so at Josh's. Call me if you can, okay? Just don't worry, I promise I'll figure it out."

Willa and I share real things beyond the eight-semester plan. We have secrets and memories we look back on, grinning. Only she knows I wrote *Josh Parker* in Sharpie on my leg in the seventh grade and that it took thirty showers to wash off. I was there when she broke her wrist teaching herself how to skateboard in the eighth grade and we told her mom that she fell from a stepladder in the library and I acted out the accident in the emergency room for P.O. I'll remind Willa of all this, after I've cleared her name—all of our names—and Willa and I will be better. Different but better.

I pull my knees to my chest and absently yank on a thread from a pillowcase. My cell vibrates on my comforter. The picture Becca programmed to show when she called lights up the screen. Her green eyes, one winking, stare at me.

I let it buzz four more seconds. I wanted to talk to Willa, not her opposite.

"H—"

"Did you hear?" she shouts.

I hold the receiver away from my ear. "That we're sneaking back to the spring to hunt for evidence and clear our names?" I say. *It was my idea.*

"Oh my God, you didn't. Listen. Ford is *missing*. Since last night. No one remembers him leaving, and his car was still there this morning. No biggie—there were tons of cars left, and Josh's moms figured kids were being responsible and getting rides. Ford's car was still there after the police station and Karen called Ford's mom to see if they needed help getting it home, and Ford's mom is all, 'I figured Ford was still with Josh.'" All this is said with a giddy lilt that doesn't match the words. Becca's pace snowballs as she continues, "No one was freaked yet, but Ford's mom started calling his cell, which was going straight to voice mail, and then she got her phone tree out and people have been calling for hours trying to find him. Some junior thinks maybe he saw Ford walking along the highway at midnight but couldn't stop because he had six drunkies in his car."

I bob my feet over the edge of the bed. "If he walked home, couldn't he be passed out somewhere, sleeping it off?" I ask, unconcerned.

"For twenty hours? Doubtful. Car and I think Maggie's killer has struck again," she says bluntly.

My stomach drops and I go still. "Why?"

"Everyone thinks it was Maggie and one of her trailer-park-hill people who got Ben, yeah? We figure it's something more dramatic and dark, like a serial killer who picked Maggie and now Ford off. I hope they do one of those made-for-TV true-crime stories about Gant. I could totally play myself."

I pull my knees to my chest. *I know the truth, Ford. You are a zombie, completely unoriginal, pathetic, feeding off your brother's popularity and nastiness, hoping that no one sees how mind-suckingly boring you are.*

"*Hellooo*, you there?"

"Yeah, I am," I say, absorbed in the previous night.

"Are you, like . . . upset? You hate Ford. You said so." A confused beat. "Ohhhh, wait a sec, is it one of those you-hate-him-because-you-think-you-can't-have-him dealies?"

"No," I say firmly, "it definitely is not. And I said I *couldn't stand him*. Hate is a lot more than that." A shudder moves through me. I absolutely hate Ford. I told him that the kids he considers friends think he's a hanger-on. He deserved it. *He earned it.* Ben used to say: *Bullies don't get to win.* Ford didn't last night.

"Can't stand him, hate him, same difference," Becca's saying. "Which is why I called Liddy a lying whore when she said she saw you guys outside. *Together.*"

I struggle to catch up. "Who?"

"You and Ford," she sighs, exasperated. "She said you guys looked super intense and that you came in with this mushy smile on your face. And then she went outside and asked him what was up, and he was all, 'That girl's always wanted to get up on me.'" I'd smile at Becca's Ford impression if I wasn't frowning.

"That isn't true," I say.

"Oh, I know. Anyway, it's sort of a compliment. People don't lie about you unless you matter," she says, a wistful quality to her voice.

I'm sick with mingling emotions after we hang up. Ford wasn't like Maggie. His actions didn't physically harm anyone. He was cruel and vindictive, though.

Maggie dying and Ford going missing feels like the universe setting itself right. Obviously, this isn't true. If the universe was going to fix bad stuff in the world, wouldn't it stop kid hunger or all the wars before it picked off the people who've been nasty to Lana McBrook of Gant Island, Washington?

The universe wouldn't bother with me.

I recline slowly and heavily.

No. Whatever remains of Ben would.

— 14 —

I t's the dark side of dawn when I lock the front door behind me. I tossed and turned last night. There was noise, unidentifiable, soft, and persistent. It was the hum of things going wrong in my head. It resembled footsteps and whispering all muddled together, and when I opened my eyes from the pillow, I half expected to see a shadowy figure swaying in my bedroom doorway. I expected Ben. The house felt occupied.

I talked myself out of it. Repeatedly. I fell asleep and would wake with a bit of a start, as if I could sense someone at the foot of my bed, observing me. Even this morning with my eyes open, it's a hard conviction to shake.

I zip my fleece to my chin. My eyes water in the brisk air. I scan the front yard before running for my car. The porch lantern's glow floods the lawn; beyond it there are the shadowy rounds and columns of tree trunks. Perfect hiding places for anyone watching. I check the backseat before slipping into my car.

Our street follows the horseshoe-shaped harbor. Houses behind brick-and-iron gates stud the shoe. I follow the roads terracing up the hill to Josh's. I pull in behind Carolynn. She's stepping out of her car in fur-cuffed suede boots, her blond hair in a French twist. *Mom* is what I think of whenever I spot a hairstyle too elaborate for me to master. Moms are the ones who teach you how to braid, twist, and pin.

It's chilly outside for August. September will mean rust- and fire-colored trees and the beginning of one long rainstorm that lasts until next summer. It means the tang of bonfires in the air will be replaced by wet earth rot. It means autumn and starting school without Ben. Instead of having to think about the dead and missing, we should be excited or dreading back-to-school. My fingers fumble popping the trunk.

I reach for the flashlight under the jumper cables of the emergency kit. I stare at the large, forest-green metal chest behind the kit. A stripe of masking tape runs its length, with *Summer Provisions* in marker. I hear the squeak the marker made as Ben labeled the box. I close my eyes for the barest second and can see what Ben did next. He wrote *Summer Provision* on an additional strip of masking tape. He peeled it from the roll and ran his fingers from one end to the other, smoothing it over the skin of my forearm. I left it there. Some feelings are as undeniable as they are inexplicable. I open my eyes, scratch my arm where the tape was once, and stare down the green chest.

We left it in my trunk after our last day on the boat. It was miserably cold, a wet February, and the week before Ben left for Guatemala. Without opening it, I know its contents: two aluminum foil balls from our turkey avocado sandwiches; one bag of unopened salt-and-vinegar potato chips; two empty bottles of root beer; one empty can of actual beer; a set of mini waterproof speakers; two rain slickers; a seagull's feather; and a flare gun kit. The day was that big. It would be our last on the sailboat for months. I am a just-poked bruise.

"Hey, you." Josh's voice makes me jerk from my thoughts. "Whatcha doin'?" he asks, rosy-cheeked in the chill morning.

I feign a smile and hold up the flashlight. "Grabbing this. You guys ready?"

Josh stands a little taller and says pluckily, "You bet." He cranes his neck, peering through the back window. "Willa meeting us there?"

I shake my head. "She isn't coming. I didn't ask her to."

Carolynn circles to join us, her eyes narrowed. "Why? All of us are going."

"I know," I say sharply. I take a breath. "Look, P.O. wasn't going to miss her sneaking out this morning. It would have caused us more trouble."

Becca warms her hands on a pink plaid thermos. Josh rocks his head side to side. "Willa could tell the cops we hurt Maggie," Carolynn says to him.

"We've already been through this, remember? She's not lying to the police," I say. "We're going to find proof that someone else was at the spring."

Carolynn and Becca exchange a look, their collective stare diverting to Josh for a moment. An unsaid agreement passes between them. I see it, gold and shimmery, tying them together. Willa and I are the outsiders. They are the core. Our four-week guest pass into their world doesn't change this. If needed, they'll strike at Willa preemptively.

We pile into Josh's Jeep to ride to the spring together. One car parked along the road will draw less attention than multiple vehicles. There is no banter, no laughter, no smiling in the Jeep's cab. The possibility that today could be the day the police decide to arrest us for Maggie's murder turns the air stuffy, unbreathable.

"If I have to listen to sports radio for one more second, I am going to kill all of you and dump your bodies in the spring," Carolynn says humorlessly.

Becca applies makeup while wedged between me and Rusty in the backseat. "I'm no fatty, but I could eat this ChapStick, it's so delicious," she says, a moment before capping it and spritzing her neck and cleavage with body spray.

"Don't get your perfume and shit on me," Rusty complains. I'm smashed against the window as she scoots toward me so she doesn't have to touch him. I'm twitchy, knees jittering, eyes resting on nothing. I shouldn't have replaced the rosary in my hiding spot. My fingerprints are on the peas. But it won't be found. Ben and I never showed another person our secret place. We never went for it when anyone else was around, and it's unlikely that anyone else saw Ben pulling a flask from it or me retrieving gummies, even more unlikely that this person turned out to be a homicidal maniac who would later hide a murder weapon there, and even unlikelier that that same person would someday have my great-great-grandmother's rosary in their possession. One unlikelihood piled on top of another.

"Ford's parents and a bunch of adults are searching the woods along here later this morning. This is the way he'd have gone to walk home," Josh announces.

I stare out the window. Is Ford there, under the brush, passed out or worse? Did someone follow him home with the aim of hurting him, or was someone lying in wait and Ford was a victim of convenience?

"My money's on Holland showing up in a day or two," Rusty says.

Duncan snickers at this. "You think he went into the city hammered, trying to score some weed?"

Rusty shrugs. "He's always getting wasted and doing dumb shit. Remember when he did a backflip off the diving board at school and fractured his collarbone freshman year?"

There are murmured *oh yeahs*.

Josh cracks his window and says into the rush of wind, "I dunno. It's been more than twenty-four hours. It's too much of a coincidence that Maggie turns up dead and then Ford goes missing. Maybe it's the same killer?"

I stay staring at the trees. The shadows between their trunks curl and twist until I see staggering, starving creatures watching the car speed past. Some of the forms bound after us, marking our trail by shedding skin and coats. I wonder if Ben's imagination bled into reality in a similar way in the moments before his death. Did he see the shadow man as I did or did he see a human face? Did he suspect that the ogre with the two-pronged tongue from one of his stories had found him? There's a little nip of my conscious mind, like my dreaming memory is stirring, poking my waking memory in a certain direction, but before I go there, the others are unloading on the access road.

We file down the path. Pockets of fog like clouds gather in the dips of the trail. The feathery masses are opaque. We disappear into them and as we emerge, I'm tingly like my atoms have been altered in some tiny way.

Glossy green leaves as big as dinner platters shine from the undergrowth. They have traceries of veins and scrolling tips. Everything is saturated, dripping, and verdant in the beams of our flashlights. The sun spills over the low points on the horizon, but the tallest pines keep the forest floor in manufactured night. The long, frilly threads of neon moss hanging from pine boughs put off bioluminescence.

In addition to our shuffling steps and sniffling, the preserve has its own symphony. The wind sings through the trees, and there are groans and creaks from their ancient trunks. There's a faint *shhhhh* from the water surging against the beach a mile away. No one speaks. It's as if they sense as I do that we're sneaking into an enchanted land, alien from Swisher Spring. We shouldn't let the natives hear us coming.

I wonder what it means that I am less and less anchored by what is in front of my face. Nothing feels real. Alone, with these five, anything—the horrible as much as the good—is possible.

My thighs get tired navigating over the slick rocks. I swipe my wet palms on my jeans after leveraging over a fallen trunk. My heart lodges itself higher in my throat. This is it. We may have only hours to clear our names. Then the police could come.

When they do, might they find my hiding spot? Having the rosary may make me appear even more suspicious. And yes, I think my hiding spot is secure, but if someone other than me or Ben put the rosary there, then maybe that someone is trying to make me look guilty? All they'd have to do is phone in an anonymous tip. I should have destroyed the rosary. Dumped it in the harbor. Anything so there was no chance I'd be tied—any more than I already am—to a murder. My instinct was to hide it again. As I said, I am a sometimes liar.

My heart is in my mouth. *Calm down. Breathe.* I need to be the braver version of me from Ben's stories. She was cool and calculating.

We trickle out on the rocks surrounding the spring. The faint light doesn't penetrate the water, only reveals the silhouette of the shore. Our flashlight beams crisscross, darting around as if the whole group can't focus. I sweep over the ferns, trying to see through the understory. If Maggie's killer watched us drag her from the water, he might have been hiding behind the waist-high hedge of green. I search for shoe prints, cigarette butts, anything left behind.

Josh's flashlight is a pendulum swinging as he paces nearby. "Hey," I whisper. The beam blinds me.

"Sorry," he mutters, working his way carefully over the boulders separating us.

He's tucked up to his earlobes in a scarf looped around his neck. It's crimson like those corduroys. "It's rained since we were here last."

He's quiet, staring intently at an unexceptional slice of matted fern. I worry he doesn't understand. I inch closer—the kind of close that allows me to identify the stitch his grandma used to knit the scarf. I don't want to start a panic. "Shoe prints and any evidence left by Maggie's killer would have washed away in the rain."

"We're screwed," he says loudly, lurching away. "We're totally fucked." Josh swings the light, flash-illuminating open mouths and alarmed eyes. "The evidence washed away with the rain. That's why the cops aren't here." He curses under his breath and hurls the flashlight at the rocks. I shrink from the hopelessness rolling off Josh. The reality of what we'll face if there is no evidence to recover has sunk in. Josh is used to things working out.

"I'm telling you, man, we say it was Skitzy-Fitzy," Duncan calls from the opposite bank of the spring. He tips his skipper hat, taking credit for what he believes is a brilliant contribution. "Who the hell knows, maybe it was him?"

Josh is motionless for a moment, and then he's scrambling over the shore. Rusty rushes to block him as Becca begins to cry in hopeless little huffs, sinking to her knees. Carolynn doesn't move from the edge of the water. She isn't deer-in-headlights still. She's hugging herself for warmth, staring at the spring, contemplative, steady. I pick my way to her. "Maggie was attached to something down there," I say. My light bounces off the black-and-blue water.

Carolynn's gaze clicks from the water to my face. Josh is shoving Rusty away and Duncan's howling about not wanting to be a *bitch* in prison and Skitzy-Fitzy probably having killed other homeless *dudes* in the past, so why can't he take the heat for Maggie this one time?

I point to the wall of the ridge. It juts up at a ninety-degree angle from the water's surface. "I found her over there. At the bottom."

Carolynn nods. "The water's higher than it was the other day."

I shrug. "The rain and the underground source that drains—" I stop short and swivel to face her. "Ben and I used to come here to look for the underground stream that fills the spring. We'd spend hours searching the bottom and the rocky walls."

She pulls her vest to her chin and nuzzles the fur. "Enough with the walk down your pathetic memory lane," she says. She isn't wearing lip gloss, and she's paler than usual without bronzer.

"It's not stagnant water," I say, "so there must be an opening. What if Maggie drowned upstream where the water runs on the surface? Or even in the sound? It's a mile away, but if she was sucked underground, she could have ended up here."

Carolynn chews her bottom lip for a spell. "That isn't totally stupid," she says reluctantly.

"We have to go under," I say. She looks skeptically from the spring to me, then waves me forward with a smirk. I roll my eyes. She crouches to unlace her furry boots. She jabs a finger at my sneakers. "You aren't going to swim in those abominations, are you?"

We're peeling off layers, teeth chattering at the air's bite, when Becca notices. "Car . . . Lan? It's too cold to swim," she says. "You'll turn to Popsicles."

At the hint of bare skin, all three boys spin in our direction. Rusty's arms pin Josh's at his sides. Duncan's blinking his left eye furiously, where Josh apparently punched him, a blow I wish I'd witnessed.

Josh shakes Rusty off and trips forward. "What are you guys doing?"

Carolynn glowers at them, continuing to slide her jeans off her hips. "While you guys are man-grappling, we're saving your asses."

"How? Suicide by hypothermia?" Becca cries. She's trying to make it over the rocks to meet us, heeled boots wobbling slowly, ankles teetering.

There are objections as we explain. We've stripped down to our underwear and bras, and I have this terrible moment where my insecurity starts screaming that I'm practically naked in front of Josh and that I'm wearing pink cotton briefs—*full butt briefs*. And then my sane self puts it into perspective.

"I'm not letting you guys go alone," Josh says, unwinding the scarf from his neck. For a split second he has the look of a boy trying to hang himself with a makeshift noose. Josh continues unraveling his clothing with the force and precision of a hurricane.

Carolynn grabs the rising hem of his fleece and yanks it down. "I used to be on swim team in middle school, remember?" She jerks her thumb at me. "Lana's already proven she can hold her breath longer than any of you ass-chaps."

Josh blinks bewildered at her. "You don't even swim anymore, Car."

"Because I don't like getting my hair wet, not because I forgot how." She secures the pins in her tresses.

The ribbon of gold on the horizon is expanding, its molten edges bleeding over the tallest trees. "It's better with only two of us," I explain. "It'll be dark below, and with more people there's more chance that someone will get hurt."

Carolynn smiles at Josh and says, "Translation: you'll kick us in the tits with your giant legs and feet." She and I are at the rim.

"I think my flashlight is waterproof. Yours?" I ask.

She sniffs under her breath. "We're about to find out."

"Maybe we should count to three and then jump?"

She stretches her arms above her head. "Whatever."

I say, "One," and she dives. Carolynn disappears under the surface. The sun's rays fracture through the fringe of trees and the water turns an unnaturally vivid violet. *Toxic water.* It must be because it's the same water that was in dead Maggie's mouth, ears, and nose. This used to be *our* place, and now it's become a killer's dumping ground. And it's because Maggie is dead that she will never be able to admit to the police what she did to Ben and who sank a knife into him.

Carolynn's kicks send ripples through the water. There's the suggestion of bodies crowded below the surface, and then the ripples fade and the water is smooth again, bodiless. I'm going mad. I give my head a defiant shake.

This is our place, and Ben would expect me to be brave. I am a shark and I can hear that hungry, daring voice, mine or Ben's, urging me on. I lunge forward. I am alive, alive, *alive*.

—15—

pop up with the slippery wall of the ridge at my chest. Carolynn's heart-shaped mouth smirks at me. A single drop clings to the tip of her upturned nose. "It's not so fun when you're not showing off for Josh, is it?"

Wet hair plasters my face, and I unceremoniously swipe it away. Carolynn's elaborate twist survived the swim. Her pins are dotted with little crystals, and they're nestled in her locks with the look of fallen stars. "I don't show off for Josh," I say.

"Please." She flicks water in my face. Her pink nails are chipped, newly neglected. "It's obvious you go for nice guys, and Josh is the nicest."

I look to the sky and sigh, exasperated, like I have no clue what she means. "You work the flashlights and I'll search the wall," I say, teeth already beginning to chatter. She shrugs, smiling like she's pegged me.

We swim in a zigzag as my fingers crawl over the rock and Carolynn sweeps our flashlights as lanterns illuminating a stormy night. Our movements and pace synchronize.

During our fourth break on the surface, Becca shouts, "You've been diving for ages. Your nips are going to fall off if you stay in longer."

Becca has a point. My skin is tight and shivering over my bones. I'm losing control of trembling muscles. Staying afloat is as exhausting as flying, and I start thinking of us as two desperate little birds trying to avoid crashing to the ground in an ice storm. We're not treading water; we're flapping our frozen wings.

Carolynn's eyes are blue rimmed, the right one twitching with cold. The only makeup she was wearing, mascara, has washed away. Without her foundation, I see she has a band of freckles on her nose like me. Her sharp jaw is set, refusing to chatter.

I lift my stubborn chin in the air. There is no quitting; no crashing to the ground. "Again?"

"Don't worry about me," Carolynn says, nimbly tucking a rogue lock into its jeweled pin. "You're the one who looks worse than an eighty-year-old stripper in Tacoma."

A gasped chuckle from me. Then we're under. My fingers skate over the rock's face as if on ice. Carolynn flashes the light, our signal for surfacing, and I shake my head. I hold up a finger. She can wait. It hasn't been long.

I kick hard and squirm lower, almost to the bottom, where a crevice forms a dark triangle. I toe the space. My foot slips into the dark. The beams crisscross and I give in, shooting up to the surface after Carolynn.

"What . . . the . . . hell . . . was . . . that?" she pants.

I try to rest my arms by floating on my back, but I keep sinking under. The dead man's float was always easier for me. "Found it," I say while exhaling.

There comes a volley of shouts from the shore. Josh's warm tone separates from the others. "Too long. You've been in too loooong."

The anxious four wave their arms vigorously. Becca brandishes the thermos, trying to coax us over with the promise of hot cocoa.

"Let's do this," I say.

Carolynn takes a deep breath and we plunge under. I fall as a rock to the bottom. The dull craving for air builds until I shove the need away and focus on more important things. *There are things more important than breathing.* The opening in the rock is knee height and no wider than my hips.

I swim lower. Carolynn angles a beam into the narrow tunnel to reveal a lone shoe. It's pink canvas with *Maggie* in Sharpie stacked alongside the lace holes. The sneaker's rubber sole is trapped in a crevice between rocks, as if Maggie was kicking, attempting to push off when she wedged it there.

A current of adrenaline sends electricity into my limbs. I take one of the flashlights from Carolynn. As my head and shoulders enter the passage, it occurs to me that what I'm doing might be the most reckless thing I've ever done. If Willa were here rather than Carolynn, she would catch a disappearing leg and drag me back. Not Carolynn. She's likely waving a middle finger at my retreating figure.

The passage is just wide enough for me. I crawl more than I swim, reaching ahead, hooking my fingers and pulling. I use the fear to move faster. I can hear Ben's voice, echoing through time to me. *Exercise your nerve and mischief, Lana.*

A shimmering, sea-green full moon takes shape. I flick the flashlight off and there's enough light to see by. The water warms the farther I wriggle. Another few feet and all the walls fall away. I push off from the floor, traveling to the surface, to the source of the jade light. Light means air. Up, up, and up. There are sharp-nailed hands in my chest, tearing at the pith of my lungs until I gag into the water.

I begin to thrash. My head breaks the surface and I gasp, legs churning, hands pressed on the rock ceiling a foot above my head. I draw mouthfuls of air from the pocket. I'm dizzy and wheezing for a minute before my surroundings stop tilting.

The ceiling is fractured and light seeps from the surface, giving it the look of a starry night sky. I must be below the ridge, under the rocky trail I've walked a thousand times. The water is still and bath-water warm. A fire-ant sting races over me as the feeling returns to my arms and legs. I tread water.

A bubbling rush surges to my right, and Carolynn hits the surface. For a minute the only noise is the roar of her catching her breath, hacking up lungs, sputtering as she searches for a place to rest. The cave is barely wider than my bedroom, and the walls are smooth and steep without a ledge to hold on to.

The water's a churning sea by the time she whirls toward me. "Jesus-effing-Christ, you stupid-ass witch," she yells. "I thought you were stuck and I was going to have to tell your sappy-eyed dad that you drowned." The water slaps our collarbones and chins. Her eyes are livid blue, and I have a feeling that if we were on land, she'd strangle me.

"I didn't think you'd follow," I say.

Her mouth twists. "You thought I'd leave you for dead?"

"Carolynn, I—I'm sorry." I paddle closer. "I saw the light and didn't think you'd worry." I try to catch her eyes. They're wild and scared, darting around, taking in the confined space. Fleetingly, her face is young and soft.

She regains her icy stare. "Stop sniveling. We're not bests, but I wouldn't let you drown."

A surprised laugh from me. Her lids are hooded, glaring. I'm delirious from the close call, from the absurdity of Carolynn following me through a tunnel that could have led to hell for all she knew, and from the pressure of Maggie's death weighing down on us. I laugh because the only alternative is to cry. I sink, submerging my mouth; chortling sends up bubbles.

"I'm going to slap you," she says. The corners of her eyes are creasing; a twitch of her jaw, as if she's fighting a smile. "Maggie could have been in here the whole day," she adds. I stop laughing. "We were here for six hours, and she only drowned in the last hour. She spent at least five here." She reaches up and pats the ceiling bearing down on us.

"Why?" I ask. "And how did she even know about this place?"

Carolynn smiles seductively and bats her lashes. "She and your bro probably had the hottest sex in here."

I stop paddling a beat and slip under before starting up again. "Why would you say that?"

Her brow furrows. "You told me that you guys used to explore the spring. I bet he found the cave with her." She licks her bottom lip. "Guys love doing it in kinky places."

I frown. I can't help frowning while imagining Ben and Maggie there. Carolynn tips her head to the side and adds in a throaty rasp, "I know what you're thinking."

I start to protest.

"You don't think Ben would have fit through the tunnel to get inside. Maybe not," she says. Her eyes run the length of the ceiling before settling back on me. "And yes, even Josh is into kinky stuff like outside hookups."

I watch her lips curl into a pouty smile. It might be that we're breathing the same air or that there's a remaining trace of a baby-bond we formed in the playpen, but I can see that like me, Carolynn's lying about who she is. Maybe no one ever looks long enough to spot the cracks in her snow-queen facade because they're afraid of what she may do. Despite all the teasing, Carolynn came after me when she thought I was in trouble. "Why do you do that?" I ask.

She glares at me like I'm exhausting her more than the treading water is.

"All this 'boys and girls are different' crap. All this 'pussies are pussy' stuff. The other day you said girls weren't made for stunts like guys are. But here you are"—I splash water in the direction of the cave's opening—"gutsier than any of them. Why pretend you aren't?"

Her eyes open a little wider before she regains control. "Look," she says in her grown-up voice she uses to tell Duncan's little brothers to get lost, "you're obviously used to hanging out with Willa, who is probably the only girl on the planet who knows less about boys than you do, and it's little wonder your life is PG, so let me give you some advice. Woman to woman." She paddles nearer and says in a confidential tone, "Guys don't like girls to show them up."

A bolt of anger goes through me. I'm sick of Carolynn thinking she can do or say whatever she wants. I'm not the same Lana I used to be. I won't keep my head down or let myself be stomped on. "Josh didn't seem to mind the other day when I jumped," I say.

She sniffs at my attitude. "Josh is freakishly nice. He's the exception, not the rule."

"And you don't like nice guys?" I ask, thinking of whatever there is between Carolynn and Duncan.

Her fingers flick water in my face, and I cough.

"Nice? I want someone who is *good* but can act . . ." She sighs through her teeth.

"Mean?"

She gives a jaded eye roll. "People aren't that simple, Lana. Good or bad. I want a guy who's interesting. I want a guy who knows where to put his hands. Josh is the nicest. Nice isn't always enough."

If Carolynn were Willa, I'd ask what she meant about a guy's hands. I try to look blasé, like her words don't set my mind spinning.

"You aren't going to tell Duncan what I said last night about not wanting to watch Bethany J. all over him, are you?" she asks abruptly.

"No," I reply. "That was a private conversation."

She opens her mouth, closes it, and shakes her head. "So why would Maggie swim all the way down here, alone?" she asks. The subject of Duncan and boys who know what to do with their hands is closed.

I swim in a tight circle. "To hide," I say. "The tunnel's narrow, and no one who doesn't know it's here would be able to follow her. No one bigger could fit." I bob my head. "But hide from who? Not us. All she had to do was swim out and we would have helped her." I say it and know it's true by the way it threatens to drag me under like an anchor. I would have helped save Maggie's life despite what she took from my family. Others might be reassured by such an epiphany. I'm disappointed. Ben deserves blind, cold revenge.

Carolynn floats on her back and twirls the tiny opal stud in her earlobe. "We can't hear anything from the surface. Maggie wouldn't have known us from the perv who poisoned her. She was hiding and waiting until he gave up and left. Maybe she didn't even know that the poison was deadly? I mean, who knows what she thought or knew?"

"The poison must have set in while she was waiting," I say.

Carolynn pushes a few tiny pebbles loose from a crack. They rain down on the water.

I try to imagine Maggie paddling for hours under here. My legs and arms feel as if I'm in hardening cement, and it hasn't been more than five minutes. Maggie was fighting for her life, though, and people do impossible things to stay alive. "You think she drowned getting caught on her way out, slowed or made sick by the poison?" I ask.

Her head sways. "Could be."

I nod. "This is the proof we needed. This is where Maggie was. The police will have to believe us." I hear Willa's voice of reason in my mind: an alternative theory isn't enough to disprove another. But it's more than we arrived with.

Carolynn murmurs assent and takes a deep breath. She dives down; her butt, then her heels rear above the surface. I take one last look at the eerie space—it has the feel of being a thousand feet under a jade lagoon on the other side of the globe.

I swim to the mouth of the tunnel and return through the narrow passage. Sediment drifts like stardust, catching the bright light of the surface. Carolynn grabs Maggie's pink sneaker. She coils her legs and shoots off the spring floor, sending wrinkles through the water. I swim from the tunnel and am about to follow when I notice a brown heap. I swim to the shapeless form.

It's a backpack, wedged between the spring's wall and the rocks that appeared to be dislodged from masking the passage's entry. It might have gotten stuck in Maggie's rush to hide.

One of the backpack's straps is under the weight of a rock as big as my head, and the other is a torn stripe reaching for the sun like a weed.

I push against the rock, but another is pinning it in place. After a lot of shoving and leveraging, the top stone tumbles away. I'm able to free the backpack from under the bottom rock. Its contents could be important. I picture Maggie, hooked on the backpack's strap, unable to free herself. Or maybe she refused to surface without it? If Maggie was panicked, the deadly poison setting in, she might have believed she had more time than she did.

Burdened by the pack and my expectations, I swim for the light.

— 16 —

I t takes Carolynn's help, our cold arms together, hooked in the remaining loop of the pack, to get it to shore. Josh hoists it from the water, showering us below. Duncan catches its waterlogged weight as it begins to slip from Josh's clenched fingers. Carolynn and I boost ourselves over the rocky lip of the spring and collapse like beached oarfish.

My hair is a blindfold. "I hate you both," Becca yells. "I'm going to murder you for making me think . . . I thought . . ." Her voice goes soft and mushy. I push the hair away and prop myself up on my elbows. Becca's slumped to the ground, crying pitifully, with Carolynn's arm wrapped around her. Little nips of jealousy needle my ribs. Willa should be here, for me.

Carolynn details the cave, and the others settle on the same conclusion we did. This is the alternative explanation we need. Moods turn lighter with relief. Josh and Duncan's argument has been forgotten, and they're fist-bumping. I roll onto my knees and crawl toward the pack.

"Nice ass." Duncan's behind me. "Is that Maggie's?" he adds as an afterthought.

I touch the zipper of the pack as I say, "Don't know yet."

"Fingerprints," Josh warns, sinking into a crouch opposite me. The zipper's already pinched between my finger pads.

"Too late for that," Rusty snorts, squatting to my left. In the pale light his freckles are more intense against his sun-pinkened skin.

"Don't worry," Josh says. His hand moves mine gently to the side, and he continues with the zipper where I left off. A glut of water rushes from the inner pocket.

Duncan groans impatiently and claps his hands. "C'mon, c'mon. Whose is it?"

Josh removes wadded up articles of clothing from the sack. Becca unfurls and holds up a black T-shirt with a tattered hem. Carolynn scowls at a pair of plaid shorts. Safety pins with no apparent purpose dangle from the pockets. Duncan pokes what appears to be a fishing net but turns out to be a pair of tights.

"Why did Maggie have a backpack with clothes in it?" Becca asks.

"She was on the run and she had to wear something," Carolynn says as she tosses the recovered pink sneaker onto the pile. "Ironic, since she would have looked better in a trash bag than in these rejects."

Becca nudges the cloth heap. "It's only one outfit. Don't tell me she went seven whole weeks wearing one hideous outfit."

"Two outfits," I say. "She had the clothes we found her in."

"Still," Becca says with disgust.

Josh continues to search through the contents. There are a few travel-size toiletries—a mini toothbrush, toothpaste, wet wipes, and a tiny stick of deodorant—and a spongy glob of what used to be paper. The fibers sag on either side of Josh's cupped hands, rivulets of water dribbling off them until they shred apart. "Shit," Josh says under his breath.

"There goes our evidence," Becca murmurs. Someone snorts.

I rock onto my heels. Anything in the backpack spent the better part of three days submerged. Anything delicate is ruined. Fingerprints are washed away. "Maybe we should have left this stuff where we found it? Let the police come and collect it?" I say.

Carolynn looks up from the backpack. "Too late now."

"Is Maggie's wallet or phone in there?" I ask as Josh searches the smaller pockets.

"Jackpot," he says, grinning.

He's removed an envelope from the bag. It's folded in half and sturdier than the individual sheets that turned to mush. The two halves are fused together. There's only a faint gray shadow where ink used to be on one side of the envelope. The shadow is a formless blot. On the flip side, drawn in thick black Sharpie, is a bird.

"It's a dove," Becca says. "How romantic. There's a little heart at its feet." She claps her hands at her chest. "I don't even remember my last sober kiss, and Maggie was writing a love letter with doves and hearts."

"There's a date in the heart," Josh says. "Three seventeen. March seventeenth." He lifts the bird for me to see clearly. I recognize it. I see Ben hunched over the patio table on the upper terrace, six long feathers arranged parallel to one another and to the top of a sketch pad. "Birds are the most challenging subjects to draw," he said. He was thirteen, fourteen at most. "The aerodynamics and the individual plumes are complicated." He spun his sketch pad around so I could see. He'd drawn four feathers in black and white and a fifth with a scarlet quill.

"Why do you draw them, then? Diane says birds are so dirty

they're basically flying rats," I said in the know-it-all tone I was experimenting with at eleven.

Ben put his charcoal down and met my eyes. I smiled uncertainly, then flattened my lips and tried to match his intensity. He blinked and laughed. "You win," he said. I always beat him at staring contests. He loved to make me compete and fight to win. "I draw birds because they're your favorite animal *and* they have wings."

"Oh," I whispered. And maybe I blathered on about fairy wings or the Pegasus stickers I'd stuck to my school binder. Who knows? I was a day-dreamy kid, infatuated with everything that wasn't real.

This depiction of a bird is unmistakably Ben's. The light reflected in its eyes makes the bird look smart, as if it's paying attention. The date is in Ben's handwriting also. The now disintegrated letter must have been written by Ben on March 17, while he was in Central America, and then delivered somehow to Maggie, either sent in the mail, though I don't see a stamp, or handed to her when he returned. But this doesn't make sense because Ben told me they didn't speak or write the entire time he was gone. He told me it was over with her once he returned. He lied. To me.

I twist around and grab for my hoodie. I tug my arms into the sleeves and zip it to my chin. There's a slight tremble to Josh's hands as he searches the rest of the pockets. Sweat glistens along his hairline. Carolynn combs his feathery hair from his forehead with her fingers. He looks up a beat to smile at her. "You know what I think? Maggie's death was an accident," she says in a way meant to comfort Josh. "All we've proven this morning is that no one held her under. She hid in the cave for hours and when she thought she was in the clear, she swam out. It was shit luck that she got stuck and killed herself."

Carolynn's theory is believable, if not for one inconvenient fact: Maggie was poisoned with a deadly neurotoxin. "How do you explain her ingesting rosary peas?" I ask. "Was she munching on antique prayer beads while she hid from us? She wasn't a closeted Catholic schoolgirl."

Duncan sniggers but thinks better of commenting.

"And *why* was she hiding from us?" I add.

Carolynn's lips move, and I know it's only a nanosecond until she has a comeback.

Josh cuts in first. "Okay, so someone *tried* to kill her at the least, and at the most, the poison is why she drowned. Maybe they meant to feed her enough poison to kill her immediately. She managed to escape and ran to the spring to hide."

"Why bring Maggie out here to poison her, though?" Carolynn presses.

I wriggle my legs into my jeans. I do this awkward half-kneeling thing to pull the waistband over my butt. "These woods are a good place to hide a body," I say, concentrating too much on the jeans maneuver to filter. All eyes are on me as I fasten my button. "They are. Think about it. No one's allowed to build around here, so you could bury someone and no one would dig them up. Parts of the forest used to be mined, so there are old mine shafts. Ben and I used to hike here, and we found a few deserted cabins that anyone could hide anything in. The preserve runs along open coastline, where you could dump a body into the sound."

Duncan glares at the woods over his shoulder, then back at me. "Remind me never to piss you off."

Josh inclines his head, working his jaw back and forth. "Lana's right. A few years ago some stoner kids used to come out here to a cabin where they could smoke and graffiti. The firehouse was freaked out that the kids were going to start a fire. A guy from my mom's station house stepped in an old well and snapped his ankle after breaking up one of their parties. That would be the perfect place to hide a body, and the killer, or *attempted* killer, didn't know Maggie was familiar with the spring. She got away, and he or she couldn't find her."

"He or she," Becca squeaks. Her hands fly to her mouth. "You don't think it was a woman, do you?"

"Here we go," Duncan scoffs. "Because girls never do anything wrong."

Carolynn takes Becca's hand in hers. "That's not what she said, Dumb-can." Her lip curls as she regards him. "It's a fact that most killers of girls are men."

Duncan looks to the ground as he adds, "Sneaky shit like poisoning is always chicks."

Rusty slaps him on the back. "Duncan's just feeling cock-blocked that Bethany J. wouldn't let him come over last night. Her parents heard about us being at the police station again."

Becca smooths her ponytail over her shoulder and is slightly cross-eyed and grimacing at thinking. "Do you guys think that we interrupted Maggie's murder? He could have been right here." She grinds a heel into the rock under her. "And he heard us coming. We were playing music on the hike in."

"Jesus," Rusty groans. "He could have been right there watching us." We look nervously to the foliage bordering the spring. If someone were there now, would we sense it?

"Sorry to interrupt your brain-gasms, but shouldn't we hurry up and get this stuff to the actual police?" Carolynn asks. "For all we know, Ford's already turned up and he's absolutely fine and Maggie's killer was some rando getting his jollies off and he's long gone. We can let the cops take it from here and get on with the last week of summer now that we're not murder suspects."

"Sheesh, Car," Rusty snickers. "Don't hold back."

Her hands fall to her mostly naked hips. "What I mean is that we have proof of an alternative theory. The cops will explore the possibility. We're off the hook. Reasonable doubt and all."

We collect ourselves and hike away from Swisher Spring. I watch the shadows on either side of the trail. I wait for a figure to take shape, familiar or not. A scavenger looking to collect lives. A hero looking for revenge. I watch for who or what chased Maggie through the woods in the moments before we arrived with our party at Swisher Spring. I watch for who or what she died trying to hide from.

— 17 —

Ben began high school when I was in the seventh grade. His first week, there were five girls, one on each day, who came to our house. I remember the fifth one, on Friday, sitting at our kitchen island, pretending that I wasn't there. She asked Ben if he thought another girl—the fourth of the week—was prettier than she was. Her lips smacked as she chewed gum. Ben's brow puckered and his eyes cut to me, as if my girlness made me all-knowing. I was pouting that we weren't out on the dinghy and that I was presently making an ice cream sundae by myself.

I stuck my tongue out at him. Ben pinched my side. I squawked and smeared caramel sauce on his chin. He grabbed my face as I reared back and wiped his chin on my cheek. By the time my attention snapped back to Number Five, she was staring at me in a way that made the laughter dry in my throat.

Ben kept laughing and opened the lid of the hot fudge for me. Number Five tossed her hair and stomped her foot. Ben shrugged a shoulder and said, "You're pretty for a blonde, but Kara's pretty for a brunette." At twelve I knew that answer was a disaster.

Number Five pushed back from the island to make like she was storming off. Ben didn't protest, and she remained roosted on the stool. A smile spread across her lips and she said in a honeyed voice, "You like Kara because she's a slut and went down on you." I had no idea what she meant, but by the way Ben's cheeks ignited and his eyes darted to me, I knew it was bad. I walked right up to Number Five, squirted the caramel sauce into her lap, knocked the hot fudge on the floor, and fled.

In my room I called Willa and repeated the exchange. Willa was baffled too, and because even twelve-year-old Willa didn't like a puzzle she couldn't solve, she consulted the Internet.

There was only the clicking of the keyboard and then she told me, her soprano gravely serious, "Holy Gertrude Guacamole Bell." Willa was going through a major archeology phase, so most of her swears, like Gertrude Bell, were explorers and archaeologists. "It's when sexual partners put each other's genitals into their mouths for pleasure."

We went on about how gross that sounded and how we'd never do anything mental like that, and there was a general consensus of horror and feeling dirty and guilty for knowing. After a while Willa got off to finish homework. I couldn't get the definition or the visual from my head. Ben was only two years older than me. I knew Ben's guilty-as-charged expression, and there was little doubt that what Number Five had alleged was true.

For a week I was jumpy around him. He plopped down on the couch and I leaped for the love seat. He sat next to me at the kitchen table and my knee jerked so hard the chair rattled.

It was the first time in two years that I was aware that (1) Ben was a boy and I was a girl, and (2) we didn't share blood. I don't mean that I didn't know Ben was a boy straight off, only that the difference between us never made me self-conscious. Ben wasn't the kind of boy who suggested that I was inferior because of my girlness. Dad taught us both to sail and bake cookies, and it was only Dad's occasional Bumblebee-this or our-girl-that that drew attention to me being different from Ben. I was hyperaware that we weren't blood siblings only when I thought about how unrelated boys and girls touch.

In the end Ben cornered me and tickled me until my knees gave out and I hiccuped. All the awkwardness fell away and he was my ridiculously long-limbed Ben, pinning me on the ground and threatening to bite me if I ever gave him the silent treatment again. "It was because of what that girl said, huh?"

I hid my face and yelped, "Yeah." I never saw Ben with Number Five again.

It didn't matter; there would be more girls like her. It was just the beginning.

I started Gant High when Ben was beginning his junior year. While I'd been mastering flying under the radar, Ben was busy getting noticed—especially by girls. The attention's side effects spilled over to me. Ben was oblivious. He didn't notice girls turning and watching as he shouted across the three hundred hall after seventh period that he was ready to drive us home. He was blind to the stares as he dragged his feet over to where Willa and I ate lunch at the beginning of freshman year in the corner of the quad.

It was one of those days in the first two weeks of ninth grade while I was still kind of hopeful and giddy that high school might not be as terrible as middle school. A whole summer had passed, and kids would be that much more mature. The new school would be a clean slate and I'd get to be whoever I wanted. It might have worked out that way, if not for my golden, attention-getting stepbrother.

Willa and I were walking to Latin after lunch and a line of freshman girls, including Carolynn, were crowded in the packed halls behind us. "They're not really brother and sister. Not by blood," Carolynn said.

"She probably wishes they were doing it," Amanda Peters, who—mercifully—moved away in the middle of tenth grade, added.

"Shut up," a third giggled, amused.

"What? I would if I had a stepbro who looked like that," Amanda said.

Carolynn stood right at my back and said loudly, "I would have thrown the giant *V* at him after my thirteenth birthday and been screwing his brains out since."

I looked over my shoulder and Amanda caught my eye. "What are you looking at, Uni-Boob? You want to tell us all about what a kinky, incestuous freak you are?"

I ditched Willa in the halls and ducked into the bathroom. I covered the toilet seat with a textbook and sat there crying for all of next period. It was easy to believe I'd done something wrong. There was this complicated and subliminal set of rules for girls. Who knew that wearing black underwear meant that you wanted sex? Or that wearing a toe ring or eating an effing banana in the school caf meant that you were a slut? I didn't. Nor did I understand why a girl who wanted sex was labeled a slut, but a boy who wanted sex was normal, *healthy*. Our middle school vice principal was always saying that so-and-so's skirt was too short and boys couldn't concentrate. It seemed backward to blame girls for boys' behavior. Medieval to act like boys and girls should want different things.

All this came crashing down on fourteen-year-old me. I figured that it must be my fault that those girls perceived Ben and me as something we weren't. I can't say why I didn't write it off immediately as more teasing from the same bitchy girls who'd perfected name-calling on me in middle school. Instead I felt fear. Would Ben hear the gossip? Would he think I was bad and a freak who didn't understand we were just siblings? Would I lose him?

There would be more innuendos from girls. There would be more whispers about what a freak Uni-Boob was to love her half brother or second cousin or whatever that beautiful boy was to that quiet, weird girl. Other kids had step-siblings at school. It wasn't earth-shattering. But remember, we were amateur siblings. We didn't know we were supposed to act as if the other was vomit-inducing and stank of boiled cabbage. Ben didn't flip me off, and I didn't whine *gross* when he touched me.

None of the girls even believed their lies. Before he started dating Maggie, a lot of those meanest to me threw themselves at him. They sent roses and candygrams, and they slipped notes into his locker. Willa and I heard about Ben messing around with girls at parties.

So, the difference between Ben and me in high school: he wanted to feel like an outsider, and I was one. Ben didn't want to fit in. He was just different enough for kids to glom onto him; for girls to flock in his direction; for guys to intone, "Classic Ben," whenever he wondered aloud if we really needed fresh sushi in the school caf when others were starving. He was not so different as to be labeled a freak. The McBrook family with our elephant of a house and Dad's money couldn't be shrugged off like a polo. Ben's popularity was a snowball, coasting downhill, unstoppable. His disinterest in it only made him more appealing. He was *different* wrapped in a pretty and confident package.

But me? WELL. I was the girl, and the world—high school and beyond—makes it so much easier to fault girls than boys. It became obvious to my tormentors that I wasn't going to tell Ben what they said. If there's one thing teenagers love more than iced coffee and candy, it's an easy mark.

I didn't stick up for myself because I was afraid it would escalate and Ben would find out. I didn't want Ben to have to defend me. I should have been able to defend myself. I also didn't want to admit to Ben just how different I was from the Lana in our stories or even that little girl with the knitting needle. She didn't exist.

It wasn't always Carolynn. It was a lot of the girls who ate with the populars in the quad. Up until December of tenth grade, it was mostly Amanda Peters. It got better once she moved away and I'd go months without a snipe. I never set foot near the populars. I grew distracted with the eight-semester plan. I didn't show my face at parties, sporting events, or dances other than freshman homecoming. I made myself small and scarce.

Right after Ben's death I didn't feel small. For most of his funeral I thought about summer provisions and that he didn't need any where he was. He would never need anything from me again. The intangible hurt grew. It was everywhere, running from my nose, mouth, ears. It helped to imagine it in a tangible way. I pictured the skin on my wrists splitting open. The blood would run and run. I'd stand in a puddle, a lake, an ocean that would flood the cemetery and fill his empty coffin. Then at least one of us would be buried inside.

It helped to think of the pain in my chest, under my skin, radiating from my organs, as coming from a specific wound.

It contained it.

It helped me believe that I would heal.

In the backseat of Josh's Jeep, behind the wheel once we pick up our cars from Josh's, on the drive to Marmalade's Café, I let myself be big. I let the relief that we're off the hook for Maggie warm me like sunbeams. I smile at my reflection in the rearview mirror as I parallel park at Marmalade's. My knees bounce as I sip my iced latte as we wait for Josh to confirm what we've convinced ourselves of: we're in the clear. The underwater cavern will be enough. The police will pursue other leads and other suspects, and who cares if they ever find who killed Maggie just so long as they know it wasn't us.

It's fifteen minutes before Josh and the blustery morning come through the door. His heavy dark-blond hair is low on his forehead as we huddle. "We did it," he says, expression stunned. "There are too many things not adding up about us as suspects." He struggles to temper his smile. "They can't figure out a motive for any of us." His eyes flick to me. I'm the only one with a motive and he knows it. "None of us, including Willa, have deviated from our story." I sink into my ribs, exhaling. "They figured that if we were guilty, one of us would fold. When we didn't, they started doubting their theory. Maggie poisoned from rosary peas has them stumped. They brought a profiler in from the FBI, and she thinks it's unlikely that a bunch of kids would kill someone that way." I don't say it out loud, but I think this profiler is an idiot.

Adults reach a certain age and they forget tasting the salt of make-believe oceans.

Josh continues, "An anonymous tip came in last night about the cave under the spring. They think it was a fisherman or hiker who's familiar with Gant's inlets. They decided not to issue arrest warrants for us after that. Their divers were waiting until it was light enough today to search for evidence. Cops were calling our parents to let them know as I walked in with the backpack."

"So we got hypothermia for nothing?" Carolynn asks, hunched forward, still blue.

"No." Josh squeezes her shoulder. "Even though my mom's cop buddy made it clear that what we did was evidence tampering, they hope they might be able to collect physical evidence from the backpack. Even though Ford is still missing, the cops don't think there's anything *serial* going on."

"Serial?" Becca asks as she bands her ponytail tighter.

"Yeah, they don't think Maggie's killer is responsible for Ford. His parents checked their bank statement, and he made a withdrawal yesterday in Seattle, and Ford's dad said they had a blowup fight right before my party. The cops think he's just trying to freak out his folks before he comes home."

Duncan and Rusty make jokes about not being bitches in prison. Becca and Carolynn talk about the start of school in less than a week. Josh is springy over Ford just pulling a stunt. "I was kind of screwed up over it," he admits. "It was my birthday he disappeared after. I would have been to blame if something happened to Holland." He laughs nervously at the close call. Me: I don't care that Ford is okay. There was a stirring in my chest when I thought Maggie's killer had gotten his hands on Ford too. It was giddy and fluttery gratitude, like finally someone was doling out revenge.

"Now that all this crap is over, we have to figure out our end-of-summer prank," Becca says, and then, aside to me, adds, "Every year before school starts we do something fantastical. Like last year we set off fireworks from the football field, and the year before we spent a night gift wrapping the school office, so when admin showed up they couldn't see where the office doors were. This year we have to top it."

"And no"—Carolynn levels a finger at Duncan—"we're not organizing a clothing-optional kegger or going streaking on the beach or doing anything nudity related."

Duncan snorts. "Did I suggest that?"

They keep batting around possible stunts. I lean back into the velvet chair and close my eyes. I let their mingling voices wash over me. This, the push and pull of the core, is what swept me along, made me feel less stuck a month ago. Every time the sadness has crept nearer, threatened to suffocate me, there's been a silly thrill to focus on. School is about to start, though. All these summery adventures will be over, and I'll be left with a small life again.

Back-to-school things shuffle through my head: girls with brand-new highlights and fish-tail braids like tiaras; a sea of tan-and-boysenberry-purple to-go coffee cups from Marmalade's; strawberry-lip-gloss-stained pouts; cake-frosting, vanilla, and berry body mists all mingling into one unidentifiable, sickening smell in the school corridors; stiff backpacks sitting too high on freshman shoulders, inviting the milk-carton bombs upperclassmen will launch at them; loner girls like me, eyes on concrete, just praying a seagull doesn't crap on their hair as they dart across the quad; and summer beefs over drunken beach hookups and the resulting fistfights and sobbing.

The first day of school is a pageant that sets the stage for the rest of the year.

"We shouldn't just do a prank to screw with people. Not this summer; not after so much has happened," Josh is saying. "It should *mean* something. When my grandpa died, my moms and I drove out to the point and we threw his ashes in the sound, and then we had a clambake right there and they drank his favorite beer and we sang his favorite campfire songs."

"I am so not doing a prank in honor of Maggie," Becca groans, fussing with her hair band again.

Josh looks expectantly at me. "What do you think about doing a prank in honor of Ben?"

I smile. I always wanted to do something for Ben—a grand gesture that he would have thought was brave and worthy.

"Oh, that's the best idea," Becca squeals, winding her finger in the end of her gathered ombré hair and then letting it feather as it unwinds.

"I like it," I say, the rightness spreading through me. "Thanks."

"Yeah?" Josh says brightly. "It's okay?"

I nod. It is. Ben deserved a better send-off than he got. He would have hated his funeral, because it wasn't for us. It was for *them*. It was for Gant. It was big and spectacular and morose with its black stretch limos and its five-course banquet hall dinner at the club.

I didn't used to understand why Ben just didn't tell all those kids to eff off if he hated them so much. I wondered why he ate lunch in the quad and not with the fringes of the school social order on the field. Why go to parties and make out with the girls and fist-bump jocks? Granted, Ben dating Maggie, the opposite of Gant, senior year was as close as he got to saying screw you all. He'd never gone out with a girl for more than a few weeks until her, and it wasn't for lack of trying on the parts of all those perky populars.

Now I get it. It's how I feel about the core. I shouldn't care what they think about me. I know better. But it's as if wanting to be accepted is in my teenage DNA. I can't resist it. I look at Carolynn and think, *I want to be friends with that girl. She's not a kitten. She's a lion.* I want to bask in her laser-beam gaze and Becca's sunshiny grin. Josh's smiling eyes are straying toward me every few seconds as the others go on about how Ben loved giving authority the finger; how Ben would have approved of a prank in his honor. With Josh's attention aimed at me, my stomach almost doesn't knot at them acting like they knew Ben.

I want to prove the five of them wrong for ignoring me—or worse—up until this summer. I want to make it really hard for them to ice me out come classes starting. I want to show them that I am brave, alive, dazzling, and full of nerve and mischief.

Ben's send-off is as clear to me as the Seattle skyline isn't on a gray, stormy day. We spend the next hour masterminding what Becca calls a giant *peace out* for Ben. Rusty and Duncan are all eager grins and fist bumps as they insist on staking out the location. It's agreed that barring disaster, we'll spring into action tomorrow night. Even Carolynn props her elbows on the coffee table, stirring her caramel-spiked coffee with a spoon, and adds to the plan.

As I walk to my car, I stare clear down the street to where it dives into the harbor. The *Mira* is docked farther down, where most of Gant's residents keep their vessels year-round. I wish I was on her now, sailing with the cold air splashing my skin. The breathless way

I smiled into it always cleared my head. I'm floating, feeling lighter than I have since we surfaced with Maggie. June hasn't crawled through July and into August to get me. The core is going to help me memorialize Ben. But Ben's killer is out there; Maggie's too. And I feel detached, like a helium balloon that's broken free from its string and is sailing away, when instead I should be grounded and disturbed that my great-great-grandmother's rosary found its way into my secret place and that a girl has died.

This is not what I experience, although at this point, I'm used to not feeling what I'm supposed to. Instead it's as if the universe has gift-wrapped a dazzling, perfect present of revenge and left it at my feet.

This is why, when I get home, I don't march to the lower terrace to destroy the rosary like I should. It's either the rosary used to kill Maggie, or else it's not and I'm losing my mind and can't remember storing it there eons ago. Either way, it looks suspicious that I'm hiding it. I won't throw it away, though, because it's a reminder that sometimes evil deeds do get punished and that villains end up dead.

It allows me to believe that the world is the way Ben imagined it.

— 18 —

Bullies don't get to win, Lana." The fire was a rosy glow on Ben's face; his nose cast a dark triangle on his left cheek.

Fitzgerald Moore had been found that morning by a woman driving her two kids to school. He was beaten bloody and unconscious on the shoulder of the road. She'd pulled over, kept the car doors locked, and called the police.

"Ethan and Max were laughing in second period, in the same way they snicker over cutting class or paying that freshman in honor society to write their term papers. This is a guy's life they screwed with, and it was funny to them, like little boys picking off the legs of a cricket."

I gave him a disapproving glare.

"Sorry. That's messed up too," he said. Ben buried his face in his hands. My fingers and their chipped purple nails had been crawling over the bag of marshmallows in my lap, bunching the plastic around the white pillows, pinching the fluff to make indents. I wasn't sure what to say or do until I thought Ben was crying. I slipped my flip-flops on and shuffled over to perch on his chair arm. My bare leg knocked into his much bigger knee, and I hugged his shoulders from the side.

"I'm sorry, Ben," I said. "Can we tell my dad to do something? Is Fitzgerald in a hospital? Does he need a doctor?"

Ben dropped his hands to his lap. I saw his face. There were no tears. His gray eyes were bottomless and angry. His square jaw was set, his teeth grinding, the muscles ticcing under the pressure. He was furious. His face softened when I stood up. His fingers slid between mine. I waited, my back warmed by the flames, my front cold and goose-pimply through my T-shirt as the wind vaulted up from the harbor.

"Don't worry," he said, his thumb covering mine. My shadow had fallen over him, and I couldn't see if his expression was as calm as his voice. "Fitzgerald's at a hospital. He'll get better. It's Max and Ethan who won't. They thought it was okay to jump a guy with their baseball bats because he's homeless and I humiliated them in front of student gov and their girlfriends. I'm sure they wanted to go after me with bats." A soft snort like a laugh. He sounded as though he wished it had been him.

It was my imagination that Ben's hand went cold in mine. Everything was going cold; night just drops on you in late September. I went back to my seat, sat there cross-legged, wishing I had a hoodie from the house and waiting for Ben to speak.

"Max and Ethan aren't much better than all those girls in your class, are they?" he asked. I froze with my teeth sunk into a marshmallow. What did he mean? Did he suspect what Amanda Peters, Carolynn Winters, and all their friends said to me? Was the truth not as buried as I thought? The marshmallow turned chalky in my mouth as I tried to swallow it. "You have no idea what I hear girls saying to each other," he added with a nonchalant shrug of his shoulders.

I forced a laugh that moved my lips like a grimace.

His eyes were careful on mine, slightly creased at their outer edges, the tiny freckle at his right hidden in the lines. "You'd tell me if anyone ever hurt you, right?" he pressed.

I fidgeted. The fire sent up a flare of spitting embers. The wind caught one and snatched it higher. It painted a wide arc in the sky. "No one's hurting me," I said.

"Not even that little witch down the street?" he continued, jerking his head in the direction of Becca's house. Ben never liked Becca. He'd noticed her coming over to swing and sleep over, and then sixth grade and she never showed again. He wasn't stupid; he knew she'd ditched me.

"I haven't seen Becca at school this year," I lied, pushing the knobs of my spine into the planks of the wood chair. Ben might have known I shared two periods with her.

"Okay," he said, rolling his shoulders back, cracking his neck as it went side to side. "Good. You only need to say the word if you ever want me to kill anyone for you." His grin was wide and sarcastic.

I cupped my chin in my hand and smiled. Amanda Peters and her minions had hissed at me the day before. Ben offing them was a satisfying thought. "How would you do it?" I thought the joke was obvious in my tone. It must not have been.

A shadow passed over his face—disappointment with me— and he sat back. He was in short sleeves like me, and goose bumps were spreading up his arms as he crossed them at his chest. "Jeez, McBrook. I was kidding."

A minute later he was challenging me to a marshmallow-eating contest—loser would buy tacos if we weren't too stuffed. I figured he'd forgiven me. He knew I wasn't serious. I was, though, a little. As much as a fourteen-year-old girl can be about killing, which depending on who you ask, varies from not at all to serious as a heart attack.

What came in the days after didn't surprise me. Ben didn't let the bullies win.

Ethan Holland's girlfriend dumped him, loudly and in the quad, for Ben—a relationship that would last a whole two weeks until it became obvious to her that Ben was more interested in revenge on Ethan than in her. Kids gossiped, and I heard that Ethan was torn up that she never tried getting back with him.

A short time after, an anonymous note arrived in every school administrator's mailbox, detailing Ethan and Max's activities: buying papers from an honor society member and plagiarizing others from the Internet. Willa had said her mom wanted to expel the boys for Skitzy-Fitzy's attack; everyone knew it was them. The police were more concerned with protecting the boys than charging them, though, and P.O. couldn't hold Ethan and Max responsible for a crime the police wouldn't. Plagiarizing was another matter, one that P.O. could dole out swift punishment for.

When the vice principal arrived to clear out the boys' lockers—school policy for those who are suspended—he discovered joints. This isn't illegal in the state of Washington but is strictly forbidden by Gant High's athletics staff. Unlike their attack on an *actual human being*, having pot in their lockers was horrible enough to get them kicked off the baseball team. No one cared that they denied it was theirs.

People whispered that the notes to the school must have been from Ben, but kids mostly shrugged it off because our classmates knew that what Ethan and Max had done to Fitzgerald was bad. Not bad because it was against the rules, like speeding on the highway; badness itself. Dozens of witnesses had seen Ethan and Max smoke at parties; it was easy to believe they were stupid enough to keep pot in their lockers. Easy for everyone who hadn't watched Ben leave our house the night before.

Ben had cracked open my bedroom door, a black beanie pulled to his eyebrows. "Wish me luck," he'd whispered as I let the book I was reading close on the comforter.

"For . . . ?" I said. The corners of his mouth tucked up, full of mischief, and he lifted a plastic bag full of neatly wrapped joints. Ben didn't smoke pot. I went to ask what he was up to, but then he was tiptoeing downstairs, heading into the night.

I thought Ben was satisfied getting Ethan and Max suspended and getting them booted out of baseball. He didn't mention either boy again, not even when the rumor started circulating that jumping Skitzy-Fitzy had been Ethan's idea and Max had been dragged along.

But on a morning a couple of months later, we sat opposite each other on the kitchen counter. I sipped an espresso and Ben ate cereal. I noticed the abrasions on his knuckles. He swallowed a large spoonful of granola. "I was going at that punching bag Cal got me in the garage." It was a lie, and by the way his eyes lingered on mine, I could tell he knew it was unconvincing. The punching bag had never been taken out of its box and was collecting dust in the rafters. "If anyone asks, you heard me last night," he added meaningfully.

"Sure," I said. "The noise kept me up super late." He smiled. And like that, I had agreed to be Ben's alibi for an unknown misdeed that had left his knuckles split. Dad was out of town; Diane had been home, but she wasn't lucid enough from the sleeping pills she took to contradict anyone.

When I saw Ethan hobbling across the quad on crutches, a raccoon-eyed look to his face, I knew it had been Ben who'd injured him. Maybe Ben had been waiting the months since Ethan's suspension for the opportunity; maybe it had serendipitously presented itself. And while Ethan was the kind of boy who would attack a vagrant with a bat, he was not the sort who'd admit to be being beat up by a classmate. He was all pride, and Ben got away with it.

Ethan ended up barely passing his senior year. He left Gant for a state college in Nebraska, his big baseball future not going to happen since he'd been kicked off our high school team. Max ended up drinking too much senior year and showing up to class one morning, stumbling. After a stay in a rehab center, his parents sent him to live with an aunt in Arizona for a fresh start. I know what happened to these boys, because when Ben died, Sweeny requested the names of anyone who'd ever had a confrontation with Ben. They'd be natural suspects. Max, Ethan, and the host of other boys Ben fought with came up. All were cleared of suspicion. The shadow man remained a shadow.

It's obvious to me that Ford chose me out of all the girls he might have bullied because of Ethan and Ben's history. Ford knew what Ben did to his brother. He thought he could hurt Ben, through me. He was wrong. Ben never even knew what Ford was saying and doing.

While it's true that I was embarrassed to tell Ben, I was also afraid. Ben took a lot from Ethan: his girlfriend and his dream of

playing on a college baseball team. And after that, Ben wasn't satisfied. What would he take from Ford? I worried it would be even
more. *I knew Ben.* Remember that we'd believed in revenge since we
were two kids in a blanket fort, shivering over bloody stories.

Ben didn't surprise me, not usually. And although it's true I kept
a bunch of stuff from him, he told me everything. At least I thought
so, until Josh found the envelope Ben gave to Maggie. Ben had no
reason to lie about talking to her while he was in Guatemala. I never
whined that I thought he should end things, or made the negative
comments about her I wanted to, or complained when he ditched
me for her.

Ben arrived home after three months away and said he was ready
to move on. Maggie's e-mails had gone unanswered. He was going
to break up with her for good. College sounded all right. In reply I
jumped in place like a kid. Ben would apply to the schools I wanted
to go to, including Dad's alma mater, and hopefully he'd get into one
of them. Maggie didn't fit into that equation. There would be college
girls. *Sorority girls,* he said in a hard-to-impress way.

Who was this Ben who lied to me and sent Maggie love notes
just before he broke up with her?

I can't let it go once I'm upstairs in my bedroom. I'm curious to
see if there were letters sent from Maggie to Ben. Ben's room is the
mirror image of mine across the hall. His window seat overlooks the
narrow street, dying at the summit of hills both ways. I toe open his
door, look around, take a deep breath, and enter. His swollen hiker's
backpack is at the foot of his dresser. I make a beeline for it. It's full
of dusty, rotten-melon-smelling clothes. Plenty of unwashed jeans;
no letters. I give up on the pack and go for Ben's desk. I intend to

flip through Ben's sketchbooks. Each drawing, the familiar style, the charcoal strokes, the way he reinvented the ordinary surreally, will be proof that I knew him.

I reach for the middle desk drawer. I go still. The desk's flat expanse is covered with dust like a fine coat of ash. At the center is one perfectly drawn handprint. I touch my palm to its palm and align my fingers. It's identical in size to mine. Stranger, though, is that unlike the desk, the print is dustless. It's been made recently. Diane's at Calm Coast. Mariella's hands are oven mitts. No one's been in the house for over a week—not Willa, or Becca, or Carolynn.

Maggie knew where our spare key was.

She might have known that our alarm code is my birthday.

I picture Maggie returning to the island after seven weeks of hiding, stealing through our house at night, and riffling through Ben's drawers. Why else bend over the desk? Why risk being caught breaking and entering? Was she searching for a piece of evidence that if found would prove her guilt in Ben's death? A note that might have shown that Maggie was furious enough with Ben to arrange his murder? She was gone, vanished, though. The police weren't looking for her. Now I wonder if Maggie didn't set the sequence of events that led to her death in motion because she returned to Gant. Would she have lived if she'd stayed away?

Our island: craggy black cliffs, periodic sweeps of gray beach, arms of fog strangling the shore, the sound's slapping waters drowning out passing ferries. It's not the pretty little snow-globe town islanders act like it is. In my head it appears cursed and cast off from the mainland. It's the kind of in-between place where a shadow man drags a boy from his car and a girl is poisoned by rosary peas. It's a lot like Ben's imagination in that way. Stories don't jump from your thoughts to lay waste to the world. All our make-believe didn't escape Ben's imagination before the shadow man pulled him from the car.

It's been weeks since I've felt suffocated by Gant. The secrets are multiplying, and the island's becoming crowded again. The rosary in my hiding spot and the rosary in Ben's story seem like too much for me to keep to myself. These secrets are a stain expanding on the ground, threatening to soak my socks as Mom's overturned wine did after she jumped. They make me feel like an island myself, and I'm dying to trust someone with them.

Not *someone*—Willa. I retreat back to my room, curl up on the window seat, and dial her. "Hey," she answers softly.

I was sure her phone would go to voice mail and was at the beginning of composing a lengthy apology message. I'm caught off guard. "Hi. You answered."

"Astute observation, L," she replies glibly.

"I mean that I thought your mom might not be letting you talk on the phone and that I'd have to leave a message begging your forgiveness. I was going to bribe you with a dozen marionberry scones from Marmalade's."

She snorts.

"One dozen every week for the rest of the year to show you how sorry I am," I try.

"Throw in an almond-milk latte and we can talk," she says. "Mom's at a meeting with the teachers about the start of classes." A pause. "You didn't call after the police station yesterday."

"I was worried that you didn't want me to, not after you were hauled there and accused of murder all because you were with your selfish best friend at Swisher Spring."

She sniffs. "I didn't want to talk yesterday."

"How about today?" I sit stiff with trepidation.

"When was the last time we went more than twenty-four hours without speaking?" The timid smile seeping from her voice has me smiling.

I exhale, stretch out, kick my foot up on my knee, and think back. "The four days you were at physics camp the summer after freshman year."

"Exactly."

A low-flying V of birds cuts over the harbor. "I'm so sorry, Willa. For this whole summer and for dragging you along to the spring and for acting like grades and college applications don't matter. They do. *You do.* And I don't know why I care about the core—I mean, obviously I have always had this crush on Josh, but I want the others to like me too. I shouldn't. I like thinking that we belong with them and that they're realizing that they were wrong not to be friends with us before, like they missed out," I say in one blast.

I hear a tapping over the line and imagine Willa's nail making contact with the bridge of her tortoiseshell glasses. She sighs after a time. "Following the loss of a family member who was important to you, it's not surprising that you'd seek acceptance elsewhere and that you'd try to distract yourself."

The heat of the house and the cool air outside steams my windows. There's the faint outline left of the sailboat. It looks lonely. I draw a fleet of boats surrounding it as I confide in Willa. I recount our hike to Swisher Spring earlier this morning and tell her about how upset I am that Ben sent Maggie a note when he swore to me that they'd had no contact. I tell her about the prank we're planning to honor Ben, my secret place, and what I found there. I try to explain Ben's stories. Every word is stupid and wrong; there's no right way to say what our make-believe meant to me; how those stories and our games grew like tree roots around my whole life.

"I was bigger than just myself because I had this fictional . . ."

"Likeness," Willa supplies.

"Yeah, this fictional likeness that was better and braver than me. And I've never told anyone about the stories, because *why would I?* They were our game, like a secret language siblings have. And it was embarrassing how important the stories were to me."

I glare at the window sweating with condensation. My hand has been busy, drawing ten sailboats. The original sticks out from the rest, though. It's a different style from my drawing. *No*—I must be drawing them differently today is all. I grab my fuzzy throw and wipe them clear. I flip to my other side. "How did my great-great-grandma's rosary get in my secret hiding spot? Am I going crazy?"

"You aren't losing your mind," she says matter-of-factly. I hear her shift position, the comforter swish, the mattress whine. "I read about PTSD—that's post-traumatic stress disorder—after Ben died because I wanted to be prepared." She says this so freely, Willa being Willa, studying for an exam that might never come. "And memory loss is a symptom. There can be a block in your memory of the traumatic event, or memories of earlier events can just be erased."

"I remember everything," I tell her, "so clearly it hurts."

"You think you do, but it's possible there are bits you aren't recalling."

194 • ALEXANDRA SIROWY

"So your theory is that I'm not going crazy, I have amnesia."

"Not amnesia, nothing that dramatic. A little confused is all. You might have put the rosary in your spot years ago. Hidden it when you were a kid because you worried your dad would see it and know you and Ben had snooped for the key and looked in the chest."

I shake my head at the empty bedroom. I would remember something like that. "Okay, but am I messing up a murder investigation by not telling the police I found it? Is it significant that Maggie was killed in the same way victims were in one of our stories?"

"Probably and unlikely," Willa says in her cool figuring-it-out voice. "The authorities just stopped suspecting you. They questioned all of us, yes, but you were the only one with a motive. The rest of us were suspected of conspiring and covering for you, Lana. The police had the motive. They needed proof." A meaningful pause. "If you turn the rosary in, one that you've had in your possession for years, there's their proof. You aren't sure how it got from your mom's chest to your hiding spot. Your fingerprints are all over it. All bets will be off. Motive *and* murder weapon. Keep it hidden where no one will find it. Once this dies down, we'll brainstorm a way to lose it for good. And the connection with Ben's horror stories, it's slim. There are a million ways Maggie's killer might have known about the paralytic properties of rosary peas. I mean, Jeannette Rankin, I think I knew as much from a *Masterpiece Mystery*."

"Jeannette who?" I laugh into the round pink pillow under my head.

"First woman elected to Congress. What are they teaching kids in US history if not that?" she groans.

"Thank you, Willa," I say. She makes me feel temporarily lighter. "For everything."

She breathes into the phone. "Of course. Thank you for not letting Carolynn or any of them turn on me. My mom was relentless at the police station. She wouldn't quit insisting that I tell the *truth*. The others were looking at me like I was a bomb about to detonate. If the five of them pointed fingers at me, who knows what would have happened?"

"I wouldn't have let them. It was my fault you were there." I trace a sad face on the window, but there isn't enough steam to make it last. "I should have seen that right away."

"I have free will, best friend of mine. I was there because I wanted to be. Even I am not immune to my teenage biology and its mad desire to be accepted by populars." By the time we hang up, things are right between us.

Dinner is with Dad. He phoned Calm Coast earlier, and Diane refused to talk with him. Her doctor made chipper promises about progress. Dad poured himself a scotch over ice. I doubt that in their short long-distance relationship before they married, Dad had noticed the similarities between Diane and Mom. Both are fragile in a way I am not. Even before Ben died she was spacey. It was eerie walking through the kitchen and spotting Diane in a black cocktail dress, glass of wine at her side, staring off at the middle distance of the harbor. After we lost Ben, I worried history might repeat itself.

"Diane needs time, Daddy. That's all it is," I say. "She'll come home."

He stares at his salmon until we give up pretending that either of us can eat and go our separate ways. I go into Ben's room, curl up on his quilt, and bury my head in his pillow, which is laced with stale hair gel and almost-gone body spray. I'm warmed from my toes to my head. Diane is a few hours away, but she seems more gone than Ben does lately. I fall asleep in this weird state, daydreaming that I'm shipwrecked on an enchanted island where stories from Ben's imagination come true.

Where Ben and I are heroes.

Where villains are separate from the shadows.

Where we don't let the bullies win.

Ever.

— 19 —

They found Ford," Josh tells me over the phone. His usually rich, bouncy voice is flat this morning.

"Oh?" I say, trying to mask my disappointment. I wasn't hoping for bad news about Ford per se, I just didn't want good news, either. The enchanted island in my mind punishes people like Maggie and Ford. I switch off the water I was running over a basket of blackberries in the sink and dump the berries into a cereal bowl. It's midmorning, and Dad is either out running errands or at his office downtown. Basel is meowing at my feet, trying to persuade me to give him a second breakfast. I usually give in.

"Can I just come over to tell you?" Josh asks abruptly after a weirdly long break.

I place the honey back on the shelf after squeezing a golden thread on the berries. "Sure," I say. My stomach's instantly fluttery. Josh and I have been alone only a handful of times since the first night he drove me home from Marmalade's. "Are we still going to meet at Becca's later to finish planning Ben's prank?" I add. I pop a berry between my teeth. Honey, blackberry juice, and Ben's prank have me feeling bright and weightless. The prank is business Ben left unfinished, and now I'm going to finish it for him.

"Uh, yeah," Josh answers, distracted. "We need to talk about everything," he ends intensely, and the sweetness of honey is diminished on my tongue.

Josh arrives just as my cell is buzzing with a call from Willa. I answer her after I've opened the door for him. "Josh just got here. Lemme call you back soon," I tell her before hitting end.

We settle in the kitchen. I lean on the counter and watch as Josh stands from crouching over Basel. I grip the counter at my waist as I see his face. "What's wrong?"

His shoulders are stooped forward as he braces himself on the kitchen island. "They found Ford."

I nod. "Okay, that's good, right? He's your friend."

"He wasn't alive," Josh says. He looks to the ceiling, blinking to clear tears, and continues. "His parents found him early this morning, before the sun came up. The police had stopped searching because of that activity on Ford's bank card. His parents worried Ford had been attacked *and* robbed. The attacker might be using the card in Seattle. They were with some other parents, walking the woods all night along the road where that junior spotted him. They got home, and their German shepherd was going crazy in the house. He'd tried to claw through the back door. Mr. Holland let the dog out and he raced into the trees. Ford's dad ran after him." Josh's features distort to make a crying face without the tears.

I am motionless and quiet. I'm listening, but what's disturbing is that it isn't Josh I'm waiting to hear from. We're the only two people in the room, and yet my ears are straining for Ben's voice: *Bullies don't get to win.*

Ford was a bully. Ford is dead. And it would be so like Ben to have had some part in that. I can almost see him sitting on the countertop, heels beating the cabinets, smiling smugly as he flicks his hair from his eyes. *You thought being dead could keep me from revenge?*

I am light-headed, sweating, weighted against the counter, Ben's gloating laugh ringing in my ears as Josh continues.

"His dad found him—can you imagine? I guess you of all people can. You saw Ben." He drags a hand down his face. "Shit, Lana. I'm so sorry." He makes a choking noise. "Ford was just on the ground . . . pale and dead."

I swallow. "How?"

"Dunno yet. Ford's mom called her best friend, who lives next door, and she works with my mom at the firehouse and that's why I know anything. The cops are over there. The scene's all cordoned off and they're searching."

"For what?"

"Evidence. Maybe for who did it."

I turn from Josh in that instant, hold either side of the sink, and try to concentrate on breathing to stop the kitchen from spinning. Basel's still begging, his meowing coming from every direction. The police are searching for *who* killed Ford. Any half-decent and mostly sane person would want a murderer found. Me: I worry that the answer to who killed Ford Holland isn't as simple as all that. I worry that being dead isn't what I used to think it was. And this matters because the person I loved best in the world isn't alive.

For someone who's dead, Ben is everywhere. He's in the sailboat that showed up on my steamy window; he's in my great-great-grandmother's rosary appearing in our hiding spot; he's in the fog; he's in my doorway;

he's at the foot of my bed; he's downtown, stargazing. Ford is dead, and I wonder if Ben was in the woods behind his house with him. What about when Maggie died? Did Ben chase her through the preserve? Is it being alive that limits you to one place? You're stuck in class, or at home blowing out your hair, or on the couch texting your best, or wherever, just so long as it's a single place, constrained by time and distance. I used to think that death limited you to zero places. You died and that was it: dead. But perhaps dead doesn't mean gone?

A hand cups the back of my neck. I start. "Sorry," Josh mutters, stepping away, jamming his hand in his pocket. "Are you okay? I was worried about telling you."

"Why?" I ask, suddenly annoyed. I hated Ford—Ford who called me foul names and whispered lurid insults in my ear. I'm glad he's gone.

Josh's brows shoot up. "Because of Ben," he explains gently. "Because it's another death and that probably dredges up . . . pain. Plus"—his eyes go around the room—"I heard that you and Ford were outside at my party toward the end and that maybe you . . . liked him?"

I frown. "No," I say. "I didn't like Ford. Not at all. Although I'm sorry for his parents. We just ran into each other in your backyard, and truthfully, he was never nice to me."

"Oh, okay," Josh says, the lines there between his eyebrows.

"There wasn't anything obviously wrong with Ford's body?" I ask. "Injuries? Signs of how he died?"

Josh rubs his closed eyelids. "Not that my mom heard, no. The coroner took him and they'll do the same tests they did on Maggie, same exam they'd do on anyone, I bet."

Josh's pocket buzzes angrily. His hand comes out with his cell.

"Crap," he says. "I was texting with Duncan and Rusty when my mom heard about Ford, and I told them. They must have told Carolynn, because she keeps calling."

"They'll be able to tell if Ford was poisoned," I say. "If rosary peas were in his stomach."

Josh looks up from texting on his cell. "Yeah, sure they will. Do you think the same person who killed Maggie killed Ford?"

My hands are jittery at my sides. "I don't know. Probably. Their deaths were in such close proximity, time-wise and both here on Gant, where there's never been anything like this before Ben."

"But who would kill Maggie and then Ford? They only knew each other from school, and they weren't even friends. There's no connection."

There is one glaring connection Josh doesn't see. Ben had reason to be angry with them both. I shrug in a vague way. I want Josh to stop thinking about it. He couldn't come up with the answer I have; he isn't increasingly uncertain about what's impossible. "They're random victims," I tell him.

His cell clatters on the counter where he'd placed it between us.

At B's. Where R U?

The text is from Carolynn.

Josh snatches it up. "We should go over to B's," he says.

I follow him to the front door. "I'll come in a few minutes. I need to call Willa." I watch Josh walk, dazed, cutting across our neighbor's lawn. I wait until he disappears, and then I sprint through the back door. My bare feet pound the stairs cut into the rocky slope, my hair comes loose from its ponytail, strands slashing what I see of the harbor. With the wind still, the water has the look of a frozen ice-blue pond. There are trails of smoke emanating from the opposite shore in the brush. A bonfire's recently been put out.

Basel meows above me from the upper terrace. I don't turn to close him inside. I go for our hiding spot. I have to see that the rosary is still there; that it exists; that I'm not crazy; that Ben's . . . whatever hasn't taken it to act out a grudge against Ford. My brain is picking at what Rusty said nights ago. Ben McBrook's ghost would have wanted Maggie dead.

I'm out of breath arriving at our secret place. My fingers shake as I slip my hand into the crevice. My fist curls around an object. I pull it out, unfurl my fingers, and stare at the rosary. It's shorter in length, by nearly a half. It would be if its peas were used to kill Ford. If the killer got it right this time. If he used enough poison for it to prove fatal.

— 20 —

I hold up the rosary, let it dangle in the sunshine. The red berries seem to pulse with their own heartbeat against the backdrop of the blue harbor. No, that's my screwed-up head, my tightening throat siphoning off air, not allowing enough oxygen to my brain. I snatch the rosary to my chest and whirl around. I'm out in the open, squinting into the sun, where anyone could see me.

I watch the coastline. I scan for a variation in the reedy sameness; a flash of fabric or the suggestion of skin. There's a distant cough, but the cougher isn't visible. A black Lab on the other side of the harbor is running down the grassy slope of his backyard. I feel his marble eyes on me. The tumbling laughter of children from far away, or maybe Ben and I are laughing in the past and the clear, sharp sound is cutting through time. I replace the rosary as soon as I'm sure I'm not being observed.

Upstairs I call Willa and ask her to meet me at Becca's. I keep the shortened rosary to myself. It's the kind of thing I should dial Dad about; tell the police. Confess to everything I think I know. At best this would get me sympathetic stares and concerned whispers. *Lana*

McBrook thinks her dead stepbrother is picking off the kids who wronged them. And what if Detective Sweeny or Dad or any adult who mattered believed me? I would be telling on Ben.

Not the Ben who was crackling with life, who blew into a room like saltwater wind, frizzing your hair with a static charge, tickling a smile out of you, but Ben as he is now.

Willa's Prius is parked behind Duncan's SUV in Becca's driveway. When no one answers, I push open Becca's door. No one bothered to lock it. Offhandedly, I think this is weird, and then I see the boys on the terrace. Josh is a blur of circuitous motion; Rusty and Duncan are statues. I discover Willa on the kitchen floor, knees pulled to her chest, back slumped against the stainless-steel fridge, fingers gouging into her temples.

I kneel beside her. "What's wrong?" I ask.

Her face has a scrubbed pink look. "I was already on my way here. Carolynn called me. Just go see."

I sidestep shards of white glass, a puddle of coffee, and Duncan's abandoned skipper hat. At the threshold I stop short. A coal-black mangy-looking bird is in the middle of a wooden plank of the terrace.

"It's beakless," Duncan says. Rogue feathers are scattered across the deck, their filaments trembling in the breeze. Off to my left the waist-high gate that connects the terrace to the side of the house is blowing open and shut, creaking and rattling with each swipe. Rusty braces himself over the railing, his knobby spine showing through his ribbed tank top. His puke smacks the rocks below. Josh has come to a stop at the side of the house, his arm propped up, bent, and his eyes hiding. Becca's dogs are at his feet.

"Dead," he says. "Winkie and Twinkie are dead."

"How?" I direct it to Duncan. He's the most composed.

He rubs his forehead with a fist. "Who the fuck knows? I called Carolynn about Ford and we came over here to find Becca hyperventilating." Duncan looks slowly from Josh to me. "She was *screaming*. She had scratches all over her arms." He runs his hand from his shoulder to his wrist. "And she was yanking her hair. It was a grade A meltdown. Her dogs are dead and there's this bird ... *butchered*. Some psycho took its beak."

"What do you mean, *took its beak?*" Josh says. He's shouldering the side of the house like he's trying to push it down.

Rusty shoves off the railing with a moan.

"I mean, it's gone," Duncan says, loud and frustrated. "Whoever killed the dogs killed this creepy-ass bird, took its beak off, and got the hell out of here." He waves indicating the unlatched side gate.

"You don't know that someone did this," Rusty says. "You don't know that for real, man. Those dogs were vicious." He points a shaky arm at them but can't look their way. "They could have attacked that bird, chewed its face off, and then ... and then ..."

"Spontaneously croaked?" Duncan says, rubbing a fist in one eye, then the other.

"Maybe the bird's poisonous? Bro, I'm saying *holy fuck*, rosary peas turned out to be toxic." Rusty pulls his baseball cap from his head and replaces it backward. His eyes bug out from his head. "We can't jump to conclusions saying someone did this, is all I'm getting at." His chest is heaving, and he forces his hands still by shoving them into his board shorts.

"Did you call the cops?" Josh asks.

"I called 9-1-1 and they chewed me out. The woman was all,

'Call a veterinarian, the police are busy with actual crimes,'" Rusty says. "Becca was losing her shit, crying about Maggie's killer being angry with us for finding her body. She kept wailing about this being revenge, and we hadn't even told her about Ford yet."

"Where is Becca now?" I ask

"Upstairs with Car," Duncan says.

Josh pulls his cell from his pocket. A moment later he's telling his mom as much as we know. Once there's a job to be done, he takes over. This is who Josh is: the protector of the core; older brother; consoler and spokesperson.

I inch closer to the bird. Its feathers are scruffy, their quills crimped. There are red puncture marks all over its back. "Those are bite marks. Maybe Rusty is right and the dogs caught it and killed it?" I say. I would prefer this explanation. Minutes ago I was hoping my dead stepbrother had poisoned Maggie and Ford because it meant he'd found a way to be on this island. And if Ben were here at all, able to poison and kill, then couldn't I talk to him? Couldn't we drive to his favorite taco truck or play Scrabble or roast marshmallows at midnight? Wouldn't it mean that he'd forgiven me for not going after him that night? For not saving him?

Duncan nudges the bird with his shoe. The bird rolls to face me. There's a red sore like a blister where the beak should be. The edges are clean, not ragged, as if the beak was removed with precision. Its black eyes gleam blindly. Its scaly black claws—four toes on each foot—are curled in on themselves. They look prehistoric, a remnant of what should no longer be here. I don't want this bird to be connected to Maggie's or Ford's death because I don't want Ben to have had a hand in this.

"Are blackbirds poisonous to dogs, like some prey are poisonous to their natural predators?" Duncan asks.

"Blackbirds?" I murmur.

He squints up at me from where he's kneeling and examining the bird. "My little bro Jeffrey's favorite book is one with all these sick nursery rhymes." There's a lag between Duncan's lips moving and his voice reaching me. "This looks like the blackbirds that broke free from a pie." Those disembodied words paint vivid black forms, flapping their wings in the air. They beat harder until their wings splinter and break against their bodies. I remember Mom's voice, rich and velvety: *four and twenty blackbirds, baked in a pie.*

The sun's voltage is hiked up. I shade my eyes, shake my head, and mutter I'm not sure what to Duncan. I imagine a wriggle under my flip-flop and I jump back, seized by the fantasy that it's the blackbird's beak, cawing for help. Dismembered and chirping.

There were blackbirds in one of Ben's stories. Correction. *Beakless* blackbirds. And the beakless body on the terrace is an echo of that long-ago childhood tale. I reenter the house. The present has a twilit feel, eclipsed by a bright long-ago moment. I can't stop hearing it, seeing it, *replaying* it.

The pink floral blanket was a canopy above eight intricately carved dining chairs. The floor was covered with brocade throw pillows that made irresistible scratching posts for Basel, some of their tassels frayed and bitten.

"You ready for a story?" Ben asked, propping a bowl of popcorn on the belly of my giant brown plush bear. The stuffed toy wore a circus collar that I eventually cut off because I couldn't stand how comical it made him seem. I nodded. "It's a bloody one," Ben warned. I grinned wider.

He recounted the story he titled, "The Lovely Scarecrow." Not all Ben's stories had names, and most I wouldn't remember if they did. This one made an impression.

A half man, half demon lived in a bank of mist in the land next to the kingdom of death. He hated girls. I can't remember why—doesn't matter, though, does it? He rode around on a mule and sheared off the noses of blackbirds to toss at the girls. Lana the brave made him pay—can't remember how. I bet he lost his nose. I remember clapping and jumping to my knees as Ben shared the grotesque ending.

People think girls aren't supposed to crave violence like boys do. Video games and toy soldiers weren't supposed to be for me. Here's a secret, though. I was hungry for the violent stories, the sheared-off body parts, the vengeful heroes, as much as any boy could have been.

The dead birds and the poisonous rosary were threads of Ben's imagination, and now they've been spun into reality. The marauding villains of Ben's stories weren't born out of air. I asked him where they came from, more than once. *Where did your stories start?* He sidestepped. He pleaded imagination. He went silent, stood up abruptly, and left me in the blanket fort. Stories have beginnings, origins. But what do they matter? They aren't real. Real is Willa's arm, hot on mine. Real is Ben, who invented heroes and villains and the means they'd fight and die by.

Soon Karen arrives from the firehouse. She brings another firefighter with her, and they're all business. Josh says that Becca's mom is on her way from work. Willa ducks into the bathroom to call her own mother. I should call Dad, but I glide up the stairs instead. Becca and Carolynn haven't come down.

The second story is wrong. Stuffy. There's a heady, nostril-burning scent I can't place. I expected to hear Becca's baying or Carolynn talking her calm. There's nothing but a white band of light under Becca's bedroom door in the dark, long hallway. I don't knock.

I should have.

The scene is jarring. Becca's in a sunshine-yellow bra and underwear. She sits on the edge of her bed, facing the door, with her fingers laced in her lap. Other than the almost nakedness, she sits prim as she would in class. Her hair has a lank, painted-on look. Water drips from the tapering ends, a scatter of spots on the silk duvet. Her bra is see-through.

"That better not be Duncan," Carolynn yells from Becca's bathroom.

I open my mouth to say it's me. I don't get that far. There are what looks like self-inflicted scratches on Becca's forearms. Three each. "Hey, Lan," Becca says. Her voice is detached and airy as a floating balloon.

"Hi," I croak.

Carolynn pops her head out of the bathroom. "Is it just you?" she asks. Her hair is wet and sticking to one side of her face. I nod and she ducks away.

I let myself slowly onto the bed. The room stinks of rubbing alcohol and the cake-frosting candle on the desk. The ceiling fan is whirling it up into a sickening-smelling twister.

Becca catches me looking at the red lines. "Don't worry," she says. "Car cleaned them. I went a little mental." She laughs softly. "I get a pass."

Carolynn's wrapped in a towel. "Showers are second only to Xanax," she says, crossing to the closet.

"Do you need something?" I ask. "Water? Josh?"

Carolynn stops pushing aside hangers. "He doesn't need to see this," she says. "Will you find B a long-sleeved shirt to wear?" She points at the dresser under a mother-of-pearl-inlaid mirror on the wall. Carolynn yanks a sundress from a hanger and wriggles it over her own head.

Dressing Becca is a lot like dressing a life-size doll. She doesn't help as I worm her noodle arms through sleeves and scrunch the fabric up so her hands pop out.

"My babies loved you, did you know?" she asks with an off-putting cheerful smile. I shake my head. She doesn't acknowledge that I'm dressing her. "You should take that as a major compliment, since they only tolerated pretty girls. I think they remembered your smell from when I used to go over your house when we were little." She rubs the heel of her hand at her temple before her arm thuds back into her lap. "Isn't that so funny?" I incline my chin. Suddenly, her eyes are swimming in tears. Her shaking fingers tuck a piece of hair behind my ear, and her wrist brushes my cheek. "You get that I'm super sorry for everything, right?" she whispers.

Her bottom lips quivers, and I think about that scared little girl on the swing next to me when we were small. I used to sing really loud to drown out her parents' fighting. Their voices echoed over the water and boomeranged back at us. "Sorry for what, B?" I ask.

She shrugs a shoulder. The neckline of her shirt is askew, and I go to fix it. She grabs my wrist hard. "Listen," she pleads. I wait. "I'm sorry for . . . like, for telling all the girls when we were in sixth grade that you had really rank BO and that I stopped going to your house because you were a smelly lesbian who wanted to make out with me and you wore a sports bra because you didn't have two boobs, just one, like a boob Cyclops." She sniffs. "They were going to invite you to sit with us at lunch, and I didn't want them to because I thought . . ."

I'm standing. All I see is Becca. Her wet hair is tucked in the neck of her shirt and her lips are curling nervously. I'm light-headed. "You thought what?"

She drags the back of her hand across her nose messily. "That you'd blab about my parents and them fighting and my dad sleeping with his yoga instructor and how I cried and everything you heard them yell. They said really embarrassing stuff."

"What are you talking about?"

"You know"—she waves a hand in the air—"all our family dirtiness. If you sat with us to eat and got invited to sleepovers, I worried you were going to spill."

I've stopped breathing. "I wouldn't have."

"I know that now. Obviously." She starts to roll her eyes but stops midway through. She exhales loudly. "I just didn't know it then. I was *only* eleven."

"'I was *only* eleven.'" I touch my collarbone. "Girls have called me Uni-Boob since. Do you realize that? I thought Carolynn was some teasing mastermind and told them to. I couldn't understand why out of nowhere she made it her life's mission to torture me." There's a snort from behind me.

Becca lifts her hands, her fingers splaying. She isn't shaking any longer. "What do you want me to say?"

"What else?"

"Huh?"

"What else did you say about me?"

Her eyes run over the room. Nothing's changed about Becca's appearance, and yet she doesn't look like a fragile doll to me anymore. She looks like a spoiled, selfish child a minute away from stomping her foot and demanding that she get a lifelong pass for cruelty.

"Car?" Becca whines, making her eyes big and innocent.

Carolynn's reclining on the window seat. "This isn't my thing, B." She shakes a bottle of nail polish. It rattles. She unscrews it and removes the brush. She begins to meticulously paint her nails while pointedly avoiding eye contact.

"Fine," Becca says with a huff. She closes her eyelids briefly, and raps gently on her forehead with her fist. "So there was the whole sports bra thing, and I told them you wore those gross pads that look like diapers because you peed like an old lady when you laughed. It was so stupid." She giggles under her breath.

I am motionless. "What else?"

She busies herself strapping sandals on her feet and glances at me like she was hoping I'd vanish. "That was enough for girls not to want you in the lunch circle. I mean, there was high school, and I said a lot of nasty things about tons of girls. I had the crappiest self-esteem in the universe." Her butt bounces once on the mattress, and she shrugs. "I was insecure, so that's like a pass, you know?"

"No," I say, "that is not a pass. You do not get a pass. What *specifically* did you say in high school?"

She chews her bottom lip, and I cover my mouth when the urge to gag becomes so strong I need to hold it in. This girl. I let her dote on me. I binged on her compliments. I let her make me glow. I *wanted* to be her friend even after she ditched me. Even though it was obvious that Becca had a talent for excluding the many and including the few.

"You have to swear not to stay pissed." She speaks quickly, and her tone is equal parts irritated and hopeful. "But I told a few girls that I saw you and Ben *doing it* on your terrace. I said I could see your deck from mine, which I can't because of my mom's hedges, but they didn't know that. It was awful and shitty of me and it was freshman year and there were some new girls and I wanted them all to want to be my friends. Can you blame me? They were all checking out the older guys at lunch and Ben walked by, and I don't know, he was the dark horse of hotness, and they were all gushing about him and it just flew out. It was like this one thing that I knew—well, *said I knew*—about the guy they all wanted. I don't always act like a good person." Her sooty lashes flutter shut with the admission.

"That's because you're not one," I say without skipping a beat.

She nods, relief bowing her lips, happy to be understood. "No, not always."

My muscles ache from holding myself stiff, and I can't believe I didn't see it before. "*It just flew out?* Ben walks by you in the ninth grade and you lie and tell girls that I had sex with him? Other girls repeated that rumor. I was terrified that Ben would hear. That he'd think I had something to do with the gossip or he wouldn't want to be seen with me if he knew what girls were saying."

She pulls her hair from her collar and fans it over her shoulders.

"Jeez, what do you want from me? I admitted it—not that I had to or anything. I'm sooo sorry, okay?"

"I thought it was Carolynn who made that up."

Becca shakes her head. "Car was there when I said it, and she just repeated it. I dunno, L. Maybe she thought it was true?"

My attention snaps toward Carolynn "Did you?"

She's parting the white gossamer curtains and peering at the street below. "Becca's mom just pulled up."

"Carolynn," I yell.

Her eyes dart to mine and her hand releases the curtain. Shafts of diagonal light pass over her features. "No, I didn't believe it. It was a messed-up thing to repeat and I'm sorry. Teenage girls are the cruelest animal."

"Yeah, they are," Becca gibbers. "See, everyone knows it."

I whirl back to face her. "You're the cruelest. Can you imagine what being called Uni-Boob felt like when I was eleven years old? Before I even had boobs? Do you know how gross and ugly it made me feel?"

Becca hooks her fingers in her lap as she stares at them. When her head snaps up, I expect another toss of her hair or a disconnected smile. Her eyes are glazed, tears sneaking out the corners. "You may not believe me, but I am sorry. As sorry as I've ever been." The back of her hand wipes a tear streaking her cheek. "I would go back in time and change it. I would shut the eff up and tell you to eat lunch with us and do all the stuff with you I should have. But I can't."

I don't get to respond because Becca's mother throws open the door and flies into the room. What is there to say? Words aren't enough. They weren't for the villains of our stories and they're not for Becca. My hands are fisted at my hips. I can't release them. I tilt against the wall. A poster's at my back. It's one of those French billboard replicas, with a half-naked girl wearing a masquerade mask as she swims in a glass of champagne. I hear it tear as I sink to the floor, and that strikes me as terribly appropriate.

"I got home from running . . . went out back because I left the dogs there . . . they pee under the table and you said I *had* to leave them out. You said that dogs belong *outside*." Becca ends in a muffled wail as she melts into her mother's lap.

I glare at the mop of Becca's wet hair. My sadness is limited to Twinkie and Winkie, with their technicolor nails and darting pink tongues. They weren't bad dogs. They could be sweet, endlessly enthusiastic no matter how many times you left and reentered a room. They didn't deserve to die, but Becca deserved to lose them.

Is this the punishment my fictive self would have doled out if I'd known that Becca was behind the awful whispers? I wasn't plotting my revenge on Carolynn when I thought she was the perpetrator, yet somehow, it's so much worse that it's Becca. Becca and I were friends. I kept her parents' fights secret. I smiled at her in the halls when she pretended not to notice me. I never held it against her. Were all those biting, passing comments Ben made about Becca because he knew what I didn't? Becca was the mastermind behind the rumors.

If there is a part of Ben on our island, it would want revenge.

I think back to that evening on the terrace when he asked if girls ever hurt me. He offered to kill them. I wondered out loud how he'd do it and he looked disappointed, I assumed because I sounded serious. Perhaps that wasn't it. What if Ben was disappointed that I asked him how he'd do it rather than tell him that I'd been plotting my own revenge? In that moment I took shape, and he saw how different I was from the Lana in his head.

At present Becca says she'd go back and do things differently. She says she's sorry. It's easy to apologize after the fact, though, isn't it? It's easy to say, *I should have been honest and brave.*

That's how the rest of the afternoon goes. I'm stupefied with fury and hurt. Becca's mom escapes for a pot of tea when it's clear that she can't console her daughter. Willa and the boys huddle in Becca's room after Sophia leaves. Josh waits for more news about Ford. The firefighters declare the cuts on Twinkie and Winkie puncture wounds, likely made by birds. They believe it's possible that one of the dogs bit the bird's beak clean from its face. The last person through the terrace's gate must not have latched it properly and the wind blew it open. None of the adults are alarmed. Dead animals are nothing compared to the body of a boy. Even Detective Ward is ambivalent when Josh asks him over the phone if this could be payback from Maggie's killer for discovering the body. The grown-ups dismiss it as little more than Mother Nature—the suburban, and therefore tame and benign, version of a lion attacking a gazelle.

"We should listen to Josh's mom," Rusty says. "Karen knows what's going on better than we do."

"Do you hear yourself? You are such a sheep," Duncan tells him, propped against Becca's bed with a corner of her duvet on his shoulder.

"I can't believe Ford is dead," Carolynn repeats for the third time. "Do you know he made a grab for my boob sophomore year at a dance?" She fans her hands over her chest. "I punched him in the face and told him I'd kill him if he ever touched me again."

Becca smashes her finger against her lips. "My mom could hear you."

Carolynn scowls. "So what? *I* didn't kill him."

Willa nudges me after I zone out. I've missed the last piece of their conversation, and everyone's attention is on me. "I won't be able to sneak out tonight. Can you, Lana?"

Becca hugs herself. "You're still in for Ben's peace out, right? I can't stay home and do nothing tonight . . . not after my babies. Pleeeease." She smiles wide. It's an alligator smile. A mask. I used to believe she was too transparent to lie convincingly about who she is. Willa would say too stupid. We were both wrong.

"We staked out the wildlife museum last night," Duncan says.

Rusty is on his feet, practicing his swing. "They don't even have a security guard or an alarm," he says. Doing something as ordinary and natural to him as swinging an imaginary bat has helped him recover since the terrace.

"I wanna do this so bad. Not just for Ben—mostly for him," Duncan directs to me, "but it'll be a declaration of life for us, too. We. Are. Alive. And we won't let nothing—*no one*—change that." He rubs his fist in his palm.

A murmur of agreement travels around our circle. On an ordinary, small day, the kind that *before* was made of, breaking into the Gant Wildlife Rehabilitation Museum would have given me hives. Today I don't need convincing. Everything that's happened has made it easier to believe that Ben could be here, somewhere in Gant, in some form. The prank is for him; he'll know it immediately. It'll make the newspaper, people will talk, or Ben will be able to sense it happened and recognize it as the message it is.

Anticipation for tonight settles into my chest. I'm dying to tell Ben:

You haven't been forgotten.

— 2 1 —

Dad is pacing in the kitchen when I get home. Like the other adults, he writes off Twinkie's and Winkie's deaths as nature gone rogue. The attacks hardly draw a contemplative sigh or an eyebrow furrow from him as he takes a final sip of his latte. Ford's death holds all his attention.

"How well did you know the younger Holland boy?" he asks. I think I hear a note of suspicion in the question, though it might be my imagination.

I wave vaguely. "We had some classes together."

"His older brother is one of the boys who attacked that poor man a couple of years back. Was Ford troubled too?"

I cringe inwardly. There's that word again: *troubled*. Dad uses it for all the teenage behavior he doesn't understand. "He wasn't an ax murderer, if that's what you're wondering," I say. This is true and the most generous thing I can say about Ford.

Dad's eyes narrow with concern. "Sounds like you didn't care for him."

"Not really," I say. A prolonged silence follows, and I try to look contrite as I wash my hands at the faucet and dry them with a paper towel. Dad's still tensed, waiting for me to continue, when I turn around and for the barest second I think he can read it all on my face. I, Bumblebee, am not sorry about Ford's death; I'm glad for it. I think my dead stepbrother has found a way to continue to *be*. I hope Ben is *existing* in Gant rather than existing nowhere in death, even if it means he's a vengeful force. Even if it means he's a poisoner, a murderer.

An incoming e-mail dings from Dad's laptop behind him, and the spell is broken. Dad spins to check it; he can't help himself. It happens just in time, because I could feel my secrets shouldering into the back of my mouth. Yarns of our stories around Gant. A handprint on Ben's desk. The rosary finding its way into my secret place. Half the peas gone after Ford's body was found. None of it comes. He wouldn't believe me anyway.

It isn't the fear of being labeled *troubled* by my father that keeps me from sharing—although he'd almost certainly use the adjective. I don't want to expose my and Ben's invented world to grown-up judgment. Sharing the stories with Willa was hard enough; confessing to Dad would be unbearable. Instead I make excuses the rest of the day to stay in my room. I let Dad believe I'm not feeling well; that I'm a normal human and all that's wrong is that I'm disturbed over the death of my classmate.

As planned, I sneak into the stillness of the night at eleven, when I'm certain Dad is asleep and won't hear me reset the house alarm. Carolynn and Becca are already in Carolynn's car down the street, and they flash their lights for my attention. The three of us drive without talking to Josh's, where we'll meet the boys.

The silver three-quarters moon is low as an afternoon sun when we climb into Duncan's SUV. Everyone argues over who brought what, who should sit where, and if it's too early or too late to head downtown. I end up with Rusty in the third row, an arrangement I'm not thrilled over, since he is not Josh. Duncan is slumped behind the wheel, his skipper hat on the dash. Josh takes the front seat to keep watch for any indication that tonight's escapade should be called off. He tried to find out from his mom about measures the police are taking to search for Ford's and Maggie's killer or killers, but he couldn't get much information without coming out and asking about possible road blocks and patrols.

"Why is every song on your phone about bending girls over or flying first class?" Becca complains, scrolling through Duncan's cell.

"Give it back if you're going to insult me," Duncan says moodily, arm reaching behind him for the phone.

Becca slaps his hand away. "Not until you defend your taste in music. OHMYGOD." Her voice is shrill. "You have old—like *dinosaur ancient*—Britney Spears on this." Her laughter peals as she thrusts the phone into Carolynn's lap.

Carolynn looks through the artists, the cell clicking like the spinning spokes of a bicycle wheel. "I didn't know you were Taylor Swift's fanboy, Duncan," she says, amusement making her words dance.

"Hey," Duncan growls, "give it back."

"Should we read your texts to Bethany J. instead?" Becca teases.

Duncan turns and takes his eyes off the road. Josh grabs the wheel as the car jounces over those plastic dots along the shoulder that look like candy buttons. "How 'bout keeping us on the road?" Josh says, righting the car.

"Nosy girls," Duncan gripes as he faces forward with his cell in hand. "And Bethany J. doesn't mind my taste in music."

Rusty's knee knocks mine as he lunges over the middle seat and shouts, "Dude, the bass. Me and McBrook are going to have ruptured eardrums back here." Duncan holds his middle finger up but turns the hip-hop lower.

Becca has a thermos of spiked cocoa for everyone to sip. Then a flask full of peppermint schnapps follows, and even Carolynn bemoans the syrupy stuff. "Why can't you ever steal a better bottle from your mom's stash?" Carolynn must remember that Becca's dogs died earlier, because she pulls Becca into her side and presses her lips to her cheek.

"This shit smells like my grandma," Duncan says.

Rusty cracks his knuckles and calls, "That's because she's always loaded."

"Then don't drink it. You're just giving us Bethany J. germs anyway," Becca says. "Hold up, no more talking about Bethany you-know-who the rest of the night." She glances sideways at Carolynn.

"You're the one bringing her up," Duncan protests.

Carolynn ignores them both. "God, it's a sauna in here. Turn on the air already. Someone smells like a circus freak."

The bickering is slathered on to cover nerves. It's sticky and as unsubstantial as that marshmallow fluff that comes in a jar. The car is roomy, but there's a cozy, crowded, overwhelming feeling with everyone shouting and frenzied. Becca's long ponytail brushes my knees where it spills over her seat back, and I push it away. I believe that Becca is sorry. Warmth is emanating from my chest at being in this car, a part of this night with these five. But Becca occupies a different space in my head now. She's in the shadowy corner with the other villains. She isn't a silly girl wondering aloud why we can't all speak British and say words like *snogging* instead of *kissing* and *holiday* rather than *vacation*. I'm not ready for her to return to sunnier shores in my head.

"Are you and your mom going to bury Twinkie and Winkie at your house?" I ask. It feels mean to bring the little dead dogs up, so I do.

Carolynn watches me from the corner of her eye as Becca shakes her head. "Nope. We're going to—what is it called when they incinerate them in a giant oven?"

"Cremate," I supply.

"Yeah, Mom brought them to the vet to be cremated." Becca sighs. "I wish teacup pigs weren't so over—they're only for losers now, though. I guess I'll get a kitten next. I've always wanted one of those famous cats on Instagram." She rests her elbow on the seat back and cups her chin dreamily.

"*Pussycat*," Duncan calls for no apparent reason other than he's Duncan.

"My cousin's cat has two hundred thousand followers," Carolynn says.

Josh twists around. "That's insane." We pass under a streetlamp, and his features sharpen in the light. "What does the cat do?"

Becca giggles. "Duh. It's cute and famous."

Josh runs a hand through his hair and faces front. He doesn't do all the posting and picture taking that a lot of boys do. He always seems *here*. He's not disembodied and existing in his phone or wondering how he looks in a picture like Duncan or obsessively texting with teammates like Rusty or wanting to tell lesser friends what a sick time he's having with his best friends.

My knees bounce. I've had two sips of schnapps and fuzziness is spreading through my veins. I am a candy cane. I am an unfocused smile and anticipation. I'm concealing a murder weapon in my childhood hidey-spot. Two people have shown up dead, and I suspect Ben of having everything to do with it. Dust is settling in Maggie's print on Ben's desk, and I haven't even started to decipher why she risked ghosting through our house. These are some of the reasons that I should be sluggish with worry. Instead they seem distant annoyances, blunted, happening to my favorite characters on television rather than me. I can easily imagine Ben sharing the third row with me and Rusty.

Rusty gulps the schnapps, pounds his chest to free a burp, and offers me the flask again. "Don't wuss out on me, McBrook," he says when I hesitate. I take the flask and tip it to my lips. He elbows my side. "There ya go. You're all right," he says offhandedly and then shouts, "Heads up, bro," as he tosses the flask to Josh.

I smile. Tonight is for Ben. And what's more, I feel like I belong in this moment. I am entrenched. I am heels dug into the ground. I know that amid the clutter on the floor of this practically new SUV is my pair of pink Havaianas, forgotten after a bonfire a week ago, the day before we found Maggie. I know that the wad of putty the color of dead flesh in the cup holder is Carolynn's grape bubble gum, and I remember Carolynn and Becca's debate about the virtues of watermelon versus grape flavoring. It ended in a stalemate. I also know that while Duncan will have an embolism when he finds it, he would drive this car into a brick wall if it would make his friends happy. It's all selfishness, loyalty, jokes, and insults delivered with the subtext *I love you*.

Their togetherness is what always struck me most about the core. How close they appeared made them seem distant, a separate species, even when surrounded by peripheral friends. They operate as a single organism. They arrive together; they leave together. They are the five stars of a constellation. They have an authentic shared history like the one Ben and I wished for. A force drew them to one another at the start of grade school. It could have been the gravitational pull of Josh's red corduroy pants.

"Did you bring the crowbar?" Duncan breaks into my thoughts.

"Bro, I said yes when you asked five minutes ago," Rusty says. He slaps my thigh lightly and thrusts his chin at Duncan. "You'd think this was the first time he ever planned a B and E. That's breaking and entering," he clarifies when he sees I'm confused.

Josh must hear because he shouts, "Is everyone wearing gloves? No one can leave fingerprints." A chorus of affirming groans and *yeah we know*s and Becca giggles. I confirm that my mittens are still tucked inside my jean pocket.

Duncan snorts. "I told you that my parents are on the board at the museum. If we get caught, no way will they call the cops and risk losing all those fat checks from Mommy and Daddy."

"Or your dad will throw us under the bus to save you," Carolynn remarks.

Duncan steers the car suddenly to the shoulder and slows. He twists to look Carolynn in the eye. "Car, I'd confess to the cops before I'd let you guys take all the heat. I may be a prick, but I'm a loyal one." Carolynn's still staring at him when his attention returns to the road.

The flask goes round and round. My lips go from tingly to numb as we drive alongside the harbor and eventually reach the south end, where commercial fishing rigs are docked. Beyond them a string of warehouses extend until Gant's downtown dies into the forest. Most of the warehouses were used by the old mining and logging companies and are now empty except when an art show or indoor festival pops up inside. The last warehouse before the preserve holds the Gant Wildlife Rehabilitation Museum.

Any woodsy rodent, bird, or mammal that's injured and rescued is delivered to the museum's vets. As the animals are nursed back to health, they serve as exhibits in the museum. Kids press their runny noses against the glass partitions, watching the furry, feathered, and scaly creatures heal.

Ben would point at a raccoon that ingested trash, or a baby hawk that fell from its nest and was stoned by a few children, or an owl that was hit by a car, and say, *See. We're a blight—a human disease—on animals.* I never knew what to say in response, but the evidence he pointed to was hard to deny. He thought it was wrong to put the sick or injured critters on display for kids. And then, at the time he started articulating how selfish he thought Gant was, Winnie, the bald eagle, became a symbol of that selfishness to Ben.

Winnie—the least majestic name an eagle could ever be christened—was injured seven years ago when she snatched a salmon from an estuary. The salmon had swallowed a fisherman's hook and so Winnie swallowed it too. It worked its way into her stomach lining and she collapsed out of the sky.

For months Winnie underwent medical treatment at the museum. Updates were printed on the front page of Gant's newspaper, and adults and kids were always buzzing over Winnie the resident celebrity. Then a bunch of environmental groups heard about Gant Island's injured bald eagle. The groups demanded to know when she'd be released into the wild. They got a biologist to write a letter to a newspaper about the town needing to protect Winnie's habitat once she was released. The scientist warned against keeping her in captivity for too long; they didn't want her to forget how to live in the wild. The groups protested every time there was another acre of forest chopped down and a fro-yo, or cupcake, or wine shop planned. Pretty soon the environmentalists were accusing Gant of not allowing enough space for Winnie to transition back to the wild. Gant's brilliant solution: keep Winnie caged for the rest of her life.

Before either of us could drive, Dad would drop Ben and me off at the museum on the weekends. I moved with the flow of kids, staring glaze-eyed at the sparrows with their wings in splints, and the baby gopher snakes learning to hunt trapped white mice. Ben stood unmovable in front of Winnie's enclosure.

He wanted to help her and to rebel against Gant and what it had done to keep her caged. I'm not sure why he never tried to rescue her himself. No matter. We'll free Winnie for Ben.

We pull to the rear of the museum, where a chain-link fence cordons off the loading dock. Duncan parks between two mammoth Dumpsters, and we pile out. During their stakeout, Duncan and Rusty watched the last employee leave and padlock the garage-style door of the rear entrance. The lock is the simple kind we use on lockers at school. Busting the padlock will be quieter than breaking a window or forcing open the front door. Besides, it's less like breaking in if we sneak in through the back.

I face the fence. The metal chain links pixelate the long building's silhouette. My mittened hands do that weak I-can't-form-a-fist thing. I believe that if we get caught, Duncan won't let us shoulder the blame, and his parents will have no choice but to protect us all to prevent him from accepting responsibility. Duncan is loyal. More importantly, we won't get caught, and this is *right*. Winnie is a captive. She doesn't belong in a cage. The wildlife museum doesn't *own* her. I stomp, driving my heel into the pavement, and flex my fingers.

Josh and Rusty are hunchbacked with our supplies. They're all wiry, lithe limbs on the gently swaying fence. Duncan is less graceful, but he gets up and over without trouble. Becca and Carolynn will stay in the locked SUV to serve as lookouts while we're inside. If they see a patrol car or anyone coming, they'll call Josh's cell and we'll evacuate.

There are gaping holes in the plan—like what if there isn't time to run through the museum and escape over the fence? Or what if someone spots the SUV parked with no apparent purpose and calls the police rather than the museum's administration? I think it's hard for everyone to be afraid of getting in trouble when there are dead bodies stacking up and we're no longer suspects. Why would Gant PD care about us liberating an eagle when there are real crimes being committed?

I draw a deep breath; the air's briny and thick without the wind. Hand crosses over hand, foot above foot, and I'm over the fence, soles striking the ground. The strength has returned to my fingers. My heart is knocking.

Rusty and Duncan are at the foot of the cement loading dock. Rusty maneuvers the crowbar into the padlock. A split second later, the lock snaps off. The metal door rumbles and creaks up. We stare at a two-foot-high gap between the door and the cement slab. A nod goes around as we silently agree to squeeze through rather than risk additional racket.

Josh steps up. "Here goes, my fellow criminals," he says, half laughing at the spectacular nerve of us. He drags himself into the darkness. We've all visited the halls of the museum but this section is off-limits to nonemployees.

"At least this might get me laid when I tell Bethany J. about it," Duncan says with a dogged grin.

I go next. It's cool and dank in the darkness on the other side. Rusty fumbles at the opening by my feet before hopping up. We navigate haltingly to Josh, who's framed by a rectangle of fluorescent light ahead. A corridor is through the entranceway, and we open doors a crack to glance through. All offices and exam rooms.

"The museum part must be this way," Josh says, moving up the hall. After one left and two rights, we dead-end into another closed door. "Here we go," Josh says, and turns the knob.

The hairs on my arms stand on end as we enter the atrium. Its lofty ceiling is a metal skeleton, webbed with glass panels that allow for natural light to illuminate the space. The moon glints off the banks of glass enclosures running the perimeter. They're small and aquarium-like. Sets of inquisitive eyes wink at us from the dark interior.

In the center of the room is one vast steel-wire cage. It extends from the cement floor to the glass ceiling, forty or fifty feet above our heads.

"Winnie," I breathe. The eagle's silhouette is stenciled black on a perch halfway to the roof. A blinking, distant airplane drifts in a diagonal behind her. We move stealthily to the center of the atrium.

"What did you get to coax her from the cage?" Josh whispers.

Rusty drops his backpack at his feet and kneels. "*Unagi,*" he says. Silence.

"Are you talking about the eel they have at Gingko Sushi?" Duncan asks.

Rusty holds up a clear plastic to-go container full of it. There's a clump of wasabi that's so green it glows radioactive beside the ribbons of pink pickled ginger. "What else was I supposed to get?"

"The bird deserves the best of Gant's Japanese cuisine," Duncan snickers.

I examine the large double doors at the front of the building. They're only five or so yards from Winnie's enclosure. They're bolted on the inside and don't appear to require a key. It will be easier for Winnie to escape through them rather than us luring her out of the twisty hallways and rear hatch. We aren't 100 percent sure that the front doors aren't connected to an alarm system, though, and while there's nothing indicating that they are, the plan is for me to wait and throw them open once everyone is in the SUV and it's idling out front for a hasty getaway.

Rusty and Duncan take turns with a pair of bolt cutters Rusty snatched from his garage. Each chain link snaps as a finger bone would in the metal jaw, and my ears prick, picking up the scratching, breathing, and fidgeting of the watching animals. Tons of little witnesses, all hungry for escape.

My mittened hands skate over the plastic container of sushi as I pick it up from the floor. The boys are about a third of the way done outlining a large rectangular window.

"Make sure you grab all the tools before you run back for the car," I remind them. "And keep your gloves on. No fingerprints." I begin dropping the bite-size pieces of eel on the floor. The trail runs from Winnie's enclosure to the front entrance. Josh wields the bolt cutters. Another few minutes and the boys maneuver the heavy section of crisscrossing bars to the floor. Winnie has the look of one of the shadow animals Ben and I used to make down at the fire pit. His hands could cast a million different shapes on the rocks.

It shouldn't surprise me that Ben found a way to stick around after he died. He was good at reinventing the ordinary. He was great at manipulating the shadows.

Winnie hasn't moved since we arrived. "I'm going to go out the front with Lana," Josh tells Rusty and Duncan as they collect their supplies. Their footsteps recede, a door opens and shuts on the opposite end of the atrium, and we're alone.

Josh and I wait halfway between the cage and the double front doors. "What if she doesn't fly out?" he whispers.

I eye Winnie's outline. The eagle appears to be looking to the sky rather than at us. "She will," I say.

He brushes the end of my ponytail from my shoulder. I feel his skin's warmth through my sweater and his glove. "How do you know?" Josh's expression is open. His blue eyes are dark and frank. I posed a similar question once to Ben. Ben was lamenting that Winnie was imprisoned in a cage. I asked how he knew that Winnie wasn't happier being fed and cared for. *Because she's a wild animal being kept in a cage,* he told me, slow and simple, like, wasn't it obvious?

Now I answer Josh: "Because the alternative is for her to stay in a cage." I hear Ben's voice speaking along with me in my head. I know that Ben felt that he wasn't so different from a caged animal. He liked to say: *It doesn't matter whether a prison looks like an island or a shack; if it has bars to keep you in, there's no difference.* I didn't point out that the boy kept in a shack would probably disagree.

Another minute passes. "You can wait with the others if you want," I offer. With each minute I'm steadier, more solid. The schnapps has either worn off or it's steeling my bones. With each breath I inhale the *rightness* of being here. I wouldn't mind if a police SWAT team stormed the building. I want the universe to know that I'm doing this for Ben; I want the universe to deliver the message to him.

Josh nudges my elbow. "I'm not leaving until you do."

I smile at him. "Thanks for following through with this even after Ford and the dogs."

"Everything is going to be okay." Josh levels his head with mine. "I won't let anyone hurt you. I promise." He slips his arm around my shoulders. I rest my head against him lightly. His chest is warm on my ear. Josh Parker's infinite charm is aimed at me. He's making promises; the sounds of our inhales and exhales mingle; we're bathed in moonshine and surrounded by twinkling eyes like stars. This is what I've been waiting for.

Winnie alights to the branch ten feet below her perch, and then another ten. Her progress is soundless; my thoughts are an uncooperative babble. The Lana from our stories would spit in the face of whatever danger Josh thinks is circling us. She wouldn't need to be held. She wouldn't need a boy to promise her that he'll keep her safe. She would keep herself safe—and probably end up saving Josh once his pluck and optimism failed him. Winnie settles on the lowest branch. I'm not even afraid, because the girl I am now believes—madly—that Ben has found his way back. Ben would never, ever hurt me.

"Call the others and let them know I'm about to open the door," I whisper, moving from Josh.

I reach the entrance and check her progress over my shoulder. Josh's voice on the cell is eager as he tells the others we're about to flee. Winnie beats her wings and skims the floor to the first chunk of eel. Her golden beak catches the moonlight and an amber eye flashes at me. She swoops forward for the second chunk before I blink. There are five pieces to go before she'll reach me.

Little shocks of anticipation fire off in my fingers as they close on the door levers. I yank inward. They groan and I realize too late that there isn't anything nearby to prop them open with. Josh has read my mind, and he runs to tip his weight against one as my shoulder blades press the other. Winnie is two chunks of eel away.

Her wings extend, and their individual feathers ripple and fan out. From the sidewalk the lampposts illuminate the spectrum of browns on her wingspan, running from damp earth to coffee made weak with cream. The wings are bent at the joint like a bat's, and then they straighten, doubling in length, longer than I am tall. The baby hairs on my temples flutter as she sweeps her wings to the ground, her impossibly white head rearing back.

At that instant, with the savage bird three feet away, her eyes trained on me as though I'm prey, the sharp hook of her beak made for tearing into skin, I understand Ben. I see him as clear as if he were standing between me and the eagle. I hate, hate, hate the museum and Winnie's captors as much as he did—*does*. She's wild and fierce and she's been reduced to living in a cage and eating sushi from the floor. And I hate myself almost as much for calling this beautiful beast Winnie, aloud or in my head, for not thinking of a better escape, something that would have allowed her to be a majestic animal, to be what she is.

Winnie makes it to the remaining limp piece of eel, a foot before the threshold. I swear she looks directly at me, daring me to try and stop her. The indigo sky looms open to her and she buffets the air with her wings and takes off, leaving the last pathetic scrap of sushi on the floor.

— 2 2 —

I am reckless.

I am a heaving chest.

I am alive, alive, *alive* and out of breath and shouting and slapping my thighs until they sting. I land in the SUV after leaping through the open door; I don't feel the impact. Duncan slams on the gas and we shoot forward. There's no alarm shrieking, and the screeching of his four tires around corners is unnecessary and potentially drawing attention to our getaway. No one gives a crap. Let the police, their sirens throwing color across the night, come after us.

"Holy fuck!" Rusty whoops. Josh punches the sky through the sunroof and howls like he's gone mad. Duncan hits the horn for three blasts.

"You should have seen Winnie up close, B," Josh says. "Her wings were this wide." He spreads his arms all the way out. Duncan slaps Josh's hand away from his face. Josh continues unaffected. "The eagle looked right at Lana." He points two fingers from his eyes to mine. "And then Winnie bowed her head like she was *thanking Lana* for her freedom." He palms his hands in a humble gesture. "The bird was in such a hurry she left the last piece of sushi!"

I bite the inside of my cheek hard. I want to say: *Why would she thank us?* She was probably cursing us for letting her rot in there for so long. She left the last piece of eel because she's a wild animal who prefers to hunt her dinner. The sushi was *beneath* her. It had nothing to do with her being in a hurry.

I frown at the seat in front of me. Josh reinvented the eagle as a tame pet, no fiercer than a dog begging for steak at the dinner table. He wanted to stay in the museum with me after he sent the others away. Josh wanted to leap into the spring and search for evidence. I usually admire Josh's confidence. But not everything is harmless. Imagining that wild animals don't bite is not the same as knowing they bite and accepting the risk. One is brave and the other is foolish.

Becca squishes her face to the window, trying to peer up at the dark sky. "Where do you think Winnie will go?" she asks after she's given up.

"Far away from here," Carolynn says.

"Where are we going? Shell Shores to bonfire?" Duncan asks over his shoulder.

"Too close to town," Josh tells him. "The police could be on patrol, and they'd see the smoke. We've lucked out so far."

"Your pool house?" Rusty hollers, throwing wadded-up paper at the back of Duncan's head.

"Veto," Carolynn says. "Let's go to the lighthouse at the point. It won't be locked and we can take the stairs to the top."

We merge onto the two-lane highway that follows the cape in the direction of the lighthouse. Duncan sews a zigzag between the two lanes. Becca spills the schnapps as she raises it to toast the eagle's rescuers. Carolynn twirls a finger in the air, but even she can't temper her smile. Five miles and a snaking gravel access road later, we pull into the lot at the base of a grassy slope. A narrow and steep staircase is cut into the rock bed of the hill. The hill's slope ends abruptly where the land collapsed into the sea. The cliffs are black and sparkling, and we studied fragments in geology during the month we learned about the unusual mineral composition of our tiny island.

At the hill's summit, Gant's historic lighthouse shoots into the sky. The tower's stones are veiny with fissures and caulked with green-and-rust-colored moss. A single scarlet door is the only entrance or exit. The tower has a medieval look, as though it's the lighthouse on a war-torn island above a sapphire sea. It's been here since Gant was feral and uninhabited. The island's rocky shelf has always been dangerous for mariners, and sailboats still capsize catching on the shallow, jagged reefs that jut out into the sound like the points of a star. The lighthouse's craggy walls, gallery deck, and gold light fracturing and banding from the lantern room are only ornamental now, since most boats are equipped with radar.

Dad took Ben and me here a few times. We liked climbing the spiral staircase, mostly because of the way it amplified our voices. It gave ordinary talk a magical resonance. Tourists with their foldout paper maps of the island line up for their turn into the lighthouse on summer days. This point is the southern tip of the island; its least inhabited cape.

"How did you know the door wouldn't be locked, Car?" Josh asks as he holds the rusted monstrosity open for us. We shuffle up the stairs. Duncan leads, the girls are behind him, then Josh and me, and Rusty last.

"This is Carolynn's special spot for all her romantic trysts,"

Becca purrs, throwing a devilish wink over her shoulder. She pokes Carolynn in the side, and Carolynn squirms away. They end up clasping hands and swinging them like little girls do. "Didn't she ever take you here, Josh?" Becca teases.

Carolynn laughs at that. "Yeah, right. Josh and I spent most of the three months we went out with his moms. Remember how they'd find little excuses to check on us in your room?" she asks. "I gained ten pounds from all the cookies they brought up."

Josh smiles at his shoes, remembering, and then says to me, "We were only fourteen, and she was my first girlfriend. My moms have gotten a lot less protective since then."

The gold light seeping through the grates in the stairs bounces off all the surfaces and gives him the look of a freshly baked gingerbread boy. He holds his hand out for me to take. I feel a blush spread as I do. Josh is straightforward and kind and interested in *me*—Lana McBrook, formerly and inaccurately known as Uni-Boob—and he doesn't care about our separate histories. So what if he's too optimistic and his bravery borders on foolish? So what if he's friends with the two-faced Becca? Josh is the kind of boy who makes you giggle dumbly, smile dreamily, and sigh like a leaky balloon. Josh Parker is why girls doodle hearts and listen to love songs on repeat. After a summer of awful, I need someone who will reinvent the world as a more harmless version of what it is.

There is constant, echoing chatter and the percussive melody of shoes as we climb. "You don't remember hearing it at sleepovers?" Carolynn asks me when she starts up about an old ghost story she swears is infamous on Gant.

"No," I say, trying to look neutral. I am not. It is because of Becca that I was excluded from all those sleepovers. I also don't like hearing that word: *ghost.*

I haven't been thinking of Ben in terms of ghosts. I haven't completely lost my grip, though I have been thinking of him in terms of *being here,* after death. Not only being here in some wispy, spirit way, but present enough to poison two people, chase one of them through the woods, and leave my rosary in our hiding spot.

"God, the story used to freak me out so bad. So there's this lighthouse guy, a keeper," Carolynn continues.

"They're called wickies," Rusty breaks in. He gets dubious looks. He tugs the bill of his baseball hat lower, and I lose sight of his bashful eyes. "I did a report in the third grade. So what? I like lighthouses. They're the catchers of the ocean. They make the calls and tell the rest of the team the way to play."

"That's not why you like them, Rusty Pipe." Duncan chuckles, craning around, his expression all smarmy self-satisfaction. Then to us, "He does 'cause they're shaped like—"

"We get it," Carolynn says. She shoves him to continue up the stairs. "Okay, so this guy lives in the cottage we passed on the access road, and he was responsible for lighting the lantern in the lighthouse each night." She skips two steps up, leading our procession with the look of a morbid tour guide. "He lived on Gant with his wife, and they were all alone because there wasn't a town here yet. This one winter his wife gets really sick. Tuberculosis." Every few steps she glances back at us to confirm she has our undivided attention. "Her death is drawn out, and he can barely leave her side without her coughing and choking on blood. But he does. Every day at dusk he sprints to the lighthouse, runs up these stairs"—she stomps her ballet flat—"lights the lantern, adds the amount of oil it needs to burn through the night, and then rushes home to his wife. He does it for thirty nights in a row, and thirty nights he returns and she's fine. The thirty-first night it's the same deal, except that he trips up these stairs."

Carolynn spins and we halt. Her eyes shine and she points to the step Duncan's on, one below her. "His boot caught right there." Duncan reverses a step hastily and then rolls his neck, making it crackle, like it was all part of one nonchalant movement. There's a stirring of a wicked smile on Carolynn's lips as she continues, "He fell to his knees and popped up, but he was slower. He limped. The trip to the top and back home took no more than a minute longer than usual." She tucks a loose lock of hair behind her ear and adds in a regretful tone, "But that's all it took."

Carolynn twirls around to continue the climb. "What happened, Car?" Duncan asks, uncharacteristically somber.

"The wife choked on her own blood. Asphyxiated." Carolynn turns for a beat to drag her finger horizontally across her neck. "The keeper burst into his house to see his wife's body spasm, one final time. He was heartbroken. Alone. It was too cold to dig a grave. He figured that the ground would thaw in time. One night turns into three, and three to five, and before he knows it, he's been inside with the body for a week."

Rusty's sneakers nip at my heels. "The corpse stinks, and he's slowly going mad. He thinks that she's coming back to life, twitching, moving." Carolynn pauses as she skips a step. "He sees her sit up. He watches her make tea. The guy was losing his shit." My chin drops to my chest. I gawk at the metal risers and grates of the stairs. Is it my imagination or is there a shadow below, soundlessly keeping pace with us? Is it listening to Carolynn's story, which might as well be about me losing my mind? "Then she begins talking to him, and she's a real vindictive nag. 'Why did you leave me? You wanted me to die.'" Carolynn intones this part in a ghostly boom. "When dusk rolls around that day, she tells the keeper not to light the lantern. 'Don't leave. The darkness will come for me.' So he doesn't go. He can't bear to desert her again. He stays beside her rotting corpse, holding her decomposing hand, having both sides of a conversation."

I watch Carolynn's bobbing head over the boys'. I've never heard her talk like this. The Carolynn of a few days ago would have said that ghost stories were boy stuff. This Carolynn is commanding an audience and licking her lips, she's so satisfied with herself. She reminds me of Ben. Not only reminds me of him, this story feels linked to ours. Carolynn makes me wonder about our island. Is Gant an in-between place where under the right circumstances, the dead aren't gone?

"On that particular night," she continues, "there was an ocean liner sailing down the sound for Tacoma. There was no light to warn them away from the island. The ship's bottom caught a shallow reef, and the rocks slashed it open. The boat sank and the passengers drowned, only a hundred yards from the coast. Clouds covered the moon, and they couldn't even see the island to swim for it." There's a tense silence. Our footsteps echo to the bottom of the staircase and then boomerang back, as if there's someone chasing after us.

Duncan is the first to speak. "You made that whole thing up."

"Did not." Carolynn stops dead in her tracks and faces us. "I swear, cross my heart and hope to die, stick a thousand needles in my eye." Her lips blur, undecided between a smile and a frown. "It's in the history books. One hundred and thirty-three people drowned. The keeper and his wife still haunt the cape."

"That is not in a history book," Duncan says. He makes a grab for Carolynn's wrist as she takes the stairs two at a time to escape him.

"How would you know? You've never read even one book," Carolynn calls back, laughing. Duncan gives us this perplexed, crooked grin and then jogs after her. Their panting and hammering footsteps surround us until they reach the top and the sounds go muffled.

I keep staring through the metal risers. The shadows below us are ours. Still . . . I feel like we're being observed. Then we wade into the lantern room's pool of light and the heat hits me like the rush of warmth that one and only time I let Becca drag me to a tanning bed in Seattle. And I sniff to myself, because even when Becca was at her nicest, she was convincing me to bake my skin in a tanning bed— basically a cancer-oven.

My eyes adjust to the brilliant light. The gas flame of the lantern is lit automatically by electricity at dusk. A thousand prisms in a hexagon surround a steel frame, and each is ablaze with refracted light. I'm hypnotized by the hundreds of flashing mirrors that make up the lighthouse's lens.

On the gallery deck the night is cold and autumn-y. The wind isn't as still here as it was in the harbor. The lantern's glow frames our silhouettes, sears their edges in bright light. I look around me at luminous faces.

Duncan and Rusty survey the ground below. The shore is treeless, only sandy, windblown dunes and cliffs that cut them off from all but the sound.

"Bonfire?" Duncan says when he's reached his threshold for contemplative stares out at the water. *Oh yeahs* and *definitelys* are traded. I've only been here once before with the core, on the beach below three weeks ago, in the middle of the afternoon. There was a wedding tent erected at Shell Shores and kids migrated up the point instead, willing to put up with the staring tourists at the lighthouse to get a little beach time in. We lit a fire in a circle of rocks that looked like a small-scale Stonehenge. Becca threw twenty party poppers, one at a time, into the flames to get them to explode. They didn't, not one. She clapped in anticipation with each try. Willa cupped her hand at my ear and whispered, *Ignorance really is bliss, huh?*

I shuffle with the others toward the helix-shaped staircase. Josh catches my hand. "Lana and I will be down in a few, guys," he tells the others.

"Wrap it up, bro," Duncan hollers from where he's descending the stairs. Rusty cracks a joke about the size of the condom needed for the lighthouse, and their laughs fade as they continue. Becca winks at me before locking arms with Carolynn and sauntering away, their hips swinging in unison.

"C'mere," Josh says, leading us to the rail of the gallery deck. Below us the waves beat the tide pools at the base of the cliff. The spray of salt water floats up into the atmosphere, and there's a fine mist that coats our faces. Little drops catch in my eyelashes. Josh exhales, ghosts swirling from his mouth. He rests his arms on the rail and looks straight out at the water. Pinpoints of light like tears in the cloth of the horizon are scattered where Bainbridge Island lies across the sound. Other than that, there's nothingness—no, not nothing, *infiniteness*.

We are infinite as the night sky and space and those bottomless caverns in the ocean that divers explore but never reach the bottom of. I start to wonder if people are like that—bottomless, boundless. No matter how much you know them, they can always surprise you.

Josh slides until there's more of my right side touching him than isn't. "You were amazing today." His voice is warm and soothing as a lullaby.

I tilt my head to find his sparkling eyes; the freckles sprayed on his cheeks from the summer sun are barely visible. "*You* were amazing. I couldn't have pulled off the museum without you."

"I don't just mean the prank," he says, half smiling. "You took care of B and Car earlier and you've been steady all night. *You* are incredible."

It's hard to hold his stare. My cheeks burn. My smile is too eager and—who are we kidding—panicked. "*You're* incredible," I say. I'm stupid with nerves. Josh's hair is stirred by the wind, and I want so badly to reach up and let it tickle my fingertips, and all of a sudden I think, *What the hell.* Tell him. "Carolynn would call me PG-13, and Becca would die at my lameness, but I want to tell you anyway."

He smirks playfully and nudges my shoe with his. "What?"

I am brave, bold, and alive. "I like you. Always have," I tell him.

There's an awful moment where his face goes surprised. Then a smile crinkles his eyes and nose in a way that makes my nose tingle. The corners of his mouth dig deep in his full cheeks. He leans until he's only two dark, blue eyes looming before me. "I wish I'd gotten to know you way earlier than this summer. And I'm not going to waste any more time," he says. "I like you, too. A lot."

Although very nice, Josh is not the sort of boy who asks permission to kiss you. Thank God, because my voice retreats somewhere into my toes as his mouth presses to mine. His lips are warm and dry. He tastes minty and full of possibility. He pulls my waist to his, and the way I flatten against him makes me present, like I exist in a whole new way, more than I used to, as if I were only a sketch and I've been painted vivid with acrylics. I'm powerful and can be anyone, go anywhere, do anything, even kiss Josh Parker, even smash my hip bones to his.

I wonder if our merged profiles are projected across the water by the lighthouse's lantern and if there's a ferry captain two miles out watching us kiss. The moment feels that big, epic, like all of Washington can feel the reverberations. I wonder if the others can see us from where they are below. I imagine Carolynn watching as the tide washes over her silver ballet flats. Carolynn's lips aren't the last that touched Josh's. Maggie's are. Dead Maggie's mouth was open as Josh heaved air into her lungs. Alive Maggie's mouth was always open and willing to Ben. If the whole island can feel what's happening between Josh and me, can Ben?

I fight to focus only on the impossible warmth of Josh. It rushes from his mouth to mine, down my throat, fills my chest, spreads bumps on the skin under my bra. I place my hand on Josh's sternum. I am determined. His heart punches my palm.

Like mine did that last night with Ben.

We watched a movie, robots and time travel, on the short sofa in the living room. We put the TV on mute to talk as we ate lobster tacos and I swigged beer. Ben turned to me suddenly. I had just finished taking a gulp from the bottle. I winced at the beer's bitter taste, even though it was this wimpy apricot-flavored ale that Diane likes.

The bottle left my hand cold and wet. I wiped it on his jeans, *right on his thigh*, and giggled over not having a napkin.

"This is my summer," he said. It was the way we told each other we were happy. Our secret code. I was so close that I could find that slight bend in the bridge of his nose. A long-ago break healed. He never told me how it happened. He never talked about before he came to the island. He went pale, or sulky, or stubborn if I asked. If I pushed, he stood up and left, so of course, I didn't push.

I smiled. "It's my summer too." We were sitting so close—*too close*—but I couldn't remember who sat down last, who was responsible for us sitting thigh to thigh? I was, I worried. I hoped that maybe—*maybe*—I wasn't as bad and dirty as I thought.

No, that's a lie.

I didn't hope to be good.

I hoped for Ben to be as bad and dirty as I wanted to be.

That Ben had moved closer to me after I sat down.

"Ben?" I said it as a question. He laid his last taco on the plate. A blond brow shot up. His gray eyes were opaque, variation-less; the color of the sound, ancient stone and moody sky. I loved that about them. They were unreadable. But I usually guessed what he thought. Not then.

I admit that I've read too many books—the kind with sea-blown green dunes, and Gothic mansions, and angry, poor boys who love who they shouldn't. Ben had told me too many stories. I was drunk off apricot beer and romantic notions. Rather than speak, I took Ben's hand and pressed his palm to my chest. Not so he'd feel my boobs. I placed it over my heart. It was hammering through my rib cage, the muscle of my chest, my skin, his hand, and into my fingers that covered his. It was pounding like his hand was calling to it. And maybe it was.

He opened his mouth to speak. The doorbell rang, three frantic whines, and he leaped up to answer. Maggie stormed in, even more agitated when she noticed me on the couch. I don't know what he planned to say; I used to think I never would. Now I'm not so sure.

"Lana?" Josh releases my waist and holds my shoulders. "Are you okay? Was that too soon?"

"No," I say.

"No? You don't want to kiss?" Josh's hands drop away.

"No, I mean yes, I want to kiss." My hands fly between us. "I just . . . I don't know. Everything, tonight, became overwhelming, and I spaced out thinking."

Josh frowns momentarily, and then the tension and lines ease. He smiles, looks to his feet, and peeks back at me. "If you let me kiss you again, I swear I won't make it so easy for you to get distracted."

A flutter of the skin on his neck. Can I see his pulse? "Yeah," I say, "let's."

I move to him and all his charming Josh-ness. I had a crush on this boy long before I knew that Ben existed. I've gone blushy over Josh since before I even understood why I was blushing. Years and years before I ever noticed the slightest deviation in the bridge of Ben's nose; or felt his laugh vibrating in my bones; or closed my eyes tight and imagined his mouth on mine so that a pressure would build, one that made my stomach ache and connected with a place I touched, shyly; or curled on my comforter, all shame and guilt and messy, useless feelings for a boy I was awful and weak for wanting.

Josh's lips are hesitant. I move mine and am dizzy that I'm kissing

248 • ALEXANDRA SIROWY

Josh, not only the other way around. He sighs. I scrunch my eyes closed because they want to open. I touch his hair. It's soft fluff, and I can feel his pulse in my wrist against his neck. I think, *Yes, this could be enough.* Could be. If I wasn't stuck loving Ben.

Ben was a strong wind, his origin mysterious, his effect as invisible as it was undeniable. Ben was necessary to me, and I want to believe that he found his way back from the nowhere place of death not just for revenge on those who were nasty to me but for what comes after. With me.

I want Ben to need me like I need him.

I want us to need each other like the summer needs sun.

— 23 —

pull back from Josh. He opens his eyes with a bewildered and good-natured smile. "Do you mind if we go down to the others?" I ask.

He grabs my hand and looks briefly serious. "I would have waited longer to kiss you if the night hadn't seemed perfect. But I've got to admit something."

I wait. Josh Parker doesn't have a confession as big as the one I do. He runs a hand through his hair and takes a breath, pupils dilating a little with the exhale. "The night I saw you and Willa at Marmalade's, and I came over to say hey, Carolynn sent me. She didn't tell me straight out that you liked me. She just pointed you out and said she heard you'd been really torn up about Ben and that it would be nice for me to say hi." His frown is so solemn.

After a long, surprised silence I say, "I can't believe she did that. Not that I'm upset over it—the opposite. It was nice of her." I don't wonder how Carolynn knew that Josh's attention would make me happy. I might have let it slip to Becca when we were kids that I had a crush on him. It's predictable; most girls like Josh Parker. I do wonder why Carolynn cared about making me happy, though.

"Car did me a huge favor," Josh says. "If she hadn't sent me over to you, then I wouldn't have gotten to know you. I just wanted to be honest, because I worried she or Becca might tell you. Full disclosure." He looks pleased at being mature.

I look toward the others. The bonfire burns bright, and the four of them move around it like they're pagans in a ritual ceremony for the goddess of fire. "I really like you, Josh. I liked kissing you."

"Hey"—he grips my hand—"school's about to start, and I don't want you to feel pressured. We can be friends or more. We can wait to figure it out when things aren't so . . . intense."

Treading down the spiraling stairs of the lighthouse, I can't help but sink into myself, to the truth. I go way, way back in time.

How did I let it get so bad? How didn't I stomp out that flicker of hope each time it stretched? I was inexperienced and silly. I was dreamy. Ben didn't help keep my feet on the ground. After I heard those whispers freshman year, which I didn't realize originated from the lie Becca told, I was awkward with Ben. My hands were gigantic swinging at my side. I couldn't find a place where they wouldn't accidentally brush his. I weaved when I walked beside him—how close was too close? My brain was swollen with words, and I'd fish out all the wrong ones. I'd blush out of nowhere.

Winter break of freshman year made it worse. Once a month, Gant's foreign cinema shows movies in English. We went. That wasn't weird. We both loved stories, so we were obvious movie freaks. We walked out of the theater, side by side, and Ben threw his arm over my shoulders. I ducked to restore the space between us.

"What's your deal?" he asked, stopping in the middle of the

crowd filtering out of the theater around us and making a divergent stream of moviegoers.

"Most step-siblings aren't all touchy-feely," I said quietly. My eyes darted over the crowd. Was someone from school observing us? "What will people think if we act like that?"

He laughed full-throated, head back and mouth open like he planned to swallow the universe. "Who gives a shit? I love you." He replaced his arm, and then added right into my ear so that his lips made contact with my skin, "And fuck everybody else."

When he said that, two things happened. The awkwardness making my hands too big for my body, the anxiety over what I was wearing, how careful I was to keep a foot away in public, vanished for the night. I had Ben and Ben had me and fuck everybody else. It returned first thing Monday morning. This would happen a lot. We would be carefree and easy on the *Mira*, or at home, or at Swisher Spring, but the instant we weren't alone anymore, I would get caught up in wondering how others perceived us.

The second thing occurred because of that sentence—*I love you*—spoken in his voice as molten as the inside of a golden marshmallow. It was the first and last time Ben said it to me; the solitary time we talked about what we felt outside of our secret language of summer.

Hearing it made all the rumors and glares worth enduring, because I loved Ben way more than I was supposed to.

And tonight, on the gallery deck of the lighthouse, while Josh's lips were on mine, I realized that I still do. Even if Ben is a vengeful force, a mere residue of the boy he used to be, it doesn't change anything. It should. I know.

As we join the others, Becca produces more schnapps from a long-forgotten flask at the bottom of her purse, and the others drain it. I don't want a sip because I can taste Josh's ChapStick. Then I grow sick and guilty thinking that Ben is somewhere and I shouldn't be holding on to this souvenir from kissing Josh. I apply my own strawberry lip balm to stop tasting Josh's. The rest of the night is like this: I teeter between giddiness over Josh liking me and hoping that Ben is on our island, waiting for me.

What happens once I sneak inside my house hours later isn't such a big leap. I stop in the kitchen to pull a tablet of paper and pen out of a drawer. The pen hesitates, and then it's all so painfully clear. A memory of a long-ago night roars in, and I know just what to write.

It was weeks before Ben left for Guatemala. Middle of the night at the fire pit. I was blathering on about not wanting to go to winter ball. *Catatonically boring*, I declared it. I might have slathered it on too thick, because I was self-conscious that Ben suspected the real reason I refused to go. I had no friends who'd be there. Girls would ask coyly where my date was—or, not so coyly, if Ben was showing up later.

Ben was quiet for a long time, and then he said, "How can you stand it? How can you let them get away with it?"

I started. "Who get away with what?"

He waited. Like usual he blinked first, looked to his hands, which were impaling a marshmallow on a roasting stick, and he said, "No one and nothing specific." He shrugged. "I just mean Gant. I'm just griping about Gant. Again. Like usual."

I laughed, light-headed with relief. "You won't always have to live here."

"I know. But what about you?" His marshmallow caught fire, and he blew to extinguish it. He was always putting them directly into the flames.

"I won't live here forever either. I'll move for college."

"Gant's more a state of mind than a place," Ben said.

I inspected the golden flesh of my marshmallow. "How so?"

He tossed his roasting stick with the charred remains into the blaze. "It's thinking that you need flavored water and two-hundred-dollar jeans and that you need to give a shit what people think about you."

I offered him the marshmallow at the end of my stick. He popped it into his mouth. "You're wearing designer jeans."

He chewed the gooey morsel. "I know." He frowned. "I'm a hypocrite." I tried to laugh it off. His expression grew more serious. "Really, Lana. I'm the worst of them. I hate this place's obliviousness. I hate that I like grape-flavored water. I hate that I drive a car Cal bought me. I hate that I might go off to college and be just like the rest of them in a few years. I hate that you're not like you used to be. Someday it'll be different. I'll get off my ass and I'll do something and never come back."

"Don't say that. You'll come back for me." I was being silly and dense, focused mostly on readjusting a log in the pit to keep the fire going so I didn't have to respond to what he said about who I used to be. I pretended I hadn't heard him emphasize those words more than the rest.

"Of course I will. I'll always come back for you."

I smiled at him. "Swear it."

"I swear on summer." The muscle of his jaw twitched. He looked so determined.

"You'll only be in Guatemala for three months."

"A lot of crap can happen in three months. Will you be okay?"

I smiled to cover up my nerves. "Sure I will. I'm Lana the shark."

"Lana the brave," he said. I didn't imagine the ironic twist in his voice.

I shake the memory off on the trip to the lower terrace. The harbor is silent, the wind holding its breath. I deposit the note in our hiding spot. Short of shouting his name, letting it travel across the water, I can't think of a better way to get a message to him. I believe he'll find the paper, somehow, wherever he is, *whatever* he is. And he'll read it or sense what I wrote, and he'll know that I've put it together: He's come back for *me*.

You swore on summer.

I go to bed, memories of Ben amassing and flashing through my head. When will he reveal that he's still here and that he's fighting for me?

There are sirens the next morning. My first thought is that we've been caught. There were security cameras at the museum. Our break-in was recorded. Duncan's parents couldn't save us all with their influence; Duncan didn't keep his promise to protect us. Or worse, the police were tipped off about the rosary in my secret place, and they're coming to arrest me for Maggie and Ford.

The minutes tick on. The doorbell doesn't sound. My room is sun heated as I pull on shorts and flip-flops. The clock reads eleven thirty a.m., later than I've slept in weeks. I band my hair into a ponytail as I plod downstairs. Dad is long gone for work. Basel paces in the foyer, his angry yowls coming almost as fast and loud as the sirens that haven't stopped. I sweep him away with my foot and open the front door. The only way I can explain my lack of urgency is this: Josh kissed me last night; I know what his lips taste like; still, I thought of Ben.

Across the street, at the base of the grassy, tree-seamed slope, there are unmarked black sedans. Detectives. It's Tuesday and most of our neighbors are at work, but a few men and women stand as spectators on porches and verandas, coffee mugs held to their chests, slippers on their feet, as they peer at the commotion on Becca's front lawn. I walk outside just as Josh's Jeep shrieks to a stop next to Carolynn's car. He leaves it double-parked. He doesn't even close the driver's-side door. He cuts a direct path up the lawn, hurdles a border of hedges, and tramps through vines, their thorny stems dragging at his jeans. Carolynn is a heap on her knees at the yard's crest. She's between Rusty and Duncan. I feel for my house keys on the table by the door and automatically close and lock it behind me.

I drift toward Becca's house, flip-flops crunching grass under me, sun scorching my bare shoulders. Summer's last stand.

Becca's mom is in the middle of her driveway, supported by two EMTs carrying her to an ambulance. Her sheer stockings catch along the cobblestones. I reach the edge of Becca's lawn fast. Must have jogged.

Josh is crouched, arms wrapped around Carolynn. Her edges blur as she trembles. I hop over a border of sharp, sparkly black rocks between Becca's lawn and her neighbor's. It's the river of tar from one of Ben's stories. A village lives along a river of fetid, boiling tar, and a faceless creature in a long white robe appears at night to coax children from their beds. It has talons rather than hands, and it holds the kids under the bubbling river until they stop thrashing, until their skin's boiled off and a layer of tar has taken its place. Lana the brave ends the creature as it did its victims.

No. See what's here, in front of me.

The sun is hot on my scalp.

Good, that's real.

There's not a cloud or a drop of blue in the sky. It's colorless, a blank canvas on top of us. Carolynn groans and buckles into Josh. He curves around her. "They won't take her down," she says. Her words are as formless as her posture. Josh hooks her hair behind her ear. She smacks his hand away and then whimpers pathetically. She wants sympathy; she can't stomach it. Her knees shuffle under her as she struggles up on them.

Duncan tries to steady her, but she slaps at his arms wildly. "I don't need help. Becca does." Duncan kneels and holds his arms out, even as she beats them away. She lifts a bit, her legs as unsteady as her voice, and collapses. Her head thuds to Duncan's shoulder like a rock dropping to the bottom of the spring. It stays there.

"She drank too much schnapps this one night and she went on that rotten slide . . . she got rusty splinters in her butt." Carolynn covers her mouth to muffle a cry. "Her front door wasn't even locked— she *never* remembers to bolt the effing door. I went inside. I kept thinking, why is it such a pigsty in here? What's on the ground? Then I saw the swing set." It takes me a second to realize that Carolynn's switched from talking about that drunken night to this morning, where Becca is somewhere *they* won't take her down from.

"It's sick. It's fucking sick," Duncan says. His hand strokes Carolynn's hair, smoothing it down her shoulder. Her eyes flutter shut. I look away. It feels like spying.

Rusty kicks the grass. "I can't see my first kiss hanging like that. She was . . . God, she was such a freaking sweetheart." He winds his fingers in his curls and yanks.

"*She is*, not was," Josh insists. His voice recedes behind me.

I reach the others and continue on. Something is very wrong. *Swing set* and *rusted slide* and *hanging* and *Becca*. I pause at the porch. There's a Fourth of July banner left in the window and wilted herbs in a planter box, and I wonder how I didn't notice either yesterday. How have these little details escaped me? I glance down. The orangey-gold object at my feet stops time, and the current moment unfolds in the endless way a complex origami creature does.

I am in time-suspended space with the beak of a blackbird.

It's the missing piece from yesterday's pageant of dead animals. This beak is as slender as a pair of tweezers, two inches in length, and hooked at the tip. Its base, where it was severed from the bird's head, is a ring of red pulp and black feather. I swallow. This token on the welcome mat appears just for me. It's plucked from our stories and left to beckon me inside.

A warm brush of skin on my arm. Willa is beside me.

"Where did you come from?" I ask, feeling only half awake.

Willa stares at the beak. "Josh texted me. I drove over. Take my hand," she adds, and it seems like the best idea, so I do.

There's a cluster of police, squared shoulders turned to us, talking off to the left in the house. They don't notice two silent girls. I keep one eye on the ground for the severed beaks. On the kitchen floor there's a clot of three, and then one a foot later, and then two a yard beyond that. "What are you two doing? This is a crime scene," a male officer, frown dimpling his chin, tells us.

He moves to block our progress and reaches to spin me around. "Ward and Sweeny," I say.

"They asked you in here? To give a statement?"

I nod, lying. Willa's hand tightens on mine. "They're outside." The officer jerks his thumb to the terrace. His wiry brows quirk up as he adds, "But maybe you should wait. You girls shouldn't see that."

I shoulder by him toward the open door. There's more resistance in Willa's arm. She's dragging. I try to release her hand; I'm brave enough to go on alone, but she holds fast. The wind comes in waves of gray mist through the doors. All surfaces in the kitchen shine with salty spray. It's much cooler than it was in the sunny front yard. That's not unusual. The harbor has its own climate, its fog and wind kept trapped by the ring of houses and steep banks. We reach the door. I hear the air go out of Willa a split second before I look to the swing set.

Becca is a porcelain doll hanging from the top beam of the play structure. The chain of a swing is coiled around her neck. Her pink toenails are suspended a foot from the ground.

Her feet are slightly turned in on themselves; pigeon-toed. A skinny cream arm dangles at her side. Her other hand is caught between the chain and her neck. She tried to wriggle herself free before she suffocated. A thread of dried blood paints a line from the corner of her mouth to her chin. Her irises are frozen rolling back into her head, leaving too much unseeing white.

I think it before I catch myself: *Becca, you made my life small, and you deserved this.*

— 24 —

I close my eyes. The nightmare doesn't vanish. Parallels suggest themselves between the tableau of Becca hanging from the swing set and the dark make-believe of my childhood. This is the conclusion to Ben's story "The Lovely Scarecrow." It's what I couldn't remember yesterday. The half man, half demon who snips off the beaks of birds falls in love with a girl and is rejected. He cuts off her nose and hangs her from a tree with bird beaks in a wreath at her feet. Even as a kid I knew that was hate, not love. Ben's Lana hunts down the wicked half man and strings him up in the same way.

I drop my hands. Becca has her nose. She wouldn't deserve that. I shake my head at myself. She didn't deserve any of this. It's as if the villains in our stories strolled out into the sun. As if Ben the vengeful hero did. He killed Maggie, Ford, and Becca's dogs. Did he come for Becca also? I make a noise, or else Willa does, because an officer kneeling with a camera looks up from his work and shouts out. A wall of police and detectives come at us.

"Don't look."

"Get out of here."

"Close your eyes."

I try to resist their tide that's carrying me into the house. "This is . . . mine," I say, pointing to Becca over their shoulders.

Willa mutters something like, "Be quiet." She doesn't recognize the vignette in front of us. She only knows about the villainous monk and his rosary. I couldn't share all our stories with her if I wanted to; there are too many to remember.

"Take her down," I say, and then Willa and I are pulled apart. We cross over the threshold as a cop hoists a plastic tarp into the air. It parachutes over Becca and the swing set.

I'm given a glass of water as I'm propped on the couch. It sloshes over the rim, trickling between my fingers. There are water lilies on the upholstery and tears seeping from my eyes, running until they streak down my neck. Sweeny offers a tissue as she crouches at my feet. I ignore it and crane to see the unnaturally blue tarp covering Becca. She can't even see the sky. Becca was a liar. She was selfish and nasty. But she wasn't a monster. She didn't deserve to be treated as one of the mad villains in our stories.

I understand why she tried to impress others with secrets. Being a girl in high school is a lot like being under a microscope, all your imperfections magnified and noted. I get not wanting to be defined by the messiness of your family. It's easier to point at some other girl and say, *Look what a loser she is.* Not right, but easy.

Still. Becca didn't deserve this ending. Not ever, but especially not after this last month. She'd say, *I've always been so jealous of your natural highlights. Your freckles make me smile. How did I survive without you before this summer?* All these little boosts built me up. Becca made me feel worthy in a way that only another girl can. She was all

THE TELLING · 261

entitlement, peppermint, and no judgment. And sitting on her lumpy couch, watching the suggestion of her body under the tarp, I forgive her. Maybe she would have grown into a better person. Maybe she would have ruined some unsuspecting girl's college experience. Doesn't matter; she didn't deserve to die.

Sweeny's hand is light on my knee. Willa is flanked by two policemen and slumped in an overstuffed chair.

"Lana, can you hear me?" Sweeny asks, enunciating in an exaggerated way. The pocket of her silk blouse is stretched open by a compact digital camera. She was photographing the crime scene. Becca loved to have her photo taken. A man in a tan suit removes the glass from my hand. Everyone's staring. "Lana, is there anything you can tell me about what you just saw?"

Panic makes me shudder. My thoughts skip from Becca's hanged form to the outline of a monk clasping a rosary. They are stories, fiction, morbid fantasy. That's the problem. They belong inside an imagination and not splashed around Gant by a vengeful hero. I wonder at what point a vengeful hero becomes a villain. Did Ben become the villain long before this and I just didn't have the heart to admit it?

"You don't understand," I mutter. "What's out there . . . it's out of my head." I jab my temple. "It doesn't exist. It isn't supposed to be real."

"Lana, do you have any idea who hurt your friend?" Sweeny squeezes my knees. "Is there anything you can tell me about the person who did this?" I want to push her hands off me. Her eyes are darting, pinched slightly, suspicious. She's right: I'm hiding something.

"I need to ask you some difficult questions, Lana." She speaks slowly and loudly. She doesn't need to. My senses are fine-tuned. I hear the swish of her silk blouse as she shifts her weight. "Your house is three down from here, correct?"

One quick nod from me.

"Did you see anyone out of the ordinary on your street this morning? Think hard. Did you hear anything?"

"No," I say. "I was in my room. I can't see Becca's house from my window. I didn't hear a thing until the sirens."

Willa's eyes are closed, her lips twitch, and her face is blotchy. She's trying not to cry. It's hard to stop thinking about Becca as the little girl with her hair in braids, her two front teeth, eyelashes, and eyes overwhelming her other features. Our friendship started with pumping our legs on my swing set, and it ends as she dangles by her neck from hers.

The tan suit slides a chair behind Sweeny. She roosts on the edge. She's taller than I am on the sunken-in couch, and it makes me feel younger looking up at a roomful of adults. "What did you mean that this is something out of your head?" Sweeny says. I make my face impassive. I hadn't meant to say that. "And while you were out on the deck, you said, 'It's mine.'" She glances toward Willa, whose eyes remain closed, and then refocuses her attention on me. "I'm certain that Ms. Owen heard it also."

The uniforms and suits wait for my answer. They're a smear of square chins dappled with whiskers and stroked by thumbs, fists on hips, and doughy waistlines that spill over belts with each deep breath. Sweeny is the only woman in the bunch. She has a better poker face. Only the sweat stains bleeding through the fabric of her blouse hint at her anxiety.

I shove my hands under my thighs to hide their shaking. Willa's eyes open. I read them clearly. *Tell them.* Willa isn't the one who needs to find words for the impossible. *My dead stepbrother used to tell stories; I might have been addicted to their gore and adventure; I think that Ben found a way to come back; he's picking off the boys and girls who were cruel to me.*

Sweeny would have to consider me a suspect. All signs point to me as a killer, acting out stories only two of us knew. What's worse is that I have a motive. Maggie killed Ben. I despised Ford. Becca spread lies about me.

"I had a nightmare about blackbirds last night," I answer at last. "We found the one with the dead dogs yesterday." I am guilty for lying, but Becca can't be helped; she's gone. I wonder how gone, though, if our island is the kind of in-between place where the dead can exist.

Sweeny watches me. "Had anyone ever told you that rosary peas were poisonous before the day Detective Ward and I spoke to you about them?" I let the couch cushions swallow more of me. I fade into their pale, watercolor world. "I'm not asking because anyone suspects you, Lana." *No, not yet.* "The coroner determined that Ford Holland, the boy who disappeared several nights ago, was poisoned by them also. These crimes are quite unusual, puzzling with surreal elements."

"I didn't know about rosary peas," I lie softly.

"Humph," she sighs. Perhaps the note of disbelief isn't really there. Sweeny leans forward. "I adhere to one principle in solving my cases, Lana. I believe that without exception everything is related and that atypical events and violent crimes should be viewed in relation to one another. Common links need to be identified. Do you understand?"

I shake my head, even though I worry I do. In my peripheral

vision, Willa cranes forward; a puzzle's been presented for her to solve.

"There have been an unprecedented number of violent deaths perpetrated on this island over the last two months. First your step-brother's in June, then Ms. Lewis's, followed by Mr. Holland's, and now this gruesome hanging. Their proximity in location and time would be enough to link them, at least preliminarily; their uniquely surreal circumstances strengthen this link. As a detective, it's my job to ask how these victims are connected. Are they the random victims of one killer? Are they connected only by location and season? Or do they have more in common?"

My inhale is harsh in my ears.

"At first glance you are a common link," she says purposefully. "There has to be a reason for that, correct?" She tilts her head, wait-ing. I give her nothing. "Why would an ordinary teenager be con-nected to four separate tragic deaths when most go their entire lives without suffering one? Detective Ward believes that you are not ordinary or innocent. He's been exploring the possibility that you are either directly involved or that you know the perpetrator and are keeping his or her name from us. We're still looking for Fitzgerald Moore. We've been told by several community members that Ben had a friendship with him and that the Holland boy's older brother attacked him several years ago.

"We've been to his campsite, and it doesn't appear that he's slept there for a week or more. The detective here believes that you may be keeping quiet because of a misguided sense of compassion for this sick individual. I may not agree with my colleague, but Mr. Moore's whereabouts do need to be ascertained." She raises a nail-bitten finger. "It is my suspicion that our focus should be trained not on you, but rather on your stepbrother."

I wait; so does Sweeny. Ward's glare pins me to the couch. They couldn't possibly suspect what I believe. I'm bewildered, and it must show, because Sweeny gives Ward a meaningful glance before she continues. "I'm operating under the assumption that Ben's death was the inciting incident to all this. It led to Maggie, to Ford, and now here, to your friend." Her eyes flick toward the terrace, where the breeze rustles the tarp. "I believe that finding your stepbrother's killer means finding the perpetrator of these related crimes. Scorned girlfriends don't usually plot carjackings. I knew Maggie was withholding information from us, and I suspected that she conspired with the unidentified man on the highway. Was the murder premeditated? Was it a carjacking gone terribly wrong? What if Maggie wasn't more than an unwitting accomplice?

"This is a theory that I've spent the last two months searching for proof of. Ms. Lewis's body being found suggests that she was under duress, perhaps to keep quiet about the identity of Ben's murderer. What if under coercion, Maggie was prompted to show up at your home as she did? Perhaps she was not the mastermind of the attack and instead was tasked with drawing Ben from home that night. If this is the case, it isn't Maggie's anger with Ben over the end of a relationship but this unknown man's motive in question. Few teenage boys have deadly acquaintances. At first I looked at possible enemies of your father and stepmother." My eyebrows pinch. I've been thinking of Ben's killer as Maggie's accomplice, her friend even. What if this isn't the case? What if she couldn't describe the shadow man's face because she was afraid to?

Sweeny's theory means that Ben shares a killer with the others, with Becca, and if that's the case, then there are no traces of Ben left over. Ben isn't a vengeful hero or villain. "Your father is well liked in the community; we didn't find any grudges against him. But Diane was more difficult to investigate," Sweeny continues, "both because there's little information available and because she wasn't forthcoming when I interviewed her in person at Calm Coast. We can't compel her without evidence that she's willfully withholding. And her doctors are adamant that she may not have the mental faculties to remember."

"She's sad," I whisper.

Sweeny frowns. "True as that may be, it's unusual when the mother of a dead child doesn't cooperate fully." An awkward moment passes. "I believe that if I find your stepbrother's killer, I will have found the person guilty of all this."

An abrupt ache is opening up in my chest and I want to touch my knees to it, curl into a ball, and go invisible. "Are you aware that Ben went to eight different schools in eight states during the six years before Diane married your father, Lana?"

My fingernails dig into the fleshy stuffing of the couch. When we were little, I knew that magical things appear out of nowhere. To me, Ben was the most magical. I wanted Ben to be past-less. It meant that there was nothing else to know about him. "No," I say.

"I obtained Ben's school records, which included the transcript from his middle school before he moved to Gant. Then I called that school and requested those records and so on. This is how I plotted Diane and Ben's progress across the country. They lived for no longer than ten months in each town. Short durations like that are unusual unless a parent has a job that relocates him or her often. I can't find any record of Diane working. None of the schools had emergency contact info for family other than Diane. The last school I located, an elementary in Atlanta where he was in the second grade, had no previous records. It's where their trail ends." She watches my reaction. "Do you know where Ben was born, Lana?"

I'm nauseated answering. "The south."

"The south where?"

"South of the country." I am lost and embarrassed at how little I know. "Don't police have access to past addresses? Can't you type in *Diane and Ben Wright* and let your database spit out the answers?"

"Not always. Not under certain circumstances," Ward says, stepping out from behind Sweeny and adding, "Did Ben ever share memories with you of his early childhood?" before I can get *What circumstances?* out. "A city or state or landmark he remembered? An amusement park or zoo they spent a day at? Someone's—*anyone's*—name?"

"I don't think so." Ben rarely shared memories. If he did, they were disjointed and brightly painted snapshots of a bizarre nomadic life. I knew they moved around; I didn't know how often or why.

"And you know none of the places Ben lived before the second grade," Sweeny says.

I squint, trying to picture what Ben might have looked like so young. Although our walls are covered with framed pictures of our family of four, there are no photos of Ben before Gant. "Ben lived with his mom," I say, and then, "I'm going to be sick. I need to go home, please."

Sweeny's expression falls, and her lips flatten into a straight line.

"I understand. Maybe tomorrow I can come by. Once we've processed evidence here, I'm sure we'll have additional questions. My condolences regarding your friend. The officer"—she waves to a policeman crossing from the kitchen—"will walk you out."

As I'm led away, I watch the shrinking double doors over my shoulder and another officer dragging the blue tarp to the ground. The swing set groans as a strong gust of wind sets Becca's boneless, rag-doll body swinging.

We were so stupid last night with our prank, bonfire, traded kisses, and peppermint schnapps. I've been so stupid to believe—*to hope*—that Ben could be here. It's sick that I was happy and grateful when I believed Ben hurt Maggie and Ford for me. I've been pathetic imagining that I can sense Ben near. Anywhere. Gant isn't an in-between place. And dead is dead.

— 2 5 —

J osh and the others are heaps on the grass, their parents scattered around, all attempting to draw their kids in the directions of waiting cars. Carolynn and Duncan stand connected by her head resting on his shoulder. Josh is doubled over. Rusty is crouched on the grass, a clumpy mess of vomit between his sneakers.

"We need to get out of here," Willa says, eyeing a Channel 6 news truck closing in on Becca's driveway.

Josh glances up; his face is red and misshapen from crying. All the pluck has been stomped out of him. I want to have the strength to kneel at his side, hold him up, comfort him. I've lost more people, although apparently, in this, practice does not make perfect. The others don't notice us, their eyes fixed on Becca's house, ghosts playing on their features as they try to will Becca into springing alive.

Uniformed officers with dogs on leashes crawl up the terraced hill across the street. A helicopter flies low over the thick brush; its propellers have the effect of a hair dryer, parting the boughs, exposing them to their roots.

The last fifteen minutes compress into fifteen seconds and play

270 • ALEXANDRA SIROWY

on a loop in my head. Sweeny's and Ward's suspicions tangle, converge, and fork. A string of murders are threaded together like the peas on my rosary.

Willa drags me in the direction of my house and doesn't stop until we're inside, the alarm set, and the doors and windows bolted. Basel is collapsed in the middle of the living room rug. He's a purring pile of rust-colored fur, tail swatting obliviously.

Willa speaks quietly on her cell. "Call us back, Mr. McBrook." She wanders into the kitchen and argues in hushed tones during her next call. Principal Owen's likely on the other line.

After she finishes, she sits cross-legged beside the coffee table. "I left a message for your dad." She hugs herself. "Out of sensitivity to your obviously overloaded emotions and rapidly firing synapses, I should give you time," Willa says. She dabs a finger at the gathering wetness in the corner of her eye. "But this whole situation is too *unimaginable*. Becca is dead. Murdered. Gruesomely. What did we just see, and why did you say it was *yours?*"

Unimaginable is the word Willa throws out. It buzzes around my head. I'm angry, sad for Becca, though what happened to her isn't *unimaginable* for me. For an awful split second I even let myself think it was what Becca deserved. Staring at my palms, I tell Willa the story of "The Lovely Scarecrow." It's difficult to look into her face and see the judgment there. Willa's always known who she is. I think that's rare, even for adults. Ben and I were two kids grappling with right and wrong; with who we wanted to grow into; with love and hate; with how to be brave in the face of our problems. We didn't watch the news back then, where coverage shows villages bombed, girls kidnapped, and people killed for what they say or for the color of their skin or for their beliefs. But we might have sensed that the world was as scary as all that. Our island was far away from the violent world, and yet there existed shades of violence around us. Perhaps we were using our stories to prepare ourselves for dealing with it?

After a long silence, Willa says, "Ben's stories were really gruesome. That didn't disturb you?" There's reproach in her tone.

My arms shield my chest. "Video games and HBO are way worse," I say defensively. "They were make-believe like that. They weren't real. We weren't being hateful. They made me feel braver than what I was: a little girl her dad called *Bumblebee*, who needed her unicorn night-light, who got bossed around by Mariella or the nanny of the week, and who missed her dead mom." Willa's lines go runny as I near tears. "And I'm not stupid. I know there must have been scary stuff when Ben was a kid and that he was trying to feel braver than all of it too."

Willa's eyes move over me and she adds more gently, "But they don't sound like the imaginary cops-and-robbers stuff kids dream up with their Nerf guns." Her eyebrows hitch up.

I shrug. "We were always the heroes. In the end, good triumphed over evil. Classic cops-and-robbers stuff, just with a surreal Ben-spin. Harmless make-believe."

"They aren't make-believe any longer, though. Someone's acting them out, and since Ben is *gone*, and you aren't doing it, there are two alternatives." She ticks them off on her fingers. "It's either someone Ben told the stories to or the originator of the stories. I'm betting it's the originator, since I don't believe the stories were made up by a kid, but rather an adult from Ben's childhood. And I think the police would at least agree that there was someone very scary chasing Ben and Diane.

272 • ALEXANDRA SIROWY

That person is the reason they spent only months in any one given place. Detective Sweeny's come to that conclusion without knowing about the link between the stories and the murders."

"Why would Ben retell stories like that? Why would he make us the heroes of them?" I ask.

"Kids get traumatized, and maybe Ben internalized them in some deep, dark place, and telling them was his therapy." I give her an inscrutable look. She throws her hands up. "So my mom reads a lot of self-help books, and once in a while I pick one up. All the head-shrinking aside, maybe they were versions of stories told to him as a kid. He tweaked them—consciously or unconsciously—to retell them to you. He may have given them their happy endings. The question is, who told Ben the stories?" Her wise gray eyes had been glazing over with the riddle of it all. They focus now with sharpened curiosity. "Where is Ben's father?"

I shift uneasily. "Ben and Diane never talked about him. I didn't push because I understood not wanting to share about a parent." Willa's expression goes soft and sympathetic. "I think Diane was a teenager when she had Ben. She's pretty young to have a kid as old as he was. You think his father stalked them across the country and then what, he caught up with them here, convinced Maggie to draw Ben out of the house that night so he'd have the opportunity to hurt him and then pick off kids who Ben had grudges against, all to echo stories he told his son?"

Willa's head sways from right to left. "Not sure. I don't talk about my dad, and it doesn't mean he's a psycho killer, just a wife-and-child-deserting jerk." Her nose is scrunched up, doing the rabbit twitch it does when she's thinking hard. "It could have been Diane's brother, or

THE TELLING · 273

uncle, or a cousin. It's likely a man, because of the physical strength
probably required to force Ford to eat poison. Would your dad know
anything about Ben and Diane's family?"

"He knows less than I do. 'Don't upset Diane.' He acted like she
was a wild animal we would spook." But again, I wasn't dying to know.
Only magical things appear out of nowhere, and to me, Ben was
the most magical. I chose not to pry. If Ben were past-less, it meant
that there was nothing else to know about him. It also meant that
everything significant included me. Thirteen-year-old me thought
about us as a Venn diagram, our circles overlapping. In class I doodled
one circle after another, right on top of each other. The idea of us as
those shapes, and all our contours touching, made me hot-faced.

"All of Ben's stuff is in his room?" she asks. I nod to her. "He may
have a scrapbook or a keepsake box or a—"

"Ben had one photo album from when he was a baby," I say. I'm
shaky and anxious heading upstairs. Willa rustles behind me as I
bend over Ben's desk. The handprint there looks dusted with snow.
My fingers tingle closing around the handle of the drawer where
Ben kept his only album. There's a jumble of sketch pads, charcoals,
pencils, and crinkled-up sheets of paper inside. Lying on top, undisturbed by the chaos beneath it, is a white envelope with my name
written on it.

"What the . . ." I hold it up for Willa to see. "This isn't Ben's handwriting." It's Maggie's graffiti-like scrawl. The same style of letters that
were in Sharpie on the pink sneaker we found in Swisher Spring.
Maggie marked her territory like Twinkie lifting his leg to piddle.

Willa rests against the doorjamb. "Open it."

These are Maggie's last words to me. Maggie would have been

able to guess that it would be me left with the job of sorting through Ben's things. If she had left the note somewhere obvious, I would have found it right away and known she'd been in my house. I would have called the police. I suspect that Maggie planned to be long gone by the time I found this.

Mentally, I tick through the accusations she might have wanted to leave me with. If Ben and I had been blood siblings, I would have escaped her endless suspicion. Maggie accused Ben of cheating on her with anything in a C cup, but she only accused him of feeling for me. *You never interrupt her. You laugh harder at her jokes than mine.* A million tiny clues added up to one unmistakable truth for Maggie. Ben didn't love either of us like he was supposed to. With a set jaw and hooded scowl, he would tell Maggie she was paranoid.

Air hisses between Willa's teeth as she waits. I slide the envelope's contents out and unfold the paper.

L—

Ben knew HE was coming. HE'd been hunting him for years. HE said HE'd kill me if I told the police what HE looked like. And HE wouldn't let me leave until now. I need to give him Ben's picture album and then I'm free. I'm sorry to be taking this from you—sorry for taking Ben.

—M

The room turns black at the edges. Why did Ben keep so many things—writing Maggie while he was in Guatemala, his childhood spent running, the origins of his stories—from me? Did he spend three months in Central America because he knew he was in danger? And if that's the case, why did he come home? Why didn't Ben or Diane tell my dad or the police that they were being hunted? My Ben was hunted. Ben knew *HE* was coming and he said nothing. Out of the confusion of questions, one is more relentless than the rest.

How did Lana the brave not see that there was a real-life villain in our story?

— 2 6 —

Ben's mattress sags as Willa comes to share the foot of the bed with me and takes the note wavering between my fingers. I motion at the handprint in dust on the desk. "If I'd investigated after seeing that the other day, I might have found the note then. Becca and Ford might be alive."

The note drops to her thighs after she's finished. "Not necessarily. The killer's motivations are a mystery; you can't say what would or wouldn't have stopped him. And I think it's a safe assumption that we're dealing with one mentally unwell killer here. Ford and Maggie were poisoned by rosary peas. Becca was hung with bird beaks at her feet. These murders were modeled off your stories. Ben's death is the inciting incident, linked to the others because the stories were told— at least to you—by him."

"And now the photo album's gone, along with any clues inside it," I say.

"Could Ben have kept the album somewhere else?"

"Doubtful," I say as she gets up to search the bookshelves. I drop to the floor and look under the bed. I open Ben's nightstand drawers. I balance on the shoe rack in his closet to get a look at the dusty top shelf. I remove the open desk drawer and dump its contents onto the bed. I pick through them and then yank the remaining drawers free. I press my wrist to my forehead as I survey the pile of sketch pads, art supplies, notebooks, trinkets, and wadded-up sheets of binder paper.

"Maggie left the note right where the album was usually hidden," I say finally. "Ben only looked through it when he thought no one was around. He treated it like *contraband*." Willa twists and peers expectantly at me. "When they first moved in, I used to spy on him. They were strangers and I was curious. Then he found the key to my mom's hope chest. He said he only had one album full of pictures when he saw how many Mom had saved. I asked to see his. He told me he couldn't remember where he put it. But see, I'd already watched him pull it out of his desk when I was spying. So I tiptoed in here one day, and after I'd seen a page or two of baby photos, Ben found me. He was furious." I hug myself, remembering his mad, glowing eyes. "Just weirdly protective over it. He didn't talk to me for two days. It was the only thing he had from being a kid."

"You don't think he moved it so you wouldn't find it again?"

I toe the corner of the Persian rug with my bare foot. "I wanted to know if Ben trusted me not to go snooping again. I looked one final time, a few days later, and found it in the same spot. While they were dating, I walked in on Maggie riffling through his desk a bunch of times. She was the queen of nosy. She must have discovered it. *He*, whoever he is, wanted the only proof Ben had of his identity."

"You think Ben had his picture?" Willa asks.

"Probably. The album is from his childhood, like the stories, like whoever was after him."

She thumbs her chin and surveys the bedroom with greater attention. "And you're a hundred percent sure that it's the only thing Ben saved? He didn't have a baby blanket? No action figures loved until their limbs fell off? No raccoon stuffed toy named Lancelot with mismatched button eyes and a torn bushy tail?"

I smile weakly at Willa; Lancelot is currently nestled between the throw pillows on my window seat in my bedroom. "He didn't have anything like that," I say, a pang of sadness deep in my chest. "When Diane and Ben arrived in Gant, they were driving this van with a smoking engine. No furniture and only a few suitcases." To me, Ben had seemed like a refugee from a storybook. His clothing had been slightly old-fashioned; he didn't own jeans or sneakers; he and Diane's suitcases were vividly embroidered carpet bags.

"You know what I don't get," Willa says. "There's this man who meant Ben and Diane harm all these years ago and he finally finds them. Why hurt Ben? Diane's the adult who's been running."

"*He* is making Diane pay." I lower my voice. "He killed her son and now he's circling."

"Circling by killing Maggie, who helped him initially and knows who he is, so that jells. But why Ford Holland and Becca Atherton? It isn't adding up, unless he's . . ." Her tongue nervously flicks the space between her front teeth.

I pick up Ben's pillow and hug it to my chest. "Unless he's what?"

Her expression is grim. "Ford was at the same party you were the night he died."

"Every upperclassman was at the party. *You* were at the party."

"Becca was with you last night. What if this person is following you now? Circling you, and eventually he plans to hurt you or your dad to continue tormenting Diane."

I grip the pillow tighter. "Biding his time until she comes back home."

"And that's why he's sticking around, risking being found out." Willa thumbs her nose thoughtfully. "He's on the island, and somehow he knew when Maggie returned. Maggie must have given an indication that she wasn't going to keep her mouth shut much longer. That's what set off this second rash of murders."

"Why didn't she stay gone?" I ask. "Returning meant putting herself in danger again."

Willa shrugs a shoulder.

Sweeny was on the right track; she sensed that Ben's death wasn't what it appeared to be. His killer wasn't a shadow man who haunted the highway. He's been circling Ben and Diane forever. And while I've been breathless and giddy over *belonging* this summer, and playing a sick game of make-believe that Ben still exists, Ben's killer has been here, on my island, under my nose. I was just too distracted by the sun glinting off the core to see.

Hands on her hips, Willa appraises the rest of the books. Dad could never swallow why someone who read as much as Ben squeaked by with Cs. Dad suspected what I knew: Ben wanted to be average. Being average is hard work when you're anything but. Ben was bright and intense, and he was hungry to ask why and to take things apart to see how they worked. I thought he refused to perform in school as part of his rebellion against Gant. Now I wonder if there was another reason. Did he need to be average to go unnoticed? Was he avoiding being printed up in the biannual issue of the *Gant Island's Times* that features the names of honor students?

"How did *he* know about the photo album?" Willa wonders aloud.

"He might have pressed Maggie for details. She might have volunteered the information to win his trust or at least get him to leave her alone."

Willa chews her bottom lip for a spell, pushes her glasses up the bridge of her nose, and frowns. "But why wouldn't Maggie just run from this guy? Why would she run his twisted errands?"

This is what Willa does; she figures things out. But right now, I don't want to wonder about this psycho's methods. I don't want to imagine the detached cogs in his head that turned him into Ben's sinister shadow; that allowed him to spread Ben's blood across the highway.

"Maybe he got her to come back to Gant with a threat? 'If you leave for good, I'll find you.' He'd hunted Ben for years." I see the timid, cowering boy who moved to Gant seven years ago more clearly. A tremble works its way into my voice. "It was smart of Maggie to fear that the same thing might happen to her."

Willa grimaces, dissatisfied. She starts organizing the supplies back into their drawers. "So either Maggie came back to Gant because he made her or else she never left and she was on Gant, hiding somewhere that no one spotted her, until this lunatic needed her again."

I watch a line of police cars coast down the street through the window. Their sirens are off and they're driving away from Becca's. "Maggie died near the spring." My voice is froggy, newly sad and sympathetic thinking of her. "Which isn't just a random isolated spot for a killer to dump a body but a place Maggie was familiar with. Maybe she was staying out there. It's out of the way. No tourists. Kids stick mostly to the spring to swim. Rangers don't patrol the preserve anymore."

"Maggie was camping?" Willa asks.

"She wouldn't need to. There are abandoned cabins in the preserve. When Ben and I explored them, there were old bottles and graffiti on the walls. Josh said that the stoner kids used to hang out in them."

"So Maggie might have known about the cabins from Ben or from other kids at school."

"Exactly. She might have been staying there for weeks or she might have only arranged the meet for the album out there, because she knew where she could run and hide if things went bad."

"What if Maggie realized the value of what she had in the photo album? She could have hidden it for leverage. 'I'll call and tell you where it is once I'm safe and long gone.'" There are twin squiggles between Willa's brows. "Maybe that's why she ended up dead? She was trying to get the upper hand. He found her, attacked her, and the album might be right where she left it." She's staring at me expectantly. Her shoe is tapping an impatient rhythm against one of the desk chair's legs. She bites the inside of her cheek and then sighs, exasperated. "I have to ask: When you started putting together that the murders were echoing Ben's stories, what did you think was happening?"

I focus on setting the pillows right on Ben's bed. "I thought that Ben was here, not entirely dead," I admit in a whisper. "Gant was this in-between place where it was possible."

It takes Willa a long, uncomfortable moment to say, "You believed that Ben had risen from the dead and was killing people?"

A tear escapes the corner of my eyes and runs to my jaw. "When you say it like that, I sound crazy."

"Is there a way to say it so you don't?"

I frown. "I'm not sure. It was more complicated in my head."

"Of course it was complicated. You lost someone. You've been in a hyperemotional state . . . sorry." She holds her hands up. "Just something else I read about PTSD."

A heavy gloom drops over me; my knees want to move like a magnet to my chest, my heels to my butt. I want to be small. Willa reasoning everything out takes me further away from when I believed something of Ben remained. "Can we stop talking about this now?" I whisper.

"Sure, Lan. We'll figure out what to do with all this information in the morning. I'll help you. Everyone's safe for now with their parents, and we're together."

With the mention of parents, it occurs to me how glaring P.O.'s absence is. "Is your mom angry that you're here?"

Willa slouches against the wall. "No. I don't know. I got Josh's call. He was on his way to Becca's and you weren't answering. Mom told me I couldn't go. She said that I've let *losers* compromise me enough. She said, 'Becca runs with a fast crowd.' I said, 'How does her going to parties explain her winding up dead?' She kept shouting about this being your influence. Then she went into my room and came out with the reading list for AP English Lit. I couldn't believe it. Two of her students have died and I'm supposed to read *Major Barbara*."

"You left?"

"At first she tried running after the car. I called her, after I tried your dad. She was . . . chilly. I told her I'm sleeping over here. It isn't for nothing, the Latin, studying, and stressing over every score, I mean. I want to leave Gant. At college I won't be Principal Owen's robotically engineered spawn."

I look at my friend. How didn't I realize how brave Willa is? She's never needed a fictional self. She's unapologetic about what she wants and how hard she works to get it. She doesn't need to point at another girl and say, *Look over there at her problems* to distract you from seeing her own. Willa isn't small. She's expansive and every bit as brave as I wish I could be.

Dad spent the day in a meeting with his cell turned off. He climbed into his car as the sky was turning moody at dusk and saw he had seventeen missed calls from me, Willa, the police, and Josh's moms. Sweeny recounts events to him over the phone as Willa and I are glaze-eyed zombies eating the pizza Dad ordered. Shortly after, he closes himself in his office. People wear sadness like they wear hats, I remind myself. People cope with fear in different ways, too. I try to keep mine under control.

He knows who we are. He watched as seven clueless kids drank beers, sunbathed, swam, and pulled Maggie's body from the bottom of Swisher Spring almost a week ago. Did he recognize me as Ben's stepsister then? Did he follow me to Josh's party? Was he in the woods, listening to my conversation with Ford? Did he watch Josh kiss me for the first time on the gallery deck of the lighthouse?

Willa and I sit on the sofa as a documentary on Mayan civilization plays on TV. This is how Willa deals with fear and grief. She keeps her brain occupied. She lets long-dead civilizations drown out the static. Willa watches and I stare out the window at our empty terrace and the night sky. The world isn't any emptier than it was this morning, and yet I feel the pull of a giant, sucking hole. Ben is gone and I only tricked myself into believing it wasn't true.

I speak with Josh over the phone. It's an awkward few minutes of taking turns asking the other if they're okay. "I'll text you in the morning. Don't be afraid. The police are going to find out who did this. We just have to trust our parents and the detectives." Josh holds fast to the belief that all will work out.

I leave Willa on the couch with the documentary's footage of Mayan pyramids in the background. She'll take the guest room down the hall from mine like always. I move wearily up the stairs and fling myself onto my bed.

I hadn't counted on any last words from Ben, and the idea of never hearing what he thought again was what broke me that first month. Then the impossible happened.

Willa left after delivering one of her you're-not-dead-too pep talks. I reached for my journal to squeeze out my first entry since he died. I wouldn't have gotten further than staring at the blank page and letting tears dot the paper. But there, tucked between the first page and the cover, was an origami crane. On the outside it was identical to those Ben had folded for me, the ones I'd tossed out, figuring that Ben was a never-ending supply of paper tokens of affection. He was all stories, origami, opinions, and belief in me.

I hadn't written in my journal since the night before Ben arrived home from Guatemala. He had five days to stow the crane there. That explained the expectant look he met me with in the hallway when I left my room. The way his brows tugged up and he smiled at me as if I scared him. There will be no more last words; no secret messages; no sailboats drawn on the sweating windows; no origami cranes.

A lot later, hours even, I reach for the journal under my mattress. My bones have settled and my muscles have sagged to fit the indents and grooves of the springs. I blink less, eyelids slowing, and my heart beats sluggishly. It would be so easy to lie here until I sink back where nothing and no one can reach me, where the only sensation is me stuck, missing Ben.

Screw kissing Josh ever again; getting asked to homecoming; crowding in the bleachers for football games with the core and flannel blankets and passed flasks of anything but schnapps (none of us will ever drink peppermint again); finally graduating Gant High with Willa. Forget everything but missing Ben.

I must not be too far gone, since there's a vicious little voice in my head screaming *no*, screeching on about making whoever took Ben from me—and Becca from the core—pay. And like I said, rather than let myself be sucked into that bottomless hole, I go for the journal, where I keep Ben's last words to me, those written on the inside of the origami crane. This note revived me once; its magic will work again.

I flip the bedside light on and stare at the words written in a younger version of Ben's handwriting on the binder paper, all creased from its past life as a crane. The note was written three years ago, right after he got his tattoo, and he either didn't have the nerve to deliver it to me or decided it was a bad idea then. He held on to it, waiting for his moment to come. He decided it had once he returned home from Guatemala.

I glance over it now and wait for it to take effect like enchanted cough syrup. This is what got me out of bed a month ago. It's what started *after*; the prime meridian of my life.

Lana—I'm an idiot. A waste of space. I don't think it even means bravery, because when the Chinese guy pulled the binder out and flipped to the foreign characters, he was smirking. Dumb white boy, he thought. I proved him right.

You cried for the three hours it took for me to get this shit tattoo, and all I wanted to do was say it wasn't supposed to be random crap. That's why it's so fucking ironic that the symbol might or might not mean bravery. I am a coward.

We got there and I freaked over what Cal would do. Cal would take one look at it and he'd think I was a perv. He wouldn't get that I know you're young. I know. Cal wouldn't have gotten that I just wanted to tell you what you mean to me. I've never had anyone who is mine and I'm theirs.

But when we got there, I wimped out and got a crap tribal tattoo that may or may not mean bravery, when all this worthless jackass wanted was to get LANA tatted on his back.

Those words were bigger than I knew words could be. They made booming thunks as they tumbled to the floor of my bedroom. The reverberations they caused traveled up into my mattress and into the side I reclined on.

There are sentiments that once expressed, alter your molecules.

I thought back to the day in the restaurant. My teeth chattered at the hornet's buzz of the needle poking into Ben's skin. Hot oil gurgled from the deep fryer, separated from where we sat in the kitchen by a curtain. The air shimmered with clouds of oily steam. Crunchy fried wontons got trapped between my teeth when we ate dinner after the tattoo was finished. Ben's shadow cast on the table flickered as the yellow lantern behind his head rocked in the wind bursting in with each new diner.

Ben's hand rested on the table like an empty cup to be filled. I always wanted to fill it. I placed mine on top. I hadn't done that since we were younger. The way his eyes lingered on our hands and then on my face . . . I should have known. But I was fourteen.

I slept in a ratty old Powerpuff Girls T-shirt and was stuck believing I was bad for liking Ben. I was dirtier than girls are supposed to be. Ben was right; I was young. I didn't have my first kiss until six months later, with Theo, the math decathlon team captain. And even then I had to concentrate really hard not to giggle. *Look like you've been here before*, my mother wrote in the margins of her journal when she was an initiate at her sorority. That's what ran through my head my first few awkward kisses. *Look like you've been here before. Like you know what you're doing.*

I was too immature to recognize that Ben loved me like that—in the dirty, bad, forbidden, wonderful way—until I read his note.

Me? I never had a shot at not loving Ben. He stomped everything else out. I walked onto the terrace and he loomed bigger than the harbor. He made the yellow sun gold and the wind scented with summer. Ben was sunshine, a boost to reach the monkey bars, the pop of water balloons tossed on the terrace, root beer bubbles making me sneeze, and a velvety smooth voice telling stories that *used to be* fiction. Even with the sun cast at our backs, his shadow was darker, more vivid.

My heart aches as though it has been kicked. Ben is gone. Wholly. It's better this way. He doesn't have a part in this dark narrative. Ben's ghost wouldn't kill Becca or her dogs. He wouldn't hurt Maggie. I'm less certain about Ford.

He wasn't just bigger than everyone else for me; he made me bigger. He never stopped acting as though I were the brave one. His last words to me made it possible to imagine that I made him more too. Ben felt what I'd felt, and if I'd been brave and confessed, we wouldn't have left to drive Maggie home that night. He wouldn't have opened the door no matter how many times the bell rang. Ben would be alive, golden, and stubborn. His opinions would sing. We'd be planning our escape from Gant Island. Together.

That's why I got out of bed, left *before* in those filthy, stale sheets. Plodded downstairs to the lower terrace. Set the fire in the pit. Stoked the flames high and leaped over them. Singed my socks and began to grin again. *Grin, grin, grin until you feel it taking hold.*

It was too late for Ben—even for Mom—but it wasn't too late for me.

That's what gave *after* its daring, hungry voice. And for the most part, I like the changes in me. What's strange, though, is that however much I've changed, my perception of who Ben was has changed more. Increasingly, he's a boy I don't recognize. He's a boy with secrets *from* me rather than *with* me. I know there's a line between what you show the world and what's inside. I was stupid to think that didn't apply to Ben. Ben was as bottomless as the next person. So how didn't I see it?

I should have known. There were signs. The sleeplessness, for one, should have clued me in. For all those nights he dragged me down to the fire pit, there were as many where I woke to see him sleeping on my window seat, his knees bent and his arms holding a lacy pillow at his chest. He rubbed the cold and the cramp from his joints as he got up. He brushed it off each time. He'd clap me on the back and make a joke. *I sleep better with your snoring in my ears*, or, *My mattress is harder than your window seat.*

I let all those times slide by. I looked forward to them. I'd crack my eyelids, and my lashes would make shapes out of the luminous streaks and the dark edges, and then Ben would appear. One of those early mornings, maybe a year ago, I slipped out of bed, soundlessly, and tiptoed to his sleeping form. Before I considered the consequences, I bent and skimmed his forehead with my lips. It was like tasting color and music. He stirred. I couldn't breathe as I pulled away and retreated before his eyes opened.

The fear must have come for him at night. Our giant house creaked. The rain and the hail hissed on the roof. The occasional car passed, headlights like coal-red demon eyes reflecting through his bedroom window. Each groan might have sounded like a creeping footstep. The branches of the trees outside made shivering shadow animals on his walls. And that very human man, who'd chased them for years, must have seemed almost supernatural in the dead of night.

— 27 —

Yesterday I was a damaged nerve. I was numb in some places and too sensitive in others. This morning I know exactly what must happen next.

I thought I was the only person alive who knew Ben's stories. I'm not. There's another, and Ben's tales actually belong to them—to *him*, whoever he is. Ben just dusted them off and added the two of us in. He spun them into his own, equipped with adolescent warriors and endings that left us satisfied. Ben made me the hero. And perhaps it's not too late to bring my braver, fictive self to life? I was weak, sad, and a tiny ball when I first suspected that Maggie had a hand in Ben's death. I was stuck in grief and couldn't unstick myself for revenge. *He* doesn't get such a feeble, broken girl as an enemy.

As I climb out of bed, I have my cell to my ear and I'm listening to Detective Sweeny's phone ring. After the eighth it goes to voice mail.

"Hi, Detective. It's Lana McBrook. I need to talk to you. As soon as you can, call me. It's important. I haven't been honest with you. I can prove that there's someone who's been after Diane and Ben. Ben knew. There were these stories that Ben used to tell, and they tie all the murders together. Um . . . uh, okay, call me, please. Thanks."

Next I dial Josh.

"Hey, you and Willa okay?" he says.

While his warm voice doesn't exactly make my resolve falter, I do feel queasy at how angry he'll be when he realizes what a liar I am.

"Hey. Yeah, we will be. I need to see you guys—all of you—ASAP. I'm not sure if everyone's parents will let them leave the house or even if the police will, but we have to figure something out."

"You don't know," he says. It isn't a question.

"Know what?" In dismay, I drop the shorts I was about to pull on.

"They found Skitzy-Fitzy. *Fitzgerald Moore.*"

I'm silent. I think it's more than likely that the next words from Josh's mouth will describe Skitzy-Fitzy's gruesome murder. I drop to the window seat.

"Someone spotted him walking along the highway last night and called it in. The police searched the surrounding area. Even my mom and some others from the station went out to help. They finally found him at four this morning. He had bird beaks in his pockets."

There's only muffled, heavy breathing for a minute. "Are you there?"

"Uh-huh."

"*Bird beaks*, Lana. *And black feathers.* The FBI profiler the cops brought in said that the crimes could be the work of someone who's not mentally all there. The police are searching the woods south of the lighthouse, since that's where they found him. My mom says that the police are being cautious, but they're pretty certain that he's the one who killed Becca, Ford, and Maggie."

"Becca, Ford, and Maggie?" I whisper.

"Yeah." He sighs like it pains him to say what comes next. "I don't know about Ben. It's the bird beaks that tie Skitzy-Fitzy to Becca, and the cops think that whoever must have hurt her also hurt Ford and Maggie, because their deaths were so . . . so out of the ordinary. It's just that Maggie said it wasn't him on the highway with Ben. I guess it doesn't matter what she said, since everyone knows she's a liar."

I shake my head to clear it. "So can I come over?"

"Oh, sorry, that's what I meant to say. The others are on their way. You and Willa should come too."

"Be there in twenty." I feel momentarily blindsided. I can't figure out where Skitzy-Fitzy showing up with bird beaks in his pockets fits into this, but he doesn't stack up as the killer. In some ways he's the obvious suspect. He's schizophrenic. Suspects with mental illness are always guilty of grisly crimes in movies. *The voices told me to do it* and all that. Skitzy-Fitzy is the obvious choice, unless you know that Ben and Diane were being followed for years and that fragments of our make-believe have been scattered across Gant in the form of murders.

I check the guest room down the hall for Willa; her bed has already been made, the fluffy duvet pulled over the embroidered pillows. I move to the staircase. Indistinct voices stream up from the living room. Dad must have made Willa her usual double-shot mocha, and I can just picture their two maddeningly reasonable and appropriately concerned faces as they mull over the events of yesterday.

I make a hairpin right at the bottom of the staircase rather than continue on to join them. I move softly toward Dad's office. Its door is cracked open, and I slip through without disturbing its creaky hinges.

The room is lined with cabinets and bookshelves stacked with yearly almanacs full of commercial real estate regulations. It's a tidy and uninteresting place. The desk was Dad's great-grandfather's, and when I think about how old that is, how many generations of McBrooks sat at it, it doesn't make me warm and fuzzy and ready to take my turn. It creeps me out, like it's seen too much.

I cut across the Turkish rug that's almost as old and go for the personal files Dad keeps in his bottom right-hand desk drawer. Dad's never told me to stay out of here, though him discovering me at his desk, with only a line of natural light seeping through where the blinds meet the windowsill to illuminate my way, would lead to an uncomfortable conversation. He'd want to know what I was looking for and why I hadn't asked him outright. I'm curious to see if Dad has information on Ben and Diane. Dad won't even discuss our family issues with me; he tiptoes around mentioning Mom. Why would I believe he'd be more forthcoming about Diane?

I glide the drawer open; its tracks whine in protest. I strain to listen for the steady rumble in the living room. It's there. I finger through the folders. This is where Ben and I found the key to Mom's hope chest under the Ms. Ben fingered a folder marked Wright, his former last name, decided not to withdraw it, and closed the drawer with a determined bob of his head. I retrieve it now.

There's a solid, sliding object within, one of those old-fashioned handheld tape recorders. There's also Ben's school transcript from the first half of sixth grade at a middle school in Savannah. Ben spent six months there; this is more than I knew. I flip the recorder over in my hand, twist the volume dial until it's turned low, hit play, and gradually turn the volume back up until it's faint but clear enough if I hold the speaker to my ear.

"And one more time, explain why you started screaming when he approached the driver's side." I fumble with the recorder as it almost drops; Sweeny's voice worms into my ear.

An impatient groan turns the recording staticky. "I already said that it was his face. It was all red." My heart knocks between my lungs. Maggie. I thought I'd never hear her I-don't-give-a-shit, nasally pitch again.

"I see," Sweeny says. Rustling of papers. "Is it possible you knew him and didn't recognize him because of the red obscuring his features?" These are questions that Sweeny asked Maggie the night on the highway. Sweeny interviewed Maggie five times in the week between Ben's death and Maggie's disappearance. These must be the recordings of those meetings. I don't have a clue how Dad got them; it's unlikely the police hand out suspect interviews. But I'm sure it was easy enough to find a sympathetic officer who'd make a copy.

"No, I've already told you. I. SAW. HIS. FEATURES. Clearly." Maggie's voice is stubborn. A palm slaps the table. "He was a stranger. He came out of nowhere. He appeared with his face covered in blood, and of course I screamed."

There's a long pause, and I study the window into the inner mechanism of the machine; the miniature tape has plenty of slack left to play.

Sweeny clears her throat. "Ms. Lewis"—there's conviction that she's onto something—"up until now you have described the suspect's face as covered in red paint. A moment ago you called it blood."

Maggie grunts affirmatively. "I was thinking about it, and it looked a lot more like blood than paint."

I go cold. Blood. Not red paint.

I jam the eject button and flip the cassette to see the handwritten label. It reads JUNE 14 INTERVIEW W/M. LEWIS. That's the last interview Maggie gave. She disappeared the next morning. She disappeared the morning after she told the police it was blood on the man's face rather than paint.

I replace the file's contents and slip it into the Ws. So: A man with a face covered in blood killed Ben. The paint sounded like camouflage; I pictured it rust-colored, near brown. Red and bloody is more vivid and bizarre. I go soundlessly from the office. I can easily think back to all those days when Ben sat on the terrace, drawing birds in charcoal. I was all chin in hand, legs swinging from the chair as I grinned into the sunshine at him. One time I was annoyed with him. How could he sit still for hours to draw? "Pelicans don't have any red feathers. You're getting it all wrong," I said, blowing through one of those bubble wands, sending a stream of glistening globes at him.

"I know that," he said, swatting and popping the bubbles.

"So how come you made that feather red?"

"Because it's unexpected," he answered.

I brace myself in the hallway. Was this detail there all along for me to snatch up? If Maggie had only recognized the blood on the man's face right away, would I have connected him to Ben's past? It isn't that I can remember a story where the villain painted his face with blood. It's closer to: I can remember remembering the image, a flash of red here and there, long ago.

Was a villain with a blood-splattered face in Ben's head and so when he was drawing in black and white, he couldn't help but let the red come through?

Willa and Principal Owen are abreast on the sofa. I stop. I wasn't expecting one of them. They're temple to temple, shoulder to shoulder, thigh to thigh. Their faces are shiny from crying. Pink-faced, all the lines that make Willa's mom look older aren't visible, and it's just their glaring resemblance that's obvious. I make out Dad's form through the windows at the table on the terrace. I reverse slowly, hoping to go unnoticed.

"Don't go, L," Willa calls just as I'm about to disappear around the corner.

P.O. looks up and, defying all odds, smiles. "Good morning," she says. "I hope we didn't wake you up." She releases Willa and dabs at the corners of her eyes. The fabric of her blouse puckers between the buttons at her chest; her pencil skirt has ridden up from sitting low on the couch; she isn't wearing heels but loafers that are deserted by the coffee table.

"You didn't," I say, inching uncertainly into the room.

Willa pats the cushion. I study her features for a trace of a fight. There's nothing but her sleepy morning smile and relief making her sag into her mother's side. Usually, she holds herself away from P.O. I roost on the arm of an adjacent chair.

"I'm here to apologize," Principal Owen says, "to both of you." I look up from staring at my knees, surprised. "What I said to you in the police station was uncalled for, Lana. I know that you've dealt with more than your share of tragedy this summer, and to throw that in your face was inexcusable." Her eyes skitter over the coffee table before landing on me. "I hope you'll accept my apology."

Willa's smile lifts up hopefully. "Uh, okay, sure," I say. I wasn't harboring a grudge. My issue with P.O. has only ever been that she rides Willa and never gives her credit for all she does impossibly right.

"I know you've been a friend to Willa," she continues, "and I don't want the two of you to think I'm not grateful that you have each other. A friendship like yours is worth preserving. When parents experience fear for their child, it can manifest in a way we don't intend. Even parents make mistakes." She lets out a short, abrupt laugh. "I hope you can forgive and forget and that we can continue looking forward to all that's in front of you girls."

I force on a smile. I see Willa's mother's shining yellow brick road of expectations going on for miles ahead of Willa, leading anywhere she wants it to, really. I'm happy for my best friend. She's lucky that her mom is here. My road isn't as certain.

I'm mostly mute until they leave. All our parents were notified as soon as Fitzgerald Moore was taken into custody. Relief and reconciliation with Willa make P.O. motherly. She offers to go back-to-school shopping with us over the weekend. My stomach drops. Becca missed senior year by *five days*. Willa doesn't explain why she's going home with her mom—it's obvious. This is what kids do. They're guided home, tucked under their parent's arm, protected long after they can protect themselves. That's what having a mother means.

I don't bother with Dad on the terrace. I couldn't handle hearing about sadness and hats. My resolve snowballs as I retrieve Maggie's note and head for Josh's.

When I arrive, Carolynn is twisted on herself like a pretzel in the

298 • ALEXANDRA SIROWY

lap of a chair. Rusty and Duncan are slumped against the fireplace's hearth. Duncan listlessly raps his knuckles against the brick. He uses too much force for it not to hurt. Only Josh is on his feet and alert. He was on the porch pacing, waiting for me as my car parked in his driveway, and he's circling the coffee table restlessly now that we're in the living room. I'm too nervous to meet his eyes.

"So, Skitzy-Fitzy," Rusty says first. His baseball cap is backward, and RUSTY PIPE glares at me, embroidered in our school colors—purple and black.

Duncan thwacks his knuckles harder. He isn't wearing his skipper hat.

"We can't believe it," Josh says. He's springy and bouncy, back to operating as the core's spokesperson; the villain has been caught and order restored. His pluck and optimism are taking a cautious gander around. "None of us expected this. We've seen that guy around for years." He palms his forehead in a stunned way. "We even gave him a six-pack once, junior year. You never think anyone could be capable of . . . of what was done to B." He ends in a whisper.

"Even the town mental patient," Duncan says.

A wisp of a groan from Carolynn, and Josh continues, "We know what to *feel*, obviously. We're broken up for Becca. Becca, Ford, Maggie, *and* Ben."

Carolynn's cheek is resting on the chair arm. A few strands of honey hair are scattered across her eyes. "Why are you so quiet?" she asks in a lifeless voice.

I've wadded my hands up in my hoodie's sleeves. Here they are, trying to make sense of Skitzy-Fitzy as the murderer, and I'm about to tell them they're wrong. Becca's killer is out there, unpunished. "I'm quiet because I can't figure out a way to say what I need to." I hesitate and then offer her Maggie's note, which is folded into quarters and slightly damp from my palm.

She reads it lying sideways. I fixate on an antique chessboard on an intricately carved wooden table in the shape of an elephant. The pieces are pale-gray stone. The queen is an inch taller than the king, and I wonder if that's the case in most chess sets. Even if she isn't always bigger, she's so much fiercer. The queen is deadly, able to sweep spaces in every direction. She homes in on her mark and then goes to battle. The king is feeble, limited in his moves and usually fatally vulnerable without the queen's defense. I stop thinking of the pieces as a queen and a king and begin to picture them as just a boy and girl.

Maggie's note travels around the group and Josh, the last to read it, lets it drift to the coffee table. Dread is splashed over their faces. My shoulders cringe.

"Tell me that Skitzy-Fitzy is somehow this *He* who had been hunting Ben," Carolynn says. She's sitting upright in the chair, gripping the arms, her nails digging into the leather.

I can't tell Carolynn that, but I do share everything I know. I explain that Ben used to tell stories and that parallels appear in the murders. I tell them about Sweeny's suspicions, Ben's mysterious past, and the stolen photo album that may possess our only clue.

This is how I end: "I'm driving to Swisher Spring. I think that Maggie was staying in one of those abandoned miner's cabins. I believe that the album could be where she left it. It's possible that she tried to bargain with him and it's what got her killed. I have to check at the least. It was important enough for him to send Maggie into my house for it. Maybe it isn't even a picture he was after? Maybe it's a bigger clue that connects him with the murders? I already called Sweeny and left her a message. After they have the album and the truth from me, they'll be able to find who really killed Becca." I spin on my heels, one more glance at the queen standing taller than the entire army of pawns, knights, bishops, and rooks. Taller than the king.

I stride to the front door. I am a ship cutting through waves. I am the queen on a chessboard. My hand closes around the knob as Carolynn catches me.

Her soft hand wraps firmly around my wrist and I face her. She releases me, brushes the hair from her wide eyes, crosses her arms, and pops a hip. "In what universe do I not go with you?" she asks.

I turn around fully to see that all three boys are moving, a bit uncertainly, but in the process of ambling to the front door to follow us.

Five minutes later we're in Duncan's SUV.

The core puts out light. I'm not talking the optical illusion kind, like glitter bouncing off a disco ball. I mean that the core puts off the molten warmth of the sun. I feel it warming me from the inside out.

My hands are doing that weak-knuckled thing as I dry them on my jeans. Carolynn is examining the spray can of Mace attached to her key chain. Rusty's baseball bat is slanted in his lap. He sees me looking and grins. "I can hit an eighty-mile-an-hour fastball. You better believe I can hit this dude's head if needed."

Duncan flexes the arm not steering and winks over the muscle. "I'm always armed," he says.

For a fleeting moment, I recognize how dangerous it is to love someone as much as I love Ben or the others love Becca. Love that strong weathers death. It makes you walk into a fight; it makes you a queen on the chessboard. It's why we're hiking into the preserve with a killer on the loose. Waiting for Sweeny to call us back, telling our parents what we've learned, and booking it to the safety of our homes is the smarter play. And the last time we felt this indestructible was just before we found Maggie. Those were the minutes that sent us spiraling out of control. But to hell with whatever we should have learned that day. To hell with the smarter play. Ben and Becca deserve this. They deserve our braver selves.

The SUV catches air bouncing over a speed bump, and as gravity smacks the car back to the road, I wonder if I'll look back in a day or seven and think, *That was my chance to love myself more than I loved a ghost, and I blew it.*

— 2 8 —

At the trailhead we take the right fork that stems from the dirt access road to the shore. The left fork snakes to Swisher Spring. We plan to veer off the demarcated trail halfway to the coast in search of abandoned cabins that rest undisturbed in the preserve. This was the same course Ben and I charted when we went in search of ruins between the trees.

"Did you ever find any?" Rusty asks. He swipes his bat at vines hanging near the trail, like he's a guide with a machete clearing a path in the Amazonian jungle.

"Yes," I answer. I hop over a creek bed with trickling water that bisects the trail and point out a fat glossy frog on a round river rock to Carolynn. She jumps to avoid squishing it with her boot and ends up alongside me. "A few. One was full of all these old iron tools, and another looked old-fashioned, like it was built out of Lincoln Logs."

"So he might have gone back and brought Maggie at some point," Carolynn says. I nod. "Do you remember where they are?"

"Not really. We just stumbled on them." Ben and I only searched together for ruins that one afternoon.

Duncan walks, staring at his cell. He says something to Josh that I don't catch, and they stop abruptly. We form a huddle around Duncan's phone. He's pulled up a map of the preserve. "We're about here," he says, thumbing a quarter mile or so past the trailhead. "Swisher Spring is a mile to the west. I say we go west, until just before the spring, and then toward the shore a few hundred yards, and then back east to the trailhead. Then, another few hundred yards up the trail, we'll walk another mile to the west. We search the preserve in vectors, so we don't miss anything. We do it until we reach the shore, and then we repeat the pattern to the east of the trail on the way to the car."

I notice Carolynn's hand on Duncan's shoulder as she leans her weight into him. He's being serious, devising a plan, sober for one of the first times since we found Maggie. This is the Duncan that Carolynn wishes he'd be all the time.

"Sounds good," Josh says with a clap.

Rusty swings the bat west to east. "We'd cover more ground if we split up into groups."

"No," Josh and I say in unison. Josh waves for me to continue. "If I'm right—and I really think I am—then whoever *He* is could be out here. Remember, this is where Maggie was poisoned. We're only safe because there are five of us and one of him. We stay together."

"Stay together, stay alive," Rusty says as a grim little motto.

Rather than walk in a line, we fan out, leaving no more than five yards between us to cover slightly more ground. We all keep in the sight line of whoever flanks us. Other than our footfalls our group is quiet.

The woods aren't as damp as when we last visited the spring.

The trees grow in varied density. We move in and out of the sunbeams that penetrate the sparser foliage. For a full minute the forest floor becomes a dark mash, and we blindly stomp through ferns and spiderwebs, their invisible threads tickling my exposed neck. The trees thin and an abrupt breeze rustles my ponytail. It flattens my hoodie, pressing it to my skin as a body slipping by me would. I check over my shoulder. We're covering more ground in this formation, but there's no one watching our backs.

Carolynn looks my way as I look hers. "It's been about fifteen minutes. Almost a mile," she says. Duncan is beyond her and Rusty beyond him. Josh is on my other side. His path has gradually veered farther from me, and I keep losing sight of him as he passes behind trees. Whereas most of the forest is made up of straight pines with boughs that appear hung with green tulle ballerina skirts, all swinging dizzily in the wind, their trunks decreasing in diameter as they grow skyward, there's a malformed group of ten or twelve trees growing in a cramped ring. Their trunks are grayish and smooth; their branches with the look of scarecrow arms, stray fingers splayed and grasping shaggy clumps of mistletoe. I notice them because the tops of their root systems are exposed. The segments aboveground look like spines with knobby vertebra shooting from the soil. A ring of skeletons digging themselves up and escaping from their graves.

My brain names them cedars—a factoid I must have picked up in biology or from Willa's encyclopedic brain. I rub heat into my arms and look up to see what Josh makes of them. He isn't there. He must have veered off on the cluster's far side. I continue on our course, but when I start to leave the mass behind, Josh isn't keeping pace.

"Josh," I call. A sideways wind scatters my bangs across my forehead as I approach the clump of trunks. They jut up, impossibly tall. Shards of light filter through their branches. "Josh?" I call louder. I check that Carolynn's stopped and is watching me. She snaps at Duncan for him to stop, and he shouts at Rusty.

Shadows pool in the space between the trunks, and I could slip through the roots and pass right through the circle. I don't want to. I walk counterclockwise around their perimeter.

"Josh?"

I stop in my tracks. He's standing with his back to me, facing the shore he can't see because there's half a mile of forest blocking it. "Look," he whispers.

I stand at his side and follow the length of his pointed finger. It's almost indecipherable from the spectrum of brown columns of tree trunks. I probably wouldn't have noticed. It's distant—maybe as far as fifty yards. The sun glints off a corner of a tin roof, and a narrow, cylindrical chimney puts out a thin white squiggle of smoke.

"Holy shit," a loud voice exclaims. Duncan's hands are on his head. "There's someone in there. There's smoke coming from the chimney."

"Shhhh," Carolynn hisses. "If you can see them, they can see you." We draw back to the other side of the small grove of trees.

"We need the police," Josh says urgently.

Duncan's the quickest draw with his phone. "There's no service this far out."

"Just like there's no service at the spring," Josh says, dragging his hand down his chin.

Still, Rusty, Carolynn, and I pull our cells from pockets, and there's a lot of holding them up an extra foot or two. Rusty jumps in place, as if that could be the difference.

"Duncan had service on the trail. We've got to go back," Josh declares.

Carolynn shakes her head. "No. What if whoever it is leaves the cabin? What if we lose him because we retreated and he has time to get away?"

"He doesn't even know we're here," Josh argues.

"You saw the cabin." She jabs his chest with her nail. "You were in his line of sight. You don't know what he saw."

"She's right, man," Duncan says, hands up in a peacemaking gesture. "Best-case scenario is we find a signal back where we looked up the map. It will still take the cops fifteen or twenty minutes to get out here. They're the ones who were supposed to search the preserve in the first place, and instead they had hard-ons to suspect us."

"Plus, they've got a suspect in custody," Carolynn says. "They found bird beaks in Skitzy-Fitzy's pockets. They'll send *one* officer out here, if we're lucky"—her thin, shaking arm points in the direction of the cabin—"and whoever is hiding will hear the siren coming."

Josh looks around our group, torn. "Okay, what if you"—he jerks his chin at Duncan—"run back to where you had a signal, and we hide in the trees to watch the house? We'll make sure no one leaves."

"Stay together, stay alive," Rusty parrots himself. He isn't being sarcastic anymore.

"The four of you will be together," Duncan says, punching Rusty playfully in the shoulder. "I can sprint to the trail and be back here within ten minutes, easy."

Carolynn cocks a skeptical eyebrow.

"Okay, twelve minutes, max," Duncan says with a wink.

There's an awful moment where we're all trading uncertain glances. It's important that the police know where we are and what we found. One cop is better than none. Duncan shoves his cell into his pocket, smashes his lips to Carolynn's cheek, whirls around, and barrels off the way we came.

"Shit," Josh says under his breath.

We shield ourselves amid the trees. The shadowy place between the circle of trunks seemed foreboding, but now their malformed roots are our cover as we keep watch. Our view of the cabin is distant and fractured. The white curl of smoke is framed perfectly by a window of blue sky between trunks.

There's the background roar of the waves beating the shore and the scampering squirrels. My hand is braced on a tree trunk until I focus on the foamy egg sacks of insects better left unidentified on the bark. I shuffle farther from it and just as I do, I catch a flash of movement out of the corner of my right eye. I turn fast. Between the trunks I can make out slim bars of the forest beyond.

Do I catch the tail end of a shadow? Or do I see a dark form because I worry that it's there? It's impossible to know, and no one else noticed, so I turn back and squint at the cabin.

I think I detect a new background noise. The buzz of a beehive, possibly. "Do you hear that?" I whisper. Carolynn moves alongside me and stretches forward so her head is between trunks. She listens.

All at once the sound is undeniable. The first sharp crack is followed by several more in rapid succession. A flock of birds shoots from the understory to the canopy. Their shrill caws spread in a relay as other birds of the forest screech in response. I blink hard. It's becoming difficult to focus on the cabin. Its lines are going runny. The air is shimmery. Only with the first puff of black smoke from the chimney stack do I connect the sound with the changing air.

"Fire," I say. I brush by Carolynn, duck under a waist-high loop of root, tear out from behind the trees, and dart toward the cabin. I close half the distance fast. There are rogue bolts of flame through its blackened windows. The chimney puts out a steady black stream. There's flickering light from the cabin's door, which appears to have been left wide open. Was it like that when we first spotted it? I can't say. That daring voice in my head just keeps howling that the cabin is going to burn to the ground, along with clues left behind in it. I take the cabin going up in flames as proof that *He's* been using it as a hideout. He's burning it to the ground because he must have spotted us. Heard us.

The sun flashes through the breaks in the canopy. I run blind for feet at a time. Messy footsteps gain on me. Rusty, who is built for stealing bases, must be at my heels. I chance a look over my shoulder. Carolynn. Josh is a few yards back, with Rusty directly behind him. The boys look intent on stopping me. Carolynn's eyes drill the cabin.

The edges of my vision pulsate as I close in on it. Embers float from the open door and land in the dirt with the look of angry red ants. I catch the black glitter of exoskeletons as spiders crawl away. The cabin's two soot-blackened windows remind me of soulless doll eyes gaping at the forest.

I pass through the open door. The heat slaps me in the face. The flames lick the walls from the floor to the exposed wood eaves of the ceiling. It's one cramped room. An ancient-seeming bench with cushions is being devoured, the upholstery charring like the flesh of a petrified marshmallow. Beside a wooden counter and a basin sink are cans and cans of crushed pineapple. Maggie loved pineapple. Her lip gloss was tropically scented, her drink of choice was pineapple-flavored rum, she'd eat the canned kind by the bucket. Maggie was here.

I step over the rotted floorboards. "Watch it," I tell Carolynn behind me. A wooden ladder leads up to a loft. I make for it. The air's full of cinders, and I'm coughing as I jump up on the first rung. The flames poke through the wood of the ceiling like dagger tips dragging and sawing. The roof won't stay up much longer. I picture Maggie sleeping in the loft, leaving her things and the album stored there. She only had the backpack with her. She must have taken more to this hideout for seven weeks in the woods.

"It isn't worth it," Carolynn shouts. I hesitate and turn on the bottom rung. Rusty and Josh are shouting from the outside, voices barely audible over the sputter of the flames. Carolynn extends her hand up to me. "Lana, it isn't worth it."

"Get out of here," I shout at her.

She makes to follow me up the ladder. There's one long groan, and then the floor under us shakes. I reverse fast. Carolynn jumps down from where she is, pauses to make certain I'm coming, and sprints for the door. I'm dizzy and hacking, tripping forward. I only see it because I'm doubled over, holding my stomach. There, by the door, resting on top of a pile of old magazines, is Ben's leather photo album.

I grab it the second before I jump over the threshold. Twenty feet away I let the album thud at my feet and brace my hands on my knees, scrunching my stinging eyes shut, hacking up smoke. At my back there's a thunderous rumble as the wood of the structure is consumed by a single, violent burst of fire. I stumble a few feet forward from the resulting push.

Josh helps me upright, his face soot-stained and grimacing. "Is that it?" he asks.

Carolynn cuts me off as she shouts, "Why hasn't Duncan gotten back?" She pitches in a halting zigzag between us and the direction of the path. Her hair is streaked with cinders and she's drained of energy, her shoes dragging. She visors her hands at her brow even though the sun has passed behind a cloud. I look up. No clouds; only a billow of gray smoke above us. "How long has it been since he left?"

"Who the fuck knows?" Rusty says. "You guys literally just made it out in time." He waves his bat at the flames.

Carolynn whirls around. "I know that, Rusty. Someone set that fire, and they weren't in there, so *where are they* is my point."

Josh spins slowly, regarding the woods.

"He's out here," I whisper. "With us."

"And Duncan's alone," Carolynn adds.

Though we're in no shape to run, we do. My feet shuffle one after the other, and I'm struck by the sense that something is very wrong. The fire was a distraction. *Look over there.* Look at the spit and spark of hundred-year-old wood breaking apart while I run through the trees, chasing down your living, breathing friend.

My thighs and lungs burn by the time we reach the path. We converge on it as one. Heads snap to the left, then the right. "Which way?" Carolynn screams.

"Toward the car," Josh shouts.

"What's wrong?"

We look up. There, coming around the bend, is Duncan. He jogs bouncily to meet us. His gelled hair is in place; his aviator sunglasses are gleaming and hooked on the collar of his V-neck. "Jesus, what happened to you, Car?" he asks. He takes us all in, legs slowing. "What the hell, guys?"

Josh doubles over wheezing, half supporting himself with a hand on a tree trunk.

"Why did you take so long?" Rusty asks, less out of breath, wielding his bat in Duncan's direction.

Duncan holds his phone up. "My cell died and I had to run all the way to the friggin' car to plug it into the charger and call the cops from there."

We drag along the path to the SUV. Every few yards I think I catch that flash of shadow in the trees again, this time mirroring our progress. Duncan is unharmed, but that doesn't mean that the fire wasn't a distraction. It doesn't mean that the fire wasn't a sleight of hand. At the very least we were drawn toward the fire while *He* escaped.

I stop a few times to squint when a shadow looks opaque and darker than the rest. I wait for a man to take shape. Nothing comes of it. The wind blows and the boughs shift and the sun refracts on the glossy leaves of a fern or stump.

We make it to Duncan's SUV; a police cruiser is idling parked beside it. An officer jumps out, his hand on the walkie clipped to his shoulder, and regards us suspiciously. "You kids know you're not allowed to light bonfires or smoke out here," he warns in that robotic-cop voice all male police seem to have.

Josh, true to form, describes the fire and the location of the cabin. The officer talks into his walkie and requests a fire truck. I check my own cell and see that Sweeny hasn't returned my call. I slump against the car door as Josh spells all our names for the cop, who wants to write them down, just in case he stumbles across the remains of a bonfire or cigarette butts. Carolynn props her elbow on the car's hood beside me and cradles her head in her hand.

"It was just there, on the top of a stack of magazines, waiting for us," I tell her quietly.

"Not waiting for long," she says. She rocks her head in her hand. "The flames would have destroyed it."

"Yes," I drag out the word as I think, "but didn't it seem weirdly easy for us to find it?"

She raises an eyebrow. A smudge of soot covers the tip of her nose, and the diamond stud looks covered in coal. "We had to hike through the preserve, brave a fire, survive a collapsing cabin, and escape whatever full-on sociopath has been killing our friends." She waits a beat, and her face stays close to mine. Her sharply drawn cheeks stand out more than usual. "Easy is not what comes to mind. Whoever we're dealing with was burning evidence. He had no idea we were there. It was the first break we've had. It was luck."

She takes the album from my hands, shakes her head in a state of irritation, and climbs into the car.

I regard the preserve's primeval green beyond the edge of the access road. All these seams of trees fill up our island with places for *him* to hide. It doesn't feel like luck that we stumbled on him at the exact moment he was destroying evidence. It feels like being outmaneuvered in a game I hadn't realized I was playing.

— 2 9 —

arolynn fiddles with the bracelets around her wrist, their charms and beads clicking faintly as the boys pile into the SUV. I stare at the cover of the album after trying three times to reach Sweeny. I'm aware of Carolynn spinning the gray and indigo square beads on a delicate gold-linked bracelet in my peripheral vision. Becca had its mate.

"I feel like we just escaped death," she muses quietly, turning each square bead on the bracelet until they're aligned neatly. "Have you ever seen those fish that are accidentally yanked up in the crab pots?" The boys stop talking. "They're all crisscrossed with rope, red slit gills opening and closing desperately, eyes bugging out because *they know*." What she says brings a gloomy dream over the car.

Duncan twists in the front seat. "What do they know?"

Carolynn looks up, seemingly surprised that she wasn't just speaking to herself. "That they're about to die."

"Morbid much?" Rusty says.

"I'm saying that that's how I felt, like Lana and I were about to die. But we didn't." She glances back to her bracelets.

"Whoever is doing this to us is about to get kneecapped, and then *he's* going to die," Duncan says. He accelerates too fast. There's the ping of rocks spitting under the wheels, and we cross the gravel shoulder to the highway.

"So that's just it?" Rusty asks. "We gave the cops our names and the fire department is going to handle the fire and we just have to wait for Ward and the lady detective to pull their heads out of their asses and call us?"

"Basically," Josh says. "That officer said they're swamped with the search for more evidence where they found Skitzy-Fitzy over by the lighthouse, and I couldn't even get through to my mom. You want to give Sweeny another try?" He gives me a hopeful look over his shoulder.

"I left three messages while we were waiting for you guys," I tell him.

His mouth winds up in dismay, and then he bobs his head, resigned.

"Why aren't you looking through it?" Carolynn asks. She nudges the album, which is resting unopened on my lap.

My fingers have been tracing the frantic design of curling vines on the front cover. "It was just before my eleventh birthday when I snuck into Ben's room to find this," I say. "I only had time for two pages before he walked in on me." Me: hot-faced and caught in the act, my hand hovering above a picture of Ben on a brightly painted carousel tiger. Ben: a wiry figure in the doorway who said in a deadly calm voice, "If you don't put that back, I'm not going to come to your party and we won't be friends anymore."

I didn't hesitate. I slammed the cover closed, leaped up, left the album where it fell to my feet, and bolted from the room. Funny, but now it's painfully obvious that it wasn't really my decision to turn Ben into a magical boy without a past. I was choice-less and made the best of it. That's me, Lana I-can-make-the-best-of-losing-my-mom-and-my-stepbrother-and-my-friends McBrook. "I might not have even remembered this album if he hadn't made such a big deal out of it," I finish aloud.

The sticky album paper with its plastic sheath crackles as I open the cover. Carolynn scoots her thigh flush with mine. Her being here, radiating strength and spine, makes my fingers shake less.

The pictures of Ben as a child and the Ben in my head don't match up. The photos capture a house of ivied brick; a maze of hedges, overwhelmed by flowering vines; a trellised garden; a terraced brick patio with a white alabaster fountain and a toddler knee-deep and shirtless in its water; a boy in a tiny wool peacoat, hugging an iron lamppost outside a horse stable; a boy on his stomach, his hands propped and cupping his chin as he looks onto an open book by firelight. There are photos on white powdery beaches with the aquamarine sea beyond, and others where the boy wears a miniature tuxedo and poses with other children who are spangled with ribbons and frills.

"Huh," Carolynn exhales. My eyes cut pointedly to her. "I did not see *this* coming." She flurries her pink chipped fingernails over the pictures. "Ben was loaded in his former life. Not Gant rich, but old-white-dude, seaside mansions, ponies, and debutantes loaded. Did you know?"

I shake my head, but it isn't enough. "I had zero idea. Diane had *one* dress when she married my dad."

Carolynn sniffs and looks—*for once*—impressed. "Whatever made them run and leave all this behind must have been really effing horrible."

316 · ALEXANDRA SIROWY

I turn back to the photos. It doesn't make sense. Ben became angry with Gant over what it had. He spit *privilege* like it was the dirtiest word he knew.

As each page turns, Ben gets a few months older. He's up to four or five by now. The pictures capture him mid-jump, leap, or monkey-dangle with two other kids. A tiny girl, about four, with large, grave eyes is usually joined in hands with a boy a year or so younger. His eyes are just as big, but rather than emitting grave intelligence, they're in a permanent state of alarm. When the three pose on a plaid blanket by the sea, the littlest boy stares at the waves, as if they're a roaring tsunami. When the three stand along a brick wall that's no more than two or three feet high, his mouth is drawn into a tight O and his eyes stretch wide, as if he's about to be pushed.

"Weird that there are no grown-ups in any of these," I mutter.

Carolynn presses closer to me and taps the photo on the right of the page. "They're always just out of the frame or else they've been cut out. This one is a weird size—square." She has a point. Many of the photos have been cropped to exclude what's just on the periphery, their edges slender dark borders.

"I haven't seen any addresses or landmarks. I guess we could try to figure out where this is by the way the beach or house looks?" I suggest.

"My money's on North Carolina," Rusty pipes up. He's been quiet this whole time, looking over my shoulder at everything we've seen. "The sand looks like it did when my parents took us to a beach house there. Why don't you just show up at the mental hospital your stepmom's in and demand answers?"

"Rusty, man," Josh says, dodging his headrest to see him. "Sensitivity training."

"He's right," I say. "I should show up at Calm Coast and demand she tell me what's happening. She won't be able to deny that she has secrets if I have this with me."

The boys prattle on about logistics. Duncan knows where Calm Coast is, across the Olympic Peninsula and on the Pacific, because he had an aunt who stayed there one summer after she got drunk one Tuesday afternoon, climbed into her car, and pinballed from mailbox to mailbox down a mile stretch of road before the police pulled her over. They argue about driving there straightaway. Rusty says that baseball practice starts this afternoon, and everyone is horrified that he's actually planning on going. I flip through the last pages, half listening to the discord, Rusty explaining that he can't let the team down.

"Do you think Ben had cousins?" I ask Carolynn. Jealousy is threatening to cut off my air supply. Here are two kids who actually have that shared history with Ben. They had summers capturing fireflies and sunny afternoons playing in the hedge maze. They even, as is evident in the very last photo, had a childhood full of blanket forts.

Carolynn responds—what, I don't hear.

I'm hunched over the final photo. There are high-backed chairs, jutting up under sheets to make a blanket tent with the look of one of those white churches you see on Greek isles. Ben and the other two kids—the kids I was envious of up until a second ago—are huddled together. Firelight reflects on their round cheeks and amplifies details. All three sets of their big eyes—a shape and shade that are too similar not to be related—are fearful and liquid. Their chins point up. Their pink doll mouths grimace. Their foreheads glisten with nervous sweat. All are listening attentively to a figure in a chair. Their little features are *tortured*.

318 · ALEXANDRA SIROWY

The adult figure is close to the camera; an edge of his rib and bottom of his elbow are all that's captured in the frame. The rest of him is out of the shot, except for his shadow, projected onto the white tent by the fire. The shadow man's head and spine are held at a manic angle. His mammoth left hand is tense and curved in the air, as if pretending to cuff a neck. His other hand is fisted higher, the arm arched and slightly bent. He appears about to plunge an invisible dagger into his imaginary victim.

Here *He* is. A shadow man cast on a white tent, tormenting three children with his stories. He was the shadow figure dragging Ben's limp body across the highway. I flip back through the pages. I don't care that the car has pulled to a stop in front of Josh's. Everyone but Carolynn has climbed out and we're sitting alone in the stuffy cab, our breaths magnified and mingling as she takes in what I point to.

I see the pictures with new eyes. The unsettling details weren't noticeable at first glimpse. Unless you were scouring the images for the dark, subtle things kids are sensitive enough to pick up on, you wouldn't notice that they're there. Kids are finely attuned to the horrible. They're always the first to see ghosts and monsters.

The carousel animals are wrong. The tiger's eyes are open and bloodshot, the fangs tipped in red. The giant purple bunny the little girl straddles is footless. "Rabbit feet are lucky." The lion the younger boy rides has a gazelle's hoof and leg sticking from its mouth. These vicious and mutilated animals were toys in their extravagant lives.

Even the pictures that appear more benign are not. On the beach, or picnicking on an expansive and velvety lawn, or knee-deep in a meadow fuzzy with yellow wildflowers, the children's eyes are red-rimmed. They don't have the injuries most kids get. There are no scabby knees. No runny noses. The kids are stiff in unwrinkled, formal outfits and staged as little life-size props rather than preschool-aged children.

The series of moments captured at the hedge maze gut me more than the rest. The four pictures were taken in rapid succession. They capture a sequence of bounding steps. The three kids are fleeing the photographer. In one, Ben is checking over his shoulder, his tiny features rearranged in horror, in another all three kids appear terrified, and in the remaining two, Ben's relatives have stumbled to the ground in their haste, and they're continuing to flee on their hands and knees.

What's pictured isn't imagined terror. I've experienced that. Kids pretend to chase. To be chased. Panic spreads and you run faster. You begin to believe that there's something at your heels. Not this. However real that feels, it isn't. I only know this now. After this summer. After I see the dread in the strange little boy's eyes and the hopeless resignation in the girl's. She knows that running is futile.

They will be caught. They know it. And they run anyway.

— 30 —

Rusty stays behind for his afternoon baseball practice and Duncan to watch his younger brothers while his parents are at work. He doesn't say it outright, but he's nervous leaving them with only their babysitter while he knows there's a killer in Gant who's managed to evade the police.

"What I can't figure is why *He* left the album in the house if he saw us coming. Sure it might have burned up, but he also ran the risk of us running inside and leaving with it. Why risk giving us this major clue?" Josh asks.

"We don't know he saw us coming," Carolynn points out.

"And is it a major clue?" I say. "What empirical evidence has it given us? His face isn't pictured."

"We know that Ben's childhood was the stuff of freaking nightmares because of it," Carolynn interjects, leaning up on the center divider from where she sits in the rear seat of Josh's car.

"Sure," I say. "We know that this is where the stories came from."

"We know this is who Ben and Diane were running from. They left two small kids behind," Carolynn adds.

"Or maybe they didn't leave anyone behind?" Josh says. I watch his profile. "Those pictures end when Ben looks about five-ish, right?" The boys pored over the photos before we left Josh's for Calm Coast in his Jeep a little less than a half hour ago. "Ben didn't show up in public school records until the second grade, according to what Sweeny told you. That's two years unaccounted for."

"Josh is sort of onto something, although he lacks the balls to say it," Carolynn says. I twist under my seat belt to face her. "Things were bad for years. It's obvious that those kids were traumatized. It's possible that Diane finally left with Ben because something happened to the other two kids. Running with one kid is a lot easier than running with three."

"You think they're dead?" I say. I keep lingering over the girl's solemn, frightened eyes. Did Ben have a *real* sister before me?

"Dead or they were cousins and Diane couldn't take them with her too," Carolynn says.

"We're sure we don't just want to wait to hear from the cops, Lana? You want to confront your stepmom without them?" Josh asks. I feel the momentum of the car slow.

"Even with that fire, I'm not convinced that the police will listen to us and investigate, not when they found Skitzy-Fitzy with evidence on him. Diane might refuse to see them. Maybe they can get a court order or something, but how long will that take?" My head falls back to the headrest, and I close my eyes a beat. "There's a better chance that Diane will talk to me. When Sweeny calls us back, we'll have a name for her." I feign confidence and turn to stare out the window.

For the first half of our drive, after we've crossed over the sound to the mainland, it's mostly gently rolling pastureland. Fields are dappled with reddish-brown cows and orchards of apple trees, their branches bowing with green fruit like shrunken heads. Carolynn dozes, fitfully murmuring Becca's name off and on. My eyelids are heavy, but as soon as I close them, I see the pictures of children fleeing through the hedge maze.

I drum my hands nervously on my thighs. I left Willa without telling her that I believe it isn't Skitzy-Fitzy. Perhaps she has enough of the pieces to figure as much, but the police finding bird beaks on Fitzgerald is compelling. I also don't want to alarm her so much that she spills everything to her mom. We don't need P.O. sending the police to herd us back to Gant. If I thought that Diane was more likely to talk with the cops, then I would call Dad and ask him to march down to the police station and demand they send an officer. Diane owes *me* the truth, and I owe her something as well. She is a mother, the fiercest beast in nature, and I just didn't see it. *She rescued Ben.*

I text Willa.

Long story. Stay with your mom until you hear from me. Be careful.

"I can't get over Diane," Carolynn pipes up. She's been stretching and doing a modified yoga pose in the backseat. "Her kid dies and she books it to a cushy 'treatment' spa?" Carolynn makes quotations with her fingers at *treatment*. "Calm Coast is where Tina Spivey went freshman year when her parents were convinced she was depressed because she painted her nails black three days in a row. She got massages and facials daily."

"Carolynn," Josh says, a frown in his voice.

She slaps his upper arm with a sarcastic little chortle. "Sign me up is all I'm saying."

Then to me, Josh says, "You don't have to talk about it."

Carolynn's bright eyes are on me, and I find that I do want to share with her. "I always thought of Ben as mysterious. Not Diane. She's alien, quiet, remote. We aren't close. I never cared, because she wasn't really any closer to Ben. They didn't really speak. When he was sick or got hurt, he never asked for her. It was weird because I'd hear her talking with my dad in the next room, laughing like a normal person, and then we'd walk in and she'd just shut down."

"I swear, having a stepmother is the only thing worse than having a mother." Carolynn laughs humorlessly. "And I have both."

"I don't really have either," I say. Her smirk loses its bite. "Although now I get why Diane's been so diluted and distant."

"It's called medicated," Carolynn says. She touches her temples and frowns. "I guess we shouldn't judge her. We might all be medicated if we'd escaped her old life."

"I have two moms and they're great," Josh says, eyeing where Carolynn is all elbows on the center divider. "They're my best friends," he adds, all pink cheeks and seriousness.

Carolynn jabs him in the ribs with a finger. "Why don't we canonize you, Saint Josh?"

I laugh.

"Is your seat belt even secure like that?" Josh asks her.

She huffs and slides back. "You don't remember your mom?" she asks.

Surprised, I face her. "Not very much. I was only four when she died."

"Those little sayings our moms had, you remember them."

"She had a chest full of old journals. I'm not sure how much I would remember if I hadn't found and read them," I admit.

"Grin, grin, grin until you feel the smile take root in your belly," Carolynn says in a singsongy voice.

"Perception is nine-tenths of everything, even the truth," I respond.

"If you're a bore, lie and say you're interesting. You can never be too skinny. There's nothing worse than being ugly," Carolynn rattles them off drily. "*God*, no wonder I'm such a bitch." I stare at her. "It's okay, I am. I have been. It's a lot of pressure, hair spray, nail polish fumes, and effort to be my mother's daughter. Sometimes I think you're lucky."

Josh's hand shoots out to cover mine on the console. "Carolynn," he blurts.

"Josh Parker, just stop sticking your nose into other people's business for one freaking second, okay?" Then to me she adds, "You know what I mean, right? Not that you're lucky that your mom died or that I wish my mom had. Only that you didn't have to grow up with all those little sayings directed at you. Her telling you to *seem* happy and *look* pretty rather than to be happy and be smart."

"You are smart," I say. "And pretty."

"And usually happy," she adds, with a flutter of her fingers.

Josh is grunting with disapproval. She smiles as she continues, "He always has to be so bloody nice." She jerks her thumb at him. "He makes the rest of us look like assholes, so what's the point of trying?"

Josh flips his mirror up (probably so he can't see her reflection anymore), peers over the dash, and says, "The point of being nice is just that: *I am nice.*"

"Oh my God, you have become so boring," she half laughs, half sighs.

He snorts and then winks at me. "I'm definitely nooo Duncan."

"Shut up," she groans, and bats his head. "I mean it, Josh."

He smiles mischievously at me. "Did you know that Carolynn wants to jump Duncan's bones, and she thinks that I'm too slow or too nice to notice?"

She throws herself back and kicks his seat. "I am going to punch you in the balls when this car stops."

"I actually did know that," I say. "And I bet Duncan knows what to do with his hands."

Josh gives me a sideways look. I start to feel that familiar heat rising in my chest.

"Okay, confession," Carolynn says. She's animated, shifting forward. This is probably how she turned to tell her secrets to Becca. "You are both sworn to absolute secrecy. Yes, I like Duncan. This is not such an epic confession, since I all but spilled to you the night of Josh's birthday." She yanks on a piece of my hair. "I have liked him since sophomore year." Her shoulders rise and fall. "It came out of nowhere. We were at Josh's—insane night—and we were playing spin the bottle." She flicks her wrist dismissively. "I know what you're thinking, but it was sophomore year and we were hammered, so it was loads of fun." I was thinking just that: *It sounds like tons of fun.*

"I spun the bottle and got Duncan." Her fingers brush her chin. "We crawled to the center of the circle and I swear to God, Lana, everything stopped." She bites her bottom lip, and there's this glow seeping from her pores that makes me wistful and eager all at once.

"We kissed for a second. Super quick, but it felt different, like no one had ever felt what I was." She smiles self-consciously. "Trust me. I know that sounds like Valentine's Day bullshit. But we each came up with bogus excuses to stop playing and met outside—not that we planned it. It just . . . *it just happened.* We were there on the porch and there weren't any lurkers, so we started going at it." She laughs nervously and gathers her hair over one shoulder.

Carolynn's words bring on sadness like a blanket of lightlessness. I will never kiss Ben. I will never experience what Carolynn is describing. I press my hand to my chest. I imagine that kissing Ben would have been like hearing a song for the first time and the lyrics skewering you. You've never been so alone and so un-alone. It's you they're singing about and expressing what you feel in a way that you were too dumb to be able to. Your chest swells and you know that you'll never be the same, your atoms have been rearranged, and you are the first and last who will ever decode the secret meaning of the music written only for you.

"It kind of ruined all other kisses for me," Carolynn continues a bit sadly. "And that attraction supersized the part of me that remembers what a sweet little boy he used to be and how I know he's so much better than he pretends he is. I told you it's his dad always demanding that he 'Be a man' and 'Boys don't cry' and 'Don't settle for one girl when you can have two.'" She mimics Duncan's dad's deep, condescending tone. "It's impossible for Duncan to please him unless he acts like an ass."

"Does he know you like him?" I ask.

"How could he?" Josh says. "She calls him Dumb-can like she used to in the third grade."

"I know. It's juvenile to tease him like that." Carolynn sighs. "I don't usually have trouble asking for what I want."

"Why don't you tell him?" I say.

"Really?" She rolls her eyes to meet mine. "You're asking me that? You?" Her nail pokes the hand I have placed over my heart.

Josh cranes for a momentary look at Carolynn. Before anything else can be said, he turns the music on full blast. He hangs his arm out of his window and taps the rearview mirror with the beat. I settle into my seat and watch the green forest, packed with trees like the bristles of a brush, streak by.

Carolynn doesn't realize that I confessed my obvious crush to Josh. Josh, I told. It's Ben I never admitted my feelings to. I'm queasy letting both boys exist side by side in my thoughts. Josh was already under my skin when Ben arrived. Josh was the boy I could giggle about with Willa; I could doodle his name on my binder in the fifth grade. Ben was different. There wasn't a centimeter that wasn't all marked up by him.

Willa texts back with a million questions, all boiling down to demanding I explain my cryptic text from earlier. I don't answer. She read it. This is enough.

A bend in the road like a bobby pin has Carolynn hanging her head out the window as she moans, "I'm going to hurl if you . . ." The wind snatches away the rest.

At two o'clock, after a little over two hours of driving, we're about three-quarters of the way there. Josh taps his gas gauge and says, "Gotta stop to fill 'er up." Twisty miles later, he pulls into the only gas station we've passed in an hour. The pumps are rusted, the square of asphalt has deep fissures in it, and we're surrounded by hundred-foot trees on three sides and the road on the fourth. The trunks reach into the sky and make everything appear stunted and short.

Carolynn hops out of the car, swings open my door, and yanks me after her. She makes a beeline for the gas station's tiny storefront, with windows so filthy only a jaundiced glow escapes. Under the awning there are vast colonies of spiderwebs, black sparkles among the garlands.

"I'm starving," Carolynn says.

"I don't want to eat anything from in there," I whisper.

"Candy is candy," she says, hitting the glass door with her butt to send it swinging inward. "Most of it doesn't even have an expiration date, so don't be a snob." There's a bell that chimes like the tinkling of laughter at Carolynn calling *me* a snob. I take one last look at Josh wiping his forehead on the hem of his T-shirt, revealing his tan stomach, before I step inside. It's muggier in here than outside, and a yellowed fog has collected in the space. There's an old-fashioned register and a woman with a bent spine on the stool behind it. She's wearing massive square-framed glasses. I smile hello. She scowls.

Carolynn already has two handfuls of crinkly neon-colored packages. "Are you a gummies or chocolate girl?"

"Neither," I say, inspecting the packaging of a granola bar. Carolynn slaps it out of my hand, and it slides across the linoleum. I look to where the bar landed in a pile of scraggly hair, dried-up leaf bits, and crimped insect legs.

Carolynn cradles her armload of candy. "Don't tell me that you're one of those freaks who don't do sugar. I hate people who don't like candy."

I stoop for the bar, closing one eye as I reach into what has to be a rat's nest made from the human hair of the sacrificed. I peer at the counter, but the woman isn't behind the register anymore. "You hate me anyway," I mutter, dusting the bar off on my jeans.

Carolynn seizes my shoulders and whirls me around. The packages she was holding drop at our feet. "I don't hate you," she says fiercely.

I try to shake her off. "Josh told me you sent him over at Marmalade's that night, so I guess 'hate' is the wrong word."

Her fingers dig into my shoulders. "Lana, I don't hate you at all. I never have. My mom talks about you constantly. About your mom constantly. It's her biggest regret not helping her, not taking it seriously when your mom moped. And I know that's why she pops all the pills and has five too many martinis and why Dad left and why she'd rather be at tennis than home with me. I got to blame you. It was easy to do that if I didn't know you. If you were just the bitch whose fault it was." Her arms flop to her side. "I'm not telling you because I think we're going to be blood sisters or anything. I feel shitty about it is all, especially with . . . with what Becca said about you." She holds herself.

In that moment I think that maybe I do remember Carolynn, her warm toddler arm hooked with mine as we skipped to the *Mira*, our parents gathered and beaming at her bow. I *feel* our shared history. "Your mom never came to visit us," I tell her.

Carolynn flicks her hair behind her shoulders. "Don't take it personally. She's a zombie."

"It helped having a distraction this summer, you know. I don't mean only Josh. You too." I brush her arm, and she smiles.

"Yeah, but Josh especially," she teases.

"How did you know?"

She stoops and recovers the dropped packages. There's the shriek of metal on linoleum, and the woman with the hunched spine is back on the stool. "Everyone likes Josh. And it wasn't charity," she says. "I wanted to go over and talk to you myself, but I knew Josh wouldn't eff it up like I would."

"You should tell Duncan," I say to her after a pause.

"I didn't ask you," she says tartly.

"He stares at you."

"Yeah." She bats her lashes at me and smirks. "Guys usually do." Her smirk fades. "But he's Dumb-can. It's embarrassing."

I reach past her and replace the granola bar. "I like gummies. Sour ones. And don't wait for Duncan to ask you out. If you want him, make it happen, before it's too late."

— 3 1 —

Calm Coast sits like a proud, painted lady on the bluffs. She wears too much makeup to hide her old age; the fissures are there through the paint and the cornices, though. One private drive, a security checkpoint where my driver's license is verified against an approved visitor list, and a reception office later, I'm signing the log and leaving Carolynn and Josh behind on worn jade satin chairs.

I didn't come with Dad when he delivered Diane here, and so I wasn't expecting the grand old house with an eastern-boarding-school feel. Truthfully, I haven't been imagining Diane anywhere other than gone, a McBrook deserter.

I'm led to a small sitting room in a wing that overlooks an internal garden courtyard. Diane's petite silhouette is framed against the crowded and diminishing greens through the glass. She's wrapped up in a gray afghan, its chunky knit doing nothing to mask the sharpness of her shoulders poking through. In a room filled with faded botanical paintings, muted sea-foam wallpaper, and beige upholstery, Diane appears to belong. It's a breakable sort of place, one that's seen better days, and so has she.

I go to her slowly, the silver hair at her temples standing out as I approach. She tracks a red ladybug crawling across the windowpane. "Diane," I say. She keeps tracking the insect. I let myself down on the cushions beside her. I brush her hand with my thumb.

With a sharp intake of her breath, she pitches back. Her eyes go wide, her jaw slides open an inch and to the side, and her arms fold, shielding her face. "Diane, it's just me," I say, patting the air between us, afraid to touch her again. She sputters, trying to catch her breath, with a wild, unfocused look in her eyes. "It's Lana," I try louder. Until she hears my name, there's no recognition.

"Lana," she whispers. She lowers her arms to her lap. "Is Cal here?" Her eyes cut to the door, dismayed.

"No." I was always struck by how little Ben and Diane resembled each other. Only their heavy-lidded and gray eyes were similar. Now Diane's are bulbous and baggy. "Dad misses you. So do I."

Her features slacken and she looks lost again. I slide closer. "I'm not here to talk about Dad, though." She tucks her chin into her neck, her shoulders fold forward, and I sense she's trying to make herself smaller. I recognize the instinct. "You lied to us—about *everything*." I wait. Nothing comes. I feel the photo album grow heavier where it rests on my knees. "Do you recognize this?" I ask, tapping its cover.

Her attention touches on it briefly, and her features spasm. "Of course I do. I told Ben to get rid of it."

I begin to crack the cover. Her four-fingered hand shoots out to stop me. "I don't need to see the photographs. I remember."

I watch her incomplete fist retract, and she hides it in the fold of the blanket. Suddenly, I understand. "*He* did that to you." My stomach opens up, and I know that if I continue to think about Diane's missing finger, I'll be sick. *"He's in Gant, Diane.* He killed Maggie, a boy from school, too, and Becca Atherton yesterday."

She pulls the blanket tighter around herself. "You don't understand," she whispers. "Your father is a kind man. He loves you, and to him that means he wants what's best for you."

"Ben's father wasn't like that?"

Her eyes become unseeing. "We were only nineteen when I had Ben. I only saw him again when he came to say good-bye at the end of the summer, before he left for school." An eerie pause. "You've heard of men described as haters of women?" She had the frailest pink in her cheeks; it made her appear girlish. "My father was a hater of everyone. His hatred was unprejudiced. Everyone was deserving. He kept us insulated in the nightmare world he created. My older sister had two children and I had Ben, and both of us were to stay there and raise them. There was no one else. Our mother died a long time before, and our father rarely left the house. He preferred us fully dependent and terrified often."

I was prepared to coax the details free. I was ready to shout and insist if she refused. Here is the truth, and I want to jam my fingers into my ears to make it stop. I wanted to throw my arms around her to protect her. "Why?"

"Would telling you that he'd been an abused child or that many of the men in our family had suffered mental illness make it any better? None of that is true." She gives a short, out-of-place laugh. "It wouldn't matter if it was. He was hateful. He was happy when we cowered. There are people like that, men and women, who want to injure the feeble and terrorize the weak." Her voice deepens. "The children brought something wicked out in him. It started with nightmarish bedtime stories. A sick game. Beheaded stuffed toys and afternoons spent chasing the children through the maze until they cried. He never raised a hand to them, not at first. There were things much worse than physical violence."

She continues after too long a beat, "He laid his nightmares into their brains and let them hatch. There was an incident where Ben's younger cousin tumbled out of the attic window and was paralyzed. Ben was in the attic with his grandfather. He was inconsolable. The week after, Ben's face was bloodied, his nose broken, and again he wouldn't say what happened. He'd been alone with my father." She removes her hand from the concealment of the blanket. "I'd known violence like that before. Thirteen years old. It was the first and last time I told him off. I couldn't let that happen to my son. We had to run. But my sister had *peculiarities* of her own; the world frightened her. This was our father's trick. He made her fear him a degree less than everything else. I tried to bring my niece with us. . . ." Her eyes go distant. "Ben—oh dear, Lana, his name isn't Ben, it's Henry, our names are Henry and Sophie Wheaton— Henry and I ran. I reached out to Henry's father's family. They gave us enough money to leave. Henry was just a small child when we began running."

I clear my throat. There's cotton there, strangling me from the inside out. "Why didn't you go to the police?"

"I tried once. In Raleigh, a day after we left. I marched into the police station. My father had a prestigious name. I overheard an officer telling his chief that I was a hysterical runaway, an unmarried mother, and to phone my father to collect me. Even if I'd made them listen, what crime had he committed that I had proof of? Ben cried

when I asked him about his cousin's accident and his nose. This"—
she lifts her hand—"had happened ten years before. Proving the
abuse would have required us to confront him, at least in court and
through lawyers. I wanted to leave it behind."

"But he wouldn't let us. There were signs we were being followed:
strange cars idling in front of our apartments; prowlers nosing
around; a woman snapping pictures of us from across the street. I
was good at watching. It was fate colliding with your father in the
lobby of the hotel I worked at." She pats the delicate graying curlicues
of her hair that frame her face. "I told him I was there for a conference; I was paid in cash to serve cocktails. My father was looking for
a mother and son. Not searching for a family of four."

I'm hot-faced, indignant for Dad. "That's why you came to Gant
and married my dad?"

"No and yes. Once I realized that we needed the protection of a
larger family, any nice man might have done. I knew I could love Cal
on our first date. I also knew that I couldn't burden him with this. He
had you. He needed to make decisions unencumbered by my secrets."

"Why didn't you tell him and the police once Ben died? You
could have prevented everything that came after."

Her eyes go glossy. "I thought I was leaving you and Cal safely
behind. I thought my father would find me. I've been waiting." She
has the defeated look of one of those fish trapped in the crab pots
Carolynn described. Diane *knows*. "I was told that the detective
called, but I had no idea of the violence of this past week. I'm here
because Ben's death is my fault.

"Two years ago I was anxious. Had he given up? I reached out
to Ben's father, who had returned to the town we grew up in to raise

a family. He told me that my father had suffered a stroke. He was confined to a wheelchair. No one thought he'd recover. I told Cal I needed to fly east to see an aunt, and I went home. My sister, nephew, and niece were gone; I don't know for how long or to where. My father was large still, but he was in a wheelchair, his jaw warped and frozen. I felt that I had won. His nurse left us, and I went right into his face. I looked him in the eye and said, 'The devil's been cleaning house for you.' He could speak out of the corner of his mouth, and he asked if I'd come to kill him. There was malice in his voice. It was how he sounded when he called me weak. I lost my temper. I said, 'I dare you, heal and come find me for a fair fight.'" She rubs at the creases on her forehead with quiet violence. "The last I heard he was seeing a doctor in Switzerland, a specialist. Six months ago."

One shaking fist punches her thigh and the shake travels through her, until she's trembling mad, furious with herself. "I spit in his face. I dared him to find us. I'd even worn my wedding ring. He knew to look for a family. He got better. He came for us."

"But we can tell the police. They'll find him. You can come home with me."

Diane shakes her head. "I don't expect you to understand this. . . . Not everyone deserves another chance. I don't deserve one with you and Cal. My son is dead. I'm not sure he ever knew what he meant to me. I couldn't pull myself out of the past enough to show either of you how much I love you. Because I do, Lana, I love you. All those other children are dead because I left."

"They're dead because someone killed them and it wasn't you. I love you too. How can I just leave you here?" I ask, my voice turning panicky.

She tilts her head, a flash of maternal warmth in her gentle smile. "By getting up and walking out," she says. Then she stands, and before I make sense of what she's doing, she's seized the iron poker resting against the fireplace. She lifts it in a high arc and sends it flying into the mirror above the mantel. Glass breaks and tinkles to the pale-blue rug below. A volley of shouts comes from the corridor, and Diane screams.

A doctor and nurse trample the glass. Diane's arms beat against those trying to subdue her. None of the jerky, wild swipes of her limbs disturb me as much as the calm in her eyes. Her focus is piercing. She throws the tantrum so that I'm told to leave.

A woman in a lab coat with a syringe advances on her. Diane's screams cut off abruptly as whatever is injected into her neck rushes into her bloodstream. Her eyelids drop, her whole body settles and sighs into a nurse's arms, and Diane is carried away.

I get up as Diane said I should. I avoid the broken glass. And I leave.

— 3 2 —

By the time the unspooling highway bisects the wildflower- and cow-dotted pastures and we're halfway home, I've spoken to Detective Sweeny three times. I have no more secrets from her, except that Ben and I were each other's summers. I think of Ben's grandfather, using the storybook words I understand best. He was a mad king; his daughters lived in isolation, pawns under his thumb. Their house was a haunted one, crafted by a rich, wicked lunatic who enjoyed filling children with fear, whispering vile things in their ears and watching them squirm.

Diane, the escaped daughter and hero of the story, dared her ailing father to heal, grow stronger, and come after her for a fight. She wasn't frightened by him any longer. She thought he'd rot in his wheelchair and that she and Ben were finally free.

With Diane's and Ben's real names—Sophie and Henry Wheaton—Sweeny says she'll be able to find his name and picture. Her officers and a forensic team are combing through the wreckage of the scorched cabin, searching for any indication of where he might be headed. He won't be able to dodge the police on our tiny island once his photo circulates. Sweeny is in the process of closing departing boat and vehicle traffic. She's casting a net over Gant.

Carolynn, Josh, and I settle into the certainty that the police will handle all. They have the pieces of the puzzle. They know it wasn't a carjacking that ratcheted out of control. Ben was meant to die all along. *He* made Maggie draw Ben out of the house that night. He poisoned Maggie when she wasn't willing to keep his secret any longer. He took the beaks off birds and murdered Becca's dogs. He meant to terrorize us because that's what he does; he torments children. He might have been peering through the cracks of our curtains, looking for his opportunity to hurt me, and Dad's erratic work schedule, or that I always set the alarm and lock the doors, fouled him up. Becca was an easier target. She never remembered to lock her front door; if she had an alarm, I've never seen her use it. We stumbled onto him destroying the evidence of his stay in Gant when we went looking for the photo album. The police are on their way to Calm Coast to protect Diane; officers have been dispatched to Rusty's, Duncan's, and Willa's houses; Dad is under police protection and a highway patrol cruiser was sent to tail us the whole way home.

If Willa had been with us during our drive home, she would have pointed out that Ben's grandfather recovering from a stroke and going on a killing spree in Gant is as fantastic as our stories. Not Josh and Carolynn. Josh steered us home, his mood gradually brightening, even in grief, because everything was set to work out as it always did. Becca's killer would pay; justice would be served; senior year would begin with new backpacks and memorial assemblies, where kids who barely knew Becca and Ford could cry over them.

I try not to let myself wonder why *He* hadn't gone for my father or me right after Ben. His motive was to hurt Diane, so weren't we the obvious victims? Was it really that impossible to reach us? Our house isn't a fortress. I'd been outside alone in the small hours of the morning. I try not to focus on the holes that appear the more I consider it; I try not to think that Willa would be pointing out all the fissures threatening to break our theory apart.

Not Carolynn. Carolynn is her mother's daughter, and she knows that people leap from terraces. Carolynn is half-blinded by grief over Becca, and all the walls she'd built to prop herself up while we tracked the killer down crumbled in the car ride home as she gave in to sadness. She balled up in the backseat and sobbed, loud shoulder-shaking cries.

Oh, the elaborate explanations I dreamed up over that three-hour drive. I built glass castles in the air, and they all came crashing to the ground as the police and my father sat me down when I arrived home.

I channel Willa's voice in my head as they tell me, in no uncertain terms, that Ben's grandfather, Jeremiah Wheaton III, died in Switzerland five months ago. He never left the clinic or his Swiss doctor's care. Sweeny confirmed his death with Interpol. Dad's already been on the phone, trying to reach a sedated Diane at Calm Coast.

The Willa in my head says: *You can't be that surprised. Even if he recovered after the stroke, he was a little old man. How would an old man drag Ben from a car or across the highway? How does an old man chase Maggie through the woods? How would he have had the strength to string Becca up from the swing set or to overpower Ford?*

Willa's voice keeps on listing all the improbabilities from the space between my ears as I look on at Sweeny's thin and troubled face. Ward stands close at her back. He brushes her elbow, and she smiles faintly.

She draws a deep breath. "Fitzgerald Moore is being charged with all four murders." Her usual thoughtfulness is switched off. "We suspect that he's been off antipsychotics for several years and out of the care of a doctor. We found the knife he used on the birds and dogs with his belongings. A psychologist is working with Fitzgerald and his public defender to ascertain his competency and ability to answer our questions."

"The stories that match up with the murders," Josh says. "How did he know them?"

"There's a witness, a man who owns Island Deli," Sweeny says. "A number of officers remembered seeing Ben there with Fitzgerald on numerous occasions. When asked about it, the deli's owner told my officers that Ben was in the habit of buying Fitzgerald lunch. The witness saw them eating outside on the picnic tables. He thought they were a strange pair and listened in to their conversation. Ben was telling him a story. One that he said was . . ."

"Full of guts and smut," Ward interjects with a flick of a judgmental eyebrow.

"Yes, thank you, Detective," Sweeny says, mildly reproachful. "Those were his words, not ours. What is significant is this: We now have a credible account that Fitzgerald Moore was told at least one of Ben's stories."

"And where there's smoke, there's fire," Ward declares.

"*Usually*," Sweeny inserts as Ward barrels on loudly.

"This big oaf knew the stories, and in his clinically unwell state, he murdered four people. Who knows? Maybe he thought it wasn't real? Maybe he had a break with reality or thought he was acting the stories out?"

"None of that really matters at this juncture," Sweeny cuts in. "Fitzgerald Moore is in police custody and there he will remain until he stands trial or is remanded to an institution."

"He was in police custody this morning. What's your explanation for the fire in the preserve?" Dad asks.

"Our fire inspector and officers had a look around," Sweeny says. "There's nothing to suggest that it wasn't a hiker or squatter using the cabin for a place to escape the cold. The fire spread from the fireplace—an accident, it would seem. No accelerant used, and it burned itself out once the structure was demolished."

"But Maggie's note," I say. Dad puts his arm around me and draws me to his side. "The cabin is where we found the photo album."

Sweeny sighs and moves so she's poised on my other side. "It's possible Maggie was using the cabin before her death. We don't understand Ms. Lewis's involvement with Fitzgerald Moore. Not yet. We will, though." There's no conviction in her words.

Willa's voice in my head is louder than those outside it after that point. A mentally ill man who knew the stories and lives in Gant is a much more reasonable suspect than an old man, who is reportedly dead. Soon Josh hugs me good-bye, murmurs that he'll call me, and leads Carolynn, who has completely shut down, from the house. The police disperse too. Dad speaks heatedly over the phone with the folks at Calm Coast for the second time, and they promise to have Diane call once she emerges from the haze of tranquilizer they injected her with while I was there.

I'm in a haze of my own the next two days. I am here in the living room, tucked under a mohair throw, staring at the fog rolling in to blanket the harbor. I am not here.

I am the Lana who nerve and mischief failed. I am June. I am barbecue on the air and blood in my mouth and my flip-flops sticking to the asphalt as the police snapped photos of my arms, torso, and face.

I am disappointed because this end to our story would not have satisfied Ben. Ben's villains were evil to their core; they weren't mentally ill and off their meds. Knowing Ben, he would feel compassion for Fitzgerald. Anger, sure, but in Ben's heart he would have blamed the world that failed Fitzgerald more than the man himself. That leaves me frustrated. I never played the hero.

I hear the rumblings when Dad is on the phone with Josh's moms or the police are in Dad's office with him. I hear the lawyer's advice when newspapers start hounding us. There are those who think Ben was at least a tiny bit to blame. *What was a boy like Ben McBrook doing befriending a man like Fitzgerald Moore?* The gist is this: If he'd never bothered to be kind, Ben would be alive, the others also. No good deed goes unpunished. I bet that's what Mom would say if she were here. She liked that adage, even though it wasn't one of her originals.

I can only stomach talking to Willa about it. She sits on the opposite end of the couch two mornings after we learned that Ben's grandfather is dead.

"I failed," I whisper. Dad is working on the terrace. Diane is coming home tomorrow. We're expecting the worst when we drive to pick her up from Calm Coast. But we'll be happy to have her. Our family will be as whole as it can be.

344 • ALEXANDRA SIROWY

"How do you mean?" Willa asks.

"I was supposed to hunt Ben's killer down. All of it, Swisher Spring, hiking back into the preserve, going to see Diane—I was just on the trail of a ghost. I dragged the others along. Sweeny and Ward found Skitzy-Fitzy. I didn't get any revenge or even justice for Ben."

"They're the police. That's their job," Willa says. "We're seventeen and about to start our last year of high school." She picks at the seam of her jeans. "Ben would understand. He would be grateful that you fought for him." She plucks my hand from my lap and laces her fingers in mine. "He would want you to move on." She raises our joined hands and emphasizes her next words. "Ada-freaking-Lovelace, Lana, Ben would want you to *live*, to go out with Josh, to make it to the homecoming dance, to get into the college of your dreams, all of it. Ben wanted that for you." Her hair is wavy and frenzied, framing her face like a lion's mane, and her eyes glow. "It's time to fight for yourself."

The ambiguous noise I plan to make catches in my throat when I hear those words, spoken in her fierce whisper. I'm less and less sure of what Ben would have wanted and who he was.

We wanted secrets. He had plenty—they were just from me.

We wanted shared history. He had more history than I knew. Our make-believe, adventures, and stories—the very things that had grown to be a part of me, like an organ that was vital to my survival—turned out to belong to someone else.

Every story is recast in the sickly yellow of a bruise that refuses to heal. As Ben fades, Willa does not. Willa is steady and determined as always. Willa wants me to fight, and I realize how much I want to. My knuckles are going weak in anticipation. That daring, hungry little voice is here, whispering, *Live, go on, dare to be happy.*

"Listen, the end-of-the-summer bonfire is tonight," Willa says.

I touch my chest and say in mock horror, "Who are you and what have you done with my best friend?"

She throws her hands up. "I know, I know, I am the last person in the universe you would expect to hear this from, but—and I swear to you that my brain hasn't been hijacked by an alien life-form that craves Jell-O shots and testosterone-fueled drinking games—I think we should go. The others—Duncan, Rusty, Josh, and Carolynn—are all going, and everyone thinks it would be good for you to get out."

"You've been talking to them?"

She shrugs. "Someone had to, since you've gone incommunicado and won't answer Josh's or Carolynn's calls. They want us to be together tonight, a united front at the bonfire. No one's thrilled about going, but school starts in *three days.*" She waves three fingers in my face. "It's either tonight or we show up for first period on Monday and it's baptism by fire."

It's difficult to deny Willa's argument. I can't put off facing the outside world much longer. I can't go back to making myself a tiny ball so that there is less of me to ache for Ben, for Becca, even for Maggie and Ford. And I don't want to.

This is why, eight hours later, I'm pulling jeans on when Josh calls, and for the first time in days, I answer.

"Hi."

"Hey." A pause, then, "This is Josh Parker . . . blond hair, blue eyes, *really ridiculously good-looking and funny.* We shared a kiss once—twice."

I laugh.

"I was just double-checking that you remember me, since we haven't talked in so long."

"Yeah, sorry about that."

"Don't apologize. Just actually show up tonight, okay?"

"I will. I'm leaving soon to pick up Willa."

"Yeah? Good. You better be there, because I'm going to hold my breath."

"I promise. I'll see you soon. And Josh?"

"Yes, Lana?"

"Thank you."

"For?"

"Being you."

A happy laugh. "I couldn't stop even if I wanted to," he says.

Dad's in the media room. I peek through the door at an old family movie playing on the projection screen. The four of us are at a ski cabin. Ben and I are hunched over a Scrabble board, with Diane laughing between sips from a ceramic mug. She comes up with whipped cream on her nose, and the camera shakes as Dad chuckles. It's possible Dad's watched videos like this since Ben, and I was just too wrapped up in my own grief to notice his. I toe through the door and hug his neck from behind. He smells like cologne that reminds me of being a little kid bundled up beside him when we'd go to watch downtown lit up in December.

He squeezes my arms back, and I see tears in the lines at the corners of his eyes. He clears his throat of emotion. "You headed to go get Willa?"

"Yeah," I say. "I'd like to watch these with you sometime."

He half turns, and I see a hopeful smile. "I'd like that too."

I go to twist the front doorknob as it occurs to me that if this is really a new start, not *before* or even *after*, then I need to do something before I leave. I flip the floodlights on for the terrace and scrunch my neck deeper into my sweater's collar.

The note I wrote Ben is waiting in my hiding place, along with the rosary Detective Sweeny never collected from me. The rosary was one of many dangling threads she and Ward left loose and flapping. I told the police that the rosary appeared shortened when I checked after Ford was found. There were frowns and under-their-breath words traded by the adults around me. Dad's been cryptic, but I've gotten the impression that the detectives were under a lot of pressure to close the murder investigations. Poisonings, stabbings, and hangings aren't great for Gant's reputation, and everyone is determined to put these events behind them, shrug them off like the flaky, dead skin of a sunburn. No one wanted to ask why or how or even if Fitzgerald Moore used my great-great-grandmother's rosary. It was easier to cast me as confused and unreliable.

Newspaper headlines—the ones I've seen on Dad's desk—focus on a sick man and his breakdown. Some even refer to him as a vagrant, as if Skitzy-Fitzy didn't live in Gant as much as the rest of us. I want to turn the rosary in even if I worry that my fingerprints are all they'll find and they'll have that much more reason to think I'm a poor, traumatized girl, manufacturing conflicting evidence. I don't want the burden of any more secrets to keep. And I need to destroy the note I wrote Ben, toss it into the bonfire, and feel that thread between Ben and me burn.

The stone stairs are slick with mist. There's music floating to me across the harbor. It echoes, and the notes become dissonant and jarring. At the lower level I cut around the fire pit. I keep the memories of all our nights spent here from creeping up. Being in that dream state where I can remember things so acutely it's close to reliving them won't help me. The Ben who I thought I knew as well as I knew myself was a figment of my imagination. All those nights we huddled around the flames would have been perfect nights for him to tell me the story of a small boy who fled his home with his mother.

My fingers jab at the cold, dry rock of my hidey-spot. A web tickles my pinkie finger just as it nudges the paper and rosary. I retrieve my hand and wipe away the spiderweb stuck to my knuckle. I unfold the note to make certain that a spider isn't hiding inside.

You swore on summer.

My words look up at me, and under them, in Ben's handwriting:

Come escape with me.

The clanging guitar chords are louder; the singer's soprano is piercing. I stagger for the stairs. My legs shake, causing my right foot to miss. My left foot loses traction on the slick rock, and I grab for the banister. My weight jolts through my arm and my knees strike the stone. I veer hard to the left, my temple colliding with a boulder on the hill. I hiss at the pain. I see shimmery white stars twinkling. After one, two, three tries I replace the treads of both my shoes on the staircase.

The pain radiates through my neck and down my spine as I hike for the terrace. I move through the house, the front door, over the lawn. I drop the car remote, bend, and catch myself pitching forward as the ground tilts under me. I retrieve it and hit the button that pops the trunk.

Eyes screwed up, I rub them with my fists. At last I open them. My head throbs and I wince, checking that I'm not bleeding. I wonder if I imagined the second line on the note because of the injury. Then I'm holding the note out, seeing that the words are still there. The fall came *after*. The trunk is nothing but a dark, empty mouth. A gaping, black ghoul's gullet. The army-green chest labeled *Summer Provisions* that we lugged aboard the *Mira* is gone.

Come escape with me.

— 33 —

shouldn't be driving. My reflexes are sluggish; brain signals muddling instructions. I flip on the blinker ten seconds after a lane change. I speed up rather than brake at a yellow light. The operations necessary to use the Bluetooth to call Willa have left me. I am one thought: *Get to where we dock the* Mira.

I screech into the parking lot for boat owners. It's mostly empty. It's just past nine, and the air around the lampposts is swarming with white, papery moths. They're the kind with fat bodies that thud into you and then swerve away unharmed. Bubble lights are inset in the planks of the dock, lighting it from either side. My feet pound over the weather-grayed wood. Fragments of thought race by: senior year beginning in three days; I'm excited to see Josh and Carolynn tonight; I could have blacked out in a PTSD haze, forged Ben's handwriting, and removed the summer provisions chest from my trunk.

I list the contents of the missing chest to bring order to my head: two aluminum foil balls from our turkey avocado sandwiches; one bag of unopened salt-and-vinegar potato chips; two empty bottles of root beer; one empty can of actual beer; a set of mini waterproof speakers; a flare gun kit; a seagull's feather; and two rain slickers.

The *Mira*'s stall is in the lane farthest from the lot. I follow the dock jutting out a few hundred feet from land. I haven't been here for more than two months. The *Mira* was like Swisher Spring in that she was ours. How wrong that she could exist in a world where Ben didn't. I pass the last vessel before her and stop short. The *Mira*'s there with her white sails tied down, pinstripe siding, weather-beaten cabin door, and strands of white lights on the mast left over from Christmas.

I drop my eyes and stare at the puddle of light I'm standing at the center of, cast by the lamppost at my back. I want it to be a portal to another world, one where things are set right, where Ben is alive. I would slip into this alternate reality and never come back. The wind picks up and the lamppost creaks; the circle of light moves with it. I'm working up the courage to climb aboard, to search for the summer provisions chest, even though it can't be here. Nothing seems quite real, and truthfully, I've forgotten how to tell what is. The bleached wood under my feet begins to resemble stone. Crickets chirp from the bank of grass separating the dock and the parking lot. The wind slips past me, rushing to arrive somewhere.

I sense him in the pit of my stomach. I raise my head dreamily. Coming out of the cabin door of the *Mira* is an apparition.

"I knew you'd find me." I catch the barest whisper from the ghost.

I stride forward, pick up speed, slow. I'm not more than five feet from the *Mira*'s bow. I must have hit my head hard. But Ben's figure isn't vaporous, about to be blown away by the harbor's next gale. The breeze whooshes in at that moment, and the boy stays solid. A faded mariner's cap is pulled low over his eyes; the wispy gold hair that

352 • ALEXANDRA SIROWY

used to curl around his ears has been sheared off. His sweatshirt
sleeves are scrunched up to his elbows, and his hands are sunk to his
knuckles in his front jean pockets. His square chin is set, and I can
make out the faint crescent scar at its center from the *Mira*'s boom
splitting it years ago.

I touch my scraped temple to see how much blood I've lost. It's
only sticky.

"You aren't real," I tell him.

He removes the cap and passes his hand over his buzzed head.
He cocks a sly eyebrow. "No?" He draws out the single syllable, molten. "What am I, then?"

I go to say *magic*, but I don't believe that anymore. Ben was the
opposite of magic. He was all smoke and mirrors. "My hallucination."

He scratches the back of his head and says, mock gravely, "I see.
Do you hallucinate me often?"

"Lately, yes." I am not ashamed admitting it. "For a while I was
sure you were a ghost and on the island."

He flashes that flirtatious smile that I was never on the receiving
end of. "You want to come aboard and tell me what I was doing in all
those hallucinations of yours?"

I frown. This wasn't our way. We didn't flirt. He didn't use that
self-assured smirk, calibrated perfectly to get out of trouble, on me.
If I were dreaming, projecting Ben on the sky, it wouldn't be this
version. It would be *my* Ben. It would be Ben whose stories and
ideas connected with the darkest and lightest places in me; who
smiled a conspirator's grin; and who I beat at most Scrabble games
and diving contests. This Ben is delivering a line and a wink. He's
an imposter, a con artist.

He's supposed to be dead, but this Ben is *alive*.

I catapult over the bow. I collide with his chest and throw my arms around his shoulders. My feet shuffle between his shoes to get closer. I attach myself like June and the Grim Reaper are coming to drag him back to death if I don't. Ben's arms move around my waist, and I hide my face between his shoulder and collar. A rough sob disappears into his chest. He absorbs it. He turns it into a smile. He smells of wind and salt, and he's impossibly solid.

"It will be over soon. *Shhh.*" He rocks back on his heels and lifts me to my tiptoes. "It's okay. I've got you." His hand curves at the base of my neck. My heart knocks louder and faster.

I pull back. Ben's gray eyes are quick to mine. Clouds pass over the moon and a stormy cast of light flickers on his cheeks. I want to be that light. I want to be bright and liquid slipping over his skin. I want this to be cosmic intervention. Ben was brought back to life or only half murdered, and he was sent to the *Mira* to wait for me. Out of nowhere, completely unbidden, I hear my mother's words in my head, *Perception is nine-tenths of everything, even the truth, Lana.* She never acknowledged that things are rarely what they seem.

Ben's palms cup my face. He thumbs away a tear. "I read about Winnie in the paper. 'Suspected Environmental Activists Free Eagle from Captivity.' Jesus, you freed that fucking eagle for me just like I always wanted to do, didn't you?"

I nod. Ben recognized it as a message. "You're here," I say, testing it out. I brush his light-touched cheek.

He holds my hand in place as his eyes dart up the dock. "I have an explanation for everything," he says, suddenly urgent. "I have a story to tell you." A hint of a smile on his lips at those words—the ones that used to fill me with anticipation but now only bring on dread. "We need to leave before someone spots us."

He takes my hand from his cheek and we walk to the controls of the inboard engine in the cockpit. He flips the switch, and the gentle puttering joins the crickets. The mainsail and the jib-stay remain tied down, and the engine revs as we accelerate backward. I dig my fingers into the cockpit seat. My eyes are glued to Ben. I am a bursting heart and an unbound smile. I don't trust that he won't disappear.

Ben shifts gears and we taxi in the direction of the sound. This is my golden, opinionated, storytelling Ben, and he's carrying us away. I can't stop thinking, though. Here he is, on the *Mira*, two days after Fitzgerald Moore was arrested. Two days after I visited Calm Coast to learn about his hateful grandfather.

Ben is dead. Bled out. Splattered all over the highway. Yet here he is. I used to be so careful touching him. What would he think? Who might be watching? I resisted, and then Ben vanished—dead, *I thought*. I lace my fingers with his. I squeeze until our bones pinch. Until it hurts. My fingers brush his wrist, his forearm, and disappear up his sleeve. My left shoe kisses his right shoe. We are ankle to ankle, knee to knee, hip to hip.

My thoughts shoulder in a queue in my head. They demand to be considered. How is this possible? Was Ben half murdered? If anyone could survive, it would be Ben. Were his injuries not as serious as the police thought? Was it someone else's blood? But that's impossible, because his DNA was in it. It was Ben's. All of it.

We cut through the water fast. I close my eyes to keep the sea spray from stinging. The memory of that night last winter comes blasting in with the wind. Ben on the lower terrace asking me how

I could stand it; how I let *them* get away with it. He promised that someday he'd do something and that he'd come back to Gant only for me. He swore on summer.

I try to be only a bursting heart and relief that Ben is here. I try so effing hard that my eyes leak. I have Ben and he has me and what does anything else matter? What does it matter that everyone thinks he's dead? The uneasiness fades. My thoughts lapse. There's only Ben, *alive*.

He's vigilant as he checks that no boats are following. He tugs his hat on and looks down at me to wink. A flutter in my chest. The sky is stormy, its gray clouds rippled with the look of squiggly brains, and I wonder what the sky thinks of us. Does the sky wonder where we're headed like I do?

We travel north, the lights of Seattle at our right, and the sound flowing into the Pacific sixty miles northwest of us. A few more miles and we weave between uninhabited bits of land and sparsely populated coastline to the east. Ben veers west until we follow the shore of a small feral island we've explored before. He cuts the engine.

"I know this place," I say, holding the railing and squinting at the pebbled shore.

Ben's shoulder rests against mine. "We camped here two years ago. We picked wild blueberries and I drank too much and ants got into the marshmallows."

I laugh. "You caught a salmon, and neither of us wanted to scale or gut it, so we let it go. We needed those marshmallows for dinner." I breathe him in with the sea air.

"It was cold at night and your teeth chattered. We didn't have a tent." He faces me. "We were back to back. I couldn't sleep." His fingers brush my hair from my shoulder. "I almost told you to crawl into my sleeping bag. What would you have said?"

"I would have pretended I was asleep." The cockpit feels very small. The edge of the stern and the slapping water are three feet away. Ben fills the universe, so of course he crowds the boat. I look toward the island. It's a state park with no houses, just a parking lot, a boat dock, a ramp, and a thin bridge connecting it to the mainland. I chew my lip. "Where have you been?" He doesn't answer. "The police said you lost fifty percent of your blood. *Five pints*," I whisper. I touch my bottom lip. "Your blood was in my mouth. It was *everywhere*."

He gives me a sad, measured smile. "You've already figured it out. I can tell by the way you're frowning. It's your frown when you anticipate a twist in a story." Those words bring on pain in my chest. I worry I won't be that surprised by what comes next. "I ordered a blood draw kit online. I researched the longest period of time blood could be frozen for there to be DNA to extract. Three and a half months at thirty-nine degrees Fahrenheit. I took three pints in the two weeks leading up to my trip. I stored it in the bottom of the freezer in the garage. No one ever uses it. I took two more pints in the five days I was home to make certain the cops would get enough fresh DNA mixed in. It was brutal but necessary." He says this as one long monotone note. He doesn't take a breath, just sighs loudly when he's done, as if in relief.

"Necessary," I repeat.

He meets my eyes, a glint of something I don't recognize in them. "To make them think I was dead."

I am light-headed. Was I expecting that? Not in the cool tone or in such great detail. I round the cockpit's seat and grip the cold rail at my waist.

"Maggie helped me. Fitzgerald too. He was the man on the highway. He had my blood, and we made it convincing." His voice is soft and precise at my back. My breath is turning gaspy. The wind and the mist roll off the waves, and I'm breathing in icicles. "I'd read a little about blood splatter. What it needed to look like to simulate a stabbing."

I close my eyes. "You let me think you were dead for more than two months." I whirl to face him.

His heavy-lidded eyes are wide open, no flirty squint to them. "I told you that I'd always come back for you."

"Come back for me?" I push off the railing. I stab at the air with my shaking finger. "You were dead. *Gone.*" I believed him, though, didn't I? He swore on summer and I thought it was possible.

He takes my hand from where it points at him. "We can leave, me and you. We can go anywhere. I have everything we'll need." He squeezes my hand. "They won't even look for us; there will be no reason to look for you. We ditch this boat." He releases me and bends to unlatch the chest on the floor. Our summer provisions. In the light of the boat's lantern I see all the things I remember, with one addition: a transparent bag and plastic tubing on top; what must be a blood draw kit. He waves at it. "We take a pint of your blood, leave it smeared across the bow. The coast guard will put it together."

I sag backward into the railing. "You want them to search for my body like they searched for yours? For my dad to think I'm dead? For Diane to?"

"We'll find a way to let them know that we're all right. I don't know how yet, but there has to be a way, when we're too far to be

358 • ALEXANDRA SIROWY

found, when enough time has passed, when there's no risk. I don't want to hurt Cal—I never did. But my mother will probably be relieved that she doesn't have anyone left to take care of. That she doesn't have to try any longer for me; she can disappear into her head."

"And who will supposedly be my killer?" I ask.

"Same as mine. My grandfather. They'll blame it on him," he says.

"Your sick, twisted grandfather," I whisper.

"God, exactly. I knew you'd figure it out. I knew that one way or another you'd find the beginning of my story." He points. I hadn't noticed the vague outline of a rowboat, anchored off the shore of the tiny island and bobbing. "We'll row in. There's a car parked. We'll drive north. I have cash, new clothes, new IDs. The cops will figure that my grandfather had another way off the boat or maybe you took him down with you. You were his next victim."

My stomach clenches. "That wouldn't work." His brows draw up in confusion. "It can't. Your grandfather is dead," I say. "The police know all about it."

Ben's features sag and melt like he's a wax boy. He steps back and, in a burst of violence, kicks the chest. It jumps and rattles. His shoe leaves a divot in its metal. "When?" he asks, shaking his hands out at his sides.

I look from the dent in the chest to Ben. "Months ago. He died in a hospital in Switzerland." I have the sense that I'm teetering on the edge. I'm at the spring and I've just realized that the water below has gone dry. And it doesn't matter; I will jump. "Why didn't you tell me about him?"

He gives an impatient, angry huff. "He was a phantom. A nightmare, Lana. Why did you need to know that someone like him existed?"

"Because he *did* exist," I say. "Because you don't get to decide what I should and shouldn't know."

"I didn't want you to think of me as a victim."

"No, you'd rather I think of you like this." I gesture at him. "You're okay with me knowing now. You wanted me to find out who he was and where you came from. Now that it's a part of this . . . this . . ."

"What good would it have done if you'd known earlier?" Ben asks. "I kept tabs on him. I read about some stroke he had on the Internet, and then he vanished. No records of what happened to him at any hospitals." He snorts. "Guess now I know why."

He braces himself against the rail, bows his head into the wind, and then shoves off. He's all mad steps and sharp pivots. "It doesn't matter that he's dead. Once you disappear, they'll have to look past Fitz. They'll let him go. That's the big thing. He was only supposed to be a red herring." He stops in front of me abruptly. He's knocked the cap from his head. "Fitzgerald bought me more time. I couldn't be sure that the cops would buy that it was my grandfather, and I needed to stick around to wait for you. I couldn't do that if the island was crawling with cops looking for suspects. I needed them to believe it was Fitz so they'd let their guard down." He rubs the back of his neck, scowls darkly at the island, and then nods resolutely. "It'll go unsolved. They won't have a fucking clue what's really happened." He smiles to himself.

Another pain in my chest. I press my hand to stop it.

He looks at me out of the corner of his eye. "God, you don't look like you," he says.

"You don't look like you," I reply.

He faces me straight on. "I watched you that day at the spring, when you went back to find evidence, and I thought, fuck, *it's working.* I did all of this for us." His tone warms to tender as he slips closer. *"For you."*

— 3 4 —

I was watching you disappear. We were kids and you were all bright colors, steady hands, and guts, and you taught me to be brave. Shit, I was such a weakling. You didn't know how fucked up I was. We'd been running. Diane"—he says her name like she's no more than a former acquaintance—"she dragged me from place to place. 'Don't make friends. Look out for strangers.' Strangers"—a bitter laugh— "which was everybody."

His eyes go round and scared like they were when we were kids, and I recognize him fleetingly. My arms twitch to hug him; I don't. "She was paranoid. Making me hide if someone knocked on the door. Never letting me play outside or over another kid's house. My grandfather was a fucking sicko, and yeah, something serious would have happened if we'd stayed, and it might have happened to my cousins because they did, but I don't know for sure that he ever tried to follow us. I never saw him. I mean, he was old even before we left. He hit me once"—he points to the bend in his nose—"because I tried to protect my younger cousin. He was weaker than his sister, an easy mark. The old bastard liked an easy mark."

"Why?"

"He was always . . . off. My mother was sure he hired investigators and tracked us along. She'd been traumatized, so who knows what was in her head and what wasn't? Didn't matter; it was real for her and she made the fear real for me." He rolls his shoulders like he's knocking Diane off them. "I didn't get that until I was older, until I felt safe"— his hand cuts across the air to me—"with you. You taught me to be brave. Fearless." I remember Ben, head dipped low, backpack hiked up, as Dad dropped him off for his first day of school. I threw rocks at bullying boys when they rode their bikes by our front yard to shout names at him. No doubt they ended up worshipping Ben once he grew into himself. Ben's right. I was fearless. I vaguely remember egging Ben on that day on the dock when he dunked Mariella's son's head under the water. Did I tell him to do it? Am I partly responsible for our particular brand of justice?

"I was watching you get stomped on," Ben says. "Middle and high school you got quieter, kept your head down, and what was worse, you wouldn't talk to me about it. I thought, maybe this is what she wants? You had Willa, and you guys had plans, and if it made you happy, what the hell." He glides along the rail until our arms meet. "But I could hear it in your voice. Willa was authentic. She only cared about getting away from her mother. I heard you whispering about that dumb fuck Josh Parker. I saw the way that monster with her yapping harpies froze you out. I knew what Holland was doing to you. And it was obvious that you wanted to belong." He nudges my shoulder until I meet his eyes. "Why didn't you tell me?"

I break eye contact.

"I realized it was Becca spreading rumors," he says. "A girl in my class overheard her and told me. It was the end of my senior year, when I really started paying attention. I couldn't believe that I'd missed it. You avoided walking through halls where certain girls had their lockers. You never came into the quad. You ate lunch in the library. If I touched you, you jumped away. You dropped astronomy second semester; you were a freaking nerd for astronomy. Then I saw you hurrying out of the classroom on your last day. Your face was red and Ford was on your heels, sneering at you. He was in that class, and you hated him more than you loved astronomy." Hearing Ben recount these times I made myself small makes me feel even smaller.

"I kept waiting for you to come clean. To ask for help. It was obvious you didn't want me to know. And then I graduated and I hoped that would make it easier for you." He wasn't wrong. Once Ben had graduated, it was harder for those girls to make my face red. Ben couldn't overhear any of it, and a large portion of me stopped caring. Carolynn had been mostly ignoring me, Becca may have continued spreading lies without me knowing, and girls who just liked spreading rumors didn't see the sport in teasing me if I didn't give a crap.

"And then Maggie," Ben groans. "You don't know what she said. We broke up, last September, and she told some underclassman stoners she smoked with that she broke it off because you kept making passes at me. She said . . . she said some really screwed-up stuff."

I cover my face for a moment. Ben was gone from school, I was good at making myself small, and yet for a week kids were snickering when I walked by. Fragments reached me: Desperate Lana . . . naked . . . in Ben's room . . . Maggie walked in.

"I confronted her. She was manipulative." He laughs bitterly. "She kept saying that maybe it was true. Why else would I be pissed that she told people? She said she knew you were the reason I kept breaking up with her. I don't know. I lost it." His hands drift to his forehead as he shakes his head, regretful. "I looked at her then, and I hated her because she wasn't wrong. Jesus, Lana, I wanted to hurt her in the way she'd been hurting you. I told her she was right. You were who I wanted. I lied, Lan." He stares wearily at me, chest heaving. "Not about wanting you. I lied and told her we'd been screwing all along." I swallow. Ben's eyes flick to my throat.

"She went nuts. She said she'd tell everybody—she'd tell Cal. I freaked. I begged her to forget it. I was a lying shit. She took me back, but I don't think she ever believed me."

Things changed their second year dating. If I entered the room, Maggie would find a seat in Ben's lap, rock her hips, make me squirm. She spent the night. I slept with a pillow over my head to block out her giggling. If Maggie and I were in a room alone, she'd obstinately kick the chair I was in or slam the fridge in my face as I looked inside. Obviously, I hated her for having Ben and for despising me for no reason. But there was a reason. She had what I wanted and I had what she wanted.

"It wasn't the Maggies of the world or those bitchy girls at school or that loser Holland. There'd be more of them," he says. "It was that you weren't yourself and you were letting them change you. The Lana I knew would have flipped those girls off. She would have kicked Holland in the balls. It was killing me to see you like that. You made me brave once. I thought I could do it for you."

"Lana the brave," I say. How comic it sounds.

"You needed an out."

"I didn't need you to rescue me," I say firmly. "I wasn't an eagle in a cage."

"No, you needed to rescue *me*. I wasn't trying to change you, just . . . just remind you who you are. I gave you a villain."

I stand, motionless, terrified of his next words.

"I faked my death because I thought if anything would jolt you awake, it would be that. I let you grieve. I was going to leave you clues once you came out of it." His voice goes desperate and hoarse. "That's all it was supposed to be. You'd follow the clues. I told Maggie about my grandfather. I made her think I was doing this to get away from him—he was days away from here. I told her I had to disappear and needed her to be able to move around Gant, to help me. I thought that it would be easier if people believed we'd broken up. I was worried about the cops piecing together that it was staged. I thought they'd be less likely to go in that direction if a burned ex-girlfriend gave a statement. No one would think she'd lie for me." Maggie and Ben planned the highway together. In the jaundiced glow of the boat's lantern, he isn't golden but yellow. The tendons protrude from his wrists as his hands run over his scalp. The sweatshirt drapes at his sides. He's depleted; emptied of magic.

"But then once she'd helped, the cops suspected her of being involved in *committing* the crime. I hadn't foreseen that. She was livid, said her whole life was ruined. I had to do whatever it took to shut her up. I had to keep her with me. We went to Seattle for weeks, and then I told her that I couldn't disappear for good without leaving you a note. Closure. She was okay with it because she thought we were leaving you behind."

"We came back to Gant a couple of weeks ago and hid in that cabin in the preserve. But do you know what I saw when I went looking for you?" He lifts my chin with a finger. "You were at a bonfire with those kids. Parker had his arm around you." His eyes go glacially cold. "You weren't pursuing my killer. You'd moved on."

I push his hand away. My throat is closing. "I was gutted," I say roughly.

"Didn't look it. You were drinking a beer and singing along to the lyrics of some pop song. My plan to frame my grandfather for my murder and then reveal myself to you so we could leave Gant was turning to shit." His voice goes quiet and his hands tuck into his pockets. "You needed a nudge. I had Maggie let herself into the house and leave you that note. Wrote exactly what I told her to. She took my photo album. She didn't care why we were doing any of it. She just wanted to go. Problem was she went through the pack I left behind and found a letter."

"Hearts and doves, dated March seventeenth," I say. "We found it in her backpack. You lied to me about not writing to her."

He looks wounded as he shakes his head. "It was to you. She came out of the house with a stack of letters I'd written and never had the guts to send. Confessions about everything I wanted; what I was planning to do. Can you imagine how pissed she was? She said if we left together that minute, she'd let it all go. I begged her to wait. She threatened going to the cops. She was going to ruin it. I thought, what the hell? *She deserves it.* You needed a bigger villain; you needed one from our stories."

My hand's at my throat. I'm agitated, can't remain still, at the holler and calm of his confession. "You poisoned her with my rosary," I say.

He jerks his head, flicking phantom hair from his eyes. "I tried, yeah. It would have been fucking poetic. It belonged to you, but no one was going to trace it to you because no one living knew it existed. I'd taken it from that old chest with some other stuff way back when we opened it. I couldn't use Maggie again to sneak into the house for it. I had to go. Middle of the day. You were out. Cal was gone. Basel growled at me—can you believe that? He knew I wasn't supposed to be there. I smashed up two of those rosary peas and put them in Maggie's canned pineapple. I thought it would be enough. She'd been getting paranoid that I was going to ditch her, though, and when she started feeling sick, she freaked out and ran. And okay, maybe I'd been watching her like I was waiting for it to kick in.

"She went for the cave under the spring that I'd showed her, knew I didn't fit. I would have waited her out, but then there you were." His expression is absorbed, watching it play out. "It was a colossal fuckup. She could have surfaced and told you everything. There was the way she died, too. You dragged her up. I worried about how long it might have taken her to drown. The police would be suspicious. When you were hauled in, I called in an anonymous tip about the cave. I'd camped across from the house and saw the cops."

Ben was there, witness to everything. A hollow, black feeling washes through me. "I'd left the rosary in our hiding spot. I don't know why." He gives a plaintive sigh. "Maybe I'm lying? Maybe I hoped you'd find it . . . guess it was me. You'd see what I was doing and you'd be happier for it. I liked thinking you were my accomplice. But with the police showing up, I thought, what if she turns it in to them? It would have had both our fingerprints, yeah. I was presumed dead, so you would have taken the heat. I would have come clean, you know that, right? I never would have let you get into trouble. You were never in danger."

I try to move around him; he blocks me.

"It had to feel real for it to work," he says pleadingly.

I grab his arms and dig my fingers through his sleeves. "Do you hear yourself? You are admitting to killing Maggie. You are confessing to *murder*."

A calm settles over him and the night, and the silence pulses in my ears before he says, "I am confessing to you. It's no different from admitting it to myself."

I shrink away. The horror of what I thought Ben had done was less when Ben was dead and returned. He was changed into some not-quite-living thing. And you don't blame a ghost for acting ghastly. Then I saw Becca and it became unforgivable. And impossible. It wasn't real just like our stories—they *weren't* supposed to be real. Make-believe allowed me to slay the monsters in my imagination; it built me up. This violence is cutting and it only tears down. Ben is not a vengeful hero from a story. He is flesh and blood and murder.

"I didn't know you were going to the spring until I saw you leave that morning. I watched you dive. You were proof, Lan. It was working. You were braver. Daring. Yourself."

I can't stand his face. His eyes ignite with the lantern light, giving him a duplicitous, cat-eyed look. I watch the light-touched clouds above our heads in the silver and navy sky as Ben's voice rumbles along like distant thunder. "I felt certain that you'd found the rosary. You were trying to put it together. But you hadn't come looking for where Maggie had stashed the photo album, so you obviously hadn't found her note yet. I'd told her to leave the note somewhere only you'd see.

"You weren't coming clean with the cops about the link between our stories and the murders. I figured it was only a matter of time till you connected the stories with someone in my past. You'd understand that whoever told me the stories would be the killer. The album was the oldest thing I had; you knew right where I hid it. Then Parker's party. I was in the trees behind the house, and there you were with Ford. I heard you tell him off. It was like you were talking directly to me, asking me to take care of him next."

"I wasn't asking you anything," I say. "I stuck up for myself. It was enough."

"No, it wasn't. He was worse than his brother. And he was out there, staggering home. Hammered. I used enough poison that time, shoved it down his throat, but it was going to take the cops a couple of days to run tests. I wasn't even sure they'd tell people he was poisoned like Maggie. I couldn't be sure you'd find out. I set Fitz busy catching all those birds. I killed those yappers to give you a push. You'd see more fragments of our stories, and the link to my past would be in your face. Undeniable." He is silent for a moment. Then he says, reluctantly, "I admit that Becca was partially because I saw you and Parker kissing that night. I had to follow you. Had to know if I was getting through to you."

"Stop," I say.

"Fuck, Lana." He tilts his square chin high, defying me. "You free that eagle for me, and then you kiss him up there for the whole island to see. *I lost my temper.*"

"I mean it, shut up," I say louder.

He does shut up. The line of his mouth blurs as he holds the admission in. He starts up again as a whisper. "I almost jumped Josh.

Except that wasn't what this was about. Maggie had gotten you to focus. Ford had it coming, and it was the revenge you deserved. You hadn't come to look for the album, which meant you hadn't found the note, which meant you hadn't searched my room. I couldn't make it easy; you had to be the hero tracking down the villain for this to work. You needed a more obvious connection to our stories. I needed the victim to deserve it—and she did—and you needed it to be someone you would fight for. Becca was the obvious choice."

I try to force the pieces to snap into place so that an alternative explanation takes shape. So that I do not have to believe what Ben is confessing to.

"You'd tell the cops that Becca's murder was identical to a story I'd told. They'd rattle Diane until she spilled about my grandfather and his stories and house of horrors. Or you'd find the note, hunt down the album that was always just waiting for you in the cabin, and demand the truth from her. Your trail, the cops' trail, they'd both lead back to him. And he was a phantom."

An alternative explanation isn't coming together. But one unlikelihood occurs to me. "I could have been hurt in the cabin fire. You would never hurt me."

He shakes his head adamantly. "I put the photo album by the door. You hardly needed to go inside. I didn't think you'd bring all of them with you. I only needed the fire as a distraction so I could get away. I knew you'd go for it. The way you looked running through the trees toward it . . . you were amazing."

"I might never have found that place."

"You knew right where to look. We explored those cabins together. It was near the spring where Maggie died. If you hadn't found it, I would have figured something else out. I'm not saying the plan was flawless. It evolved. It was a moving target."

I want to slip into the water below; make myself scarce and invisible. If there is less of me to listen, there will be less of me that knows what Ben has done. "You killed three people."

"It saved you." His profile is silhouetted against the lantern. He's still exquisite. "I'd do it again and again to bring you back."

"You killed two innocent little dogs. You killed birds. How could you be capable of all that?" I tangle my hands in my hair and pull. "How could you say you did it for me? It's hateful. Becca, Ford, and Maggie were people. Becca had friends. She had a mother who's alone now. Maggie and Ford might have grown up to become decent people," I say. "You ended their lives."

"They were villains," he says emphatically. "The hero kills the villains. And those kids you've been bashing around with? You think I didn't see them at parties or at school? You think I don't know Carolynn Winters or Rusty Pipe or Duncan Alvarez? Becca, Ford, and Maggie were cruel to you. They went first. Maybe I should have picked Carolynn? Or Parker?"

"Josh never did anything to me."

"You had it bad for him for years and he didn't know you existed until ... until ..."

"Until what? Until your murder was spooky and people were whispering about it? Until the tragedy reflected on me and made me more interesting to them?"

"You said it, not me. I didn't want to hurt you. None of this was to hurt you."

He reaches for me. I slap his hand away. "What about Fitzgerald?

Was this supposed to hurt him?" I yell. "He's being charged with four murders."

"I told you. He was only to buy me time. He knows everything. He hates this place. They've treated him like an animal. *Worse*. I was kind to him. He knows I won't leave him in there. You disappearing with me *is* his fail-safe. You vanishing will be enough for them to know they've got the wrong guy."

"You are a lie." I move from the railing. I'm gathering courage as I grow angrier.

"I didn't know the truth well enough to tell it." His voice breaks, he swallows, and then he continues steadily. "I didn't know which parts were Diane's paranoia and sickness and which were her father's. Those stories—his stories—stuck inside of me. He infected us with nightmares. There were no heroes. I had to get them out of my head or else I'd explode. I gave them the endings we deserved.

"I would brood over Gant and stop just short of telling you that I couldn't stand to hear you trying to convince me that you were happy. I wanted to tell you. I was so close. 'Hey, Lan. My universe is shrinking here, watching you shrink.' I went away for three months thinking that I could get over you. If I could breathe without you, I wouldn't need to go through with it. I'd forget you existed. Except every fucking day there you were." He jabs two fingers at his temple. "You were here. Always. What food you'd like. What you'd call the color of the sky. I'd wake up in the middle of the night, thousands of miles from you, and think I heard you breathing. I got back and you were electric at the airport. Laughing and talking on and on. The instant we drove off the ferry, you disappeared. It was Gant. It was killing us both, but you wouldn't leave with me. That little girl with the freckles down her nose and the shifty eyes and the quick hands that could always steal cookies, she would have left. That girl would have followed me anywhere. The letter in your journal was a last-ditch effort. Spill it all; risk everything."

"I didn't find it until a month ago. It's the only reason that I got out of bed," I whisper. It feels like a memory of a memory I had in a dream.

"I hoped it would have that galvanizing effect before I *died*," he says. "I couldn't stand that you couldn't—that you wouldn't—admit what you wanted from me. Here's the awful truth, Lana." He opens his arms and says in a booming voice, "I am selfish. I was sick and boneless without you. I need you with me. I did this mostly so that you'd be brave enough to admit what you want from me."

I shake my head. "I don't want anything from you. How could I?"

"That last night, you were about to tell me. But Maggie showed up half an hour early. She was nervous about having you in the back-seat. She was scared that she wouldn't be able to keep you in the car and that you'd get out and ruin everything."

"Why would you do that to—"

"To someone I love?"

"To me," I say. Love seems too straight a word. If this is love, then it's the crooked kind.

"You had to see it. It had to be terrible and *enough* to jolt you into yourself. You were supposed to be awake. I was going to get out of the car; the attack was going to start on the road, from a distance, so you'd see the red face but you wouldn't recognize Fitz in the dark. The kid safety locks were on, and Maggie was going to crawl behind the steering wheel and drive you away. But you were asleep and listening to music. We went for something more dramatic, spraying the blood in the car; it would be scarier, better. I miscalculated, though, and you couldn't make out the blood on Fitz's face, and Maggie screwed up calling it paint. You didn't connect it to the story."

"You told me to come. To save you. How could you be that cruel? You knew I'd see you dying. Maggie drove us a mile away and I crawled through the window to escape the car to get back to you."

He brushes his thumb down my limp arm. He flattens my palm to his chest. The thump is there through his sweatshirt. "I did this for you and me." He ducks his head. "I am cruel. And I'm going to hell for it. You are my summer. It has been you since we were two stupid kids in a blanket fort. Tell me you don't hate me. Leave with me. You don't care about Gant. Cal doesn't know you. Parker isn't good enough." He smiles crookedly. "Neither am I, but at least I know it. *I know you.*"

He floats, blown into me with the wind. This is Ben. For a moment, as giant drifts of fog block out everything but the boat, and it's possible to pretend that we are alone in the world, I am only Lana, who is unforgivably in love with a boy who killed for her. I am Lana who loves Ben best, most, always. His hands close on my waist. For once mine aren't awkward and oversize; I place them on his shoulders. My bottom lip fits to his bottom and my top to his.

Little bursts run down my neck to spread through my chest. My hands slip over Ben's arms and skate under his sweatshirt's hem to touch his lower back, and I might as well be hanging upside down doing this; I'm dizzy from the rush of blood. I am a million tiny blazing nerve endings that are not angry with Ben in the slightest. I am everything I should have done six months ago. His mouth on mine makes me alert, like jumping into the deep, cold water of the sound would. I am fresh and raw and aching and alive, alive, alive.

Then, like the cold, his kiss sets in. The blood pounds in my ears and I hear the warning: this love is dangerous. One of his hands curves around my hip bone and the other moves into my hair and it occurs to me that this isn't my Ben. My Ben told stories and played games; he was compassionate; he could see the good in people.

I come apart from Ben, intent on our summer provisions chest. My hand connects with the flare gun, which is exactly where it always is. I bring it up to his stomach before he reacts. There is nothing but cold air slapping my heated cheeks and our traded inhales and exhales for a long minute. His face hovers so near mine it's impossible to make out more than the light in his eyes. I taste the saltiness of his lips left over on mine.

"Get away from me," I say.

"Lana."

"This will absolutely rip into your stomach and the force and heat will probably burn the skin from my hand," I say. A shudder travels through me. I grit my teeth. "Move away."

He strides in reverse until he reaches the starboard side of the boat. I expect a scowl, or betrayal, or disappointment to seize his features, twist them until he looks like a monster. Instead he has a dazed, intoxicated smile and he's nodding his head, thumbing his stubbled chin like he's watching fireworks or me making a seventy-six-point Scrabble word.

"There you are," he whispers. "Lana the brave." He tilts his head back and laughs full and hard at the clouds coming apart in the sky. "I'm the fucking villain, and heroes kill villains. Isn't that right, sweetheart?" he asks, chin dropping.

There's a sharp twinge and then a pop in my chest. I am a twice-broken heart. Ben did this so I'd be the Lana from his head. She wasn't real, though. The girl who would have killed Becca for the rumors she spread never existed. Neither did the Lana who would hurt Maggie or Ford. Even now, looking on at this wicked and sick boy, I'm leaking love everywhere. It's oozing from my pores and drip-dripping on the deck of the *Mira*. I worry I might slip in it. I love Ben. I loved the trembling Ben who showed up with the tabby cat. I loved the Ben I watched die on the highway. I loved him too much for it to be chipped away by awful deeds.

"Don't think about it," he says. His eyes travel from the flare gun to my face.

"Leave," I tell him. "If you ever come back to Gant, if anyone ever spots you, if anyone else gets hurt, if I feel you watching, I will tell the police everything."

"That won't work, Lan. Are you crazy?" He pounds a fist to his sternum. "I killed three people for you. I'm not going to disappear. Even if I go, I'll come back. I'll try again in six months, and six more after, and again after that. I will find new ways to tell you that you're my summer. And you will change your mind. You won't tell anyone, least of all the police."

"I will. Do you hear me?" I shout. "Whoever you have in your head that could be with you after you killed Becca and . . . and all of them, *I'm not her*."

One foot shuffles forward. "We are a pair." Certainty is glimmering in his eyes.

I shake my head hard. "We're not anymore. You're just my dead stepbrother. You have to be my dead stepbrother," I end, pleading.

He points at the flare gun. "Then do it, because there's nothing beyond this for me. You'll see me again and again, and it will get harder. I know you. I know that I'm your summer too."

"Stop it."

"Pull the trigger, Lana." His whole frame shakes.

My free hand claws at my sweater collar, which is constricting my neck. "No," I say.

"If I get any closer and you do it, you're right, the heat will burn you. It's going to blow off your hand. Do you understand?" His gaze holds mine steadily. "If I reach you, I am throwing it in the water. I'll know that it's only a matter of *when* you'll come with me."

"Please stop."

"Please?" He takes a threatening step closer. "You think I care if you say please?" His eyes go hooded. "Do you know that that's what Becca kept saying? Please . . . please . . . She was whining the whole time, it never even occurred to the idiot to scream." He makes his voice whiny and high. "*Please*, she begged me."

My finger compresses. There's a hiss with the release and a rough cry in answer. Ben pitches back. A shower of embers sears the space between us, running from one point to the other, connecting me to the person I love. My nostrils flare with the smell of singed fabric and skin.

I hit the floor at Ben's feet. The flare is a burning orange circle in his abdomen. The sweatshirt around the wound is tattered, its edges blackened so that I can't tell charred skin from fabric. Blood, liquid and black, seeps from the circular wound. Ben stares at me, faraway and detached from the hole in him. The flare is burning, it will burn through him. It will burn through my Ben, and then it will burn the *Mira*.

My throat hurts, and I realize that I've been screaming, "I take it back," since I pulled the trigger. I sense that I've been thrown in time, to the beginning, to the black, oily highway shining as a river in the headlights, to Ben, injured, dying, taken away from me.

Ben grinds his teeth. His spine sags in a spasm that leaves him seeming diminished. He's slumped to the deck, and his hands close around the rails behind his head. There are two feet between the bottom rail and the boat.

"What are you doing?" I panic. His knuckles flex around the metal. I try to reach for him. I scramble forward and seize his arm. He's already pushing himself over the side, though. Gravity is working against me, and I'm not strong enough to stop it.

On the tail end of his splash, I catch, "Shhh, it's okay."

I say, "No, no, no," that one syllable repeated over and over as he begins to convulse, as his mouth expels a glut of blood, as Ben disappears into the sound.

— 35 —

We cook dinner on the beach at Shell Shores on Friday, end of the first week of senior year. Josh, Rusty, and Duncan kneel, stoking orange flames that are licking the two-toned sky of late afternoon. They argue over stabbing the hot dogs with sticks or putting them to grill directly on the burning wood. There are other kids scattered up the shore. Their celebrations are giddy over being seniors, top of the school food chain, tempered only by the occasional self-conscious glance thrown the core's way. The others keep apart from us.

The week was full of whispers and stares. Not merely the ones that come with being seen with the core, although there have been those, too. The whole island has heard about Becca hanging from her swing set and institutionalized Fitzgerald Moore. Bits and pieces of my account of Ben's confession to the police have trickled into public ears. Adults go tight-lipped; give their heads a shake that could mean they think I'm crazy or that they don't care to discuss something as unpleasant as the boy who wasn't even from Gant picking off the island's sons and daughters.

A convoy of cheerleaders led by Liddy cornered me at my locker the first day back. They made sad doll eyes as Liddy said in her shrill soprano, "So like, we heard Ben was attacking you and you fought him off. And you had to shoot him or else he was going to strangle you, and we just wanted you to know that we never thought he was all that hot. God, what was his damage?"

Carolynn intervened. Her eyes fixed on Liddy like laser beams, and the cheerleaders retreated. Unfortunately, that trick doesn't work on teachers, or Principal Owen, or the counselor, and the host of other adults who've relayed their sympathies and then kept one uneasy eye on me. No one knows what to believe.

Am I the girl with the stepbrother who lost it and tormented our idyllic island over a summer that will be hastily forgotten? Am I the little stepsister who had to lodge a flare in her stepbrother's abdomen to stop his killing spree? Or am I the *troubled* and lying victim and witness of a rash of mysterious crimes? At least now, everyone gets the step-thing right.

"Are those tofu?" Carolynn asks as Josh skewers the hot dogs on sticks.

He gives her a goofy smile and answers, "No."

"Thank God," Carolynn groans, and reclines on the blanket we're sharing. She wears oversize sunglasses. They've covered her watery eyes for much of the week.

"You want one or two, Car?" Duncan asks. He stays awake at night with Carolynn on the phone. Becca would be happy; Bethany J. is basically blacklisted. Carolynn holds two fingers in the air.

Willa's reading a book from AP Lit. She rests on one elbow and holds the volume to shade her face. She didn't skip a beat performing in class. As I stared glassy-eyed out the window in stats, Willa spoke more than the teacher. Good. My best friend deserves her yellow brick road of scholarly accomplishments. She deserves for it to lead to Oz—or Brown.

I stay sitting, just watching the boys. It's harder than it sounds. It's hard not curling up and sinking into grief. It helps to remember who I am and who I want to be.

I am Lana McBrook. Not *before Lana*, that saggy-spined minnow who let the world walk all over her, who was authentically loved by her best friend, Willa Owen, and who Ben McBrook killed three people and faked his own death to change. Not *after Lana* with her big Josh-loving declarations, beloved stepbrother, and her silly notions about who she had to be.

I am *just Lana McBrook*, the girl who loved her stepbrother in all the dirty, gross, and wonderful ways; who murdered him with a flare gun when she realized that eventually she would leave with him, she would become a monster to love the one he'd become; who leaped into the icy, black water of the sound to try and save him once she had.

He was gone.

The current was strong, the water deep, and the night dark.

I am Lana who thought she believed in revenge, until I saw what it looked like: Becca hanging from her swing set. And for an awful moment, like a sickness, I felt what it was to be happy for the violence visited upon her. Truthfully, though, I've believed in forgiveness since I was a four-year-old whose depressed mom leaped from a terrace. I'd forgiven her right away for leaving me. I'd forgiven Dad for departing in his own way shortly after. I've been the forgiving kind before I was old enough to know how hard forgiving can be. Before I understood that there was an alternative.

I am still a sometimes liar. It can't be helped. I haven't said aloud that Ben created a villain in Gant to turn me into the girl from our stories. Or that I loved him. Or that he succeeded in jolting me brave. Ben did know what I needed. It worked. *It worked.* How awful is that?

The police, Sweeny in particular, have wondered at Ben's motivations. After I was half-drowned from the search, I climbed up the ladder onto the *Mira*. I called the coast guard and then Sweeny. She was waiting for me at the dock when the coast guard delivered me there. I sat with her on the bank of grass by the parking lot. I shivered under the blankets I'd been given. I told her what Ben had done. I told her that he wanted me to fake my death and disappear with him. I admitted to shooting him with the flare gun.

Sweeny held my hand as Ward lingered behind us, pretending not to listen, but training an ear in our direction. Self-defense, she proclaimed it quickly. I had no choice, she assured me. Ward looked less convinced, but he nodded anyway.

Ward had been suspicious of me at the start. Back in Seattle he'd spent just as much time ruminating over the details of Ben's killing as Sweeny had. Neither of them was as startled to hear the truth as I thought they'd be. They'd sensed something wasn't stacking up. It's why they'd continued asking me if I was protecting someone else.

The police called Dad and he showed up, frantic and frightened. After we got home, he spent most of that night on the phone with Diane. Dad believed me without hesitation; no matter how fantastic my story. Diane hasn't returned from Calm Coast, although this time, I don't blame her. We would all rather not know that Ben was responsible. I would rather miss Ben without the guilt weighting me from the inside out. I would rather not replay the night on the highway, searching for cracks, indications that it was a ruse.

Ben was controlled and calculating. Maggie showed up and he feigned surprise and irritation. I was about to confess my feelings. No matter, he continued with the plan. He and Maggie staged their fight. Ben didn't want me to suspect that they were colluding or reuniting. He begged me to go with them. He knew I wouldn't say no. The attack he planned was meant to connect with the part of me that had loved our childhood stories and adventures.

Ben parked on the highway. Fitzgerald was armed with the blood bags, and they sprayed the interior as quietly as possible. There was no real chance there'd be another car on the road. It was Sunday, right before midnight. Maggie played her role magnificently. I didn't know she had it in her. She screamed. I woke up. Ben was being dragged. The child lock kept me trapped. Maggie sped away before I could clamber through the window.

As we fled up the highway, Ben and Fitzgerald emptied the blood bags along the road. They used a butcher knife and left blood splatter as if Ben had been stabbed. They let it trickle over the rocks, leading the police to deduce that Ben had tumbled into the tide pools, before he was swept away. They absconded into the woods. Ben had had years of practice traversing Gant's forests, exploring and on our adventures; Fitzgerald had even more practice going unseen. They made it to the *Mira*, where Fitzgerald showered and went on his way. Ben stayed below until the coast guard lifted the ban on boat traffic two days after his supposed death; he knew Dad and I wouldn't be sailing in the aftermath. The one person who knew where Ben went next is dead.

Perhaps I should have seen it from the beginning. I don't mean all of Ben's brooding over Gant; he was right about the nature of this place. I don't only mean after all those stories or when the crimes echoed them. I mean, I should have sensed his anger way before that. My memory of the nights Ben asked me how I could let *them* get away with *it* and if I wanted him to kill them burns me at both ends. What was to come suggested itself there. It was foreshadowed. I ignored it. Did I know way down deep in my toes? Did I white-knuckle the lies and stomp the truth?

Mom wasn't completely wrong about the power of perception. You can see heroes where there are villains. You can see love where there is hate. It's often harder to see what's really there. I am the Lana who wants to try.

I am tired of hearing what anyone but me thinks I should be. I want to define myself.

If I am small, it's my choice.

If I'm daring, it's because it's who I am.

If I'm good, fine.

If I'm bad, that's on me.

I struggle with how I hurt Ben. I don't label it self-defense in my head, because Ben was never going to hurt me. I wonder why he told me to pull the trigger. Was he calling my bluff? Did he believe that I would put the flare down and go with him? Was he certain that he knew me right up until the second I proved he didn't? Or was Ben telling the truth? Did he understand that he'd become a villain? He saw the girl he'd been searching for the moment she drew the flare gun and he realized the foolishness of what he'd done. It's rosy and optimistic, but I want to believe that Ben was freeing me in a way. He realized his cruelty. He said what he needed to so that I could leave him behind, so that I wouldn't become a villain also.

I'm furious with Ben for how he hurt Becca. I'm angry with Ben for going overboard and making me wonder if he did it in the confusion of death or if it was to keep the flare from burning the *Mira*. Was his last thought to save me? I'm even furious for Maggie and Ford, who didn't deserve to be drawn into his designs. There's no way to tell Ben any of this. He's gone.

Mostly, when I think of Ben, I am a middle finger flipped to the sky. He acted hateful and labeled it love. He only succeeded fleetingly in turning me into the bloodthirsty girl he believed I was when I killed him. I wasn't her until the moment I decided that he deserved to die. I stopped being her at the precise second I did what I couldn't take back.

When I am not a middle finger flipped to the sky, I listen for the noise Ben made in the world. I catch my ears straining for it. I wake up with the sense that I've just said his name. I whirl around on the terrace, half expecting to see his silhouette. I am always waiting to catch his shadow in my periphery. Maybe it will fade. I doubt it. Ben was not the sort of person who does.

I want to tell fewer lies. So here is the truth, here is what I've hidden inside myself, in the place I used to guard my affection for my golden stepbrother. I didn't refuse to leave Gant with Ben at the end because I love it so freaking much or because I couldn't bear to leave Willa or the core. I didn't stay for Dad and Diane. Ben still crowds them out. Even the Ben I see now through a kaleidoscope, his pattern ever changing. I can't always make sense of him. I don't always want to. I didn't stay in Gant because I'm goo-goo eyed over Josh Parker, although, as I watch him make a rock skip three times on the surface of the sound and celebrate with a fist in the air, I do think I could be. Someday.

On the deck of the *Mira*, I pictured leaving with Ben. As his mouth covered mine, everything else dropped away. We could leave Gant. We could escape anyone who knew us and anyone's expectations but our own. We could have one endless adventure and we could love each other and make no room for anyone else. I could find out what Carolynn meant about a boy knowing what to do with his hands. We could leave the violence behind—except we couldn't. It was in him. I would always know it. I would find a way to ignore it again.

I tried to send Ben away alive because there was a slice of me that was jittery, grateful, and loved him that much more for killing Maggie and Ford.

I couldn't go with him because he was dangerous. The stories meant different things to us. They made me strong and brave; they taught me that the line between a vengeful hero and a villain is narrow and gray; they entertained me, like stories are meant to.

Ben didn't just invent the world as something less ordinary in a story or sketch, though; he made the world malicious and violent with his actions. He was too good at manipulating the shadows. The abuse was rooted in him, making him grow crooked. It wasn't the stories, the make-believe, or the pretend terror. It was Ben's grandfather, the violence, and the real terror. Not the grand strokes but the subtle details I should have seen.

With Ben, that's how it would always be. The world would be painted extraordinary. People would be cast as heroes and villains. I would be weak-kneed over a boy who killed for me. So: I compressed the trigger.

I want to decide for myself how I see the world. So far it's full of good and evil, the difference between the two not always obvious, friends and enemies, love and loss, and new beginnings. I'm better off in between Carolynn and Willa. One will keep me gutsy and the other smart. Josh will keep us good and optimistic. Duncan will keep Carolynn happy. Rusty will keep us laughing. The memory of Becca will keep us tethered to earth, bound by gravity. And I hope that I'll keep my friends safe.

I will always wonder. In moments of weakness, rather than doodle us as a Venn diagram, rather than pen *summer* in thick black letters down my wrists, on my thighs, or in places only I'll see, I'll pretend that despite his injury Ben made it to shore. Somehow. The flare wound wasn't fatal, as it appeared to be. He found a doctor and he's alive. Alive, alive, *alive*. Like me.

I will close my eyes into the rush of wind on the *Mira* and imagine Ben digging a well in a buggy field, some balmy place south of here. I will pretend that he's baking in the sun and making up for all the bad he did. He'll try to make amends with the universe.

Summer days perfumed by marionberry blossoms will remind me of him, golden, his opinions singing, and he'll have nothing to do with the screeching beaks of blackbirds.

Acknowledgments

At its heart, this is a book about bravery. And so I must thank the numerous women and girls who have inspired me with their courage. In particular, thank you to my mother—a more passionate, creative, and loving person does not exist.

Thank you to my clever and perpetually game editor, Navah Wolfe. Thank you to Justin Chanda, Lizzy Bromley, Valeria Shea, and the entire Simon & Schuster Books for Young Readers team.

Thank you to my wise, creative, and classy agent, Brianne Johnson of Writers House.

Thank you, CB; I still believe.

Thank you to my aunt and uncle, Toni and Al, for their support and encouragement. Thank you to my friends Melissa, Tika, and Andrea for their steadfast support. Thank you to Greg and Jamie for getting it (for getting everything) and being family.

Thank you to my mother and father for teaching me that I am brave and of consequence. Thank you to my sister, Elizabeth, the grandest woman I know. Thank you to my little brother and golf champion of the world, Andrew.

And a profound thank you to my husband, Joe. Thank you for being whip-smart, damn handsome, superlatively kind, and the best partner anyone could have. This book is yours. What a marvelous life. Thank you.